The Island Wife

The Island Wife

Jessica Stirling

St. Martin's Press ⚏ New York

Library of Congress Cataloging-in-Publication Data

Stirling, Jessica.
  The island wife / Jessica Stirling.
    p.   cm.
  ISBN 0-312-19289-4
  1. Mull, Island of (Scotland)—History—Fiction.
I. Title.
PR6069.T49717   1998
823'.914—dc21   98-35162
                                     CIP

First published in Great Britain by Hodder and Stoughton, a division of Hodder Headline PLC.

First U.S. Edition: December 1998

10 9 8 7 6 5 4 3 2 1

Contents

ONE

The Coming of the Sheep

Out beyond the skerries the sea lay smooth as cornsilk in the oppressive heat of the August afternoon. Inshore, south of the farm, great beds of kelp and bladder wrack heaved sluggishly against the ledges of basaltic rock that slack water had exposed. In the bay itself there was no motion at all, save where the burn fanned into the sea's edge like a tuck in a seam, as if, Innis thought, the island itself had shrunk in the hot spell and needed restitching.

She disliked the hot, breathless days, the brassy evenings when the sun hovered long over the Treshnish Isles and made the big blue mountains of Skye seem sullen and ominous. Fortunately such spells were rare on the west coast of Scotland. This one had lasted near a fortnight, though, and had rendered Innis and her sisters bad-tempered. They would girn and grumble and might even have given way to wrestling on the grass, like Neil and Donnie, if their mother had not been there to remind them that not only were they supposed to be ladies but that there was work to be done.

Heavy work it was too in that dusty summer of 1878. In the field on the shoulder of Olaf's Hill the oats and barley crop was almost ready for the sickle. There were calves to be weaned and hay stooks still to be brought in. The running of the farm was left to Vassie and her daughters, for her husband and sons could not be expected to sacrifice so much as one day's fishing, not even to help erect the boundary wall. To hear Vassie speak of it, digging out a drystone dike that had lain half buried since long before the Campbells had set foot on Mull was hardly more than casual repair work. But apart from drawing milk and gathering

1

eggs, farm labours had been put entirely to one side while Vassie and the girls unearthed the ancient wall that divided the fields of Pennypol from the rest of the Fetternish estate.

Shrouded in weeds and bramble-thorn the wall ran from the edge of the pine wood to the shoulder of the burn. From the outset the girls had known that it would test their strength and stamina but the advent of sultry weather had turned the task into racking drudgery.

What they could not have foreseen was the strange effect that uncovering the ancient stones would have on their sister Aileen who had grown hardly at all in stature or intelligence since her tenth year – she was now fifteen – and who could not read, or write more than her name. Until recently Aileen's simple-mindedness had seemed harmless. In the past year, however, it had taken on a sinister tone, for she was for ever sneaking off to kneel among the standing stones or hide in the ruins of the old fort at Dun Fidra to commune with the people under the hill. She claimed that the fairies spoke with her and played the *timpan*, the fairy harp, for her benefit and, in payment, she fed them curds and gulls' eggs and offered them wild flowers and berries to appease their mischievous natures.

'Well, now,' Father had said, when Vassie expressed concern about Aileen's mental state, 'Aileen would not be the first in your family to be going the way of the devil.'

'Do you think it is the devil that is in her?'

'Since it cannot be the fairies, who can it be but the devil?'

'Is it not yourself, Ronan Campbell, who has been carried away by the devil?' Mother would say. 'The devil that comes out of a bottle. There is nothing wrong with Aileen that could not be cured by a better example.'

Ronan Campbell was as broad and bulky as a bale of wool, Vassie as thin and sharp as clipping shears. When they argued about the children or the future of the farm, Vassie's voice would rise like the squeak of a nail on wet wood and Father's patient sighs would become wheezy. She would scrape away at him all night long and squeeze no more out of him than a slow, lop-sided grin that was so smug and arrogant that Innis did not know whose side to take and, unlike her sister Biddy, wound up taking no side at all.

The Coming of the Sheep

In temperament if not appearance, Biddy was very much her mother's daughter: all teeth and temper. At twenty she was still without a husband in spite of her beautiful auburn hair, sea green eyes and statuesque figure. While the look of her attracted men like bees to clover, there was within her a devouring quality that soon withered the horns of male lust. Only Aileen, with hair as pale as bog-cotton and eyes as blue as infinity, could render Biddy speechless, for Biddy stood in awe of her little sister and treated her if not with affection at least with caution. There was precious little time to fret about Aileen's antics during August, though, for work on the wall consumed all the girls' energy and attention.

Biddy handled the pick and Innis the spade. Hair spiky with sweat and eyes vacant, Aileen dug out the smaller stones and washed them in the buckets of salt water that Mother lugged up from the sea. She washed them as if they were objects of great value and would croon over them and cradle them in her arms for a moment before she chipped off a rough edge or shaped a coping with the little road-mender's hammer that her father had found for her.

Weather-brown face shiny with sweat, Vassie did most of the lifting and setting and only the biggest of the stones defeated her wiry strength. One hundred and eighty-eight yards of stock-proof boundary wall were gradually redeemed from the earth at the rate of twelve paces a day. Eight days in the fortnight were scorched by bright, glary sunshine. Six were dunned by grey, oppressive heat. Ronan and the boys would come up from the shore in the evening and inspect the wall and, nodding, would stoop and lift a flint or a pebble, fit it into a crack or little vacancy and give it a delicate tap. Then they would step back and murmur with self-approval as if that one stone was all it took to make the women's work complete.

But there was more to unearthing the old stones than Vassie Campbell had imagined. The wall did not end at the Pennypol burn. It swarmed away across the moor and up over the clifftop and across the ridge that led to Quinish and inland to Dervaig, and, for all the Campbells knew, continued on to Mornish and Calgary and the shores of Loch Tuath. If all the buried hummocks and mounds had been unearthed a great chain of stones might have been found to link the lost communities of the Hebridean coast and unite the fragile settlements that the landowners' greed had all but swept away.

Biddy and Innis were too exhausted to consider the wall's historical significance. All they wanted to do was flop on the grass and idly watch the clouds form overhead. They could no longer be bothered to enquire what strange creatures Vassie expected to come trotting down the glen to snuffle at the dike that they had helped her build.

They were two or three yards short of the burn when the first of the sheep stuck its head up out of the bracken. Perched on a short wooden ladder, Vassie stiffened and yelled, 'By God, they are here already,' then she stepped backward into space, landed like a cat and sprang for the dump at the back of the house before Innis and Biddy even knew what was upon them.

Biddy stood motionless, hands on hips, staring inland towards Crove while the bleating came closer and dust from the drove road rose in a pall like smoke. Innis glanced out to sea in the faint, fond hope that Father's boat might come winging around the headland; of course, it did not. So, stirring herself, she scampered down the slope to help her mother with the rusted harrow that she, Vassie, was dragging up from behind the house.

Vassie had knotted a tattered rope to the broken frame. She dragged it like a sled, bouncing and snagging on the tussocks, and yelled at the pitch of her voice, 'Keep away. Keep away,' as if it were Vikings pouring over the hill to pillage and rape and not just a flock of knee-weary sheep seeking green grass.

The first thing Innis saw of Baverstocks' invaders was a rough-coated black and white collie. It reached the wall top with a sharp little scrabble of claws and peered down at them curiously, tongue lolling and tail wagging. Then there was a whistle, and a shout in the English tongue, 'Roy, come down at once.' The dog twisted round in a dainty half-circle and leaped out of sight.

'Quick, quick, we must be quick,' Vassie cried. She yanked at the rope and brought the harrow – and Innis with it – to the gap at the end of the wall.

The wooden frame, split in an ugly vee, was not as high as the wall but its spikes would be enough to deter any sheep, however nosy, from breaking through. A rake of stones and brushwood would finish the job well enough. Dipping and ducking through the bracken, the Baverstocks' sheep emerged in single file, silent at first, then, when they reached the turf that lapped down from the moor, breaking into a loud baa-ing and bleating that grew deafening as the flock coagulated, bewildered and rowdy, against the base of the wall.

The shepherd was a spare young man, not much more than twenty-five years old. He was sallow, with jet black hair, sleek as sealskin. He wore a flannel shirt open all the way down so that his lean, hairless chest showed and his flat, hairless belly, down to the belt that supported his breeks. He had no hat on his head and carried nothing but a crook. He said nothing as he approached and did not smile. He seemed as neat and solemn and as out of place as the big, spongy sheep that he drove before him or the lithe collie that tripped obediently at his heel.

Biddy was first to find her voice. She addressed him in English, not Gaelic. 'What is it you are wanting here?' Hands on hips, hair like a mane, bosom heaving, she was so tall and haughty and handsome that even the collie, never mind the shepherd, stopped and blinked.

The incomer answered in English. 'I want nothing here.'

He was no islander, Innis felt sure. He was more like one of the young lairds that came to open the cattle show or one of pursers off the steamers that plied the sightseeing route round Staffa. He had a clean, scrubbed look to him, an expression not so much patronising as patient. In case he was more educated than he looked, though, she tried him in her native tongue. 'Do you not know whose land this is?'

He shook his head and shrugged. He did not understand.

Innis could smell the sheep now. Two hundred Cheviots had a different smell to the handful of little Blackfaces that had once cropped the neighbouring pastures. She had seen enough of Cheviots to suspect that they would not fare well on Fetternish.

'I don't speak the Gaelic, miss. I'm sorry.'

Biddy said, 'Are you an Englishman, then?'

'No, nothing as bad as that.'

'I asked if you knew what place this is?' Innis said.

'The estate of Fetternish, I believe.'

Although his voice lacked the formal quality of island speech it was quite comprehensible, unlike the grating of gruff Glaswegians or the twang of Aberdeen trawlermen whom Innis had encountered on visits to Tobermory. And, thank God, it was a far cry from the mewing of the southern gentry who spilled across the Hebrides in such profusion every summer.

'Aye, sir, the ground upon which you are standing may be the estate of Fetternish,' Vassie said, 'but if you are taking ten more steps then you will be on my ground and I will be putting you off it as a trespasser.'

'Are you afraid I'll eat your grass, Mrs Campbell?'

'So you know who I am, do you now?'

'I've been told who you are. And what you are.'

'And what is it that I am then?' Vassie demanded.

'You are the proprietor of Pennypol, so I'm informed, and as fine a farming lady as is to be found this side of Morven.'

Vassie gave no sign that his flattery pleased her. She was still quivering with the effort of hauling the harrow up the hill. Innis, though, hid a smile behind her hand, for she realised that the young shepherd had been instructed, probably by Mr Thrale, not to antagonise the quarrelsome Campbells.

'It is my father, Ronan Campbell, who is the owner,' Innis said.

This, of course, was a lie. Ten minutes' conversation in the McKinnon Arms at Crove would supply the incomer with the whole truth about Pennypol, whether he wished to hear it or whether he did not. Land, house, stock and plenishings, such as they were, belonged to Vassie not Ronan Campbell. His sole possession was the boat. The arrangement was unique on the north part of the island and the fact that a crofting woman owned land in her own name and in her own right was considered somehow shameful.

'What is your name?' Biddy said.

'My name is Michael Tarrant.'

'What are you, Mr Tarrant?' Biddy went on. 'A hired drover, or have the Baverstocks appointed you to look after their flock?'

'I'm here to stay, if that's what you mean.'

'Where did you come from?'

'Up from the pier at Calgary.'

'She is meaning where is your home,' Vassie said.

The Coming of the Sheep

'I was raised in the Ettrick Hills in the Border country.'

'Is that where these damned sheep also come from?' Vassie said.

'They were bought at the Perth sales, so I'm told.'

'Were you not there when the purchase was made?' Biddy said.

Michael Tarrant shook his head. 'The purchase was made by Mr Thrale, who I think you already know.'

'Aye, we know Thrale only too well,' Vassie said.

'Will you be settling on Fetternish, Mr Tarrant?' Innis asked.

Uncertain of his bearings, he gestured towards Olaf's Hill. 'In the cottage over – over in that direction.'

'Then we will be neighbours,' said Innis.

'Friendly neighbours, I hope,' said Michael Tarrant.

'We will never be friendly neighbours,' Vassie informed him. 'You are with the Baverstocks and the Baverstocks will not be our friends, neither them, nor their hirelings, nor their damned sheep.'

'Have you met the brothers, then?' Michael asked.

'No, I have not met them,' Vassie answered. 'Nor will I be likely to meet them since they are Edinburgh gentlemen and will not be wishing to hob-nob with humble folk like us.'

'Well' – Michael shrugged – 'I haven't met them either, Mrs Campbell. But by all accounts they are honest enough and intend to do well by Fetternish.'

'To do well for themselves, you mean,' said Vassie. 'I do not have to be meeting them to know that they will be no different from all the other lairds that have come to ruin the Highlands.'

'Because they cleared the crofters' land to make way for sheep, do you mean?' Michael Tarrant said.

'Because they destroyed what was here before they came.'

'And what was that, Mrs Campbell?'

'Crofts and townships . . .'

'And poverty?' Michael Tarrant said. 'Dire poverty?'

'Poverty!' Vassie yelled. 'Do you dare to talk to me of poverty? I tell you I have seen the people here who would eat the husks of the oats and gnaw at the tips of the heather plants to fill their empty bellies. I have seen folk standing in Loch Cuin on a winter's day dredging for crabs that even the herons would not take, just to have something to put in their children's mouths.'

Innis had heard the accounts of the enforced evictions so often that she could recite the litany of suffering in her sleep: Calgary in 1822. Mishnish in 1842. The scouring of Ulva in '51. Treshnish in '62. The callous deceptions that had been perpetrated on the crofters of Dervaig to cheat them out of their grazing land. The cottages of Sorn burned down to make way for sheep.

Only a mile or two along the coast, a certain Mr James Forsyth had erected the towering castle of Glengorm, a monument to arrogance and ambition. Though Forsyth had not lived to occupy the place it had become a landmark for every salt and sightseer who rounded the Point of Ardnamurchan or slid past the rocky corner of Ardmore.

Fetternish too had been cleared. Nothing remained of the old communities now except heaps of stones and patches of bright green grass where the middens had been. Fetternish had changed hands several times since then, for none of the owners had been able to make it thrive. Now the long spit of cliffs and moorland had changed hands again, had been put up for auction and sold to two brothers who had never set foot on Mull and who knew little or nothing about farming.

'I'm sorry, Mrs Campbell,' Michael said. 'I didn't mean to offend you.'

Innis felt a certain sympathy for the incomer. He had much to learn about the pride of the islanders and the scars that history had laid upon them.

'Go away,' Biddy shouted. 'We are cattle people and have no dealings with sheep or with shepherds.'

Michael Tarrant regarded Biddy with interest. He watched her shake out her auburn mane and swell her breast and, Innis thought, present a picture that was both alluring and ridiculous at one and the same time. She wondered if they had girls like Biddy on the Ettrick Hills or if, like so many things on Mull, her sister was unique.

'I see you have built a fine wall here, Mrs Campbell,' Michael Tarrant said. 'But, like all walls, it has two sides to it.'

'What is that supposed to be meaning?' Vassie said.

'As you have pointed out, it'll keep me and my sheep from straying on to Pennypol but it will also keep your kye from straying on to Fetternish. The grazings belong to my employers now. I have every right to remain where I am until every blade of grass, every buttercup and docken has been devoured down to the root. Here, where I stand, is not your ground, Mrs Campbell. You have no right to shout at me to move on.'

'I am not shouting at you,' Vassie yelled. 'I never shout.'

'Then all I can say is that conversations on Mull must be conducted at very long distances,' said Michael Tarrant. 'Frankly, Mrs Campbell, I have heard railway engines make less noise coming out of tunnels.'

Vassie had never seen let alone heard a railway engine. Even so the meaning of the insult was clear. She opened her mouth to protest but no words came only a little 'uh-uh-uh,' like a ewe in labour. She leaned against the broken harrow and pointed at the shepherd as if she hoped that she might put the sign of lightning upon him and shrivel him on the spot for his audacity.

Biddy was less backward. She rushed at the incomer with her fists raised but before she could deliver a blow Michael Tarrant tripped her neatly with the tip of his crook and caught her as she fell. He held her as no man had ever done, very tightly, smothering her flailing arms with his hands and deflecting her knees with his thigh to prevent damage to valuable parts of his anatomy.

'No, Miss Campbell,' he murmured. 'No, that will not do at all.'

'Let me go. Let – me – go.'

'If I do, will you behave yourself?'

'Let me . . .'

He put his cheek against her cheek, not affectionately, and whispered something into her ear.

Biddy was still in an instant. He released her and stepped quickly away.

'I'll be going now,' he said. 'Not because you have ordered it, Mrs Campbell, but because it is high time I got these poor sheep on to the home pasture. How soon will it be dark?'

Innis opened her mouth to answer but Biddy got there before her.

'In four hours.'

'Thank you, Miss Campbell.'

'Biddy. I am called Biddy.'

'Bridget – an Irish name?'

She blushed, gave her hair a shake and nodded. 'After my grandmother.'

'A very pretty name,' Michael said. 'And you, miss?'

'Innis.'

'And what about you, wee lady?' Michael said.

None of them, apart from Michael, had noticed Aileen. She had climbed the inside of the wall and rested her forearms on the coping, her chin supported on cupped hands. Without a trace of fear she stared down at the collie, at the milling sheep and at the stranger. For once her vacant blue eyes had a glitter of interest in them. She did not answer the shepherd's question, though. Instead she giggled, lifted her shoulders, and cocked her head so that her face was coyly veiled by strands of fine, pale hair.

'She is called Aileen,' Innis said.

'There now,' Michael said. 'Have I met you all?'

'Aye, Mr Tarrant, so you will be knowing who we are and how to avoid us.' Vassie had found her voice again. 'There is nothing here for the likes of you.'

He smiled for the first time, a broad grin that showed white, even teeth.

'I would not be so sure of that, Mrs Campbell,' Michael Tarrant said.

It was late in the evening before Ronan Campbell and his sons, Neil and Donnie, returned to the jetty at Pennypol at the end of a profitable day's fishing.

August was the best month for lobsters and the haul from the pots strung out along the reef had been good. They had ferried the catch straight to the slipway at Croig where Mr Drury, a fish agent from Oban, was on hand to pick up the best of it, and servants from the big houses had come to buy fish and shellfish straight from the boats. Since this was the height of the shooting season the island was thick with visitors all demanding to be fed, and the lobsters had fetched higher prices than usual.

There was no inn at Croig but it was just a short sail to Fergus Haggerty's turf-roofed cottage under the cliffs at Arkle where

Fergus kept a still going in the byre and maintained a reputation for being able to supply whisky untainted by an exciseman's gauge. The whisky was very dark and tasted of seaweed and peat ash but it was palatable enough after you got the first glass down. Some lairds even claimed to prefer it to the stuff that came out of labelled bottles and presented it to their hardier guests as 'the real McKay', by which they meant that it could lay you on your back faster than a blow from a ten-pound hammer.

Fergus's illicit whisky – any sort of whisky – was good enough for Ronan Campbell. Forty odd years of imbibing the stuff had numbed him to its injurious effects. Nobody could recall ever having seen Ronan the worse for drink, possibly because nobody could ever recall having seen Ronan completely sober. The equitable haze that enveloped Ronan Campbell's mental faculty was the sole reason for his popularity. It was impossible to argue with him, to rouse him to disagreement, let alone passion. He seemed so easy-going that even sharp-witted fish merchants and wily cattle dealers could not find it in their hearts to cheat him by much and he appeared to drift through life without a care in the world. No money either, of course. Never a penny to spare to give to his girls to buy earrings or a card of petticoat lace. Never a sixpence left to put into the bank for a rainy day. The farm fed him, the fishing supplied him with money for drink, and as far as Ronan was concerned this system worked just fine.

Whatever small luxuries the Campbells had acquired had been wrested from Ronan's clutches by stealth and deception. Lying was endemic to Vassie's relationship with her husband. It had spilled over into the girls' relationship with their brothers too, so that at times it seemed as if there were not just two sexes sharing the Pennypol cottage but two warring clans. Only on the rare occasions when farm labour demanded more muscle than women could provide would Ronan forsake his creels and lines.

With a sigh, Ronan would say, 'Well, now, Vassie, I suppose you will be needing us for the cutting tomorrow. What do you say, lads? Do you think we should be lending a helping hand?'

'We will have to be thinking about that,' Neil would say, frowning.

'The crop will not wait for you to do your thinking,' Vassie would say. 'It is ripe for the sickle and the weather is dry.'

'It is a pity that there is such a fine run of lobsters on. Still' – the smile, the sly, crooked smile – 'still, if that is the way of it I suppose it will just have to be. And a bit of a rest from the boat will do us no harm.'

'It is a pity about the lobsters, though,' Donnie would put in.

'A pity, a great pity. But that is the way of it, is it not? We will just be having to put our work aside to help out the women with theirs.'

The building of the wall elicited no admiration from Ronan and his sons. It was treated as another idiosyncrasy, another of Vassie's fancies. However much it might appear to the contrary, though, Ronan and Donnie understood only too well the importance of having a barrier to keep out the sheep. Even Neil, a huge lummox of a boy, was intelligent enough to suspect that the sale of Fetternish to strangers would alter things on Pennypol and that the establishment of a boundary wall was no whim but a necessity.

Norman McAlpin, the last owner of Fetternish, had been a farmer of sorts. Consequently he had understood the struggle to make ends meet and had been easy in his dealings with his neighbours. McAlpin, though, had overextended himself and had run into debt. To avoid a shameful bankruptcy he had put Fetternish up for auction in the library of the New Athenian Club where, according to rumour, it had been knocked down to the Baverstocks for a song. The Baverstocks were a different kettle of fish from McAlpin. They were businessmen, not farmers. Their wealth stemmed from tweed cloth production. They had inherited the family manufactory in the Border town of Sangster but prudently left the management of the place in the hands of their brother-in-law, Alister Paul, whom they had made a full and active partner.

The fact that Fetternish had brought three previous owners to their knees did not deter the Baverstocks. They had, of course, an immediate outlet for any quantity of wool that Fetternish might produce and would not be at the mercy of brokers and dealers. They had retained Hector Thrale, McAlpin's factor, to manage the estate and, so it was said, had grand plans to refurbish and extend the 'big house'. The coming of the sheep was the first sure sign that the Baverstocks meant business, however, and it was not until Ronan and his sons walked up from the jetty and saw the pale shapes of the Cheviots dotting the hillside that they were willing to concede that Vassie had been right and that it was no bad thing to have a wall behind you after all.

Dusk had come down. The rim of the sun, round as an orange, showed beneath a lid of cloud. Swarms of gnats had risen from bog and beach and hung in spirals in the fetid air. From the calf park and along the shore the roaring of tormented cattle rose loud and prolonged. Inside the cottage a haze of peat smoke and sweltering steam from cooking pots kept the midges at bay and the only annoyance came from the glossy black flies that crawled over pots and plates, impervious to Vassie's irritable attacks with the back of an iron spoon or a rolled-up copy of the *Oban Times*.

Curved around the stones of the open fireplace, the Campbells' dog, a portly lurcher named Fingal, opened one eye, contemplated the arrivals and, by way of greeting, broke wind and yawned.

'I see that they are here then.' Ronan seated himself at the table that occupied the centre of the room. 'Who drove them across from Calgary? Thrale would it be?'

'No, a shepherd, a new shepherd,' Biddy answered. 'He comes from a place called Ettrick.'

'Aye, like his sheep, I'm thinking,' Donnie said.

Donnie was his father's double, small-boned but muscular, with a square cleft chin and small, almost prissy mouth. His grandmother had been a famous Irish beauty and Donnie's lashes were embarrassingly long, his neck so slender that it made his head seem top-heavy. He was the oldest child of the family, twenty months older than Bridget, who was twelve months older than Neil.

The men occupied the chairs around the table. Aileen perched close to her father on a high four-legged stool that she had used since she was a baby. Ladling and serving were brisk. Broth first of all, then a dish of boiled cod done with potatoes and a thin butter sauce; hard bread sliced thick and tea, tea as black as boiler tar, to wash it all down.

Biddy, by right, took the last chair. Seated on low rush-bottomed stools that placed them beneath the level of the table, Vassie and Innis ate from bowls balanced in their laps. Women as well as men ate quickly, hungrily. Supper was over in ten minutes. Bowls and plates were removed and put outside on the grass for the hens to peck at or for Fingal to lick clean.

Through the open doorway Innis looked out at the darkening sky. The sun had gone down into cloud. There was no iridescence on the surface of the sea and the waves, such as they were, reflected no light in the smothering gloom. There was the sound of them, though, for the doldrums never stilled that rhythm, that soft 'pah-daaah' that on calm nights seemed almost like the beating of your heart.

She was sticky with sweat. Her petticoat clung to her hips and her breasts were pasted to the lining of her bodice. Even her bare legs felt prickly, as if she had walked through nettles. It would be a hot night again too, lying in the vee-shaped loft just under the thatch with Biddy on one side, Aileen on the other and the straw sticking into her and the blanket rough and itchy.

She put down her teacup and, saying nothing, went outside. She did not take the lantern. Later, she would accompany her mother to the calf park to inspect the beasts that had been dropped that summer. Then Mam and she would return arm-in-arm by the back of the byre to see if they could spot where the hens were roosting and where, in the morning, the eggs might be found. There had been a time when Ronan and Vassie had made this last tour of the farm together, in the gloaming or in the dark, but not now, not for years now.

Innis walked to the gable of the cottage and glanced up at the shadowy undulations of the dike. There was no sign of moon or stars, only a faint smear of light in the sky and a slight, almost undetectable cooling in the night air. She unbuttoned her bodice and let the air surround her body then, quickening her step, made for the shallow pool where the burn checked above the beach.

The turf was so dry and hard that it seemed to ring beneath her feet and even on the shoulder of the burn the grass was brittle and slippery. She removed her bodice and heavy outer skirt and, clad only in her shift, felt for the edge of the pool with her toes. The water, spring-fed, was cool and, sighing with pleasure, she stooped and cupped her hands and brought up a little quantity of water and let it trickle over her breasts and down into the waist of her shift. She stooped again and splashed burn water up on to her face, her throat and breasts.

When she straightened she saw him standing above her, a solid grey shape in the half-dark. She was startled but not frightened.

'I'm sorry. I didn't mean to alarm you,' Michael Tarrant said.

'You did not alarm me, Mr Tarrant.'

She stepped back on to the bank, groped for her skirt and bodice and, finding them, pressed them against her breasts.

'Is this fresh water?' he asked.

'It is,' Innis answered. 'As fresh as any you will find on Mull.'

He perched uncertainly on the bank above her then, as if to indicate that his purpose was entirely innocent, lifted his hands and shook the two galvanised pails that he had lugged the half-mile from Pennymain.

'Mr Thrale neglected to tell me where I could find the water supply for the cottage,' he said.

'It is in the hollow just behind your house. It comes out of a pipe in the bottom of the glen. You would be hard put to find it in the dark,' Innis said. 'Besides, the flow will be slight in the drought, or may have dried up altogether.'

'It's not for me, you understand. It's for the dog. He's parched. I didn't know where else to turn.'

'This is our water, Mr Tarrant.'

'Oh!'

'When my grandfather first came into possession of Pennypol he made sure that the boundary was drawn beyond the burn so that nobody could steal the water from us or divert it for their own use.'

'Are you saying that I can't have water?'

'No, Mr Tarrant. I'm saying that you may have your water tonight, and welcome, but that my mother will not allow you to draw regularly.'

'Is fresh water scarce on Fetternish?'

'Far from it. Mull is a wet island. Only in the worse droughts do the streams dry up and then, sometimes, there has to be a pump carted up to the Fetternish lochs for watering stock and supplying the big house.'

15

'Thrale didn't tell me that.'

'I wonder what else Mr Thrale did not tell you?'

'Well, he didn't tell me about . . .' He let the sentence trail away as if, Innis thought, he could not bring himself to fashion another compliment.

Although she was only seventeen, Innis was not inexperienced in recognising interest in a man's voice. Michael Tarrant was no silver-tongued seducer, though, of that she was sure. He was more likely to be the sort of man who would keep his emotions under tight rein and would surrender control of his passions reluctantly.

'Where,' he asked, 'is the best place to draw the water?'

'Here, where I am standing,' Innis said. 'If you will allow me to step away, I will make room for you.'

'Thank you.'

He turned his back on her, allowed her to slip into her skirt and tie her bodice. She was less modest than he might have expected. She was not embarrassed by the situation. She lacked the pettiness that governed manners in the towns. She watched the shepherd crouch by the pool and fill one of the pails. She took it from him and held the cool new metal against her stomach. She could feel the heat going out of her for the first time that day, a strange, passive coolness transmit itself from the pail to her body. She watched him fill the second pail and took it from him too. She waited while he dipped his face in the flow of the burn, drank, bathed his neck and hair, then rose, dripping, and took the pails from her, his fingers touching her fingers, his arm brushing her arm.

The last of the twilight had faded. Darkness wrapped them like a cloak. She could hear the kye roaring on the foreshore, hoarse and distant.

She watched Michael adjust the water pails, one to each hand. He lingered as if he wanted to ask her more questions. Then she realised that however self-sufficient he might appear to be he was lonely for home, for the place he had left behind, for his mother, his sisters and brothers and – a sudden thought – his wife and children?

'I'll be on my way, then,' he said.

'Is there no – have you no wife?' Innis blurted out.

16

'Not I,' Michael Tarrant told her. 'I'm quite used to doing for myself.'

'How will you find your way back to Pennymain?'

'I'll follow the line of the wall and the track will lead me from there.'

She was tempted to offer to accompany him but decided that it would be too forward. Besides, she had a feeling that she would encounter Michael Tarrant quite often in the days ahead, that this might be more of a new beginning than anyone, even her mother, could possibly have foreseen.

'Goodnight to you then, Mr Tarrant.'

'Goodnight, Miss Campbell,' he said and, turning, set off along the burn towards the wall with the water pails splashing at his sides.

Somehow Biddy and Innis contrived not to discuss the arrival of sheep on Fetternish or, more particularly, the arrival of the personable young shepherd. It was not that they had put Michael Tarrant out of their thoughts – far from it – but simply that neither was willing to reveal to the other that, in spite of the acrimony of their first meeting, she had been attracted to the incomer. For once, Innis had one up on Biddy: that secret, late-evening encounter with Mr Tarrant. While she was half inclined to boast about it and make more of the incident than it deserved, she decided to say nothing. An exchange of confidences with Biddy might wind up setting the shepherd on a pedestal to be fought over like a silver cup at the Mull and Morven Agricultural Show and Innis knew that she could not compete with her sister when it came to attracting the attention of a man.

Biddy's auburn hair and full figure, not to mention her ruby red lips and high, arching eyebrows, had a cohesion that Innis felt she lacked. She would study her features in the shell-backed mirror that Grandfather McIver had given her, trying to make the bits and pieces all come together the way they did with Biddy but they never did. All she had to offer was a nose with a narrow bridge and too much snub, eyebrows that had hardly any curve and a mouth that was – well – just a mouth. Her eyes were not sea green like Biddy's but indeterminate brown. As for her hair, it was McIver hair, so fine and granular that the only time it seemed to stay in place was when the wind blew hard and it streamed straight out behind her like sand from the top of a dune.

When it became obvious that she was not going to grow up to look like Biddy, Innis concentrated on making herself a more 'interesting' person. She doubted if it would do her much good, though, for men were invariably more attracted by the curve of your hips and the prominence of your bosom than by subtle shades in your character. In addition, Mother had no truck with how her daughters looked, only with their ability to pass themselves off as 'ladies', to be well regarded by the very class of person that she professed to despise.

There was no one to whom Innis could turn for consolation – except Grandfather McIver. He always seemed to know exactly what troubled her. He had had a great deal of experience of women – far too much, according to Vassie – and was very good at offering advice to his granddaughters. It seemed odd to talk of matters of the heart with such a hulk of a man, for Evander McIver was so old and grizzled that Innis tended to think of him not as a person at all but as a sort of immutable geological formation, like a sea-stac or a skerry.

In the past couple of years she had seen little of him, for there was no love lost between Ronan and he, and Evander McIver did not often leave his home on the tiny island of Foss. Every now and then, though, a passing boatman would deliver letters or packets from Foss to show that Grandfather had not forgotten them. While Aileen showed off her latest trinket, a brooch or a ring, and Biddy chirped over a spool of silk ribbon or a card of lace, Innis, with a pleasure quite incomprehensible to her sisters, would unwrap the books that her grandfather had chosen for her. Stout treatises on the anatomy of the horse or the management of cattle, historical biographies, scientific monographs, novels or poems; Innis had no special preference and would devour instructional manuals with the same rapt attention as she read the tales of Meredith and Blackmore.

If she had been a boy, or if the boys had been more like her, perhaps Grandfather McIver would have tried to educate them too, but Neil and Donnie were Campbells to the core. They made fun of old Evander, dubbed him 'the laird of nowhere', and failed to appreciate that his tiny island was in fact a kingdom from which you might survey the whole wide world.

When word came that Norman McAlpin had gone broke, that Fetternish had been sold yet again, Grandfather McIver sailed over from Foss. He had taken Vassie aside and had told her what she must do to protect Pennypol, not only from the predations of new owners but from the idleness of the man with whom she shared bed and board. He had advised her to build the head wall, for whether it was sheep the Baverstocks put on to the ground or whether it was shooting parties there was bound to be change in the air and Pennypol would have to be kept safe from it.

Biddy and Innis were anxious lest Grandfather's predictions were correct and the winds of change would blow away the only way of life that they had ever known. Now that the sheep had come to Fetternish, however, it was difficult to see where the threat lay. There was certainly nothing threatening in the sight of the Cheviots peacefully nibbling the grass on top of the ridge or in the thin column of smoke that rose from the shepherd's cottage where Mr Michael Tarrant was cooking a lonely breakfast and – perhaps, perhaps – dreaming of the girls on the farm next door.

Sheep or not, shepherd or not, it was still dry, still hot and there was still work to be done. Hay had been made in the last week in July, late for a grass crop, but the stooks had been left in the field and not brought into the hay loft. It was that task that now occupied the Campbell women.

The hayfield lay north-west of the calf park on the back side of Olaf's Hill. It was shaped like a Valentine heart, squashed at the top by a broken dike and a straggling blackthorn hedge. From the crest of the field you could watch the red funnels of MacBrayne's paddle steamers cleaving up from Staffa and Iona and see the black sails of the luggers drift fishing beyond Coll or the big jibs of east-coast smacks chasing down the herring shoals.

As a rule the girls would lift their heads and glance out to sea whenever one of the funnels went past or, more rarely, one of the scuddy little steam-lighters that were beginning to take over the coastal trade. But that morning Biddy did not look out to sea. Poised with hay on the fork or a stook in her arms she would stare up at the hill and the smoke that rose above it and would arch her eyebrows so high that she seemed to have no brows at all. And Innis would smile to herself – not in triumph, not yet – but because she believed that when it came to Michael Tarrant she was already one point up in the game.

The grass had been cut just past bloom and laid out evenly in wind-rows. The rows had been stacked into conical heaps to keep the hay from bleaching while the wall had been constructed. Now Vassie was eager to have the hay brought to the loft before the first autumn storm flattened everything in sight. They did not use the wheeled cart. The ground by the field gate was soft and sandy and an old-fashioned peat sled was best for the job. One of the farm's sturdy Highland garrons was attached to the shafts, Aileen in charge of it. She was less adept at handling animals than Innis but the pony was patient and understood what was required of it. It permitted Aileen to hang on to the rein and yap out instructions while it got on with the job at its own even pace.

It was half past eleven o'clock before Vassie allowed the girls to break for dinner, by which time half the stooks had been transported to the steading. Dinner was brought up in two pails, one containing bread and smoked fish, the other cold unsweetened tea. The pony was released to crop the grass and drink from a bucket of fresh water while Vassie and her daughters flopped on the fringe of the hayfield in the shadow of the thorn hedge. They ate the smoked fish and buttered bread washed down with tin cupfuls of astringent black tea. They listened to flies buzzing in the bracken and the unfamiliar bleating of sheep from somewhere just over the ridge and, on the surface, the day seemed quiet.

Then a voice said, 'Aye, sir, that is them.'

'You, I say, you there.'

Men and dogs formed a tableau on the hillside below the coppice of larch and pine. For a fleeting instant Innis knew what it felt like to be a hare or a rabbit. She would not have been surprised if the man with the shotgun under his arm had snapped it to his shoulder and fired at them, shouting, the way some sportsmen did, when the pellets struck home. She rolled over and struggled to her feet. Vassie was already upright, her thin brown arm extended.

'So it's yourself then, Mrs Campbell,' Hector Thrale said. 'You and your lassies will be taking a breather, if I am not mistaken. Is it not on the late side to be drawing in hay, though?'

'When I draw my hay is none of your business,' Vassie told him.

'And how are you today, Biddy? Are you keeping well?'

Put out by the presence of Michael Tarrant, Biddy ignored the factor's question. The shepherd stood behind the others, the collie at his side, while two monstrous liver-coloured hounds slavered and snuffled about the Baverstocks' shins. The men were obviously brothers, angular and tall, with large, long-fingered hands. The elder sported a trim beard with a trace of grey in its brown strands, while the younger made do with a dainty moustache. They were clad in identical brand-new Norfolk jackets and plus-two trousers tailored from stiff herring-bone tweed and, in spite of the heat of the day, wore tweed caps with buttoned ear flaps. Their leather boots were too new to have been broken in and Innis noticed how they hirpled as they clambered down the hill with the big, ungainly hounds snuffling and lolloping before them.

'Far enough,' said Vassie, then paused and added, 'Mr Baverstock.'

'Hah! I do believe we have been recognised, Walter.'

'I do believe we have, Austin.'

'Pleasure to make your acquaintance, madam.'

Michael remained where he was, the crook resting against his shoulder and one hand held down to let the collie lick his fingers.

He met Innis's eye and gave her a faint smile.

'Will you be good enough to do the honours, Thrale, old chap?' said Walter Baverstock, advancing down the bracken-clad slope. He had the gun cracked open, the barrel pointed downward. The shotgun, Innis saw, was as new as the Norfolk jacket, as smooth and oily as the gentleman himself. He had small sharp white teeth and his eyes had that far-away look that she had noticed before in men of a certain class, as if they were gazing beyond you at something more interesting.

'Mrs Vanessa Campbell, of Pennypol,' Hector Thrale announced.

The factor wore an old black serge suit and stiff-collared shirt.

You might have thought that he had just emerged from church if it weren't for the big round-toed brogans on his feet and the soft-brimmed, sweat-stained hat. He was of an age with Walter Baverstock, somewhere about fifty; Austin, Innis reckoned, was three or four years younger.

The long arm, the long hand came over the thorn, the long, bearded chin thrust out, the smile fixed under a remote gaze. 'I am Walter Baverstock and this is my brother Austin.'

Vassie scowled and hesitated. She held up her skirts, showing wrinkled stockings and worn boots. Her hair was tangled, her bodice patched with sweat. She looked like what she was, a peasant woman whittled by weather and hard labour. She was by no means indifferent to the power that these men wielded, however, or to her own little handful of power. She was no mere tenant or crofter, no tacksman's wife eking out a living on the edge of the shore. She too owned land and did not have to grovel to any man, a fact of which the Baverstocks were well aware.

Innis watched her mother wipe her hand on her skirt and reach across the thorn to shake Walter Baverstock's hand. She did the same for Austin and then, at the lairds' request, brought Biddy and Innis forward and introduced them too. When Biddy dropped a curtsey, the remoteness went out of Austin Baverstock's eyes. He no longer seemed to be gazing towards the horizon and thinking of other things. Biddy usually had this effect on strangers and, Innis thought, it would take more than heavy tweeds and a shotgun to protect a man against her sister's wiles if Biddy chose to put on the swank.

'There now,' said Hector Thrale. 'Is it not better to be neighbourly?'

'That remains to be seen,' Vassie said.

'The little one, the child, what's her name?' Walter Baverstock asked.

'She is Aileen, sir,' Biddy answered. 'My other sister.'

'What – if I may ask – is she doing?' said Austin Baverstock.

'Drinking her tea,' said Biddy, as if it was the most natural thing in the world for a young girl to crouch on all fours and lap from a tin cup like a pup. 'She says it tastes better that way.'

'How pecul – I mean, well, perhaps it does. Perhaps it does,' Austin Baverstock conceded. He glanced at Thrale who, with a motion too slight to be offensive, shook his head. 'The menfolk, Mrs Campbell, where are they?'

'They are at the fishing,' Vassie replied.

'Ah, I see,' said Austin Baverstock. 'They attend to the harvest of the sea while you have the farm to keep you busy. An excellent arrangement, Walter, don't you think?'

'Very practical. Very sound.'

At that moment one of the hounds spotted a rabbit on the edge of the hayfield and swarmed over the broken dike and raced away down the slope, its partner on its heels.

'Stay, Roy,' Michael Tarrant said sharply, as the shepherd's collie seemed about to forget his training and rush off through the bracken in pursuit of a quarry that had already vanished. The sheepdog obeyed instantly. He peered up at his master with a puckered frown, then settled on his haunches with an air of virtuous disdain.

'Thor. Odin. Heah. Heah,' Walter Baverstock shouted.

Fishing a silver whistle from his breast pocket, he stuck it in his mouth and blew a summons that the hounds ignored. The sound was sufficiently shrill to rouse the Campbells' lurcher from noonday stupor, however. It brought him padding round the gable to see what all the fuss was about.

'Thor, come to Papa this instant.' Austin added his voice to his brother's. 'Odin, bad dog. Bad, bad dog.'

The daft young hounds would have none of it. They dashed into the bracken where the rabbit, or a memory of the rabbit, lured them and, finding nothing, bayed and bellowed like lost children then, thrashing through the ferns, emerged upon the wrong side of the drystone, in Fingal's territory.

'Do you keep a dog, madam?' Austin Baverstock asked.

'Oh, aye,' said Vassie.

'Is that him?'

'Aye, Mr Baverstock, that's him.'

The hounds quivered into and out of view, tails up and heads down, heads up and tails down, while Fingal, forelegs stiff, ruff bristling, muzzle curled and teeth bared, stalked them confidently. Baying turned suddenly to whining, followed by a fierce frenzy of snarling and yelping. Then the hounds reappeared. One almost on top of the other, they scrambled over the coping, thumped down and raced off, not towards the sound of the silver whistle and the friendly smell of tweed but away across the burn and into the moorland heather.

'Odin.'

'Thor.'

Fingal appeared at the harrow-gate, planted his forepaws on it, stared uphill at the fleeing hounds for a second then slipped back, gave himself a shake, and lay down, satisfied.

'His name is Fingal,' Biddy informed them while Aileen, attentive now, bounced up and down and clapped her hands.

'What shall we do, Thrale? Have we lost them?'

'Hounds, Mr Baverstock, should be able to find their own way home.'

'Unless they run into Mr Clark's sheep,' Biddy said.

'Sheep?' said Austin Baverstock in alarm.

'A hundred and twenty Blackface,' Vassie said.

'Mr Clark has a gun too.' The men stared at Aileen. 'Mr Clark shoots doggies that worry his sheep.'

'Surely he wouldn't shoot a pedigree hound?'

'Bang!' Aileen cried, gleefully. 'Bang, bang, bang!'

'If you will take my dog back to my cottage,' Michael Tarrant said, 'I'll have a tramp over the moor and see if I can lead the hounds in.'

'Would you, Tarrant? Good suggestion. Jolly good suggestion.'

Michael unlooped a length of twine from about his waist, collared Roy with it and handed the lead to Thrale.

Innis said, 'Do you know what is over there, Mr Tarrant?'

'No, I admit I do not.'

'Then I will come with you.'

'Innis!' Biddy swung round to appeal to her mother. 'Has she not got work to do like the rest of us?'

'Go with the man to the top of the hill,' Vassie said. 'Show him the lie of the land but be back here without fail in half an hour.'

'Aye, Mother,' Innis agreed, then, with a boldness that was more show than anything, beckoned Mr Tarrant to follow her across the strip of the hayfield and up on to the breast of the moor.

*　*　*

The Coming of the Sheep

For their first excursion to the wild west coast of Mull the Baverstocks had travelled light. They had left their town-house servants behind in Edinburgh and had brought with them only a cook and a boot-boy. The latter person had been borrowed from their sister, Agnes, who had charge of the family mansion at Sangster. It had been a good twenty-five years since Willy Naismith had been a 'Boots', a fact that the Baverstock brothers somehow managed to ignore. To Walter and Austin, Willy Naismith was and always would be the Boots, a smart, sly, often truculent orphan who, even before he'd reached his teens, seemed to know more than his master's sons about the real world and how it wagged. During school holidays, Willy had led the brothers into many scrapes and adventures, earning not so much gratitude as dependence; which was why, for the grandest adventure of all – the purchase and establishment of a Highland estate – Willy had been summoned from Sangster to serve them once more.

What the Baverstocks did not know, and what Willy certainly wasn't going to tell them, was that he'd been damned relieved to be yanked out of Sangster that August. The summons had come at a most opportune moment. Willy's masculine efficiency had run him into trouble with yet another young kitchen-maid who was letting it be known that she had given her all to Mr Naismith on the strength of a promise of marriage and that she was not going to be fobbed off with a groom or a gardener instead.

Eight years ago fate had dealt Willy a similar bacon-saving hand when his wife had been carried off to the bosom of the Lord. He had grieved for Prudence, of course, had worn widower's weeds for months, had even sworn off random intercourse for a while. But Pru's departure had conveniently erased the accusations of adultery that had kept the mansion's staff on tenterhooks, and had opened up for Willy a whole new chapter of seduction.

Willy had four daughters living in Sangster, all happily married. He had two other daughters and a son born out of wedlock to servant girls, all of whom were, or soon would be, employed in the tweed cloth manufactory. To the good citizens of Sangster it seemed like a miracle that Willy Naismith remained a servant of the Baverstock Pauls and had not been dismissed for moral turpitude. Willy could have told them that it was more a mistake than a miracle but he was not the sort to brag about his conquests, upstairs or down.

Mull, however, was the perfect place to lie low while the latest whiff of scandal cleared away and he had travelled to join the brothers in Edinburgh with a light heart, leaving his women and his problems behind.

Whatever his moral failings Willy was a diligent and attentive servant. It didn't surprise Austin and Walter to find him waiting on the doorstep of Fetternish House to relieve them of their caps and jackets, usher them to the bench in the alcove behind the door and, kneeling, haul off their boots and place them – the boots not the brothers – into a tall-box for cleaning.

'Did you have a satisfactory morning, Mr Austin?' Willy enquired.

'No, William, we did not have a satisfactory morning.'

'Too hot for you, sir?'

'Far too hot.'

'I've just the medicine for that, sir,' Willy said and directed the gentlemen into the great hall where it was dark and quiet and cool and a jug of gin and tonic and two tall, chilled glasses waited on the table before the empty fireplace. He had the gin poured before Austin or Walter could hobble across the creaking wooden floorboards and settle themselves into the furniture.

Austin eased himself into a Georgian wing chair, one of a pair, stretched out his legs, waggled his toes, and sighed. Willy slid a glass into his hand, a moist glass, deliciously chilled. Austin drank.

'It's cold collation for luncheon, sir. I thought that'd be best on a warm day. Cook's made a salad to go with the last of the veal pie and there's a fresh raspberry mousse to follow.' Willy placed a glass into Walter's outstretched hand then knelt and massaged his master's stockinged feet. 'Now, we can have it in the front room at the big table or we can have it, *al fresco*, in here.'

'We lost the dogs, William,' said Walter.

'Lost them? How?'

'They ran off,' said Austin.

'Will the Thrale person find them for you?' Willy said.

'The shepherd,' Austin told him.

'So Mr Thrale will not be joining us for luncheon then?'

'No. No, no,' said Walter.

'He'll be back at two o'clock,' said Austin. 'He has some notion to break another piece of ground for cultivation and wishes us to approve his choice of the site. I cannot think why.'

'What does he wish us to cultivate, sir?' Willy asked.

'Root crops,' Walter said. 'Turnips, I believe.'

'What do we know about turnips?' Austin said.

Sod all, Willy thought. That's what you know about most things agricultural. He placed Walter's foot down gently, crossed to the hexagonal table and refreshed the glasses.

'Sheep like them, I suppose,' Austin went on, after a pause.

'Nourishment,' Walter told him. 'Winter feed.'

Staring into the empty fireplace that reared before them like a bishop's tomb the Baverstocks nodded in unison. A pace or two behind the chairs, Willy waited, jug in hand. He wondered, not for the first time, what the languid city gentlemen were doing here, what they thought they were playing at in buying a run-down rustic property. Fetternish House was chalk against cheese compared to the Baverstock Paul mansion in Sangster or the brothers' elegant town-house in Edinburgh's Charlotte Square. What had possessed them to bid for this bleak old dwelling on an estate composed mainly of bracken and broken rock? The house didn't even have a distinguished history. The plumbing was primitive. There was, of course, no piped gas. The nearest store, let alone a telegraph office, was two miles away across the heather.

'What did you think of her, Walter?' Austin said.

'Who?'

'The Campbell girl. The redhead. At the hayfield.'

'Oh, the Campbell girl,' said Walter Baverstock, vaguely. 'Yes.'

'Stunning, what?' said Austin. 'A solitary reaper.'

'Come now, Austin, don't get carried away.'

'No.' Austin sighed and cupped the tall glass in both hands as if, Willy thought, he was clasping the waist of the little island chick who had already caught his fancy. 'No, I suppose you're right.'

A moment's silence. Walter said, 'What was her name again?'

'Biddy.'

'Are you smitten, old man?' Walter enquired.

'You know,' Austin answered, 'I do believe I am,' while a step or two behind the brothers, wily Willy Naismith immediately pricked up his ears.

Innis led Michael Tarrant on to the ridge that overlooked Loch Mingary. He walked behind her, not so close that he could not admire the swing of her hips or the shape of her calves if he had a mind to, but more likely out of politeness. She walked with a young woman's gait, swinging her shoulders. Now and then she glanced round to make sure that Michael had not been left behind and noticed how neatly he moved, body upright, head erect and vigilant.

She said nothing until they reached the summit of the ridge. It was marked by a single standing stone ten feet in height. She stepped into the sheep hollow that surrounded the stone, rested her shoulder against it and beckoned Michael to join her.

'Does it have a name?' he asked. 'The stone, I mean.'

'Aye, she is called Caliach.' Innis used the Gaelic pronunciation.

'What does it mean?'

'Old wife. She is the Old Wife of Mingary.'

'Is there a story about her?' Michael said. 'There must be. There's always a story attached to a standing stone. Is she good or evil?'

'She is neither good nor evil,' Innis told him. 'But there is a story about how she came to be here.'

'Tell it to me.'

Innis wondered if he was teasing her, if, like so many incomers, he thought that Gaelic lore and legend was just so much fanciful rubbish.

'No,' he said. 'I mean it.'

'Thousands of years ago,' Innis said, 'the Norsemen came and stole Caliach's children to take back to Norway. She ran after them, cursed them and called on the winds and the waves to turn them round and drive them back.' Innis shook her head. 'Surely you do not want to listen to all this nonsense?'

'It isn't nonsense,' Michael assured her. 'I want to hear the story.'

He had come down into the hollow and stood by the stone, looking up at it. While she spoke he brushed the rough surface with his fingertips as if the faded grey medallions of lichen could be read like an alphabet of the blind.

'Is it too shocking for the ears of an incomer?' he said.

'No, no,' Innis said, and continued. 'One of the sea gods, or it may have been a druid, struck a bargain with Caliach. He told her that he would bring her children back safe if she would agree to become his watch-woman.'

'And did the god, or the druid, keep his word?'

'She is here, is she not?'

'Indeed,' Michael said. 'And her children, what happened to them?'

'The Norsemen were drowned in a sudden squall but all Caliach's children were saved to become the original people of the isles. Because she was a woman of her word, Caliach stands guard upon this part of the coast to this day,' Innis said. 'In winter mists and at dusk sometimes they say you can hear her call out to those of her children who have gone on their journey westward.'

'What does she say to them?' Michael asked.

'She calls out to assure them that she will be waiting for them whenever they choose to return.'

'Have you heard the Old Wife's voice?'

'No,' Innis answered him. 'Not yet.'

'Some day you will?'

'Some day, perhaps.' Inclining her head, she said, 'See, there are your dogs, playing by the sea's edge.'

'I know,' Michael said. 'I spotted them from the top of the hill.'

'Had you not better be fetching them before they drown themselves?'

'Aye, they're daft enough for it,' Michael said.

The Baverstocks' hounds were sniffing about the fringes of a rock pool, oblivious to the fact that they were supposed to be lost.

'I must be getting back now,' Innis said. 'The hay will not wait and I cannot be leaving all the work to Biddy. Do you know where you are, Mr Tarrant?'

29

'I'm not sure I do,' the shepherd said, then laughed. 'Aye, Miss Campbell, I know where I am.' He rested his shoulders on the stone and surveyed the landscape before him. 'It's fine country, though very different from where I come from.'

There were no fences and few walls, only the shape of the sea loch, like a butter-knife blade and, up towards the head of it, dark clusters of oak, fir and pine. Smoke purled upwards from the Ards, Mr Clark's house, from farm buildings scattered over Quinish and, faint in the distance, tinted the sky above the little township of Dervaig.

Innis said, 'Will you be staying, Mr Tarrant?'

'On Mull?' He glanced at her and pushed himself away from the rock. 'Well, from what I gather it's not accommodating country for a shepherd. I've even heard it said that Mull can break a man's heart.'

'That depends on the man, Mr Tarrant,' Innis said.

'What do you think, Miss Campbell? Do you think it'll break my heart?'

'It might, Mr Tarrant,' Innis answered him. 'Aye, it might at that.'

TWO

A Sunday Lunch

Even Willy Naismith, bred to the great indoors, was sufficiently country wise to realise that the weather was on the turn. He didn't need the experts in the McKinnon Arms to inform him that when the hot spell broke the summer would break with it and that winter would soon be at their throats. He had been listening to farmers' patter all his life and had no sympathy with men who, however bountiful nature had been, always managed to look on the black side; men who believed that for every good thing that happened there would be a price to pay. He had always assumed that Border sheep-farmers had no equals when it came to wallowing in gloom, but, before the end of his first week on the island, Willy was ready to concede that for sheer, dyed-in-the-wool, down-in-the-mouth pessimism Mull's crofters really took the biscuit.

Willy left the Baverstocks lolling in armchairs in the great hall. Fresh air, scallops, poached salmon, venison, and plum tart had rendered them drowsy and, fortified by a bottle of twelve-year-old malt whisky, the brothers could not have cared less where the boot-boy was going or what he intended to do when he got there. In fact, Willy set off for Crove in search of two things: women and information. He didn't really expect to be met with open arms by a bunch of sonsy lassies or even to receive much of a welcome, though, for Crove was a dour wee village with Church of Scotland granite glowering over one end of the main street and the Free Kirk's sandstone over the other.

The McKinnon Arms was the first building at the head of an unpaved cul-de-sac set between facing rows of whitewashed cottages. Crove's public house was hardly a magnet for travellers and even unfastidious cattle drovers preferred to tramp on the extra couple of miles to Dervaig, for the McKinnon was shabby and down at heel and put out no welcome mat for visitors.

On the grass outside the front door were two or three wooden benches which were occupied by local farmers and fishermen. Willy nodded amiably as he approached. The men stopped drinking and puffing on their pipes and regarded him as if he were an object of no more interest than a crow. Somewhat nonplussed, Willy hunched his shoulders, ducked under the lintel and entered a room so shrouded in tobacco smoke that he could barely make out the bar. Heads turned towards him and conversation ceased, leaving only the lonely creak of Willy's shoes on the floorboards to accompany him to the counter.

He cleared his throat. 'Pint of your best beer, landlord, please.'

McKinnon, if that's who he was, bore no resemblance to any landlord with whom Willy had done business. He was thin-faced, weedy and pale. He was dressed in a stiff, collarless shirt fastened at the throat with a tin stud and had dark, streaky hair plastered across his scalp.

'That will be fourpence,' he said.

'Fourpence?'

'It is the cost of the transportation, you see.'

'You mean you don't have a brewery on Mull?' Willy said.

'There is whisky if you would be preferring it?'

'Is it cheaper?'

'It is much the same sort of price.'

'I'll take the beer.'

Willy counted out coins from his purse.

McKinnon tapped beer directly from a barrel into a none too clean glass and passed it to Willy across the counter then he, the landlord, murmured something in Gaelic that drew a snigger from his local clients.

'What did you say?' Willy asked.

'I was wishing you the good health,' the landlord said, innocently.

'I see. Fine. Well – good health to you too.'

He held the glass in both hands and sipped from it. The beer was flat, lukewarm and weak enough to have been watered.

Willy said nothing by way of complaint. He slaked his thirst, wandered from the counter into the body of the room and then, prompted by the silence, carried the glass outside.

No lamps had been lit along the length of the main street though the air was sooty with dusk. Clouds of midges swirled overhead and on the bench by the wall were three fishermen, a man and two grown boys.

One of the boys was huge with the sort of shoulder span that you usually associated with Highland bulls. The other young man was smaller and had a cool, cunning look to him. They had a jug of beer and a bottle of whisky on the bench beside them. Seven or eight empty pint glasses littered the grass at their feet and the spiralling midges did not seem to bother them at all.

To Willy's surprise the man spoke to him in English.

'Well, now, sir,' the man said, 'I see that you have found your way to our hostelry. Tell me, what do you think of Mr McKinnon's beer?'

'I've tasted better,' Willy said.

'It is best taken with a drop of whisky.'

'I'll remember that in future,' Willy said.

'No need to be waiting for the future. Let Neil strengthen your glass.'

For some reason Willy was chary. He sensed that the fisherman was not offering him hospitality out of the goodness of his heart. The young man lifted the whisky bottle, rose from the bench and towered over Willy like a giant.

'You will be taking a drink with us, will you not now?' he said.

'Well, since you're offering, aye. Many thanks.'

Whisky trickled into his glass. At the same moment he felt the first nip of the midge cloud on his brow and the backs of his hands. It was all he could do not to scratch and slap at the biting insects. He forced a smile, lifted the glass and let the fiery liquid trickle down his throat.

'You will be from the big house at Fetternish, will you not?' the man said.

'I am.'

'You will be a friend of the Mr Baverstocks then?'

The fire in Willy's throat was matched by the scalding of insect bites. How long do you have to live on Mull and how much local whisky did you have to consume to become immune? Willy wondered and, in the hope of escaping the tiny attackers, stepped closer to the bench.

He said, 'I'm man-servant to the Mr Baverstocks.'

'And where are your gentlemen tonight?'

'At home. I mean, at Fetternish.'

'Uh-hmm,' the man said. 'Were you sent down the road to see what Crove had to offer?'

'Aye,' Willy said, 'and it isn't much.'

'Well, we are just simple folk here, you know.'

Willy's inner voice whispered a warning: Be careful, William. This chap's trying to intimidate you.

Moving closer, he realised that the man was not so young as he appeared to be, nearer fifty than forty. He was dark-haired, smooth-skinned and with a roundness to his features that reminded Willy of tide-washed boulders. His brown eyes were soft but watchful. The dark-haired lad with the feminine eye-lashes leaned forward. 'Where is it you come from, Mr–'

'My name's Naismith. And you?'

'Oh, we come from down the shore a piece,' the lad answered. 'Are you from the gentlemen's residence in Edinburgh?'

'No, from the family house in Sangster.'

'Sangster? Now where would that be?' the father asked.

'In the Borders.'

'Uh-hmm, I see. Have you been employed by the Baverstocks for long?'

'Long enough,' said Willy.

The blond boy stood before him, blocking out the last of the light. He drank from the beer glass in deep practised swallows, Adam's apple bobbing in the column of his throat. He wiped his mouth and said, 'So you will be knowing them well? The Baverstocks, I mean.'

'Well enough,' said Willy, cautiously.

'Would you be saying that you are in their confidence?' the father asked.

'I'd say that, aye.'

The young man with the long lashes leaned his elbows on his knees and gave a little nod as if everything was going along nicely. Willy's caution increased. 'It is a fine flock of sheep they have bought.'

'They seem satisfied with them,' Willy said.

'Will they be bringing more on to the land, do you know?'

'They might.'

'Are you not acquainted with the shepherd?'

'Tarrant.'

'Oh, is that his name, now?'

'That's his name,' said Willy. 'I haven't met him yet.'

'Have you not?' The man seemed surprised. 'I thought he might have let it slip to you just how many of the sheep are coming on to Fetternish.'

'He hasn't,' said Willy.

'And what he thinks of his neighbours.'

Willy shrugged and, in spite of his resolve, clawed at the back of his hand. His cheeks above the line of his beard were burning. He had encountered midge clouds often before but he had not felt anything quite so bad as this. It was as if he were being eaten alive.

'How long will they be staying here?' the man persisted.

'Until they're settled in, I expect,' Willy got out.

'Will they not be going home to Edinburgh for the winter?'

'I doubt it,' Willy said. 'I think they're here to stay, Mr Campbell. You are Mr Campbell, aren't you?'

'And will you be staying with them?'

'Where they are, I am,' Willy said.

He could not decide whether it was the agony inflicted upon him by the midges or the fisherman's wheedling tone that finally eroded his patience. He drank the last of the whisky, got to his feet and said, 'Are you the father of the red-haired girl, the one called Biddy?'

Ronan Campbell started. 'What sort of question is that to be asking?'

'You seemed so interested in what the Mr Baverstocks had to say about their neighbours, I thought . . .'

'Biddy? Do they talk about our Biddy?'

'If she's the good-looking redhead, aye, they do.'

The blond boy moved. If Daddy Campbell had not caught his arm then he might have punched Willy, knocked him flying.

35

There was more to it than the defence of a sister's honour, Willy thought, something that he had no knowledge of yet, some dark secret about the girl that made the Campbells bridle at the very raising of her name.

'Uh-hmm,' Ronan Campbell said. 'What is it they are saying about my daughter, Mr Naismith? Will you be telling me that?'

'No, I will not be telling you that, Mr Campbell,' Willy said. 'Some things are best left to the imagination. Now, if you'll excuse me, I've had enough of your questions and your midges. Thank you for the dram. I'm off home.'

He would have stepped away if the blond boy had not barred his path. Red-eyed, red-faced, young Campbell looked more like a bull than ever. His huge hands balled into huge fists.

'Try it,' Willy said, quietly. 'Go on, son, just try it.'

'Let him go, Neil,' Campbell said.

Reluctantly the boy stepped aside and, to his relief, Willy found himself free to leave. He walked quickly away from the Arms and out of Crove and soon felt the faint, refreshing breeze off the sea loch brush his brow and cheeks and scare off the last of the midges. The evening had not been entirely wasted. Without effort or intention, it seemed that he had made enemies of the Baverstocks' neighbours. What did he care? He owed the islanders no loyalty, no respect. And if and when his chance came for an encounter with the red-haired girl he would seize it now without a qualm.

Whistling, and not in the least depressed by his encounter with the Campbell clan, Willy headed home towards the big house on the hill.

It was a little after midnight and Biddy could not sleep. She lay on her side with Aileen fitted into her back like a spoon in a velvet box. The heat that the little girl generated was ferocious even on cold winter nights and in summer the sheets, blanket and mattress grew damp with her perspiration. Not so long ago cattle had been stalled below the loft, for cottage and byre had been one and the same, and cows, calves, ponies and hens, not to mention the odd stray cat, crowded under the long roof so that you never knew what sort of beast would be sharing your bed when you wakened in the morning.

A Sunday Lunch

It was only after the timber-ship *Tobago* had foundered off Tiree and equinoctial tides had washed great rafts of unstripped logs into the Pennypol coves that Vassie had acquired enough wood to build partitions, a lean-to for the ponies and a solid wooden water-closet that, unlike its predecessor, did not blow over in the wind and spill its contents, and its occupant, out upon the grass.

Biddy still missed the closeness of the cattle. Their coughs and splutterings, wheezings and shiftings had been comforting in the dead dark hours of the night, much preferable to Aileen's squeaky little snores.

Biddy did not like small things. Frogs, moths, caterpillars, spiders, mice all made her flesh creep. She preferred creatures to be on the same scale as she was herself. She had inherited her size from Grandfather McIver, her beauty from her Irish grandmother; an uncomfortable mix. Grandfather McIver had told her that her good looks were a gift from God and that she should be grateful for them; that one day she would be able to choose a husband from a host of admirers instead of having to make do with whatever drifted her way.

It was not until her seventeenth year, when faint but persistent yearnings possessed her, that Biddy finally matured, became attractive to and attracted by men and curious about sexual matters. If only they had made their intentions less obvious perhaps she would have surrendered her virginity to one of the lusty young drovers who plagued her at the cattle show or to one of the lynx-eyed fishermen who hung about with Neil and Donnie.

She had been proposed to four times, molested twice and had laid Sonny McKinstry out stone cold with a blow from her fist when he offered her money to go into the woods with him. Until that sultry day when Michael Tarrant had held her in his arms, however, she had never known what it was to yield to a man. She could not imagine why a perfect stranger, who had succeeded in ignoring both her temper and her beauty, had affected her so much, why she could not stop thinking of him and dreaming of his touch.

Aileen wakened suddenly and sat up. There was no light in the loft. The glimmer of the peat fire in the room below had long since faded.

Biddy could hear nothing, not cattle roar, not wave beat, not even the faint whisper of the wind. She could just make out the shape of Aileen's face framed by a shock of near-white hair.

Innis lifted herself out of the darkness and said, 'What ails you, Aileen?'

'Do you not hear it?' Aileen said.

'Hear what?' said Biddy.

'The rain,' Aileen said.

Biddy strained to catch whatever tell-tale sound had wakened Aileen from sleep. She was tense and nervous. In three or four days it would be her time of the month and she had been thinking too much of Michael Tarrant, the feel of his arms about her. 'I hear nothing,' she said. 'Go back to sleep.'

'Rain,' Aileen chanted, softly. 'Rain, rain, rain. Rain's coming.'

'Are you sure?' Innis asked.

'I feel it,' Aileen said. 'Do you not feel the changes in the air?'

Biddy looked up at the pinewood slats that supported the roof. She put up her hand and touched the wood as if to feel the coming of the rain. But there was nothing, no spot, plop or tremor, none of the thrilling little vibrations that usually stirred the house when tides of wind ran in before the rain cloud.

'She's dreaming again,' said Biddy.

Aileen giggled, flung herself across the loft and, wriggling like a sand eel, vanished down the ladder that led to the kitchen. A moment later Biddy heard the front door scrape open.

'Go after her,' Biddy said.

'Go yourself,' said Innis.

'Is it the rain at last?'

'How do I know?' Innis said and, flinging off sheet and blanket, backed to the ladder and lowered herself down it.

Biddy lay back against the bolster, relieved to be alone in the loft. She listened for the voice of the thunder but could hear nothing save the pulses beating within her. She was so hot and restless that she felt as if she might explode. She lay back, spread her bare legs across the mattress, braced the back of her head against the angle of the roof and tried to imagine what it would be like to have the shepherd lying on top of her.

'Biddy?'

She rolled on to her stomach and clawed guiltily at the sheet just as her mother's face appeared at the top of the ladder.

'What is going on here?'

She wrapped the bedsheet around her and flattened herself against the mattress, sulky with guilt. 'I'm – I'm – I am trying to sleep.'

'Where are your sisters?'

'Gone out, I think. Aileen heard . . .'

'Come down,' Vassie said. 'Come down and see this.'

Lamplight bloomed in the kitchen. She could hear her father crooning instructions, Donnie answering him. She peered at her mother's face, fierce in the underglow, wiry hair sticking out about her head, the lamplight moving below her in pale, flat patches. The lurcher, Fingal, growled, then barked.

'What's happening? What are they doing?'

'Bringing up the boat.'

'Why?'

'Come down,' Vassie said again, and vanished.

Biddy crawled to the top of the ladder and peered down into the kitchen. Father, still in his night-shirt, was tugging on his sea-boots. Neil, like a gigantic spectre in his knee-length shirt, was paring a tallow candle to stick into the lantern. Clad in under-drawers, an oilskin slung over his bare back, Donnie was propped in the doorway, looking out into the night.

Biddy snatched her skirt from the cord at the back of the loft and, hugging it to her, climbed down the ladder. By the time she reached the floor everyone, even the dog, had gone. She hesitated, struggled into her skirt then wearily followed the family outside.

There was some light in the sky now. A thin horizontal smear, the colour of buttermilk, separated the black Atlantic from a ceiling of pure black cloud. The haziness had gone from the air and the blackness was glossy like the skin of a whale. The heat was suffocating. Biddy put her hands to her face and stripped sweat from her cheekbones. She wiped her eyes with her knuckles and peered down towards the beach.

Her father and brothers were scurrying towards the jetty to untie the boat and drag it high up on the sand. They had lost a boat the year before last, smashed by a storm, and only a loan from Grandfather McIver had saved them from ruin, for Father

39

didn't believe in wasting money on insurance. Mother and Innis were halfway to the calf park, the dancing light of a paraffin lamp charting their progress. Before her, though, stood Aileen with Fingal at her side. The dog was bristling and barking while Aileen shouted gleefully and waved her arms as if she were stirring a gigantic, invisible pot.

'What is it?' Biddy cried out.

'There.'

Aileen pointed to the north where a huge spreading flicker of blue-white light opened and lingered and faded, opened and lingered once more. Sheet lightning: far off, far out to sea but so brilliant that Biddy could clearly make out the silhouette of each of the small isles and headlands, matt black against the nothingness beyond. Even before the flash had faded she heard a distant mutter of thunder and felt against her cheeks, at last, the first cool stirring of the wind that, in an hour or less, would whip and whirl the cloud mass hard against the coast and drive the sea up to their door.

Aileen spread her arms, shrieked in delight at the feel of the wind and then, with Fingal bounding at her heels, darted off towards the beach, after her father and the boys.

Biddy stood where she was, letting the breeze melt against her skin, then, turning from the waist, she looked up through the darkness to Olaf's Hill behind which, in his sheltered cottage on Pennymain, Michael Tarrant would be safe and snug, and all alone.

'Biddeee.'

'I'm coming,' Biddy shouted and started out towards the calf park to help her mother fetch the little creatures into the safety of the byre.

Minutes after they had steered the calves into the byre the rain began.

Innis shooed the hens into the byre too, then Biddy and she hurried around the sheds and roped all the doors; autumn gales were often worse than winter ones and could strip the steading of everything that was not tied down. Father and the boys, wet through, were back indoors before Innis tumbled into the kitchen and, with rain beating in great sheets against the facing

A Sunday Lunch

wall, flung herself against the door and barred it against the elements.

Even in the kitchen the atmosphere had already cooled. Donnie had tossed three or four lumps of peat on to the fire to make it blaze and Fingal, stinking wet, lay curled before it as if summer had been nothing but a dream. Vassie filled the kettle from the bucket and hung it on the hook to boil while the boys took off their boots and jackets and towelled themselves down. Innis was no longer sleepy. In fact, she was more alert than she had been in weeks. Covered with a shawl, she sat cross-legged by the hearthstones and listened to the rain beat against the tiny windows and felt curiously content.

She watched her mother lay out a sugar jar, the tea caddie, cups and spoons, the brown earthenware teapot. Aileen had climbed on to Father's knee and put an arm about his neck. She rubbed her nose against his cheek, kissed his mouth, hugged him fondly and hummed the tuneless little air that she claimed the fairy folk had taught her.

'There will be no fishing for us tomorrow, I'm thinking,' he said. Donnie and Neil growled in agreement. 'Are the oats ready for the cutting?'

'No,' Vassie answered.

'They were sown too late,' Ronan said. 'Now, most likely, you will be losing the straw. What will you do for winter dressing then?'

'I will buy in from Mr Clark,' Vassie said, 'if he has any to spare.'

'What will you be using for money?'

'We will not lose the crop,' Vassie said. 'But if we do then I will sell all the calves.'

Ronan wrapped an arm about Aileen's waist and said, 'I was talking to one of the Fetternish servants tonight. He tells me that the Baverstocks would not be averse to buying us out.'

'Do you expect me to believe that a servant knows the Baverstocks' business?' Vassie said.

'I wheedled it out of him,' Ronan said. 'Did I not, boys?'

Donnie cleared his throat. 'So you did, Father, so you did.'

'If I have told you once, Ronan Campbell,' Vassie said, 'I have

41

told you one thousand times; I will not be selling my land just to keep you in idleness.'

'What will you do if there is no feed?'

'I will find the money somehow.'

'It must be a fine thing to have a wealthy dada to spoil you,' Ronan said. 'However, it will soon be the time for the girls to be taking husbands of their own. How will you be managing then, Vassie?'

. It had been several years since Ronan had seriously tried to talk Vassie into parting with Pennypol. When Mr McAlpin had first arrived on Fetternish there had been many quarrels on the subject, arguments that had ceased only when it became apparent that Mr McAlpin had no intention of taking on more ground, and had no cash to pay for it; or when Ronan's persistence had worn Vassie down and she had screamed at him to shut up and he had struck her, not sadistically, but coldly as if he were killing a salmon or a cod: a single, cold, thudding blow to the side of the head that caused her to stagger and fall.

Now, to Innis's dismay, it was beginning again.

Sometimes she wished that they were not landowners but just the same as other folk; that Biddy and she might be courted and married and taken off to crofts of their own without the burden of Pennypol hanging round their necks.

She knew why Grandfather McIver had settled the holding upon his daughter, not upon one of his grandsons. He had done it to protect Vassie against Ronan Campbell's shiftlessness, to give her something to cling to if her marriage foundered. The deeds were so entailed that even if Vassie had wished it she could not sell one acre without Grandfather's permission. Why, Innis wondered, did her father persist in urging her mother to do something that she could not do? Why, when nothing was required of him, was he so keen to be rid of the place?

She had fallen out of love with her father as soon as she was old enough to see through his charm. The soft-voiced, smiling bonhomie that went down so well with men hid a cruel, cold nature. At home he raised his voice less often than he raised his fist. He never shouted, never roared; instead he punched or, when he was out of drink, would unbuckle his belt, wrap it around his knuckles and strap whoever in the family had displeased him. She remembered the horror of being stripped and whipped for no reason; of standing before him, all displayed, while he held mother back and snapped the leather across her naked buttocks, welting them, and the boys, even the boys, looked away in shame.

It was even worse for Biddy. He would take Biddy away, leading her by the hand and if she resisted he would catch her by the hair, push her down and make her hobble after him, half crouched and half naked. He would take her into the back byre or the hayloft and they would hear the *whack-whack-whack* of the leather strap and the silence after it, for Biddy would not cry for him, would not shriek as she, Innis, did. Those stubborn silences were the worst of all, for those who listened knew that he would go at her again and again until there was nothing but silence, not even sobbing, and they would imagine him stooping over her, talking soft into her ear, telling her how much it pained him to have to punish her and that she must do as he wished her to do in future, even if she did not know what he meant or how she might best please him.

Neil and Donnie suffered too. Their punishments were sudden and perfunctory: a punch, a blow to the face with an elbow, a knee driven upwards into the belly, a kick between the legs. Once he drew blood from Donnie's water and once made Neil vomit. The strange thing was that the boys respected him for what he did to them, for when he punished them no more they knew that they were men at last, and his equal.

'Do you not hear me, Vassie?' Ronan went on. 'What will you be doing when your girls are gone? Do you think that you will be able to hire hands to do the work for you?'

'Perhaps,' Innis heard herself say, 'we will take husbands who will live here instead of taking us away.'

'Live here?' said Neil. 'Where would you all sleep?'

'Aye, and what would you all eat?' said Donnie. 'There's barely enough to keep us going as it is.'

Vassie went about the tea-making without a word. In the dim light of the kitchen the worry lines were etched deep into her flesh. Innis felt sorry for her mother but she could not always bring herself to take Vassie's side, to stand up boldly to her father. There was no sense to his demands. His prejudices were ingrained. It did not occur to him that he could ever be wrong. Tonight, though, she felt that she must speak out.

She said, 'Pennypol cannot be sold whatever Biddy and I do. Mother cannot sell so much as one acre without Grandfather's permission.'

'He'll not live for ever,' Donnie said.

'The old bugger will have to go sooner or later,' Neil said.

'He could live for fifteen or twenty years yet,' Innis said.

'Then,' Ronan said, 'you will just have to be patient, will you not?'

'Patient?' Biddy said.

'Patient, and unmarried,' Ronan said.

'Would you be keeping us here to work for you under threat?' Biddy said. 'What will happen to Pennypol if I choose to leave Mull altogether?'

'It will either run to ruin, or it will have to be sold,' Ronan said.

'Because you will not work it?' Biddy said.

'I am a fisherman, not a farmer.'

'Other men manage to be both,' Biddy said.

'Yes, well, that is other men,' Ronan said.

'But you eat the bread and the beef that the farm provides and take shelter under Mother's roof,' Biddy said. 'When we are gone away – Innis and I – you will still have the roof over your head, and the boat.'

'It will not be enough for a living,' Ronan said.

'It will have to be enough,' Biddy said. 'While we are on this subject, will you tell me what you will do if your precious sons marry and set up homes of their own?'

'What?' said Donnie. 'Who have you been talking to?'

'Oh, I have heard about you,' said Biddy, making her brother blush. 'I have heard about you and MacNiven's daughter.'

'MacNiven?' said Vassie, with interest. 'Which MacNiven would that be?'

'MacNiven, from Leathan,' said Biddy.

Ronan rounded on Donnie. 'Is this true?'

'No, there is not a word of truth in it,' Donnie answered, hotly. 'The girl may have an interest in me but I have no interest in her.'

44

A Sunday Lunch

'That is not what *she* says,' Biddy informed him.

'She may say what she likes. I made her no promises, no promises at all.'

Crimson-cheeked, Donnie scraped back his chair and slouched off into the alcove at the back of the house where Neil and he slept.

For a long minute there were no sounds but the beating of the wind and the battering rain. Stray drops of water crept along a rafter and dripped to the floor below. The patchwork thatch had dried with the heat and had not swollen enough with the new rain to seal itself. It would be worse in the loft, Innis thought, but she did not care. She would pull the blanket over her head and sleep anyway. She felt cleansed by the coming of the rain, refreshed by the way Biddy had turned the tables on her father and the boys.

Ronan slid Aileen from his knee. The girl went reluctantly, her thin arms trailing from him like seaweed, until, with his forearm, he pushed her finally away. He looked at Neil. 'Which of MacNiven's daughters is it?'

'I – I canna say, Father.'

'Is it the young one?'

'Muriel? Aye, it might be.'

'Why was I not told?'

'There is nothing to tell. It is not a courtship.'

'Does the girl think it might be?'

'I canna say.'

'Where did you hear this news, Biddy?' Ronan said.

'At the church,' Biddy said.

'Did the girl tell you that a promise had been made?'

'No.'

Ronan made a signal with his hand. 'Has he done anything to her?'

'She would not be telling me the likes of that,' Biddy said.

'Is she a strong girl?' Ronan asked.

'She is very like her mother,' Vassie said. 'I am sure you will be remembering her mother since you once had a fancy for her.'

Neil too had gone through the canvas curtain that partitioned off the boys' bunks from the kitchen but Innis could see his fingers upon the fold and she knew that both he and Donnie

45

would be listening to every word that was said in the kitchen. She remembered Muriel MacNiven well enough, a small, dark-haired girl, unremarkable in appearance, whose father and brothers worked for MacBrayne's steamship company on the mail boat routes while the women tended the croft at Leathan which they rented from Mr Clark.

It was the first Innis had heard of Donnie's interest in the MacNiven girl. She was annoyed at Biddy for not passing on the gossip. She saw what was on her father's mind, though; how he might replace daughters with daughters-in-law as farm labourers until such time as Grandfather McIver died and Pennypol could be sold. At least, she thought as she hoisted herself to her feet, Biddy has given him something to think about, something to take his mind off us.

She watched him stoop and fumble beneath the bench for the whisky bottle. He picked it up and pulled the cork with his teeth. He was not looking at them now, at Aileen or at Vassie. As he lifted the bottle to his lips his eyes had the same sort of vacancy that Aileen's had when she heard the fairy music.

'I'm going to bed,' Innis said from the base of the ladder. 'Goodnight.'

No one, not even her mother, bothered to answer her.

The Baverstock brothers were Edinburgh to the core. They had lived in the city for most of their adult lives and spent their time tinkering with shares and pretending that they were active partners in the manufactory from which their basic income derived. They had been educated at the High School of Edinburgh and had sown remarkably few wild oats before settling into lives of comfortable ease. They were members of several clubs, patrons of art and letters, staunch churchgoers, make-weights at dinner parties and soirées in New Town society and, in spite of their stodginess, were subtly courted by all the high-toned hostesses who had unmarried daughters on their hands, blandishments that the brothers – Walter more readily than Austin – always managed to resist.

On the backside of Olaf's Hill on a hot August morning Austin and Walter Baverstock might appear to be fools of the first water but when it came to matters of business, to getting and spending, they were shrewd enough not just to survive but to prosper. However offhand they might appear to be about the management of Fetternish they embraced at least some of their responsibilities with efficiency and gravity.

On that morning of wind and rain Thrale expected his new masters to be still in bed or, at best, in that drowsy state in which his first employer, Cecil Ainsworth, had usually begun the day. Ainsworth hadn't lasted long on Fetternish. He had been rooked by the stonemasons and carpenters who had been employed to repair the house and deceived by every moocher who hobbled into the hall. What had finally driven Ainsworth back to civilisation, however, was the hostility of tenants who did not understand his English ways and who were having none of his 'latest agricultural improvements'.

Next into the firing line was Donald Pottinger. He owned land in Angus, knew a great deal about arable farming and might have made a go of Fetternish if his pretty, bone-china wife, Geraldine, hadn't threatened suicide if he did not remove her from that god-blighted, rain-drenched peninsula. 'It's me, Donald,' she had yelled – Thrale had heard her say it – 'it's me or it's Mull. Make up your mind.' To give him his due Pottinger had pondered the worth of a wife against a half-developed estate for several weeks but in the end he had gone back to his bland little mansion in the rolling hills of Angus, with his mad little wife chuckling all the way to the steamer. Thrale continued to manage the estate on Pottinger's behalf but the owner never set foot on Mull again and for four long years Fetternish House lay empty.

It was eventually sold to a wealthy English cattle merchant who had no interest in living on Mull. He had claimed his rents, raised cattle on the grass and had left everything else to Thrale, who had revelled in the power thus given him. The cattle merchant had died suddenly, alas. His heirs had promptly put the place up for sale again and Norman McAlpin had bought it.

McAlpin had not been a gentleman. He had regarded Mull as a beast to be tamed, an enemy to be defeated. With two or three thousand pounds more in the bank he might even have conquered the problems of poor soil, harsh weather and recalcitrant tenants. But time, tempest and temperament had been against him from the start and, in the end, he had lost not only heart but head and had put Fetternish up for auction.

Consequently, Thrale had good precedent for supposing that his new employers would be dependent upon him when it came to the hiring of servants and so he had arrived, dripping, at the stables that lay in the hollow north of the terraces, put up his horse and strolled up the steps to the side door that led to the office.

The broad, wood-panelled room was more dusty and mouldy than it had been in Ainsworth's day and had taken on the yeasty smell of seed bags and the damp-fur smell of the trophies that lined the walls. The corridor that led from the terrace to the big hall was crowded with tenants and servants who, when Thrale appeared, fell absolutely silent. He knew them all, of course, all their secrets and weaknesses. Women in bonnets, men in black suits and earth-stained boots, boys in baggy trousers, girls in bedraggled shawls; servants and labourers desperately in need of the security that a steady wage would bring.

Thrale took off his hat and oilskins and hung them on a peg at the corridor's end. They were all watching him, every head turned deferentially towards him. They knew that a quiet word from Mr Thrale to the new masters would ensure them work and wages for the next twelve months or send them, perhaps, to the Tobermory workhouse.

Thrale puffed out his chest, elevated his chin and surveyed the throng. And then he noticed the letters, not one or two but a dozen of them. Some were folded lengthways, like tapers, others were opened out flat, as if that sign of neatness would be a point in favour of the recipient. He had heard nothing of letters. The matter of letters had not been discussed with him.

Thrale snatched a sheet of paper from the hands of a young dairymaid.

'Have you all got letters?'

'Aye, Mr Thrale, that we have.'

He glanced at the document. Couched in the simplest possible terms, it offered forty days' notice to be followed by a fresh contract on the same terms.

Thrale gestured to a woman from Salen. 'Have you got one of these?'

'No, sir. I have come on speculation.'

Hector Thrale inhaled deeply. Old hands had probably already realised that he, the factor, had not been consulted on the matter of contracts and might already have concluded that Mr Thrale was not so important a man as he thought himself to be.

'Well now, we will have to see about all this,' he said, 'as soon as the Mr Baverstocks put in appearance.'

'Oh, but they are here, Mr Thrale.'

'What? Where?'

'In there.'

He glowered at the closed door of the office, knocked upon it, thrust it open and found to his astonishment that the Baverstocks were already in session.

Not only were they out of bed and wide awake, they were dressed to the nines in slope-fronted morning coats and diamond-check waistcoats. Walter's beard had been trimmed, and Austin's hair so flattened down with pomade that it looked as if he had been standing out in the rain, which, of course, he had not. Walter was seated behind a square teak-wood desk. Austin was to his right, seated too, legs crossed neatly at the ankles, arms folded. Standing behind them was Naismith, the valet, who, even as Thrale stepped into the room, bent forward and whispered advice into his master's ear.

Before the desk stood Margaret Bell, a dreary, long-bodied young woman who had been day-maid to the McAlpins.

Thrale closed the door firmly behind him and said, 'I see that you have started without me.'

'Ah, Thrale, yes,' said Walter Baverstock. 'In view of the weather, we—'

'What weather?' said Hector Thrale.

'The rain. It seemed churlish to keep everyone waiting outside in the wet.'

'They are used to it,' Thrale said. 'This is not the way it is done.'

'Pardon?' Austin recrossed his ankles. 'What's not?'

'You should have gone around to the houses,' Thrale said. 'If you had consulted with me, Mr Baverstock, I would have told you how it is done.'

'No, Mr Thrale,' Walter Baverstock said. '*This* is the way it will he done in future. Have them in, sign them up and be done with it. Then everyone knows where they stand.'

'What are they signing, if I might ask?' Thrale said.

'Articles of employment,' Walter answered.

'On paper?'

'Of course.'

'In the past it has been done with a handshake.'

'Really!' Walter said. 'Well, that is not how it's done now, nor how it will be done in future. We – my brother and I – prefer to have everything in writing as protection for both parties in the event of a disputation.'

'Black and white,' said Austin. 'Cut and dried.'

'Half of them cannot read English.'

'That's why Naismith is on hand,' Walter said, 'To read out the clauses, if required, and to act as witness to the signatures.'

Thrale groped for a chair, plumped himself down and glowered at Margaret Bell, as if she and not his employers had challenged his authority.

She was no girl but a woman of twenty-eight whose appalling shyness had kept her off the marriage market. She stood before the Baverstocks like a slave on the block, head bowed, eyes downcast.

'Bell?' he snapped.

The Baverstocks glanced up while the woman responded with a thin, serpentine coiling of the upper body and a little nervous twitch of the head. She was dressed in a plain but clean fashion and wore a maid's muslin cap as if to signal her position.

'Bell, can you not stand up straight?' Thrale said, testily. 'How do you expect these gentlemen to take you into their service when you slouch like that?'

Valiantly the woman attempted to pull back her shoulders and, by stiffening her spine, give herself presence.

'What position are you after?' Thrale went on.

'D-day-m-m-maid, sir.'

'Aye, it is all you are fit for, Margaret,' Thrale told her. 'In fact, I'm doubting if you are even suitable for that post.'

'I – I did it for Mr M-McAlpin, sir.'

In full swing now, Thrale got to his feet. Spread-legged, his big, square hands with their bitten fingernails pressed against his thighs. 'What did Mr McAlpin pay you?'

'I – I canna remember.'

'Well, I can remember. You were paid ten shillings for the month, and a free dinner on weekdays. Is that not right?'

'Aye, if you – if you . . .'

'If I say so? Well, I do say so,' said Hector Thrale. 'I also say that you were not worth so much and that the Mr Baverstocks will be generous if they offer you eight shillings in the month.'

Soundlessly and undemonstratively, Margaret began to weep. Whether it was the loss of twenty-four shillings a year in wages or the fact that she had been forced to open her lips and engage in conversation was immaterial. Her reaction appeared to embarrass the Baverstocks but, authority restored, Thrale rocked on his heels and stared at the woman without compassion.

'Eight shillings, Margaret,' he said.

'But – but—'

'The lady,' said Willy Naismith suddenly, 'has already been offered ten. I'm sure the Mr Baverstocks are not going to go back on their word. Besides, the signatures are already on the document.'

'William's right,' Walter said. 'That will be fine, Miss Bell, the arrangement as agreed. Ten shillings. Six dinners. Sundays off.'

'Sundays off?' Thrale said.

'Yes. You may go now, Miss Bell,' said Austin, gently.

'Wait.' Willy came around the desk, handkerchief at the ready. 'If you'll allow me, Miss Bell. We can't be sendin' you out to your ma in such a state. What would she think of us, eh?' He placed a forefinger under her chin and lifted her face up. He wiped the tears from her cheeks then, stepping back, soberly contemplated his handiwork. 'There now, that's better.' He was rewarded with a shy smile. 'We wouldn't want folk to go thinking that the Mr Baverstocks are tyrants.' He glanced at Hector Thrale. 'Would we?'

'No, sir,' Maggie Bell agreed.

'There you are then, Margaret,' Willy said. 'All right now?'

'Aye, sir,' the maid said as Willy ushered her out of the office and Hector Thrale, deflated, groped for his chair again.

West-coast rain came in forty-eight varieties but on that particular morning it was fairly ordinary stuff that descended from the crumpled skirts of cloud that the storm had dragged in its wake.

Out to sea there were whitecaps as far as the eye could see and all the headlands were drenched with spray. By southern standards the wind would have been classed as a half-gale but to islanders used to the real thing it was hardly more than a breeze and certainly not stiff enough to keep even small boats from putting out. Salty weather did not prevent Ronan and his sons from loading on the lobster pots and the cut bait and skulking away in the *Kelpie* along the landward side of the skerries that lay off the mouth of Loch Mingary.

Innis was glad of the big wall. It had not occurred to her before that Vassie's dike would offer such good shelter that she could milk the cows behind it without having to drive them all the way back to the byre.

Byre milking was a chore, for it was difficult to keep the stalls clean and nobody liked having to muck out. Innis enjoyed outdoor milking, though. When she leaned into a cow's belly, rested her brow on the flank and reached in for an udder, she did not resent the beast's occasional moans or indiscriminate splatterings but waited for it to settle with a patience that neither her mother nor Biddy could emulate.

On that August morning, though, she was a wee bit less patient than usual and hurried the animals from the park to the shelter of the wall, briskly stuck the stool under the first of them, shook the lid off the wooden pail and slid her hands to the udders.

Over her head and shoulders was an old canvas sack, cowled into a hood. She had reconciled herself to a wet morning but at least the air was clean and the cows, sheltering by the edge of the hayfield, were frisky now that the heat had gone and the flies had been blown away. The sky was still filled with broken cloud and the rain persisted but the storm had come to nothing and no damage had been done even to the oat and barley crop. Mother and Biddy had gone off to the burn to fill the washing tubs. Clothes that had been allowed to pile up during the past weeks would be washed and by dinner time the interior of the cottage would be dripping with shirts, stockings and petticoats roped between the rafters to dry.

If she got through the milking quickly Innis hoped to steal a few spare minutes to slip away over the hill and call upon Michael. If he was not at home, which was quite probable, she would leave a can of fresh milk on the table and slip away again. She would leave no message, just the milk.

She leaned into Rosie and stroked milk from the udders. Rosie was no longer young and her teats had lost their suppleness. The strone of milk was slow and had to be coaxed. Innis sighed. She felt a sudden flicker of anxiety at the thought that even now Michael might be setting out for the grazings on the Sorn side of Fetternish where she would never find him. With difficulty she resisted the temptation to finish with Rosie and run back to the house with the pails.

She did not know what the strange conglomeration of feelings and shifts of mood signified. In the past few days she had become more fickle than spring weather. She could not decide whether it was the novelty of having new neighbours or something more devious that troubled her. Rain dripped from her canvas hood. She shivered, though she was not cold, and peeped past the cow's flank at the hillside upon which, this morning, no sheep showed. And then she saw him. And her heart gave a leap in her chest, so forceful and surprising that she released the teat and sat back on the stool.

He stood on the path between the larches in exactly the spot where she had first seen the Baverstocks. When he saw her he raised his hand and waved with an enthusiasm that seemed oddly out of character. Unable to disguise her pleasure, she waved back and it was not until he reached the edge of the field that she realised that it was not Michael Tarrant at all but a stranger.

Rosie swooped her head around and lowed mournfully as the man clambered over the broken dike and came across the field towards them. It was all Innis could do to finish the hand-milk, to tap shut the lid of the pail and draw it from under the udder. She stood up. Rosie did a little dance, hoofs thumping, and turned square-on towards the man who, undaunted, swept off his hat and bowed first to the cow, then to the lady.

'Willy Naismith, at your service.'

Strong, craggy features, manly and handsome in spite of, or because of, the full black beard. He wore a pea-jacket, corduroy trousers and pair of hand-lasted boots. He was so vigorous and lively that Innis had difficulty in determining his age.

'Did Mr Tarrant send you?' she said.

'Mr Tarrant? No, no, no.'

'Are you from Fetternish?'

'Aye, I'll admit to that.' He mimicked a constable by licking an imaginary pencil and holding it poised over an invisible notebook. 'Name, please?'

'Innis Campbell.'

'No relation to the Duke of Argyll?'

'None.'

'Daughter to Vanessa then?'

'Yes.'

He scribbled in thin air. 'Sister to Bridget?'

'Yes, and to Aileen.'

'Aileen? Haven't heard of her.' He made a mark on nothing. 'Brothers?'

'Two,' Innis said. 'I think you've met them, Mr Naismith, if you are who I think you are.'

'And who do you think I am?'

'The Mr Baverstocks' servant.'

'I prefer to think of myself as a messenger of the gods.'

'Do you now?' said Innis. 'Like Mercury?'

'Aye, like Mercury.'

'Well, I am sorry to disappoint you, sir, but in this part of the world we only receive messages from Hermes.'

'Oooh,' he said. 'An educated lass.'

'What did you expect, Mr Naismith?'

'Certainly not a girl who could swap classical allusions without a blush.'

'Oh, we are a very clever family altogether, Mr Naismith. My sister can mow hay and recite *The Rape of the Lock* at the same time.'

'The what?'

'*Tam O'Shanter*, then, if you prefer it.'

His little piece of play-acting had petered out. He put his hand in his pockets and studied her with more doubt than drollery. She noticed how the rain slithered off his skin, as if he had been waxed, like an expensive overcoat.

He said, 'She must be a remarkable young lady, your sister.'

54

'Is it my sister you have come to call on, Mr Naismith?'

'What?' he said again. 'No, no.' He hesitated. 'Unless, of course, she's readily available.'

'She is up to her oxters in dirty water right now and I think you would find her disinclined to receive a visitor.'

'No matter,' said Willy Naismith. 'You'll do.'

'Will I? Are you sure?'

He laughed, a fuzzy little chuckle. 'My, my! But you are prickly.'

'No rose without a thorn, do they not say?'

'So they do,' Willy Naismith agreed. 'I tell you this, though; if I was half the age I am I would not be averse to getting my finger pricked.'

'What age are you, Mr Naismith?'

'I've daughters older than you.'

'How many?'

'Too many.'

'Does your wife think that too?'

'My wife, alas, is serving in the mansions of the Lord. She's been dead these several years.'

'Is that why you came to Mull?' Innis said. 'To escape sad memories?'

'God, no!' He chuckled once more. 'I came to Mull with the brothers to – to escape other things.'

'Like daughters?'

'Aye, like daughters.' He reached into the breast of his pea-jacket and brought out an envelope of pure white manila. He protected it from the rain with one hand held above it. 'Be that as it may, Miss Campbell, what I have come to Pennypol for this morning is to deliver this.'

He offered the envelope, still sheltered in cupped palms.

Innis wiped her fingers on her apron while she peered at the envelope. A trickle of apprehension went through her, triggered by echoes of a past that she had never known; her mother's past, her mother's history, when the arrival of a hand-delivered letter could only mean eviction.

One word – Campbell – was handwritten across the envelope in a loose, spidery style that would surely have had Mr Leggat, the schoolmaster, reaching for his ruler to rap knuckles.

'What is it?' Innis asked.

'An invitation,' Willy Naismith answered.

'To what?' said Vassie.

She held the paper up to the daylight so that the watermark – Baverstock, Baverstock & Paul – shone out of it like a magic trick. Suds trickled down her forearms, catching in the fine hairs and mounding up like sea-foam against her knotted sleeves.

'Luncheon,' Innis told her.

'Luncheon?' Vassie shrieked.

'What well-to-do people have at midday instead of dinner,' Biddy said.

'Do you think I do not know what luncheon is?' Vassie retorted, still staring at the sheet of paper as if she hoped that something more informative than a monogram would emerge from it. 'When does it say this "luncheon" will take place?'

'On Sunday,' Innis informed her. 'We're all invited to a Sunday lunch.'

Vassie would have none of it. 'We are at the kirk on Sunday.'

'After kirk,' Innis said, patiently. 'Lunch will be served at a quarter past one o'clock at the big house.'

'A quarter past one o'clock?' Vassie girned. 'What sort of hour is that to be feeding folk their dinners?' Biddy grabbed for the letter. Though reading was not her strong suit, Vassie would not yield it up. 'What exactly does it say?'

' "Messrs Walter and Austin Baverstock request the pleasure of—" '

Vassie interrupted. 'Some pleasure it will be, I am sure.'

' " . . . request the pleasure of Mrs Vanessa Campbell and her family at luncheon at Fetternish House at a quarter past one o'clock on Sunday 31st August. RSVP." '

'That means' – Biddy craned over Mam's shoulder '*Répondez s'il vous*—'

'I know what it means, Biddy. It means they are wanting an answer. Aye, well, I am knowing what sort of an answer they will get from us.'

'Mother!' Biddy cried in horror. 'Surely we are not going to refuse?'

'Do they think that we are starving and have need of charity?'

'Ma-am, we have to go.'

'They will not be getting around me with their damned luncheon.'

'Very well,' Innis said. 'I will write and tender our regrets.'

'What will you say?' Biddy demanded. 'What excuse can you offer that will not seem insulting? It is not as if we will be working. They have found out that we will be at the church and they have arranged—'

'Yes, we would be dressed up for church, anyway,' Innis said, 'and we would be back here in time for evening milking. But Mother's right. It is not proper for us to be breaking bread with the Baverstocks. I will find some paper and write immediately.' She teased the letter from her mother's fingers. 'It is a pity, though, since everyone else will be there."

'Everyone else?" said Vassie.

'Mr Leggat. Mr Carmichael. Mr Clark, of course. And their wives.'

'How is it that you are so well informed? It does not tell you all that in the letter, does it?'

'No, Mother.' Innis peered ostentatiously through the steam that hovered above the washtubs. 'Now, where did I put my paper box?"

She moved a little, the stiff white paper held negligently down by her side. Clothing and bed sheets, blankets and shawls swagged from the lines between the rafters, dripping water on to the floor. There was no sign of Aileen, or of Fingal, both of whom had sensibly taken refuge in the byre. As she brushed past Biddy, Innis squeezed her arm to reassure her sister that all was not yet lost.

Vassie said, 'Mr Clark will be there, do you say?'

'So I was told.'

'Who told you?'

'Was it Michael?' Biddy asked.

'No,' Innis answered. 'It was the servant who delivered the letter. His name is Naismith.'

'Is the doctor going to be there too?' said Vassie.

'It is a lunch for all the important people round about, to extend the hand of friendship to neighbouring landowners. It is how it is done these days,' Innis said. 'But you are right, Mother. It is not for the likes of us.'

'What's wrong with us?' said Biddy. 'We are landowners too. Please, Mother, please say we will go.'

'Your father will have none of it,' Vassie said. 'However, since he is the man of the house it would not do to rush to reply without giving him his place.'

'If Dada agrees?' said Innis.

'We will go,' said Vassie.

If he had not known the reason for it, it might have given Tom Ewing quite a turn to see the entire Pennypol clan assembled before him.

In eight years of ministering to the parish, he could not recall having witnessed such a thing. Ronan Campbell was known to be a godless wight to whom worship meant nothing. Campbell was not the only man who left his spiritual welfare in the hands of his wife, of course. Indeed, on that August Sunday the Reverend Ewing was confronted by several less than familiar faces, men whose appearance in the kirk at Crove had less to do with religious zeal than the promise of a free dinner at Fetternish House.

If he had been a less generous sort of man, and had not himself been invited to the Baverstocks' luncheon, Tom Ewing might have seized the opportunity to pour scorn on the heads of the prodigals. He was, however, a practical chap and resisted the temptation to mock for fear of offending the ladies who made up the backbone of his congregation. Besides, as a bachelor, he was dependent upon the generosity of farmers and fishermen, poachers and smugglers too, alas, to supplement his diet and he was not too keen to antagonise his benefactors by waxing sarcastic at their expense.

If Ronan Campbell and his sons were strangers to the kirk, Vassie and her daughters were not and while it would be wrong to say that Reverend Ewing lusted after Biddy he was not entirely oblivious to her charms.

Now and then, when boredom overcame him, he would cover the margins of his sermon book with arithmetical calculations which showed that at thirty-six years and four months he was not really that much older than Biddy; that when he was seventy she would be – let's see – over fifty which, given the mortality rate and taking away the number you first thought of, did not seem too bad. He made similar calculations regarding Innis too but he could never contrive to make those sums come out in his favour, not even by resorting to algebra.

Pity! For of all the children whom he had watched sprout from the Sabbath School benches Innis Campbell was the one who interested him most.

In the solitary hours of a winter's night, after his housekeeper, Mrs McCorkindale, had trudged off home, the minister might speculate what it would be like to have Biddy tucked up in bed in preference to a warming pan but, as a rule, when he thought of the Campbells of Pennypol it was the middle sister, Innis, who came most often to mind.

Her intelligence set her apart from the other girls: a calm, uncalculating quality which he regarded as the essence of the Gael. Innis, of course, denied that she was in any way different from her peers. She had, in fact, said as much: 'What do you want with me, Mr Ewing? Why do you keep pestering me with these peculiar questions?'

He had winced a little at the word 'pestering'. It had not occurred to him that he had begun to single her out. He had experienced a wave of guilt at the notion that he had offended her. Then he'd realised that she had turned fifteen that summer and had become sensitive to the differences between man and woman and that he had better row with muffled oars until she passed through her awkward, self-conscious phase. In the past year or so, however, Innis had changed once more. She was no longer a bashful young girl, ruled by self-doubt and suspicion. She would never be a beauty like her sister but she had a fresh, attractive quality that Tom Ewing – if he had been younger – would have found difficult to resist.

He concluded the morning service twenty minutes early. He stepped down from the pulpit, whisked into the closet at the rear of the wee stone building, jumped out of his preaching robes and into his overcoat and hurried round by the side of the church just in time to offer his customary handshakes to members of the congregation and to greet the Campbells one by one.

'Are you all going to Fetternish then?' he asked.

'Yes, Mr Ewing, we are,' Ronan Campbell answered. 'I had thought that we might be seeing the Mr Baverstocks at the worship.'

'They are, I believe, Episcopalians,' Tom said.

'Indeed, indeed!' said Ronan Campbell. 'And they did not send a carriage for us either, it would seem.'

Tom said, 'I am taking the dogcart, Mr Campbell, and would be honoured if your ladies would join me for the ride.'

'Just the ladies?' Ronan Campbell said.

'It's a very small cart,' Tom pointed out.

Fifteen minutes later he was propped on the board of the dogcart with the four Pennypol females crammed around and behind him. It was fortunate that the dogcart was more wagonette than gig for the load was heavy and the road out from Crove rough. Tom had inherited both the cart and the pony from his predecessor, Reverend Brodie, also a bachelor, who had expired, aged seventy-nine, at the reins of the conveyance and had been transported, stone dead, not to the manse but, oddly, to the door of the McKinnon Arms where he had fallen, not for the first time, down upon the grass.

It was a dry day, just, with a strappy wind that whisked the clouds along at too great a pace for rain. The dogcart had no hood and the pony, though strong, did not care for such a severe load and adopted a stubborn, plodding pace in spite of Tom's eloquent urgings. The road was smooth for the first mile but when it split from the Tobermory highway it became as bumpy as a burn bed. Brambly old pine woods cancelled out the views and it was not until the road climbed out of the wood that the coast spread out before them and Fetternish House was exposed in all its glory, proud and stark on the headland.

The women chatted quietly among themselves. The little one, Aileen, sang songs to herself and waved to this tall tree and that stunted stone as if they were friends and acquaintances. Tom found nothing appealing in the girl-child's naïveté which was too pagan for his taste. He was conscious of Biddy, though. She shared the front board with him, one shoe resting on the knurl, her knees swathed by the broad sash of her dress, her kilted skirt clinging to her figure. Her hair was startling: no chignon, just a mass of auburn curls turned back and fluffed out around her ears. On top rode a tiny wee hat, like the puff bonnets his sisters had favoured a dozen years ago. Biddy, however, was not at all like his sisters. She had a throat like Juno, a bosom as proud as the prow of a schooner and sea green eyes that seemed to eat away at him. She made no effort to engage him in conversation, however, and at first he felt quite cut off from the Campbell women, not because he was a man of the cloth but because he was a man at all.

'It is very kind of you, Mr Ewing,' Innis said, at length.

'Oh, it is the least I could do.'

'It has not been very quick, though, has it now?' Vassie remarked.

'The pony isn't used to . . .'

'Who's here? Can you see who's here?' Biddy stretched, heel planted firmly against the iron, thighs taut under the skirt. 'Who's that at the door?'

Tom cleared his throat. 'Mr Leggat, I believe.'

'Is it? I thought he was Free Church?'

'Episcopalian,' Tom told her, 'like the Baverstocks.'

'There will be no Free Church folk here today,' Vassie said. 'They'll not be ones for breaking the Sabbath by "lunching".'

'Do you see any harm in it, Mr Ewing?' Innis asked.

Tom shook his head. 'What harm can there be in having guests to lunch on a Sunday afternoon? It's a very practical arrangement, except insofar as our Free Church brethren cannot join us, of course.'

The rear wheels of the cart lurched on a boulder. The minister's precious cargo listed to one side. The dogcart went skidding down towards the crescent of gravel that fronted the doorway of the house.

'The new shepherd,' Biddy said. 'I wonder what denomination he is?'

Something in her tone alerted Tom; the question was less casual than it seemed. He glanced at Biddy and then, turning, at Innis. 'I do not think I have had the pleasure of meeting the new shepherd,' he said. 'Do you know what his name is?'

In unison the Campbell girls blurted out, 'Michael Tarrant,' then, embarrassed, looked in opposite directions as if the headlands that they had seen a thousand times had suddenly become fascinating.

'No,' said Tom, soberly. 'I do not believe he is one of us.'

He was tempted to press for more information about the incomer who had so affected the Campbell girls that they could not utter his name without blushing. He was prevented by a strange little pang of jealousy, not monstrous or green-eyed, to be sure, but wistful. Sighing, he flicked the reins and rumbled the dogcart down to Fetternish House.

The Baverstocks were not snobs but neither were they milk-and-water liberals. In Charlotte Square, Edinburgh, they would have known precisely how to arrange the lines of social demarcation so that nobody would take umbrage. In Charlotte Square, of course, the brothers would not have laid on a lunch at all. They would have organised a garden party or hired a caterer to set up a dinner for forty in the ballroom of the Caledonia Club or the upper room of the New Athenian.

On Mull, though, the brothers were less sure of how things were done and, heeding Willy Naismith's advice, elected to treat their tenants and servants to a sit-down, slap-up meal. No dainty canapés, no fragments of chicken balanced on toast, no salmon, green salads or glossy little sorbets; no lobster claws, scallops or stuffed crabs. Their guests would be properly fed on beef broth, rich mutton stew, hot meat pies and, for those of delicate palate, six or eight roast grouse. Plum duff, date puddings and apricot flans drenched in whipped cream would finish things off, all washed down with keg beer, tea and, for the younger element, fruit-flavoured cordials glamorised with crushed ice.

Estate workers would be served at trestle tables in the almost unfurnished drawing-room while those of a certain status in the community would be propped around the great slab of oak in the dining-room where enormous floor-to-ceiling windows looked over the weathered balustrades and terraced lawns to the mighty hills of Ardnamurchan.

In all, forty-two folk would be fed and watered. The food would be cooked by Mrs McQueen and two assistants, including the woman from Salen, and served by eight girls employed for the afternoon. They would be presided over by Mr Naismith who wore tartan trews and a military-style cutaway that lent him the crisp authority of a sergeant-major. Chairs were brought up from the old 'communal hall', tables from the schoolhouse, all of which necessitated a great deal of effort and organisation for which, Hector Thrale predicted, the Baverstocks would receive very little thanks.

According to the factor, hospitality was not the sort of thing that tenants expected from lairds. There was a grain of truth in Thrale's assessment, for the dearth of 'proper' furniture suggested that the Baverstocks might be no better off than McAlpin and that those whose livelihoods hinged on estate work had better not become too dependent upon employers who were, perhaps, already on the slippery slope to ruin.

Ronan Campbell, for instance, sidled across the hall, glass in hand, his sons trailing loyally behind him, and announced that he for one would not want to be living in this barn of a place when winter came and that it would be nothing compared to a stone-built croft for warmth and comfort and practicality.

'I do not know, at all, what they want to dwell in castles for,' he muttered. 'Castles are not places where a man can be at ease.'

'No, Father.'

'You're right, Father.'

'Once you have got such a place into your possession, och, what a millstone it can become. Servants needed to keep it clean and constant worry about where the money will be coming from to pay for it all.'

'Aye, Father.'

'It is better –' he drank from the glass – 'to be as we are.'

'Father.'

'What is it, son?'

'I think they are calling us to the dinner table.'

Ronan turned from contemplation of the staircase and, catching sight of Austin Baverstock near the doorway of the dining-room, advanced with his hand thrust out. 'Why, Mr Baverstock, it is indeed an honour to be invited into your home. I have just been saying to my sons what a fine house it is and how fortunate it is for all of us that Fetternish has found such generous owners.'

'Ah, yes. Well, thank you. Mr . . .'

'I am Campbell. Your neighbour.'

'Really?'

'Aye, really. My sons, Mr Baverstock – Donald and Neil.'

'Pleasure, pleasure,' said Austin, politely.

Although he shook hands with them Austin Baverstock did not make eye contact with Campbell's sons, for he was anxiously scanning the ground-floor corridor for sight of Campbell's daughter.

She, Biddy, had taken her sister to the water-closet and would at any moment return and he did not want to miss an opportunity to talk with her. Behind him he could hear the rattle of plates, the sing-song of conversational Gaelic as the guests became less intimidated by their surroundings. He could smell cooked meats, the oniony aroma of beef soup and taste the pre-prandial brandy with which he had tried to allay his excitement at the prospect of encountering the red-haired girl again.

He had watched Biddy arrive in the minister's dogcart. She resembled, he thought, a maiden from a painting by Millais or Rossetti. He had to confess that she seemed somewhat less enigmatic after she'd climbed down from the cart. Even so, a certain aura of fecundity – he could think of no other word for it – more than compensated for her forthrightness. Reluctantly he had passed her on to his brother but, five or six minutes later, he had spotted her once more as she escorted her little sister to the ground-floor water-closet.

If only he'd had the nerve he might have directed her to the splendid master bathroom upstairs. There a window of tinted glass threw petals of pink and purple into the air above the pedestal and he could have thought of her next time he sat there, could have shared that intimacy with her in his imagination.

Dragging the child-like girl by the hand, Biddy appeared in the gloom of the corridor. Her chin jutted upward and her lips were pursed, a severe expression that Austin put down to nervousness.

He fashioned a stiff little bow.

'Ah, Miss Campbell. If you are ready, may I escort you to the table?'

'Aye,' the girl-child said. 'I'm starved.'

'Where are we?' Biddy said.

'I beg your pardon?'

64

'In here, or in there?'

'Oh, the dining-room, Miss Campbell, the dining-room.'

'Where is Mr Tarrant?'

'Mr Tarrant?'

'I wanted to speak to Mr Tarrant about – about the sheep.'

'What's wrong with the sheep?' said Austin.

'To see how they are faring.'

'They are . . .' Austin hesitated, 'they are faring very well, I believe – for sheep, that is. Tarrant is seated with the servants. The dining-room is not for servants. It is reserved for guests – friends, I mean.'

'Starved,' the girl-child repeated.

Austin offered his arm. 'Miss Campbell?'

The door to the drawing-room was wedged open, the double doors to the dining-room folded back so that both interiors were visible from the hall.

Serving had begun. The woman from Salen hurried past from the kitchen stairs bearing a huge tureen of soup. She was followed by shy Margaret who carried a tray of bowls and by a boy whom Austin had never seen before clutching a quiver of knives and forks in his fist, like a cupid.

'Who is that?' Austin asked, frowning slightly.

'Barrett,' Biddy answered off-handedly. 'Barrett from Crove.'

She inclined her head and peered into the drawing-room.

Austin followed the line of her gaze and found himself observing the shepherd, Tarrant, who, with the window behind him, appeared not so much blurred as radiant in the soft afternoon light.

Tarrant was dressed in a blue two-piece and an old-fashioned shirt with a starched collar. He had just dipped his spoon into his bowl and, spoon dribbling soup, looked past the row of his fellow estate workers and gave Biddy a smile and a nod of recognition.

'When you pull the brass handle in there,' Aileen said, 'it all goes swooshing away with the water. Is that where you do it, Mr Baverstock?'

'Beg pardon?'

'In there,' Aileen said, pointing back along the corridor. 'Where we . . .'

'Enough out of you.' Biddy snatched at Austin's arm and wrenched him so close that he could feel the swell of her bosom against his forearm. 'Take me in, Mr Baverstock,' Biddy said and, with Aileen scampering before them, allowed him to lead her into lunch.

Innis dabbed a fleck of cream from the corner of her mouth with her handkerchief and said, 'I know what you're thinking, Mr Ewing.'

'Really?'

'Are you not thinking that this is a queer way for folk to behave?'

'Well, they are from Edinburgh,' Tom Ewing said, then, frowning, added, 'How did you know what I was thinking?'

'It's the second sight,' Innis said.

'Oh, come now. Surely, you don't believe that nonsense?'

'I was not meaning the Baverstocks. I was meaning us,' Innis said. 'Look at us, dining here in Fetternish House as if we belonged.'

'There are those among us – here and next door – who think that we do belong, who would declare that we have more right to enjoy the fruits of the land than any incomer, however prosperous.'

'Would that not be politics, Mr Ewing?'

'Dangerously close.' Tom glanced at her and winked. 'I'm not above enjoying the fruits of the land, though, whoever provides them.'

They were seated side by side at the nether end of the long oak table, a considerable distance from Austin Baverstock who was flanked by Biddy and Mrs Leggat, the teacher's wife. Towards the centre of the table Mr Clark talked crops with Vassie and fish with Ronan while Donnie and Neil vied for the attention of Miss Penelope Clark, aged eighteen. She spent the best part of the year with a great-aunt in Glasgow and attended something called a 'finishing school', which gave the impression to the lads of Mull that she was regularly subjected to scraping, sanding and caulking, like the keel of a suspect trawler.

Thrale and his massive wife, Freda, were in consultation with Dr Andrew Kirkhope and his massive wife, Jessie, while Aileen and young Peter Kirkhope - another refugee from schooling on the mainland - seemed to have formed a bond of interest in the composition of a date stone which they were trying vainly to crack open with the back of a spoon.

It was now approaching three o'clock. Outside, a band of sunlight flitted across the lawns and, a moment later, lit fires in the windows of the cottages on the distant shore of Ardnamurchan. In an hour or so Tom Ewing would have to leave to prepare himself for the taking of evening worship. For the moment, though, he was content to sit at the grand table in the grand house with a pretty young lady by his side.

Innis had a point: it was rather odd to see master and man gathered together around the groaning board. Not for a moment, though, did he believe that the harmony would last. He knew the islanders, even if he did not know the Baverstocks; knew how they would find grievances even where none existed. In fact he was not at all sure that the Baverstocks had not erred in making this gesture of good faith towards their employees, some of whom would regard it as weakness, not generosity. They were a strange lot, the folk of the isles, none stranger than those who dwelled on Mull. He had grown used to their ways in the last eight years, though, and could not imagine himself living anywhere else. He would never be one of them, of course, not if he lived to be a hundred, but at least he was tolerated. They were, on the whole, a tolerant race, the Gaels, tolerant of almost everything except change and strangers.

He became aware that Innis was studying him, a little furrow of concern upon her brow. 'What?' he said, with a tiny throaty chuckle. 'What's wrong?'

'Nothing.'

'Yes, there is. Tell me.'

She leaned closer. Her hands were slender, not muscular, and bore a multitude of little scars upon them. She had none of the immediate appeal of her sister, but then few women did. Biddy always made him think of Sarah, Abraham's wife, and Innis of Ruth, Ruth in the fields of Boaz.

'May I ask you something, Mr Ewing?'

'Of course.'

'What do you think of me?'

67

Surprised, he sat back. The question seemed thoroughly out of character. He had never suspected Innis of being vain, though he did not regard vanity in young women as an irredeemable sin. God had made them as they were, he supposed, and God must answer for their idiosyncrasies. There must be a point to her question. A man, there must be a man behind it. The young shepherd, probably, the new neighbour, mention of whose name had caused both Campbell sisters to blush like beetroots. Poor Innis wasn't begging for compliments, only for something to arm her against her sister.

He glanced up the length of the table and saw that Biddy had made yet another conquest. Even sagacious bachelors of long standing were not immune to Biddy's auburn charms. In the room next door the shepherd would be polishing off his apricot flan, oblivious to the fluttering hearts.

Tom thought for a moment, then said, 'Not so long ago I encountered a man from the Long Island who told me that he had once met a young woman who was perfect in herself. He told me that her eyes were pools of quiet and the sea-sweetness rang in her voice and that when she smiled it was always the month of June.' Tom paused. 'At the time I did not know what the man meant, Miss Innis Campbell, but I'm beginning to think that I do now.'

He watched her eyes widen, her brows arch.

'Do you mean it, Mr Ewing?'

'Of course I mean it. I would not have said it otherwise.'

'Then I thank you for it. It is a very great compliment.'

'No more than you deserve,' he said, then, clearing his throat, asked her to pass him the cream jug so that he might polish off the flan.

An hour later, just before he took his leave, Tom noticed Innis strolling on the lawn in the company of a small, neatly packaged man whom he took to be Michael Tarrant. He also noticed the magnificent Bridget with Austin Baverstock hovering at her side. She was leaning like a queen against the balustrade, no doubt fuming at the march her sister had stolen over her in the deadly game of hearts. Unless he missed his guess, there would be more than the coming of the sheep to keep the Campbell girls occupied and the community supplied with gossip this season. Chuckling to himself at the small part he had played in evening up the score, Reverend Ewing shook hands all round, climbed into the dogcart and, with the sunlight fading over Fetternish, rode off to attend the business of the Lord.

THREE

The People under the Hill

Evergreens had spread from the back of what had once been formal gardens into the narrow gully that went by the Gaelic name of Na h-Vaignich – the Solitudes. It was a gloomy place of weeds and nettle beds with dense tangles of bramble and blackthorn in which a lamb or even a ewe could easily become ensnared. It had been fenced at one time but the posts had rotted so all that remained now to prevent an inquisitive animal straying into the depression were remnants of rusty wire trailing through the undergrowth and, thirty yards behind the shepherd's house, a wicket gate on sagging hinges.

Eight flat stones led down from the gate to the spring that bubbled from a pipe in the bank at the head of the glen. The flow was not consistent. It changed with the weather from a peaty brown trickle to a milky gush or, after storms, into a torrent that filled the glen with spray. On that particular day the spring was quiet and Innis could hear nothing but the din of the flock as she passed the gable of Michael's cottage.

It was a fine, bright morning, a good drying day for the straw that the Campbell women had stooked in the week following the Baverstocks' luncheon. The drought had kept the barley hard and the oats were thin and short but there would be enough to provide feed and bedding for the animals during the winter, provided spring did not arrive late.

Innis had seen nothing of Michael Tarrant since she had walked with him on the lawn of Fetternish House. Every day since she had stolen a quarter of an hour from the morning to deliver a canister of fresh milk to the shepherd's isolated cottage,

71

hoping that she might catch him at home. She never did, though. She would find the cottage door unlatched and yesterday's canister, washed and polished, standing upright upon the bare, scrubbed, deal table. So tidy, so clean, so empty was the cottage above the Solitudes that it reminded Innis of a house in a fairy tale. She would find his bed neatly made, his bowl and cup washed, his shoes tucked away beneath the wooden rocking-chair by the hearth and, in the hearth itself, a pyramid of peat to keep the room warm until he returned at dinner time or in the evening.

Yesterday there had been a posy of wild flowers tied to the canister on the bare deal table, however; no note of thanks, only the delicate little bouquet of sea-lavender and fruited asphodel and pale blue forget-me-nots to express his gratitude. She had come now to thank him for the gift.

She had learned from Donnie that the new shepherd intended to dip his masters' sheep that day and that the flock had grown by one hundred and forty head that had been ferried over from the Morven peninsula. Donnie also informed her that many local experts were unhappy about Tarrant's methods, for it was rumoured that he was about to subject the Fetternish flock to the ordeal of an arsenic bath. There was great fear in the district concerning new-fangled methods and it was said that if the poison got into the rivers it could wipe out the salmon or turn seals so mad that they would eat their pups, like cannibals. The crofters' prejudice took no account of cost and labour, though, for Innis knew that there was a mighty big difference between smearing a dozen little Blackfaces with butter and tar and doing the same thing for three hundred-odd Cheviots.

She found Michael down in the glen. He was assisted by Barrett, a youngster from Crove, and by Barrett's grandfather. Thrale was there too but he would not deign to get his hands dirty and stood up on the bank with his pipe stuck in his mouth and a look on his face so black and furious that he seemed about to explode. 'I have never seen the likes of this, Tarrant,' he shouted, the pipe wagging between his teeth. 'Never in all my born days. You will be killing them with the smell if you do not drown them first. Or if you do not drown them they will be dying of the chill when the wind gets them.' He glanced across at Innis, nodded curtly and went on with his harangue. 'It was not done this way even by Mr McAlpin and he was a very progressive gentleman. Smearing it is that keeps sheep safe from the cold, do you not know?'

Shouting to make himself heard above the baa-ing and bleating, Michael called out, 'Aye, Mr Thrale, and ruins their wool in the process.'

'Never, never! There is nothing better than butterine—'

'At ninepence a head. Ninepence, Mr Thrale,' Michael interrupted. 'Think of that when it comes to balancing the books. If he heeded your advice then it's small wonder that McAlpin went to the wall.'

Thrale removed the pipe from his mouth and spat. He glanced at Innis, nodded again, then launched himself into the argument once more.

Innis knew that it was not a serious disagreement. Hector Thrale might be a man of some education but he was an islander through and through, subject to the changes of mood that marked the Gaelic temperament, sudden swings between gaiety and melancholy, dourness and volubility. In spite of appearances, Innis reckoned that old Hector was enjoying himself. She could not be so sure about Michael, for she did not understand incomers, whether they hailed from Aberdeen or Glasgow or that strange land south of the River Tweed.

'Are you telling me, Tarrant, that I do not know how to manage the estate?' Thrale bellowed. 'I have been working these acres man and boy for half a century. I know more about what is good for sheep than you ever will.'

'If that's the case,' Michael shouted, 'why don't you step down here and show me what I'm doing wrong.'

'I would not be soiling my hands with that poisonous stuff,' Thrale said.

'What poisonous stuff?' Michael said. 'Do you mean work, Mr Thrale?'

From her position above the dipping-trough Innis saw old man Barrett smile. Even the boy, a moon-faced lad hardly much older than Aileen, grinned. They did not dare talk back to Mr Thrale, of course, but the new shepherd obviously had no fear of losing the factor's favour, of being tumbled out of his cottage next quarter day without a penny.

'It is the policy that is wrong, the policy not the practice,' Thrale shouted.

'Then you must tell the Baverstocks,' Michael said.

'Is this how dipping is done where they come from?'

'No,' Michael shouted. 'Where they come from it is done with ink.'

'*Ink?*'

'Pen and ink. Facts and figures. Tell me, how long does it take one man to smear three hundred and eighty sheep with rancid Irish butter, Manchester brown grease and Russian tar? And how much do you lose per pound on the sale of the laid wool?' Michael leaned on the larch-wood hurdle that guarded the trough. 'Well, Mr Thrale?'

'I cannot be telling you all that off the top of my head.'

'Mr Walter Baverstock can.' Michael glanced at Innis. 'Indeed, so can I. One man can do a score of sheep in ten hours. He would use forty pints of smear. That is, thirteen working days for one man or the best part of a week for two men and a lad. I will dip three hundred and eighty head by nightfall, if, that is, you will take yourself away and leave me to it. Or, better still, peel off your coat and step down here and help us.'

Thrale stuck the pipe back into his mouth and said nothing. He scowled again but not so ferociously as before. He watched in silence as Michael *heyed* the next batch of sheep from the temporary pen at the top of the glen and had the collie drive them neatly through a line of light wooden hurdles on to the ramp of the old farm cart that served as a waiting station.

Beyond the cart, half buried in firm ground beside the burn, was a cast-iron water trough eight feet long and three feet wide. It was filled with the greyish-brown swirl of whatever patented carbolic-acid dip Michael favoured, fed by a soft, full trickle of water siphoned from the stream via a rubberised hose. Beyond that again was another little hay cart. Its wheels had been removed, its tailgate lowered to the edge of the tub and a ramp of turf and bracken stalks built up to the level of the board.

Young Barrett checked the sheep then he gave one a shove or a tap on the rump and projected it into the trough. Michael dipped its back and hindquarters with a forked pole. Old Barrett, strong as a pony, lugged the dripping sheep half on to the tailgate, let it scramble up to the draining floor from which, shaking itself and bawling, it trotted down the ramp and off to a drying pen that had been assembled at the nether end of the glen.

The method displayed all the advantages of speed and efficiency and even Innis could see that Michael knew just what he was doing – at least when it came to sheep. He wore a wide oilcloth apron, like a herring-gutter, and thigh-length canvas boots. His sleeves were rolled up almost to the shoulder. His arms were thin and hairless and there was not a pick of spare flesh on him anywhere. In the sunlight, with the pole in his hands, he looked far too young to be in command of such a large and valuable flock.

Innis hunkered on the bank, watching, while a knot of six sheep were run through the trough in as many minutes. In the tub, grey-brown water swirling up to their throats, their eyes rolling in panic, the ewes looked so helpless that she felt almost sorry for them. But when they clambered on to the draining board they became comical, fleeces plastered to their ribs, ears flicking and tongues vibrating indignantly. If the stench of the tar-acid solution was anything to go by there would not be a scab mite or maggot fly left on any of them and the flock would remain clean throughout the winter.

Thrale had seated himself too. He squatted on the slope on the other side of the glen from Innis, puffed on his blunt little briar and watched the proceedings sullenly, without comment.

Only when the batch had been treated did Innis slip down the slope to the fence. Michael's brows were sprinkled with droplets from the tub and his eyes were red and watering from the effect of the fumes. Even so, he seemed pleased to see her.

'I came to thank you,' Innis said.

'For what?'

'The flowers.'

'Oh, it's you who brings me milk every morning, is it?'

'Who else would it be?'

'I thought it might be – well, your sister.'

Innis felt a little gulp of disappointment in her chest. It seemed stupid, almost perverse of Michael not to have realised that Biddy did not put herself out for anyone. 'Is that why you left the flowers – for Biddy?'

'I left the flowers for - well, whoever did me the kindness.'

'Did you not guess that it was me?'

She felt heated now, her mood shifting. She was aware of Mr Thrale perched on the bank above, watching and listening, of the Barretts pretending to be busy with the hose. The fumes from the tub made her eyes sting. It was all she could do not to rub them, which would only make matters worse.

'I thought it would be you.' Michael Tarrant paused. 'But then . . .'

Innis was suddenly overcome by loathing of the artificial ramp and the maze of temporary pens and fences. She looked up at the ribbon of pure blue sky that floated above the throat of the glen, then at Mr Thrale who, as if he knew what doubts assailed her, nodded and blew out a plume of tobacco smoke.

'You hoped it might be Biddy?' Innis said.

'I hoped nothing of the sort,' Michael told her. 'However, since is was you, you have my thanks. I will leave you more flowers tomorrow or the next day if you like. Whenever I have time to gather . . .'

'Please, do not be bothering yourself, Mr Tarrant,' Innis said.

Pushing herself away from the hurdle, she turned and ran up the weed-strewn banking and out into open pasture. She felt better at once. Her eyes stopped stinging, her throat smarting, her heart pounding.

She was just embarrassed enough by her rudeness to pause on the edge of the gully and look down at him. She intended to give him a conciliatory wave, some small signal that she had not meant to be so sharp with him. But Michael had gone back to dipping and, though Innis lingered for two or three minutes, he did not look up again and gave no sign that he even knew she was there.

Throughout her married life Vassie Campbell had lived at odds with the cycle of the seasons. She was such an anxious person that she could not be at peace even when the hay was in, crops gathered, calves weaned and the hens laying well. She would fret about dearth in lean years or, in fruitful times, about the low prices that a glut would bring. Before one task was complete she was worrying about the next. She worried too - though with more justification – about her husband, her sons and her daft daughter Aileen. Most of all she worried about Biddy for, try as she might, Vassie could only regard Biddy's good looks as a potential source of disaster. It scared her to think that Biddy might succumb to her passionate nature as she, Vassie, had done so many years ago, that Biddy too might have to live with the consequences of her mistakes. Until the arrival of the new shepherd, however, Vassie had no reason to suppose that Biddy would throw herself away upon a scoundrel. If anything, it was Innis who was making the running with Mr Tarrant and that fact worried Vassie too, not because she thought that Innis would make a fool of herself over the man but because Biddy would be piqued. And Biddy piqued was Biddy dangerous.

At first there had been only blushes when the shepherd's name cropped up, but after the Sunday luncheon her girls had taken to squabbling more openly, a situation that Ronan and the boys had thought hilarious but which filled Vassie with trepidation. She had tried to persuade her daughters to make peace but they would not. She had tried to keep them apart but that was impossible. Both Innis and Biddy denied that they were in the least affected by the presence of the young man across the hill or cared a jot whether he paid court to either of them, or neither.

Vassie lost her temper and shouted. Biddy lost her temper and shouted back. Innis took to skulking in the byre with a lantern and a book. And Mr Michael Tarrant, cause of all the fuss, wisely gave Pennypol a wide berth for a week or two and kept himself, and his preferences, to himself.

The nights were beginning to draw in. Dusk came in over the moor before supper was finished and in the early mornings the dew was cold on the feet. The haws had ripened and the brambles were plump and the cow, Dandy, was huge about the belly and would let no one except Innis come near.

Some days were brisk with a spit of rain, others hazy and still. But it did not matter to Vassie, who was already depressed by the change of season and the prospect of losing a daughter, let alone a son, before spring came round again.

She might have taken herself over to Foss and asked her father what to do for the best. He was generous in offering advice. Unfortunately, she was not alone in finding Dada McIver sympathetic. It galled her to see how effortlessly he supported himself on his little green isle, surrounded by women and fat cattle, blissfully ignoring the fact that most men of his age were either past it or dead. There was something disturbing in the way her father defied the progress of the years, something unnatural in his optimism and the manner in which he was able, still, to look towards the future, not backwards into the past.

Vassie found her father's equanimity in the face of death quite distressing, for she, not much more than half his age, was already afraid of the darkness that lay beyond and of a future in which she would have no say at all. So she kept her concerns about Biddy, Innis and the new shepherd bottled up within her while she applied herself to feeding cattle and to weeding and hoeing the onion beds and potato quarters.

She liked the feel of the soil under the hoe blade, a sandy tilth, not deep. She liked being out in the vegetable plots and when the onion beds were cleared at the month's end she would spend whole days there planting out cabbage for the spring. She worked rapidly, with sharp little stabbings of the blade and agitated flicks of the wrists. Sometimes when the peace and pleasure of the task threatened to annul her foreboding, she would curse under her breath, rip the weeds out by the roots and hurl them away as if they were offshoots of all the cares that burdened her.

She did not see Donnie until he was almost upon her. He had come out of his way to reach her. He might have gone on up the track directly to the cottage but instead he had veered along the top of the high-tide line to the paling that kept the kye from eating the green tops. Only when he had reached the fence did he call out her name. Vassie swung round. He stood by the paling, left wrist cradled on right forearm. She would not have known that there was anything wrong with him if it had not been for the stain on his sleeve and the drips of blood that fell softly from his hand to the grass.

'Mother,' he said. 'I'm hurting.'

'What is it? What have you done to yourself?'

'Ach, it's the knife again.'

He tried to be stoical but Donnie was not like Neil. Neil would have hugged the pain to himself and let none of it show. Donnie might be his father's son in other ways but when it came to needing help it was his mother he turned to. He held out the injured hand and let her see the wound that cleaved the mound of flesh at the base of his thumb.

'The gutting knife?' said Vassie calmly.

Donnie nodded. 'Opening a clam.'

She put down the hoe and climbed over the fence. All the agitation had gone out of her. As she peered at her son's injury she seemed almost serene.

Inside, though, was terrible panic. Had he severed a tendon? Would he lose the power of the hand? Would gangrene set in and poison his whole system? Would her lovely Donnie die in agony in hospital far away, like Mairi Henderson's man, who had been taken in that manner five years back?

'Suck it,' Vassie said.

Obediently he stuck his hand to his mouth, sucked and spat blood on to the grass. He extended his hand again. The wound gaped, clean-lipped. Vassie could see where the blade of the sharp-edged knife had parted her son's flesh almost to the bone. It was not the first such wound she had treated, and it would not be the last. It was not so bad as a rope burn or a tear inflicted by a hook, not near so bad as a crushed finger, a jerked shoulder or cracked rib which might have laid him up for weeks. She would not need to stitch it to make it heal, not this time.

'Can you fix it for me?' Donnie said.

'Aye, son. I can fix it,' Vassie said lightly, wishing that all the little wounds and injuries that afflicted her family were so clean and so easy to cure.

She took him to the cottage which was quiet indoors at that hour of the afternoon with nobody at home but Fingal who, as always, was drowsily guarding the hearth.

She sat Donnie down at the table, wrapped a cloth around his hand and poured him a dram from one of Ronan's hidden bottles while she rummaged among the squills, pills and worming powders in the cupboard of the pinewood dresser. She brought out the gentian, cotton strips for binding and the big, dusty pot of common plaster and Burgundy pitch that, warmed up, would hold the dressing firmly in place and allow him freedom to work.

Vassie pulled up a stool, seated herself and set about her doctoring.

Now that his mother had taken charge, Donnie seemed stoical and unconcerned, almost detached. He drank whisky from the glass in his right hand and looked out of the open door at the sky.

He made no sound as she cleansed the cut, pinched the lips of the wound together and ran a thin smear of pitch across them with the tip of her forefinger. She laid the bog-cotton pad upon it and, leaning into him, knotted the end of the bandage about his wrist.

Then he said, 'I have it in my mind to marry.'

'Is it MacNiven's daughter, from Leathan?'

'It is.'

'Will she have you, son?'

'Aye, I believe she will.'

Vassie's voice was soothing. 'Do you love her, Donnie?'

'Well enough,' he said.

'Well enough to live your whole life with her?'

'Yes, well enough for that.'

She pulled the cloth strip tight and looked into his face. He frowned slightly and shook his head, let her tighten the binding further.

'Will she come with anything?' Vassie asked.

'Nothing very much.'

'Have you told your father?'

'No.' Donnie hesitated. 'I have hinted at what is on my mind but you have heard him for yourself, what he thinks of it. He will want me to bring her here to work on the farm.'

'Do you think I will not make her welcome?' Vassie asked.

'Oh, I know that you would welcome her,' Donnie answered. 'But it is not the right thing for Muriel or for me. It is a place of my own I'm after, a place of my own and a boat of my own.'

'Donnie, are you betrothed?'

'No, not yet.'

Vassie sighed and, forcing herself, returned to bandaging his hand.

'There are empty cottages at Pennymain. Perhaps the Baverstocks would rent one out to you.'

'That would be costing money,' Donnie said.

'Would you not be earning money from the boat?'

'If I had a boat,' said Donnie. 'If I could borrow the money to buy a boat then I think everything would be fine.'

'Borrow money?' said Vassie, unable to hide her alarm. 'It is not a good thing to be starting your married life on borrowings.'

'Perhaps Grandfather McIver would lend me something.'

'I would not ask him,' Vassie said.

'Do you think he would not lend it to me?' Donnie said. 'He might even give it to me, to get me started.'

'Donnie . . .'

'Aye, I know. He does not like me. He has never liked me. I cannot say I blame him for that.' He winced as Vassie tugged the bandage tight. 'The other thing I could be doing is to go away on the boats, like Muriel's brothers. They have been after me to apply to MacBrayne's for a job. It would not be the same as a boat of my own but it would be money coming in every week.'

'Where would you live?'

'I would have to think about that,' Donnie said, then added, 'Not here.'

'Why not here?'

'I would not want to be bringing a wife here.'

'It seems,' Vassie said, 'that you are determined to leave Pennypol.'

'There is no choice in the matter for me, Mother. It is a case of marry and go, or not marry and stay where I am. Unless . . .'

'Unless?'

'I had a boat of my own. I could stay then, not here but nearby.'

She had hoped to talk to him of other things, to confide her fears about the future of the farm, to ask what he knew of the shepherd, Michael Tarrant, and what Biddy might have said about the man. But Donnie was only concerned with himself and with what would happen to him. It was in the nature of the young to be selfish. It was how they got on in the world.

At least, she thought, as she tied the final knot and applied a slathering of plaster to the bandage, at least he is not so much under Ronan's thrall that he will make himself a slave for life.

And, for that, she felt a strange little glow of gratitude towards MacNiven's daughter.

She wiped her hands on her apron and carried the bowl to the doorstep.

Donnie stayed where he was at the table, stock still, staring at her.

'Have you no money to give me?' he said.

She threw the slops out of the door in a wide arc and watched the hens scutter towards the spot and, after a peck or two, heard them cluck in disappointment. They waggled away, crooning and clucking huffily. Vassie stepped back into the kitchen.

He was still exactly where she had left him, bandaged hand resting square and flat on the table, the empty whisky glass beside it.

'It will all be for them, I suppose,' Donnie said.

'What will?'

'Your money,' he said. 'You will be saving it all for them.'

'Donnie, I have no money.'

'You could get me a boat if you wanted to.'

'No, son, I . . .'

'For my sisters, not for me.' He slammed the injured hand flat upon the table and flinched at the pain. Then he stood up. 'I will be getting back now.'

'It would be better if you rested.'

'Rested?' he said. 'What rest will there ever be for the likes of me?'

He lifted his hand and turned it this way and that, studying it. In spite of Vassie's attentions a faint seep of blood showed through the bandage, coaxed out by the blow. Deliberately he closed his fingers and kneaded them into his palm as if to undo all Vassie's careful doctoring.

'Does it hurt?' Vassie asked.

'Aye, it hurts,' said Donnie.

The big moons of the harvest month had a strange effect on Aileen. In September her wanderlust became rampant and she could not be restrained from roaming the twilit moors or flitting away to Dun Fidra as soon as her day's work was done. There she would listen for elfin footsteps or the strains of the fairy harp or the soft little whistle that her lover gave before he appeared out of the heather.

She was not afraid of her lover. She had never been afraid of him, not even the first time. He was as familiar to her as the stones of the fort itself. She would lie trembling under the harvest moon and wait eagerly for the little whistle he would give to warn her that he was coming.

No matter where she lay he would find her as he had found her that first time. In the moonlight of the harvest month she would see him loom out of the heather, would hear him snuffling and whistling, and she would become so excited that she would almost die from it.

She would grab her skirts and haul them up so that he would not be kept waiting. He would stand above her, looking down, and at that moment he would seem to have no more substance than the scent of wild thyme or the cry of the owls that hunted the field's edge or any one of the thousand and one things that filled Aileen's head in lieu of thought. But when he knelt over her and touched her with his fingers he became as real and earthy as if he had indeed clambered out of the chambers under the hill.

He never spoke. He never once uttered her name or called her his sweetheart or his darling. He would put his arms beneath her back, hoist her up and enter her. After a minute or two she would feel the weight of the earth change to a breaking of waves and would hear the laughter of the people who lived under the hill. It was as if she were giving them all pleasure by what she did with him. He would pant and grunt and she would arch her back and try to clasp him to her, to keep him. But she could not keep him. He would pull back, kneel over her, touch her again, rubbing his fingers over her. Then he would be gone.

And Aileen would lie motionless and think of the little fishes that she left upon the stones and how the people under the hill left nothing of her gifts except bones and how they scattered the shells and let the flowers wither willy-nilly. And she too would feel consumed and withered, and then she would hear their laughter and she would not know whether they were mocking her or rejoicing for what had been done to her and, for a moment, she would become one with them and was honoured to share their secrets. At other times, reason would spoil it for her. She would know what the secret meant and she would run away at the sight of him, run away to the rocks or into the hayfield and wish that it was harvest time again as it had been when he had first taken her down with him, like the king he really was, the king of the people under the hill.

'Where have you been?' Biddy would say. 'Look at your skirts. My God, what a rag-tag you are, Aileen. What have you been up to? Rolling in the muck again?'

'She will have been with the fairies,' Donnie would say.

'Aye, or the fairies have been with her,' Neil would add.

Vassie would shriek at the boys to hold their tongues. Biddy would serve soup and thrust the bowl at her and she would climb up on to the high stool and, hurting sometimes, would eat, not sullenly but slyly, holding the bowl up to her breast and keeking at them out of the corner of her eye, pressing her knees together, holding in the secret.

'Where *have* you been?' Innis would say. 'I came looking for you but I could not find you.'

He would be eating too, supping fish stew with a spoon or cutting meat with a knife. He would frown a bit and glance up from his plate and would say, 'She's fine. Leave her alone.'

She would feel better then, would lean into him, rub herself against him, pressing her knees together.

He would feed her a mouthful or two from his plate before pushing her away again. And Neil would nudge Donnie and Donnie would say, 'And did you see the fairies tonight then, Aileen?' And she would answer shyly, 'Yes,' and not mind at all when they laughed at her, because he never laughed.

He never laughed.

Willy Naismith contemplated the distance between the gunwale and the rock. No more than two feet at most, shortening with every lurch of the ocean. Below it, though, the water was deep and dark and heaving with stuff that made Willy think of octopuses. Poised on the rock's edge, elbows cocked out behind him as if he were a fledgling cormorant about to test its wings, he hesitated nervously.

'For God's sake, man,' Ronan Campbell said, 'have you never

been in a boat before? Jump, jump. I do not have all day to waste.'

'I – I can't swim.'

'You do not have to swim. If you could swim you would not be needing my boat, now would you? Jump.'

Willy cocked his elbows, rocked on the soles of his fine leather boots and stayed where he was, land-locked and lubberly.

He wished now that he had made some less hazardous arrangement with Campbell, one that didn't require a pick-up from an isolated rock tucked off the point below Fetternish House. He was losing face by the second but even pride couldn't move him forward and when the water slopped over the rock he stepped quickly back in case his fine boots got ruined.

'I am going now,' Ronan Campbell declared. 'I am leaving.'

'No. Wait. Here, give me your hand.'

'My hand?'

'Help me.'

Campbell had no intention of leaving him high and dry, of course, and Willy, sucking in a deep breath, finally took the bull by the horns and leaped down into the belly of the little craft just as Ronan reached out to assist him.

The oars rose and fell with a slap and the fisherman, for all his expertise, had to grab at the starboard oar to prevent it leaping the rowlock. Without a shred of dignity, Willy landed on his spine among the creels and herring-boxes. He felt the boat take off beneath him, sliding away from the rock even as he scrambled to steady himself and claw his way to the seat amidships.

The rock, the land receded and already seemed far out of reach. Above the line of cliffs Fetternish House appeared, tower and turrets first, then floor by floor until even the windows of drawing- and dining-room were visible and, hardly larger than dolls, Queenie, the cook, and shy Margaret picking peas in the sheltered garden. Willy sat bolt upright. He clutched the varnished board. It felt wet and slippery. He slithered this way and that as Campbell dug first one oar and then the other into the water, brought the bow around and headed out across the arm of the bay towards the skerries that fringed Quinish.

There was low cloud upon the horizon and a stiff breeze plucked at the canvas sail that was roped loosely against the mast. Willy was tempted to ask Campbell why he preferred oars to sail but even he could see that the wind was set against them. He tried to appear calm and unflustered but the proximity of the deep black water disturbed him. He had never been this close to the sea before and it felt – what? – ravenous, as if it might suddenly suck him over the side and devour him. He kept his eyes firmly fixed on Ronan Campbell.

He said, 'It's kind of you to take me.'

'I thought you were going to pay me,' Campbell said, the rhythm of the oars faltering. 'Is it not to be a financial arrangement?'

'Oh, certainly, certainly,' Willy said. 'A bargain's a bargain.'

'Five shillings, you said.'

'Five shillings, it is,' said Willy. 'Do you want it now?'

'I was surprised when you approached me at the tea-party and asked me to do this service for you, since it did not seem that we had got off on the right foot at all.'

'Life's too short, the island too small, to harbour grudges,' Willy said, trying to grin. 'Besides, I reckoned you of all people would know where I might find what I'm looking for.'

'Aye, well, that is true,' Ronan Campbell said. 'There are not many things go on hereabouts that I do not know of. Is it for your masters or for yourself that you are wanting the stuff?'

'For me,' Willy answered. 'If it's drinkable at all, that is.'

'Oh, it is drinkable,' Ronan told him. 'It is no worse than what you would be buying out of the bottle at McKinnon's place.'

'That's not saying much.'

'And it is a damned sight cheaper. How much would you be wanting?'

'If it's palatable, enough to see me through the winter.'

'A gallon?'

'Or two,' said Willy.

Ronan Campbell nodded. To judge by his pallor a gallon of poteen or moonshine, or whatever illicitly distilled whisky was called in these parts, would hardly see Campbell through the week never mind the winter. Beneath the weather tan a web of broken veins had begun to spread out from his nose and his eyes were washed out.

Campbell was still robust enough to apply himself to the oars, however, and the boat fair flew over the sea. Willy could feel the thrust of each pull and the shudder of the waves against the bow. On the skerries the seals basked and paid not the slightest heed to the boat and even the cormorants and shags, propped like candles on the rocks, did not fly off, as if Campbell's boat were so much part of the natural scene that they hardly noticed it.

'How far is it to Arkle?' Willy asked.

'Not far. Are you sick to the stomach?'

'No.' Willy told the truth. 'I'm absolutely fine.'

In fact he was beginning to enjoy himself. He felt safe and confident in Campbell's hands. He lifted his chin, let the breeze tickle his beard and, posing a bit, surveyed the contours of the coast as if he were Henry the Navigator or, perhaps, Columba, the famous missionary, scouting for converts.

Apart from a few sheep on the higher grazings the coast was devoid of life and habitation. Willy could readily understand why Fergus Haggerty managed to conduct his business without interference. Revenue officers would find it impossible to approach the distiller's bothy undetected. Willy had no doubt that Haggerty kept his eyes peeled for strange craft during the four or five days when the still was running. Besides – Willy had done his homework – the west coast Preventative Force had been much reduced in recent years and the low alcohol tax and the availability of cheap grain whisky of the legal variety had all but killed the smugglers' trade. That, however, was about to change.

Willy was a dedicated reader of the parliamentary reports in *The Times* which the Baverstocks had delivered, albeit three days late, to Fetternish. What Willy knew that the bumpkins of Pennypol did not was that the malt tax was under review and would soon be abolished, after which the smuggling of whisky free of duty would become a highly profitable business once more. Even so, his trip to Arkle was no more than a reconnaissance, a voyage of exploration, for he had not accumulated enough information to put a proper scheme together yet and for the time being he was content to let Campbell think that he was just another down-trodden wage-slave with a permanent thirst.

The boat moved in towards the shore.

The Island Wife

Long ribbons of froth curled across the water and seabirds flocked over the hummocky hill where, Willy reckoned, the tiny hamlet of Croig was situated. At first he thought that they were headed for the mouth of the little sea loch, but he was wrong. They were steering for another inlet, an opening in the barrier of rocks so narrow that it appeared it could hardly accommodate the boat at all. Then Ronan with one strong pull upon the oars propelled the *Kelpie* through the gap into a bay that seemed hardly larger than a fingernail.

The tiny bowl-shaped beach was guarded by two columns of black basalt. Above it hung a little saddle of bright green grass upon which three or four goats grazed and above that again the cliff-face was split by a crack so even and unwavering that Willy almost expected to see an axe-blade buried in it.

Far above, on top of the cliff, were woolly wisps of grass through which two Blackface ewes peered down reproachfully at the landing party.

'Arkle?' Willy asked.

'Arkle,' Ronan answered.

'Where's the bothy?'

'In the cave.'

'Where's the still?'

'In the bothy.'

'Who's that?'

Ronan shipped oars and skiffed the boat forward on to the sand.

'That's Fergus Haggerty.'

'What's he doing?'

'Waiting for us.'

'How did he know we were coming?'

'I told him.'

'Oh!' Willy said. 'I see.'

Then, stepping awkwardly over the bow, he padded up the sand towards the ragged little mannikin who sat on a rock like a leprechaun, puffing a small Burmese cheroot and reading – rather ostentatiously Willy thought – yesterday's edition of *The Times*.

Just at first Innis supposed that it was one of the Baverstocks who was coming over the hill. She was concerned that he might have brought the disobedient hounds with him. The autumn cow, Dandy, was close to calving and the last thing she needed were dogs bounding about the pasture.

It was not a Baverstock at all but Michael Tarrant. He had replaced his corduroy trousers with tweed plus-twos and long stockings and his shirt was hidden beneath a knitted jumper that made him appear almost sturdy. He carried no crook and was not accompanied by the collie, Roy. He was very intent, very purposeful in his stride and vaulted over the head dike and advanced towards her as if he were pressed for time or – the thought startled Innis – as if he intended to pick her up and carry her off with him.

She was standing by the back of the cow, for she had been feeling the gristle that ran from each side of the tail to the pin bones to see how slack it had become. Very slack, as it happened; Dandy would calve before the day was out. She lifted a hand and signalled, pointing to the animal and gesturing.

Michael slowed his pace for, whatever urged him on, he was not ignorant of beastly antics and the moodiness that pregnancy brought with it. He made a little detour to let the cow see him clearly and came close to Innis before he opened his mouth. 'She's near her time, I see.'

'Yes, she will drop about dusk or shortly after.'

'In the field?'

'No, I will take her in.'

'In case of chilling?'

'Yes.'

'Do you think there will be rain then?'

'On a south-west wind,' Innis said, 'it is possible.'

'And you will be with her to comfort her?'

'I will,' said Innis.

'Aye, my brother, when he was a cattleman, was just the same.'

'How many brothers do you have, Mr Tarrant?'

'Just one,' Michael said. 'However, I did not come over to discuss my family – or cows for that matter.' He paused. 'It seems I have offended you.'

'No,' Innis said. 'I have not been aware of it.'

'Then why have you stopped delivering milk?'

89

'Oh, so that's what's wrong with you, is it? You are missing the milk?'

'The milk's not important. I can have milk from the big house just for the asking.' He planted his hands on his hips in a manner that reminded Innis, oddly, of her mother. He glowered at her. The blandness had gone out of him. Irritation added character to his features. 'If I have offended you, I would like to be told what I've done.'

'Why?'

'So that I can make amends.'

'There is no need for you to make amends.'

'I upset you, didn't I?'

'No.'

'On the day of the dipping, I upset you. Whatever I said or did, it was certainly not intentional.'

'You were very busy. I should not have been there at all.'

'What was it?' Michael persisted. 'Was it the flowers?'

Innis was tempted to tell him the truth but would not confirm his opinion of women by admitting to jealousy. 'Oh, the flowers?' she heard herself say. 'Biddy's flowers, do you mean?'

'So that's it? I knew that was it.'

'Should you not be apologising to Biddy instead of me?'

'God!' He shook his head in frustration. 'I'm not apologising, not to you and not to your sister. There's nothing to apologise for.'

'Biddy's in the kitchen, if you want to call on her. Baking bread, I think.'

He glanced towards the house and rubbed a hand over his chin which, Innis noticed, had been shaved as smooth as a pebble. There was even a tiny snow-white dab of lather drying on the lobe of his left ear, a blemish that diminished his neatness and somehow gave her hope.

'I am sure she would be pleased to see you,' Innis said.

The cow, Dandy, uttered a low groan, in discomfort not pain. She was rocking a little, rolling her head this way and that, though still with a mouthful of the new hay that Innis had carried out to supplement the thinning grass of the pasture. The byre was ready for delivery, the calf-pen scrubbed to prevent the risk of infection. Innis had spent the morning at the task. It occurred to her that she probably still smelled of disinfectant. The realisation did not detract from her feeling of superiority, for her teasing – if it was teasing – had Michael on the hop and she was not about to relent.

'Are you always like this?' he said abruptly.

'Like what?'

'Unreasonable.'

'Am I unreasonable?' Innis said. 'Perhaps it is because I am busy with the cow.'

He rubbed his chin with his hand again and when he withdrew it she saw that he was smiling, nothing cheesy or overconfident, as if he had realised that he was in the wrong and that she was entitled to take revenge upon him.

He said, 'Is Biddy really at home?'

'Yes, baking bread.'

'Perhaps I will call upon her then, since I have come this far.'

'And since you are so nicely got up,' Innis said. He glanced down at the knitted jumper and the tweedy trousers as if he were surprised to find himself thus clad. 'If you are going calling on my sister, though,' Innis went on, 'it might be as well to be nothing less than perfect, Mr Tarrant.'

'Hmmm?'

She wiped her hand on her skirt, wetted her pinkie and stepped close to him. She dabbed the fleck of shaving lather from his earlobe and wiped it delicately away. He did not flinch from her touch, did not ask the reason for it. He looked straight at her, head cocked to one side.

'There!' she said. 'Now you are just right. By the by, my mother and Aileen are also at home so you will be able to impress them all at once.'

'Innis,' he said, 'be quiet.'

'Mr Tarrant . . .'

He kissed her.

There was nothing she could do about it. He did not ensnare her waist with his arm, did not clasp her shoulder with his hand. He leaned forward and kissed her on the mouth as if there were no other way of making her obey him. His lips were warm and he smelled of shaving soap. She knew then what it was that Biddy had found so attractive and why her sister, for all her tantrums and tempers, had fallen under Michael Tarrant's spell that very first day up by the wall. The kiss vibrated through her like the sound of the sea in a cave and she gasped when he pulled away.

'I will not apologise,' he said, softly. 'Not for that, at any rate,' then, as if his business here was done, he turned around and headed back towards the little wall that separated the Campbells' property from the base of Olaf's Hill.

Shaken, it took a moment for Innis to gather herself. She put a hand to her lips and then to her breast and, hurrying a few steps after him, called out, 'Michael. Michael, what about Biddy?'

'Another day,' he shouted. 'Another day,' and retreated into the bracken without breaking stride.

It was the queerest dwelling that Willy had ever seen. Built of driftwood and stones held together by mortar and rope, it was tucked into the mouth of the cave and reeked of peat smoke and malted barley. If he had been a Customs' officer he would have needed no more evidence of illegal brewing than one whiff of the air within. And, Willy was willing to wager, there wouldn't be a gull roosting within a mile of Haggerty's house unless it had developed a fondness for whisky fumes. The only smell that distinguished itself from the effluvia of sour mash was that of Fergus Haggerty's cheroot which Willy followed like a lifeline into the gloom.

The house had several doors but no windows. It was surprisingly comfortable inside with a proper fireplace and a long tubular funnel which soared up through the roof in lieu of a chimney. Pots and pans were everywhere. Shelves were laden with meal sacks, jugs and jars and assorted bottles. Strings of onions dangled from the rafters, along with haunches of ripe venison, smoked pork and ribs of beef. Tubs of new potatoes, beans and cabbages were piled against the wall and draped neatly on a string across the prow of the Irishman's bed hung six or eight pairs of glossy brown kippers.

'Me humble abode.' Fergus Haggerty flashed a grin that displayed brown teeth, pink gums and a sleek little tongue like an adder's. 'Ye'll be takin' a tocht o' the Aquavity, nae doot, since that's whit ye cam' fur?'

'Pardon?' said Willy.

'Aquavity – a draught frae the Well o' Bethlehem.'

'The Well of Bethlehem?'

'Whaur David o' the Bible suppit.' Fergus Haggerty frowned as if the visitor's ignorance of Scripture was reprehensible. 'Or, as Jamie wroted tae the twelve tribes o' the dispershun, "Doth the found-tain send forth frae the same openin' both sweet water an' bitter?" ' He reached to a shelf, whipped down a ginger-beer bottle and plonked it on the table. 'Sweet's the answer, Mister Namesmith, as ye'll be findin' oot for yersel' in a wee minute.'

The table, barely knee high, had been fashioned from a single piece of split oak. Following religious principle, Willy knelt before the bottle. Fergus set down a glass. The bottle was of glazed, pale grey stone, sealed with a cork cut from a fishing float. Willy pulled the cork, trickled liquid into the glass, sniffed it and held it to the light.

Behind him the Irishman was still blathering. Willy was not taken in. No, he said to himself, this man is no more fool than I am. This is an act, a deliberate ploy to trick me into thinking he's simple-minded, to put me off my guard. He might be citing the 'Epistle of James' right now but in five or ten minutes he'll be quoting just as confidently from stock market reports in *The Times*. Even the rich polyglot dialect was intended to deceive and Willy, as he lifted the glass to his lips, focused his attention on the clouded liquor and blotted Haggerty's contrivances from his thoughts.

He drank. He held the firewater on his tongue for a moment or two then let it slip gradually down his throat. Membranous tissues crinkled under the onslaught. Fire changed to heat, heat to warmth and through the suffusion came the distinctive flavour of pure malt. He put the glass down quickly.

'Is it not to your liking then?' Ronan Campbell asked.

'For what it is, it's fine,' Willy said.

'Will ye be havin' a wee tait more then?' Haggerty offered.

'No, I think I'll be leavin' that tae stronger heads than mine,' said Willy, lightly mimicking the accent. He remained kneeling, his back to the islanders. 'How large is the capacity of the still?'

'Forty gallons.'

'Do you buy in the malt?'

'No, I malt myself.'

'Where?'

'Back there, in the cave.'

Willy swung on his hip and leaned an elbow on the table. Haggerty and Campbell were watching him anxiously. He'd been right in his assessment: the meeting *had* been set up between them. They had probably guessed what was on his mind. Had he become so transparent that his every move was obvious? Dealing with these foxy islanders would soon restore his edge.

'Where do you buy your barley?' Willy asked.

'Frae – from farms in the south of the island,' Fergus Haggerty answered, shedding the false accent at last.

Willy administered his most penetrating stare and rapped out his questions without preliminary.

'Why doesn't he buy barley from you, Mr Campbell?'

'It is cattle fodder my wife grows, not fit for the making of whisky.'

'And your yeast?'

'From Belgium,' said Haggerty. 'Only the best, you see.'

'What's your season?'

'October into May, if the weather is cool.'

'How much do you produce in that time?'

'Only what I can sell.'

'Are there other distillers on Mull?'

'None.'

'Are you sure?'

'I am sure,' Haggerty said; Ronan nodded in confirmation.

'Do you send any whisky for sale on the mainland?' Willy asked.

'No.'

'Why not?'

'It's not worth the trouble,' Haggerty said. 'What is your proposition, Mr Namesmith?'

'My name's Naismith – and my proposition is simple. When the malt tax is abolished at the back end of the year then making and selling illicit whisky will become a highly profitable business.'

'Aye, the thought had crossed my mind,' Haggerty said.

'As an inveterate reader of *The Times*,' Willy said, 'you'll no doubt realise that it'll take time for the Office of the Excise to train a new force of Protective officers. There's been some correspondence about it.'

'I did catch somethin' o' the sort, aye.'

'You have a still in working order,' Willy said. 'It may not be of large capacity but it's big enough to produce a hundred and eighty to two hundred gallons a month.'

'I do not have the malt for that sort o' output.'

Willy did not take up the point. 'How often do excisemen come sniffing round Arkle?'

'Never,' Ronan answered. He glanced at Haggerty who nodded. 'The land belongs to Mr Duffertin who is a friend of Mr McNab, who is the officer responsible for the protection of this coastline. Mr Duffertin and Mr McNab are very fond of Arkle whisky.'

'Aye, Mr Naismith,' Fergus Haggerty informed him, 'there is a sayin' hereabouts: *Is fada Arkle bho lagh.*'

'What does that mean in plain English?'

'It means, "Arkle is far from the law," ' said Ronan. 'The trouble is, Mr Naismith, that Oban is far from Arkle.'

'Not by boat it's not,' Willy said.

'I would not be wanting to take a boat laden with whisky down the Sound of Mull, not even in the quiet season,' Ronan said. 'There are too many inquisitive people—'

Willy interrupted him. 'Have you thought of taking it down the west coast instead?'

'It can be very wild—' Ronan began.

Again Willy interrupted. 'You're not the only boatman on Mull, Campbell. I'm sure there are plenty of others who'd be willing to make a fortnightly trip to, say, Eilean nan Boghan, via the Sound of Iona –'

'It is dangerous water, with shoals and rocks,' said Ronan.

Willy continued without a pause, ' – for seven or eight pounds the trip.'

'Seven or eight pounds?' said Ronan. 'Well, now!'

Willy was confident that the distiller would do his part. But he needed Campbell's co-operation to make it profitable. There was no real money to be made in selling the product of the pot still locally; real money would come only from regular sales to a mainland broker.

Ronan Campbell seated himself on the table. He folded his

arms across his chest and considered the matter. In the light of the paraffin lamp his eyes were sly. Even now, Willy reckoned, he would be doing sums in his head and greed would be struggling against laziness. The Irishman took down a plywood box and extracted a black Burmese cheroot. He did not, Willy noticed, offer the cigar box round. Instead he filled three glasses from the ginger bottle. Ronan drank the spirit as if it were no stronger than cocoa. Willy waited. He was still seated on the earthen floor, elbow propped on the table like a Roman emperor.

Something about the queer wee house in the Arkle cave was very conducive to secret negotiation. When trippers from Iona or Staffa passed on the steamers they would see only the gable and a piece of the roof and would remark how 'quaint' it was and imagine some hermit living a simple and contented life there. Little did they know what went on under the sod roofs of Mull's cottages on dreary winter nights, a lot more than plying a spinning wheel or practising the chanter or telling tales by the peat-fire flame.

At length, Ronan Campbell said, 'And what is it that you would be doing, Mr Naismith? How will you contribute to the making of all this profit?'

'Apart from finding buyers, do you mean?'

'Yes, apart from that.'

'I'll fund the venture. I'll put out the money for barley purchase and I'll buy every drop of whisky that Mr Haggerty produces at an agreed price.'

'Then it will be your whisky?'

'It will,' Willy said.

'And the profit will be yours?'

'No, the profit – and the risk – will be shared,' said Willy, patiently.

'How will *you* be taking any risk at all?' Ronan said.

'If a cargo is lost, if the broker welches on payment, if the Protective officers come breathing down your neck and the load has to be jettisoned, the loss will be mine.'

'Aye, but it's not you who will appear before the sheriff and go to jail.'

'No, and it won't be you either. Not if you're careful.'

'Eight pounds the trip?' Ronan said.

'Seven or eight, yes.'

It was Haggerty who grasped the bull by the horns. The Irishman was far more astute than the fisherman. He seated himself on a little three-legged stool and leaned back against the wall. He rocked forth and back for a moment, the cheroot clenched in his teeth, then he said, 'Tell me, Mr Naismith, have you done this sort of thing before?'

'Not with whisky,' Willy said, 'with other things.'

'Do you have the capital that you say you have?'

'I have the money.'

'Not saved from a servant's wage?' said Fergus Haggerty.

'Hardly,' Willy said. 'I do have the money, though, and once I've made arrangements with a mainland buyer then I'll be looking for sixty or eighty gallons to be delivered within the week.'

'Cash into my hand, in advance,' said Haggerty.

'On delivery of the first run,' Willy said.

'What do you say to it, Ronan?' Haggerty asked.

'I say that we should be discussing it,' Ronan Campbell answered.

'Are you in favour of the principle of the thing, though?'

'Aye, I am inclined to be in favour.'

Willy got up suddenly. 'That'll do me,' he said. 'I would have been disappointed in your judgement, gentlemen, if you hadn't been cautious. You have heard my proposition. You may give me your answer to it at your convenience, preferably before the end of the month. Is that agreed?'

'Agreed.'

'Now,' Willy said, 'there's only one thing more I require of you, Mr Haggerty: two bottles of your excellent whisky to offer to potential buyers.'

'O' course ye do,' said Fergus Haggerty.

Rising, Haggerty produced two pint bottles from an alcove cupboard and put them down upon the table. As Willy reached forward to lift them, however, Haggerty laid a little brown claw upon his shoulder and grinned.

'Four shillin's please,' he said.

And Willy, without quibble, paid.

It gave Innis a bit of a turn to see the Baverstocks' man-servant leaning on the door post and she wondered how long he had been there, observing her.

She had been fully occupied for the last hour of the afternoon. Dandy had been brought into the byre just in time to eject a fine, sturdy little bull calf without assistance at the tail end. Innis had rubbed the calf with dry bracken and had steered its wobbly progress two or three steps to the pen. She had given Dandy an oatmeal drink, almost two gallons of it, and a rack of hay before reporting to Vassie. Vassie had come round to inspect the calf but had soon gone away again, for it did not do to have the cow disturbed before she had got rid of the cleansing. Innis had drawn a pint of first milk from each of Dandy's teats and had finger-fed the calf and she would draw again before she went to bed at eleven and, in the morning, empty the udder completely.

She had been so wrapped up in her work that she had had no time to think of anything else, not even of Michael and that sudden, impromptu kiss. But as the darkness came down over the sea she had lighted a lantern and had paused to stare into the candle flame and had imagined Michael coming from the hill to his empty cottage and what it would be like if she were there to greet him, not just tonight, but always.

'It's a bonnie sight, lass, right enough,' Willy Naismith said in a quiet voice. 'She'll keep you in butter for the best part of the winter, unless I'm much mistaken.'

The door had been left open to give the beasts fresh air, for the books all said that coddling a cow after calving was bad policy. Next door, just through the wooden partition, Innis could hear Biddy rattling pails in readiness for the chore of evening milking out in the field.

'Are you here with another invitation, Mr Naismith?'

'Alas, no. I'm on my way home, in fact. I've been out on the mighty ocean in your father's boat and he set me down here at your jetty since it was roughing up and the Fetternish rock did not appeal to him.'

'Where did you go?'

'Not far. Down the coast, in and out of the islands, observing the seals.'

'And were you impressed?'

'Not greatly. They reminded me of the pigs on Circe's isle.'

'What an education you have, Mr Naismith. Did you think that you were Ulysses and get my dada to rope you to the mast?'

He laughed, white teeth in the curly black beard. 'That was hardly necessary, since neither Sirens nor Circe could take my mind off my stomach. I've learned a hard lesson today, Innis: I'm no small-boat sailor.'

She had guided him out of the byre. They stood on the flagstones at the threshold of the outbuildings, listening to Biddy in the dairy clanking and clinking the dishes about. She was singing too, without much tune to it, not one of the mournful songs that the islanders loved, but a busy little reel.

Innis said, 'Did my father show you one of the great sights of the coast?'

'What would that be?'

'Mr Haggerty's cave.'

Hesitation, a tug at the beard. 'Aye, lass, he did.'

'From the inside?'

'I admit that we did draw in for a glass or two.'

'For which you paid?' said Innis.

'A fair price for an afternoon out,' said Willy.

He was easy to talk to, relaxed in manner, not so much roguish as jocular.

Innis said, 'Will you tell your masters where you spent your holiday?'

'No. The Baverstocks have gone to dine with Mr Leggat.'

'Do they know how to drive a gig?'

'They're not so dizzy as you might suppose, that pair,' said Willy, then, as the door to the dairy opened, glanced casually to his left. 'Why, if it isn't Miss Biddy, the songstress of the north.'

Biddy carried two empty pails, one under each arm. Not at her glowing best, she was not amused by Mr Naismith's teasing remark. She scowled and snapped, 'What do you want?'

'To enquire if you will be gracing the Harvest Home with your presence?'

'Of course I will.'

'Will you put me down on your card for the Reel o' Tulloch?'

'Card? What card?'

It was on the tip of Innis's tongue to explain the allusion to the elegant balls that took place in Edinburgh but she had no wish to embarrass her sister in front of the gentlemen's gentleman.

'Tell me,' Willy said, smoothly, 'who else will be there?'

'Everybody,' Biddy said. 'Except those who consider ceilidhs immoral.'

'Oooo,' Willy said. 'I'm glad you warned me.'

Innis chuckled and Biddy, still scowling, said, 'What?'

'That the hall will be filled to bursting,' Willy said. 'I'll make sure that we all get there early.'

'We?' said Innis.

'The Baverstock boys, Queenie, shy Margaret – and me.'

'And who is Queenie?' said Biddy.

'Our cook. Loves a right good fling from time to time does our Queenie. She's a great one for the heuching and cheuching,' Willy said. 'I'm not averse to it myself, come to think of it.' He raised his arms above his head like a sword-dancer and executed a few lumbering steps upon the flagstones. 'Be warned, though, ladies, I like it fast an' furious.'

'Well, Mr Naismith,' said Biddy, not quite in touch with the conversation, 'I will see if I can fit you in.'

Willy opened his mouth to let out a guffaw, thought better of it and, covering his beard with his hand, bade the Campbell girls goodnight.

'What is wrong with him?' Biddy asked as soon as Willy had left.

'Nothing,' Innis answered.

'What did I say to offend him?'

'Nothing, nothing.'

Biddy sighed. 'I'm thinking he does not approve of me.'

'Oh, no, Biddy,' said Innis. 'He does, he really does.' Then, cheered by the prospect of the Harvest Home, she went back to attend the cow.

FOUR

The Harvest Home

In his declining years Colonel Murray Wingard of the 93rd Sutherland Highlanders, who had taken a musket ball in the hip at Orléans and a wife in Dublin, retired to live with his daughter, Rose, in the village of Crove. Rose's husband, William Gardiner, was less than delighted to welcome the old war-horse into his home but Colonel Wingard was by then a widower in his seventies, had nowhere else to go and was not, in any case, expected to live long.

Gardiner himself was an incomer. He had purchased Crove House and a small parcel of land around it early in the century and, being an architect and engineer of sorts, had transformed the original crumbling farmhouse into a solid castellated mansion-house in the Scots baronial style. Patience was not William Gardiner's strong suit, though, and when old Wingard did not pop off after a couple of hard, wet winters, he took to baiting his father-in-law which, of course, was exactly the sort of tonic that the splenetic colonel needed to resurrect his interest in staying alive.

Nobody in Crove liked Gardiner. Everybody in Crove loved the whisky-sodden old colonel. The local community was soon divided over and diverted by the Wingard-Gardiner feud which spilled on for the best part of twenty years and into the age of the Clearances. In the struggle against dispossession the colonel took arms on the side of the peasants. Ignoring the fact that half the new landowning class were Scots, he did what he could to keep them from excessive suffering at the hands of 'those thieving English blackguards'. He led meetings of protest in the back room of the McKinnon Arms and when he finally died, aged ninety-four, and ten weeks after his son-in-law, he endowed the community with enough money to build a hall on Crove's last piece of common ground.

Thus the Wingard Memorial Hall came into being. Thus the annual celebration of the Harvest Home slipped from control of the Kirk and became instead a communal rant. Customs change with less subtlety and a deal more speed than folklorists would have us believe, however, and it wasn't long before the Harvest Home ceilidh established its own set of traditions which, before a decade had passed, had become as time-honoured as anything on the Christian calendar. Nominating the Committee, Calling the Meeting, the Election of Chairman, the Appeasement of the Treasurer swiftly became part of community fabric and, by displacement, eradicated for ever many of the old customs by which Crove's forefathers had paid homage to the crown of the seasons.

The important issue now was not who would cut the last sheaf of corn but which band would roll up on the back of a farm cart and which famous piper would be ferried in from Coll or Tiree to skirl out reels and, after sweat and whisky had oiled the tear ducts, heart-breaking laments.

'Have you heard yet?' Molly Maclean would enquire breathlessly as she dived into the shop at the end of the main street. 'Is it to be McPherson or is it to be Dunlop?'

'Neither, Mrs Maclean,' old Miss Fergusson would tell her. 'I have heard that it is to be none other than McFee himself.'

'Calum or Alisdair?'

'Calum.'

'He is out of the jail then?'

'Out of the jail and never looking back.'

'And the band? Is it to be Morrison's again?'

'No, it is not to be Morrison's. After last year Mr Ewing said he would not be providing accommodation at the manse for any of that drunken rabble, not if he had to take out his cornet and play for us himself.'

'It would be the two young ladies that they found lying in the graveyard afterwards that would be hardening his heart against Morrison, I'm thinking,' Mrs Maclean would say, frowning. 'Who will it be then? Not the fiddlers from the Seaman's Lodge, I hope?'

'No.' The voice would drop, the shoulders would come forward, the hand would come up to cover the mouth and the head turn away to squint through the dusty window into the empty street. 'The Kildonan Volunteers.'

'Them with the flute?'

'Aye - and the thingummy.'

'Oh, what a treat will be in store for us, Miss Fergusson.'

'What a treat, indeed, Mrs Maclean.'

By noon word of the selection of the band was all over the parish and half-way out to sea and, in certain quarters, like the girls' school in Dervaig, excitement knew no bounds. The Kildonan Volunteers! My, but they were famous the length and breadth of Mull, so well thought of, indeed, that they had even been invited to Glasgow to play at the Highlanders' Ball. The Kildonan Volunteers coming to Crove for the Harvest ceilidh! Who would be paying for that, I wonder, who would be footing that part of the bill?

'Well, Mr Ewing,' Austin Baverstock said, 'my brother and I may not be, strictly speaking, the owners of Crove but I suppose that we are what you may call "lairds" and that we must accept our responsibilities in that direction.'

'It's exceedingly generous of you,' Tom Ewing murmured, through a mouthful of seed cake. 'I'm sure the parish will be very grateful.'

'Everyone will be there, you say?'

'Every cowman, ploughman and shepherd this side of Salen,' Tom assured him. 'Only those who consider dancing an invention of the devil will boycott the proceedings. As for the rest, wild horses won't keep them away.'

'There will be drink, of course?'

'Mild ale,' said the minister. 'Fruit cordials for the children.'

'Nothing stronger?'

'Alas, yes,' Tom said, shrugging. 'It would not be a Harvest Home without frequent libations of whisky. Officially, however, no strong drink is allowed in the hall.'

'If I may say so, Mr Ewing, you're very liberal for a minister of the Gospel,' Austin Baverstock told him. 'Is that a personal characteristic or is it a quality that you've had to acquire since coming to Mull?'

'A little of both, I suppose,' Tom said. 'Although the Presbytery and one or two of my elders do not entirely approve of my "laxity", my parishioners seemed happy enough with the bit of rope I allow them. Thanksgiving services on the Sabbath will be almost as well attended as Friday night's ceilidh, I'm happy to say. I will bless the sheaves, the cheeses and the baskets of herring without feeling that I'm committing sacrilege for, like the good Christian folk around me, I sincerely believe that the Lord God is a Great Provider – even if I do not subscribe to the theory that He was originally a Lewisman and fashioned the Gaels out of different clay from Adam.'

Austin Baverstock chuckled. 'Is that what they believe?'

'It's what they'd like to believe,' Tom said. 'And, I confess, there are times when I stand on the hill on a fine summer's evening and look out to the horizon when I'm also tempted to believe that there is a land just beyond the Hebrides where a man might find eternal peace.'

'Tir-Nan-Og, do you mean?' said Austin Baverstock.

'The Isles of the Blessed, Land of Eternal Youth,' Tom said, 'where there's no poverty, no ageing, no pain or suffering – and no organising committees. Which,' he said, 'brings me back to the purpose of my visit. To thank you on behalf of the board of management of the Wingard Hall for your generous donation.'

Talk of an earthly paradise had brought a wistful smile to Austin's face. He had turned his gaze to the window of the drawing-room, to the heaving grey-green sea which lay, that afternoon, under a lid of cloud.

'Will Miss Campbell be there?' he said.

For a split second Tom thought that Austin Baverstock might still be dreaming of the Blessed Isles. He frowned and tapped a finger to his chin, then said, 'Ah, at the ceilidh, you mean?'

'Yes, at the ceilidh.'

'Which Miss Campbell?'

'Bridget.'

Tom cleared his throat and removed a crumb of seed cake from the corner of his lips with his napkin. 'Biddy, yes, Biddy will be there. Are you – ah – interested in Miss Campbell, Mr Baverstock?'

'Oh, no, no, no. I wouldn't say that,' Austin replied. 'She is, however, rather a remarkable - a striking young woman, I'm sure you'll agree.'

'Without doubt,' Tom said. 'You're not the first gentleman in these parts to make the observation. One would have to be blind not to notice Biddy Campbell.'

'I'm sorry. I didn't mean to cause offence.'

'Offence?' said Tom. 'Good heavens, Mr Baverstock, I'm not in the least offended. It's not as if Biddy were - well, *that* sort of girl.'

'Oh, dear me, no. Certainly not. She's seems very modest, very well mannered.'

Tom kept his reservations on that score to himself, for he sensed that thin ice lay not far off and he had no wish to alienate the Baverstocks who obviously had much to contribute to the commonwealth of Crove.

'Have you known Bid - the family for long?' Austin asked.

'Since I first came to Crove. Eight years since,' Tom answered. 'She was as pretty as a picture even then.'

'I wonder why - I mean, it's curious that she has not married.'

'She has a fiery temper, Mr Baverstock,' Tom said, 'which some men find off-putting.'

'She has never been - I mean, never betrothed?'

'Not to my knowledge.'

'Perhaps the right chap hasn't come along yet,' Austin suggested.

'That's probably the reason,' Tom Ewing said.

'An older man. Steady.'

'Yes,' Tom said, 'I'm sure that's it.'

Austin Baverstock nodded, pleased by the minister's tactful assurances and as eager now as any man for Friday night to arrive.

Unlike Morrison's reprobates, who had visited every pub on their way through the glens, the members of the Kildonan Volunteers band turned up sober and on time; so sober and so on time, in fact, that they were ensconced in the Wingard Hall and warming up before anyone knew they had arrived. There were seven of them; three fiddles, a cornet, flute, piccolo and a 'thingummy', by which was meant a gigantic double bass. They had travelled in their own conveyance, a wagon pulled by two horses but somehow, in appearance at least, they did not live up to their grand reputation.

There was nothing military about them except their uniform of kilts, sporrans and starched white shirts. Squat and stout and middle-aged, they sat square on their chairs on the platform at the hall's end, a bitter disappointment to the girls from the hill farms and spinster ladies of a certain age to whom anything in kilts was, as a rule, irresistible. What's more, they used music clipped to huge mahogany stands that added a formality more in keeping with an orchestral concert than a village-hall dance.

For a half-hour after their arrival they tuned their violins, tootled on cornet and flute, trilled on the piccolo, sawed away on the boat-shaped bass and now and then burst into twelve or sixteen bars of 'The Linton Ploughman' or 'Jenny Dang the Weaver' with such force and volume that cattle bolted on the hill, sheep scuttled for cover and all the crofting lads and lassies, who were already intoxicated by anticipation, cried out, 'Hurry, hurry,' and dragged their parents to the door.

'Callous' Calum McFee, the piper, who had arrived over from Coll and was quietly partaking of a liquid supper in the back room of the Arms, would lift his head at the sound of the Volunteers' rehearsal and with the cock's feather in his bonnet bobbing menacingly, would glower and growl, 'By God, if it is just noise they are wanting, I will be showing them who is the boss.'

The Campbells arrived from Pennypol. Vassie and the girls came on foot, skirts kirtled up, white stockings and dancing pumps carried in bags over their shoulders. Donnie had ridden off on the garron to pick up Muriel MacNiven, while Neil and Ronan had left early for the McKinnon Arms where most of Crove's menfolk had assembled to honour the spirits of the corn in their own inimitable manner.

The hall was more than half full by the time Innis stepped out of the water-closet at the rear of the building, stockings gartered and kidskin slippers – a present from her grandfather – laced to her feet. She was buoyed up by the sight of the lamps that blazed in the hall and the lanterns that hung among the boughs of the two little holly trees that flanked the entranceway. Even Crove's dismal main street had a cosmopolitan air, she thought, with everybody dressed up fancy. On nights like this she was always amazed at the number of folk who appeared out of nowhere. Pennypol and Fetternish seemed so empty for the most part, the land lying bleak and desolate with never another person in sight; yet fairs and markets and dances brought out a whole jolly regiment of friends and acquaintances, like one great sprawling family.

She paused just inside the door and peeped nervously into the hall. The band were not upon the platform. Their instruments occupied the vacant chairs under the corn wheels and barley whirls that hung above the dais. In the back room women were already laying out trays of pies and sandwiches and the corn cakes, dabbed with jam, that miller Sloan donated. Kegs of light ale, bottles of ginger beer and bowls of 'Temperance Punch' were being arranged on a long table and all the odd chairs and benches had been peeled back from the floor and set about the sides of the hall. Children skated across the empty space, working in the water that had been sprinkled to lay the dust, and those young men and women who were already sweethearts stood awkwardly together in one corner, waiting for music to give them an excuse to embrace in public.

A hand cupped Innis's waist. She swung round, heart leaping at the thought that it would be Michael and that she would be carried into Courtship Corner and everyone - including Biddy - would see just whose girl she was.

'Innis, how are you tonight?'

'Oh, I'm fine, Mr Ewing.'

She tried to hide her disappointment. The minister had touched her without any romantic intention. He had merely moved her out of the way of the bandsmen, who had been relieving themselves in the trees, and trooped past her now back into the hall.

She looked down the length of the hall. There was Nancy Pritchard with Fraser Lamb. She was sporting his ring and, some said, already carrying his bairn. There was Horace 'Hovan' Watters who had tried to kiss Innis long ago when they were hardly more than seven years old and whose innocent familiarity had reduced her to tears. Donnie and Muriel were here, defying propriety by holding hands in public. And, down by the platform, Michael, Biddy and Mr Austin Baverstock were huddled in a group that did not, at least to Innis's way of thinking, seem quite comfortable with itself.

The band settled stiffly and stared out over the expectant faces while Mr Ewing requested silence and intoned a prayer; while Mr Sloan, current chairman of the Hall Committee, welcomed one and all to the *hairst*, then they raised their instruments and blasted forth with 'The Corn Rigs', just to get the feet stamping and the blood tingling. But before Innis could move forward to let Michael see her, Reverend Ewing arrived at her side and, with a bow, led her out to form first couple for the reel.

It was all Willy could do to separate himself from shy Margaret long enough to introduce Ronan Campbell to the man from Glasgow. He was not dismayed by Maggie's attention. To tell the truth, he was quite flattered by it, for she looked unusually pretty in a silky white dress and scarlet sash and when he danced with her she threw herself on to his arm with an enthusiasm that was anything but shy. In fact if he had not made an arrangement with Jack Stockton he would have been happy to dance every set with Miss Margaret Bell.

He had invited Stockton to Crove, however. He had coaxed the broker from the comfort of a Tobermory hotel specifically to finalise arrangements for the purchase of Fergus Haggerty's whisky.

Jack Stockton was a tall, powerfully built man in his thirties with a full moustache and a twinkle in his eye that, Willy thought, probably belied his true nature, for he had never met an agent yet who didn't have a heart of stone. He had located Stockton in the Marine Hotel in Oban, where he had been directed by the publican of a backstreet dram-shop. Willy's reason for being on the mainland was ostensibly to oversee the despatch of a freight-load of furniture that the Baverstocks had ordered from an Edinburgh wholesaler, but he had completed that task very quickly and had spent the rest of the evening seeking out a broker.

Stockton, it seemed, was one of those fellows who could get you anything from anywhere, at a price. Buying and selling was his business and as soon as he realised that Willy was trustworthy, he had bragged about the size of his warehouse in Glasgow and the volume of untaxed trade that he did up and down the west coast of Scotland, in wool, beef, pork and out-of-season game as well as wines, beers and spirits. He was no stranger to Mull and claimed to have regular clients in Salen and Tobermory.

To the villagers of Crove Mr Stockton appeared friendly and outgoing. He engaged in conversations with Mr Thrale, Reverend Ewing and, of course, with the Baverstock brothers to whom, he hoped, he might one day be of service. He also talked for some time with Biddy. He danced an Eightsome with Freda Thrale – it took a brave man to do that – a strathspey with Mrs McQueen and he might have carried Margaret into the Circassian Circle if Willy hadn't spotted Ronan Campbell heading for the side door and, with a tug on Stockton's sleeve, steered him out of the hall into the grass yard near the water-closets where Ronan, bottle and glass in hand, awaited them.

Stockton and Campbell shook hands. Ronan poured a glass of whisky and passed it to Stockton who, although he had already tested the product, took in a mouthful, rolled it round his cheeks and then, to Ronan's consternation, spat it on to the grass.

'Is it not to your liking then, Mr Stockton?'

'It is very much to my liking. Once I'm done with it, it will taste as good as anything that comes out of Glenlivet.'

'Once you're done with it?' said Ronan.

'Once it's been matured in oak casks for six months.'

'Oh, is that what you will do with it?' Willy said.

'Never mind what I'll do with it,' Jack Stockton said. 'What can you do to ensure a regular supply? How much can you make, Willy?'

'A hundred proof gallons a month.'

'I need more than that to make it worth my while.'

'Very well. One hundred and sixty. October to May.'

'Fine.'

'What price are you paying for it, Mr Stockton?' Ronan enquired.

'That doesn't concern you,' Willy said, sharply. 'What you are here for, Ronan, is to devise a method of shipment that will not attract the attention of the Protection officers.'

'A drop on Bucks' Island,' Stockton said. 'Do you know where that is?'

'At the mouth of Loch Buie on the Firth of Lorne,' Ronan said. 'Will you be sailing the boat?'

'Of course I won't be sailing the boat,' Jack Stockton said. 'You won't even meet the boatman. What you'll do is unload the cargo as fast as possible, then make yourself scarce.'

'The firth can be rough in winter.'

'Where did you find this specimen, Willy?' Jack Stockton asked.

'I can be doing it,' Ronan said, hastily. 'I am not afraid of a rough sea. How will you know when we will be there?'

'Telegraph, Jack?' Willy suggested.

'Fine.'

'I know nothing about telegraphs,' said Ronan.

'You don't have to,' Jack Stockton told him. 'All you have to do is ferry each consignment to Bucks' Island, land it on the brown beach on the Loch Buie shore and stack it in out of sight against the rocks.'

'Bury it?'

'No, man, you don't have to bury it.'

'How will I get paid?' said Ronan.

'I'll pay you after each trip,' Willy told him. 'Now, is there anything else you need to know from Mr Stockton before we go back inside?'

'Will I not be seeing you again?'

'No,' Jack Stockton said. 'You will not be seeing me again,' then, shaking his head, he returned to the dance and left the ugly little fisherman, with his bottle, loitering outside.

Every village had one and Crove was no exception; Lachlan Gorum was his name. He was the half-witted 'natural' whose poems and songs were regarded as works of genius by those who knew no better. Even at his best, Lachie was not very prepossessing. In middle age he had lost the innocence that had originally made him tolerable. Having taken the lad to its bosom, however, the community could hardly cast him off and had to endure several new renditions from the 'Bard of Crove' at every social function.

For his platform appearances Lachie sported a great greasy swathe of tartan cloth – his 'plaidie', he called it – a moulting sporran and an old blue bonnet. He clumped on to the platform, knocking music stands askew, as if entitled to interrupt the dancing whenever he chose. The younger lads whistled and cheered and the older women, those of Lachie's vintage, seated themselves and muttered, 'Aye, pair laddie, pair laddie. He has naught in this life but the gift God ga'ed him,' while everybody else gritted their teeth at the prospect of being on the receiving end of the gift God ga'ed tae Lachie.

Biddy was certainly not one of Lachie Gorum's admirers. Feign – as Lachie might have put it – would she have sidled outside with a glass of light ale and a ham sandwich in her fist. But she was trapped by Austin Baverstock who, for the first time that evening, took his eyes off her long enough to stare, blinking in disbelief, at the bardic apparition. Being illiterate as well as 'a natural', Lachie had committed his latest composition to memory, so nobody could tell whether it would be a couplet or a quatrain or whether, as had happened once at a Lammas Fair, it would turn out to be an epic that would last for half an hour.

Lachie pushed the fiddlers back, fondled his sporran in a manner that would have had a lesser man arrested for indecency, raised his arms above his head and in the angry, declamatory voice that he had developed for performances, launched into his laureate production.

'*Ferst yer hells an' then yer toes . . .*'

'What?'

'*That'll be the wey the po-orkers goes . . .*'

'Porkers? What's he talking about pigs for?'

'Polkas. It's "polkas".'

'Quiet,' hissed Mr Ewing.

'*Then yer toes an' then yer hells . . .*'

Even as Lachie opened his mouth to deliver the poetic de-nouement, every young man and half the lassies in the hall chanted in unison, 'THAT'S THE WAY TO DANCE THE RELLS.' Lachie stopped, arms raised like a drowning man's, then, unpredictably, he grinned and in an accent as smooth and round as a water stone, said, 'Reels, you fools. Reeellls.'

'REEELLLS, LACHIE. REEELLLS.'

Biddy would have laughed along with the rest. But at that moment she felt a hand brush the outside of her thigh and slide provocatively against the material of her dress.

If Austin Baverstock had not been in plain view she might have suspected that he had forgotten that he was a gentleman and she a lady. She put her hand to her side, felt fingers close on hers, the contact hidden by the crush of her skirts and the bodies clustered around her. She glanced round and then, instantly, back at Lachie. Michael Tarrant leaned into her. Chin almost touching her shoulder, he whispered into her ear and, as if to wring a reply, tugged urgently at her fingers. Without turning, Biddy nodded.

'Jump aboot an' then a-wey...'
'THAT'S THE WAY TO DANCE STRATHSPEY.'
'Jump it, jump it, jump it big...'
'THAT'S THE WAY TO DANCE A JIG.'

Austin Baverstock's eyes grew moist at the warmth of the rough islanders and the pathetic innocence of the Bard of Crove; then he let out a hoot of laughter and clapped his hands while Lachie, quite taken with this novel form of appreciation, pranced and hopped and groped his sporran until Mr Sloan stepped on to the platform to calm him down and claim for the poor, delighted soul a hearty round of applause.

'Wonderful! Wonderful, Bridget, don't you think?' said Austin, glancing behind him, only to discover that Biddy Campbell had disappeared.

'Oh, there you are,' Innis said. 'I was wondering where you were hiding.'

'I'm not hiding,' Michael said. 'I came out for a breath of air.'

'I was not looking for you,' Innis said. 'I was looking for my sister.'

'Which one? Aileen?'

'No, Aileen is inside, eating all the corn cakes she can lay hands on.'

'I haven't seen Biddy, if that's who you mean,' Michael said. 'Your father was here but he's gone down to the public house to find the piper.'

Innis let out a little glitter of laughter, quite insincere. 'That

will be like sending a fox to bring home a chicken, I'm thinking.'
Michael did not smile. He seemed tense, almost afraid, as if
that impulsive, open air kiss had been an aberration or, more
likely, had put him off her completely. Inconsistency was not
what she had expected from Michael Tarrant.

He wore a suit of navy blue worsted, buttoned neatly up to
the middle of his chest. His shirt had a starched collar and long
conical cuffs that jutted over his wrists. He swayed, like a little
bear, from foot to foot, his hands stuffed into his jacket pockets
as if he were ashamed of them.

'I thought,' she said, 'that you might be giving me a dance.'

'I'm no good at dancing,' Michael said.

'A waltz or a valetta are easy enough.'

'No.'

'Do you not want to dance with me, Michael?'

'It's not that,' he said, still rocking a little. 'It's just that – well,
I'm not very sociable, Innis. I don't much care for the noise or
the crowded hall.'

'One dance?'

'I'm thinking of going home. I've an early rise with the sheep.'

'We all have to be up early.' Innis struggled not to let her
disappointment show. 'Still, if that is how you feel – I just thought
that when you kissed me . . .'

'That was a mistake,' Michael said.

'Oh!'

'I don't mean a mistake. I mean . . .'

The door of one of the upright wooden water-closets creaked
open. Innis and the shepherd turned simultaneously towards the
sound. He took a hasty step in the direction of the closets as if
he hoped that he might screen from Innis's view the person
who emerged from it.

'Michael,' Biddy said. 'Michael, I'm ready to . . .'

He glanced from Biddy to Innis and back again and, in spite
of himself, fashioned a gesture that gave the game away. He tore
one hand from his pocket and held it up, a warning sign that
she, Biddy, should say no more.

There was something so ridiculous in the background of
water-closets, upright as coffins and smelling of urine and
disinfectant, that Innis's hurt was suspended. She felt almost

sorry for them, for their furtiveness, for the fact that poor Biddy had been taken in by Michael Tarrant, who was no more subtle than the rest of them when it came to getting what he really wanted.

She should have known better than to trust an incomer, a Lowlander, a man who tended sheep not cattle.

'Innis . . .' Michael began, while Biddy, smoothing down her skirts, did not dare to meet her sister's eye.

'It's all right,' Innis said. 'Really, it is,' and then, 'I don't care what you do, either of you,' and then, with less dignity than she intended, she darted through the side door of the hall.

'Innis,' Michael called out.

But Biddy pulled him back, saying, 'Let her go, Michael, just let her go.'

Ten minutes later Biddy returned to the hall, alone. By that time Callous Calum McFee had been persuaded to leave the comfort of the McKinnon Arms and present himself, bagpipes unfurled, at the door of the Wingard from which, on a signal from Mr Sloan, he would make his entry and, giving big licks to 'Demeter's March', would lead the folk behind him to partake of harvest supper.

Calum's face was beetroot red by the time he had inflated the bag. His belly stuck out against the broad polished belt that kept his kilt up. He looked every inch the piper as he took tune and, with Mr Sloan and Hector Thrale throwing open the doors before him, carried into the Wingard that true-blue Scottish spirit that the Volunteers, for all their volume, lacked. As if to acknowledge defeat the Volunteers rose as one, trooped off the platform and out of the side door where, it was rudely suggested, they would make water together, probably to the tune of 'Lumps o' Pudding' or possibly 'The Sailor's Hornpipe'

Supper was served. The evening was already halfway over, though for many – Innis was not one of them – the best was still to come.

Reverend Ewing put a mutton pie on her plate, dipped a ladle into the punch barrel, filled a glass, handed it to Innis and, frowning, said, 'Those are not tears, are they?'

'No, Mr Ewing, just – just perspiration.'

'There's enough of that to fill a river,' Tom Ewing conceded, raising his voice above that of the pipes. 'But you are not looking too happy with life, Innis, and I am not going to be palmed off with a lie.'

'No, no, Minister, I am fine, I assure you.'

He had been standing by the end of the long trestle table from which supper was being served but he stepped away with her now, not towards the piper or to the chairs where, in the manner of picnickers, the hungry throng were feeding themselves from plates and cups and glasses, but towards a quiet corner on the nether side of the door. She looked so depressed, so lost, that he had an inclination – which he resisted, of course – to put an arm about her shoulders. She stopped by an empty chair, set plate and glass upon it.

'Eat something,' Tom advised.

She lifted the plate and held it against her breast, lifted the pie from the plate and bit into it. No matter what sufferings and sorrows afflicted the young, Tom thought, they never seemed to lose their appetites.

'More,' he said.

'I am not from the workhouse, Mr Ewing. I'm not in need of stuffing.'

'Is it your father?'

'What about my father?'

'Is it, then, the young chap from Fetternish who's upset you?'

'Michael?' She seemed surprised, perhaps alarmed, at his perspicacity. 'I don't know what you mean, Mr Ewing.'

'Oh, I think you do, Innis,' Tom Ewing said.

Behind him was a rattle of plates and clack of glasses, the hubbub of conversation and, over all, the skirl of the bagpipes as Calum played away quite happily to a circle of appreciative young pipers.

Innis hesitated, then said, 'He prefers Biddy's company to mine.'

'Are you sure?'

'He has been outside in the yard with her.'

'Perhaps,' Tom said, 'he was rescuing her from Mr Baverstock.'

She glanced at him quickly. 'Do you think so?'

'It seems to me that Mr Baverstock's attentions might be just a little overwhelming, shall we say, for your sister's taste.'

'She has never had any trouble in dealing with unwelcome attentions before now.'

'True.' Tom recalled the efficiency with which Biddy had dealt with suitors in the past. 'On the other hand she has never had a gentleman like Austin Baverstock paying her court before.'

'Is that what he's doing?'

'You just have to observe how he looks at her.'

Innis considered the minister's theory. She realised, of course, that he was trying to comfort her and she was wary of being too easily taken in. It did not occur to her that it was a very strange conversation to be having with a clergyman. 'Perhaps his attentions are not unwelcome,' Tom went on, 'just, as I've said, overwhelming.'

She scanned the hall, found her mother seated by the platform, Aileen half seated, half sprawled upon Vassie's knee, the pair of them sharing a glass of ginger beer, sip and sip about. Biddy was clinging to Mr Baverstock who in his soft, almost elegant way, was plying her with titbits from his plate. Of Michael there was no sign at all.

'Do you see what I mean, Innis?' the minister said.

'Yes, I do. But . . .'

Intelligence was no defence against the pangs of unrequited love, Tom knew well enough. He rubbed his hand to the back of his neck, hesitated, then said, 'Innis, what do you know of Mr Tarrant?'

'He is a good shepherd.'

'Forbye that,' Tom said. 'About his history, his background?'

'Very little. Why?'

'He's not for Biddy,' Tom Ewing said. 'He's not for Biddy and he's not for you, Innis. Take my word for it.'

'He seems . . .'

'He is not what he seems.'

The piping had ceased, leaving an odd, muttering quietness in the hall as if the villagers had all been engaged in conversations which, in the absence of sound, had become embarrassing.

'What do you mean, Mr Ewing?'

'Michael Tarrant's a . . .'

At that precise moment the doctor and Mr Sloan strode up to

consult the minister about some crisis in the distribution of the pies. Then the Volunteers were trooping back in a perfect line like a covey of partridges. In half an hour or so Miss Valerie Mair would sing a mournful song, Callous Calum would play one of his own compositions, and a choir of sisters and brothers from a croft near Glengorm would deliver a nippy version of one of the old Hebridean shanties and, for encore, a lullaby, before the final set of reels and strathspeys.

For Innis, though, the evening had turned stale. As soon as Mr Ewing left she put out of her mind all that he had said and, with Michael gone, ate the rest of the mutton pie and the whole of a corn cake all on her own in the corner by the door until Aileen came and dragged her reluctantly back to the fray.

Willy Naismith steered well clear of the peevish little argument that took place between the Baverstock brothers a quarter of an hour before the singing of 'Auld Lang Syne'. The cause of the spat was obvious. Walter did not approve of his brother's association with the redhead who, now that she had Austin's interest, was acting more aloof and arrogant than ever.

If Biddy Campbell had been his daughter, Willy told himself, he would have knocked the conceit out of her with a sound spanking. He would also have informed her just what Austin Baverstock was really worth, would have pointed out that she would not do better on this island or anywhere else, and reminded her that good looks don't last for ever. Willy, though, had enough on his plate with Margaret Bell, whose doe-eyed adoration promised compliance when he, the object of her veneration, requested a sacrifice out there in the woods when the dance was over.

Jack Stockton had ridden back to Tobermory and Ronan Campbell had drifted off in the company of the piper and when Willy approached Mr Walter, and asked permission to escort Miss Bell home to the stable cottages, Walter just glowered at him and said, 'Has she no relatives who will take her?'

'None, sir.'

'How far is it to the stables?'

'Two or three miles, I believe.'

'Oh, very well,' Walter Baverstock conceded.

Willy had her by the arm, her shoe-bag over his shoulder, and was out of the Wingard and out of Crove before anyone, least of all Margaret, could question his motives.

She had thrown a shawl over her shoulders and put on her Sunday boots but the silky dress was smooth and white even in the darkness and when the track emerged from the woods a wisp of moonlight added glamour and shone through shy Maggie Bell as if she were a glass lantern and he, Mr William Naismith, valet to the gentry, a taper needing only a spark to set him alight. She laced an arm about his waist to guide him, for Willy had never travelled this particular track before, and it was about then that Willy began to wonder if Maggie was quite so shy as folk believed her to be.

'It's a braw night,' Willy said.

'It's all that, Mr Naismith.'

'Don't call me Mr Naismith. Call me Willy – at least when we're alone. Are you warm enough in that skimpy dress?'

'Aye.'

'Do you want to stop?'

'What for?'

Oh! Willy thought. If she doesn't know what a man means by 'stopping' then she's hardly likely to know what a man expects from a woman when he's alone with her in dead of night in the middle of nowhere.

'To rest – in case you're out of breath,' he said.

'I'm not out of breath – Willy.'

'Uh-huh!' Willy said.

He experienced an unfamiliar twinge of guilt. How could he tell her that he had taken a score of girls home after fairs and dances and that he had never yet failed to find his target.

'If you're out of breath, Willy, I'll wait wi' you.'

Yes, I'm out of breath. Why don't we rest here by the side of the path? Why don't you spread your shawl on the ground and sit beside me? What am I doing? I'm only doing what nature commands me to do, Margaret. I cannot resist you.

'Do you really need a rest?' she asked.

'No,' Willy said. 'I think we'll just push on.'

The strategies of seduction waned. He was her superior, her protector. Her liking for him was – unfortunately – based on trust.

As if to confirm his judgement, Margaret said, 'It's nice having a friend.'

'Is that what – I mean, aye.'

'I have never had a proper friend before,' she said. 'A man friend to walk me safe home.'

'Uh-huh,' Willy said.

There was still time to take advantage of the situation. He had never been reluctant before. Fetternish stables, where the estate's horses and ponies were looked after, would abound in secluded spots where he could draw her down or prop her up and kiss her to his heart's content.

'Are you – are you my man friend now – Willy?'

'Aye, I suppose you could say I am.'

The track rounded a rocky corner by the tail of the ridge. Fifty yards below, house, outbuildings and fenced paddocks rose out of the darkness. He heard a horse snicker, saw the animal rise and trot to the wooden paling. Lamplight in the ground-floor window of the two-storey house suggested that her parents were still up. Margaret removed her arm from about his waist and clasped his hand in hers. She gave it a squeeze.

'You will be coming inside, Willy, will you not?'

'What?'

'To take a dish of tea before you go home.'

'I – I – how far is Fetternish House from here?'

'No distance at all,' Margaret said. 'You can see the tower.'

Willy had often slept with parlour maids in their own beds, crouched under the blankets with the girl saying 'Ssshhh, ssshhh,' every five seconds and strangling his passion by fear of discovery.

'Since you're my special friend, Willy, you can come in if you like.' Margaret held his hand in a vice-like grip, stretched out a slender arm and cocked the latch on the front door. 'You will be safe with me,' she whispered. 'You mustna be frightened,' and drew him into the house.

There were five of them: two males, two females and one whose gender was, to say the least of it, indeterminate.

They were seated in a semicircle on upright chairs as if they'd been disturbed in the middle of a seance. Behind them was an oval table draped with a muslin cloth so lumpy, Willy thought, that a small corpse might be hidden beneath its folds. One miserable lamp with the wick turned down, a puny wee fire in the grate indicated parsimony mingled with an air of piety that almost made Willy choke. If he had been less of a man, he might have turned and fled. Instead he stood there like a fool and endured the Bells' scrutiny.

The males had horsehair clinging to their trousers, hands scarred by hot iron and burning coals. The women were shrouded like Rechabites in dun-coloured shawls and scarves. The androgynous creature had the square jaw and broad cheekbones of a male and the dainty hands and feet of a girl. She – for it turned out to be a woman – was the matriarch, Margaret's great-grandmother, a Macleod who could trace her ancestry back to the barons of Lewis and who, Willy was proudly informed, would be one hundred and three come Martinmas.

One hundred and three? Willy felt like yelling. Is that all?

'Mother, this is Mr Naismith, who is my man friend.'

One of the women nodded. The fold of her shawl slid back an inch. Willy was permitted a glimpse of a face that was just as broad and mannish as that of the matriarch and seemed, he thought, hardly much younger.

'So you are for Maggie, are you now?' the woman growled.

'I – I'm . . .'

'Sit.'

The stool was already in position on the base of the semicircle as if the spot had been measured with geometrical instruments. Willy drew the tiny rush-bottomed object under his buttocks with a degree of self-consciousness that he hadn't experienced since he'd escaped from dame school. He tried to remind himself where he came from, how superior he was to these sullen, stone-faced peasants. But it was useless. He had been 'brought home' by the daughter of the household, carried in like a little piece of prey from the jungle that lay beyond the hill and if he so much as wriggled, let alone tried to escape, they would tear him limb from limb.

'You will be having a cup of tea, Mr Naismith?'

'Well, it's late. I – I really should be . . .'

'No, Mr Naismith, you *will* be having a cup of tea.'

Behind him shy Margaret brushed the nape of his neck with

her fingertips and, in a tone of voice that made Willy's blood run cold, said for all to hear, 'My man. My man.'

From the moment she had followed him into the yard outside the Wingard and he had put his hands upon her breasts and kissed her, she had known that he would be her lover and that she would give herself to him willingly. The lies she had told to Innis, the lies Innis had told her had nothing to do with it. She did not have to convince herself that Michael Tarrant was in love with her or that she was deeply in love with him.

She longed for Michael Tarrant urgently and selfishly, the way men longed for her. When she slipped out of bed, climbed down the ladder and went out of the cottage, she carried no burden of fear. She did not care if she was found out, if her father beat her and her mother screamed and Innis refused to speak to her again. Once it was done, there could be no going back and the family's recriminations would be meaningless, for she would have mutated into something new, something different, like a butterfly from a chrysalis.

She ran, barefoot, towards the faint glimmer of the lantern in the bracken behind the calf park. The cold wind from the sea made her nipples stiffen. She wore only the shift in which she had pretended to sleep. The wind plastered the shift against her body. She could feel her breasts taut against the material, her belly and thighs pressed against the pocket of cold air. She stumbled, righted herself, ran on along the cattle path that skirted the low shore, the line of the new wall to her right, the sea to her left ribbed by waves that broke out of the darkness on to the moonlit sand.

She ran as fast she dared towards the lantern that Michael had lit to guide her. She saw him before she reached him. He was leaning on the wall at the bottom of Olaf's Hill, legs spread apart, as if the hill was tilting him towards her.

'Biddy,' he called out softly. 'Here.'

When she reached him she found that he was open and ready. She went forward into his arms. He staggered, braced himself and dragged her against him. He had taken off his jacket. His shirt was open all the way down to his belly, as it had been that first day. Her hands went round his waist beneath the shirt and she grasped him tightly. He thrust up and up, into and against her and, as he did so, enquired in a flat expressionless voice, 'Are you cold, Biddy?'

'No.'

'I have a blanket.'

He pushed her towards the wall. He could not bring himself to release her. As she tried to find the gap in the wall, to clamber through it without hurting herself, he thrust against her once more. The lantern below her in the bracken made the bracken fronds all brown and bronze. The blanket was crushed among the stalks the way outlaw clansmen slept in the days before she had been born. When Michael cupped his hands to her breasts and pinned her with his hips, she felt as if she had been captured by him. That she would be his prisoner as well as his lover. That whatever happened to her now would not be her fault.

She stretched out an arm to steady herself while he nuzzled against her, murmuring into her hair, 'God, my God, but you're beautiful, Biddy Campbell.' Then he drew away. She felt a rush of panic at the thought that he might be done with her. Then he gave her another push. She stepped over the stones into the bracken. Bare feet slithered on damp grass. He steadied her, hands clasped to the small of her back, his legs wide apart.

'Have you done it before?' he whispered.

'No. But I . . .'

'Lie down.'

'How?'

'On your back.'

'On the blanket.'

'Yes.'

She lay down, all the way down, then propped herself up on her elbows again to watch him strip off his clothing, everything but his shirt. She had seen bulls and rams in arousal often enough and knew what to expect. She was not afraid of him, nor was she disappointed.

'Have you,' she said, 'done it before?'

'Yes.'

He dropped to his knees, slipped his fingers under her shift, lifted the garment and furled it over her stomach. She felt the material catch against her breasts, the strange pleasing tug as he freed it. She studied her body almost inquisitively as Michael crouched over it and kissed her breasts. She could smell the candle in the lantern close by her head and glimpse its crescent aura.

'Who with?' Biddy said.

'Bridget,' he said, 'be quiet.'

Hands in her hair. Tugging. Hands on her knees. Stretching. When he dropped across her she felt so weak that she sank back under him. She stared up at the sky, black as a river above the bracken fronds. His face came down. Frowning, he peered into her eyes. She felt him rub against her, strong and thick. She arched her spine, tightened her muscles. Caught her breath. He said, 'Am I hurting you? Tell me if I'm hurting you.' She could do nothing but shake her head. Then, riding on a wavelet of pain, he was suddenly inside her.

It was not as she had imagined it would be, not swift and sore and sudden. She did not know whether or not it was Michael that made it so. She could not begin to think what the sensation signified. At first it seemed intolerable. Then, just as she was ready to cry out, it gathered and melted within her and she was transported not out of but into herself and knew then that, with or without love, she had finally been fulfilled.

Cold came with daylight, not the chill of summer rain or the nip of clear autumn mornings but cold, wintry and biting. Innis could feel it on her nose and the tips of her ears as soon as she wakened; inside her too as if it had seeped into her in that grave, grey hour when darkness reluctantly yielded to daylight. She knew, even before she opened the door or peeped from the window, that there would be a thick layer of cloud along the horizon, the sea bristling with waves sharper than whetted steel.

Aileen knelt on top of the blankets with her head cocked and the tiny knowing smile that Innis so hated on her lips. Curled up under the lion's share of the blankets, Biddy slept like something dead. Nothing of Biddy was visible except a strand of red hair and the knuckles of one hand on the blanket's edge, but her shape seemed different, not stretched but indrawn, her knees drawn up to her stomach. When Aileen skiddled towards the ladder Innis caught her by the wrist and pressed a forefinger to her lips to make her be quiet.

In the wake of the ceilidh there would be many a sore head in Fetternish, many a man vowing that he would never touch strong drink again or linger outside a barn or byre for hours wooing a reluctant lady-love. Some, like her father, would waken late, reach for the bottle under the bed, trudge off to the water-closet and return, muttering that the need to labour was a curse and how fine a thing it would be to have a servant to do your work for you, then, over breakfast, would decide that the sea was too rough or the weather too windy to put the boat out and that the earning of bread must be delayed.

Innis felt a bit light-headed from lack of sleep but otherwise she was well enough. She did not hold Biddy responsible for what had happened, for, Innis told herself, she had seen nothing to indicate that Michael and her sister had been up to mischief. Besides, Michael had left early and Biddy had returned home with the rest of the family. Perhaps if she had been more like Biddy she would have nursed a grudge. But she had never been like Biddy. The incident had simply proved to her that what she thought she had felt for Michael Tarrant had been a groundless emotion.

Why had he kissed her? That question must remain un-answered.

She hastened through the household chores and, wrapped up well against the snell wind, left Aileen to coax the fire into a blaze while she went off to milk the cows and, as soon as that was done, to carry a canister of fresh milk across the hill to Michael's cottage.

The light on the sea was marble green, the wind cutting. At any season a north wind was always bold and dangerous but for one to arrive on Mull, teeth bared, before the back end of October did not seem right. It made the cattle restless and even the cows were thrawn and would not come to the shelter of the wall at first. Even so, her weariness left her as she worked with stool and pail, with the wind pushing against her back like an open hand, cold even through five layers of woollen clothing.

It was still early when she capped the lid on the milk canister and set off across the hill through the tossing bracken. The sound of the wind came low and deep out of the Solitudes. The Fetternish sheep had tucked themselves under the lee side of boulders or down in the earthy scrapes that scarred the edge of the pasture and they stared at her indignantly as she steered through the heather to Michael Tarrant's cottage. There was no smoke from the chimney, no sign of life until she heard the collie scrabbling behind the door of the shed. The scratch of his claws against the woodwork and his thin, uncertain whining followed her to the cottage door. She listened for a moment then thumbed down the latch and stepped into the kitchen.

Bottles littered the table along with plates, cups and glasses. A kettle, burned black, had been tossed on to a pile of bedding and a blanket, ticked with bracken straw, lay wrinkled against the table legs. A trail of clothing led to the cot where Michael lay under a blanket, with his face buried in a bolster.

He did not stir when Innis entered the room.

She placed the canister gently upon the table top. She glanced at the remnants of a meal: bacon rind, egg shells, the heel of a loaf, whisky in a glass, tea leaves in a cup. She resisted the temptation to clear the dishes into the washing tub and moved quietly to the bed. He was fast asleep and she could see little of him, nothing but a bare shoulder, a wisp of dark hair. The bolster was pressed so tightly against his face that she experienced a moment of panic at the thought that he might be dead.

She shot out her hand to touch him, then checked herself. She could see veins in his neck, the pulse of blood, a movement of the sheet that indicated that he was still breathing. Even as she watched, he sighed and opened the fingers of one hand in a gesture as instinctive as that of an infant groping for the teat.

Trickling through his fingers was a fine silver chain to which was attached a jewel or ornament that remained hidden in his palm. Innis leaned closer. She longed to lift back the blanket, to slip in beside him so that when he opened his eyes he would see her face, and only her face.

Instead she retreated, hurried away, carrying the canister of new milk back with her over the hill to Pennypol.

FIVE

A Midnight Courtship

The place that Austin Baverstock liked best on all the rough, rolling acres of his estate was a palm-sized piece of grassland tucked above the black rocks of Fetternish Point. There had been cultivation here probably not so long ago and the ruins of a croft, backed by a stand of trees, gave some shelter from the rains that came marauding up from the sea.

He would come here, wrapped in his no-longer-new tweeds, to train the dogs and teach them some manners. The dogs were just an excuse for getting out of the house, however. He could not abide being cooped up in the office with Walter and Hector Thrale for long stretches or for dolefully viewing the landscape from behind the big windows of the dining-room. So out he would go with Odin and Thor, a pocketful of biscuits and the long leather leads that he had purchased in Tobermory and do his best to make the dogs obey him, not because he was a bully but simply because the hounds were young and required some discipline to make them bearable.

At first he had liked the hounds even less than he had liked Mull. He had no affinity with dogs and even less with the lonely coastal outpost of Fetternish. Oddly, though, the dogs seemed fond of him even when he wasn't bribing them with biscuits. They would pad up to him, put their huge paws on his knees and nudge each other for the privilege of licking his face and, much to Walter's consternation, he would admit them to the great hall or the drawing-room every evening to sprawl at his feet while he drowsed in his chair before the hearth.

From consulting an old map in the estate office Austin learned that the ruined croft was named An Fhearann Cáirdeil which Innis Campbell told him meant 'The Farm of Friendship'. Initially he had asked Biddy for a translation but Biddy had been dismissive and had informed him that there was no English equivalent for the Gaelic; as if he had no right to probe into what had been here before he came, as if Mull's history, like the land itself, was something which the islanders preferred to keep to themselves. He had liked going to An Fhearann Cáirdeil from the moment he had stumbled upon it, but after Innis had told him what the name meant he liked going there even more.

The remnants of a barley patch brought in rustling clouds of small birds and if he sat still he could watch them feed on the ears until Thor or Odin, not maliciously, scared them off again. He watched buzzards circle high over the tree line and kestrels hover over the cliff edge and once, just once, glimpsed five roe deer grazing on grass that was by law and deed, he supposed, rightfully his. It was all he could do to hold 'the boys' that afternoon, for the hounds smelled the deer before the deer detected them and the jerk on the leads had almost taken his arm off. For the first time he had experienced the thrill, not of the chase, but of discovery, more mysterious and exciting than anything he had known in a long time; and when the pretty, white-scutted creatures had gone bounding off he had felt a pang of regret and a need to apologise for disturbing them.

Soon after that he took to going out in the mornings too. He would ramble along the shore and over the ridge or, as he grew more energetic, would scramble up the steep defile that led into the glen called Na h-Vaignich where sometimes he would meet with Michael Tarrant or old man Barrett and would stop and pass the time of day with them. He also went to Olaf's Hill, of course, in the hope of encountering Biddy. But after lunch, each and every day, he would head for Friendship Farm, for he was almost as keen to glimpse the deer again as he was to meet up with the red-haired girl.

'What,' Walter said, one evening after dinner, 'has got into you, Austin?'

'Hmmm?'

'Where do you go every day? What do you do with yourself?'

'I told you, I'm just keeping an eye on things.'

A Midnight Courtship

'Spying on the Campbell girl, you mean.'

'Really, Walter, that's quite uncalled for.'

They had just finished dinner, not in the dining-room but in the hall. In the past few weeks the weather had been so cold that the huge front rooms had become inhospitable, and it was easier for Willy and the maid to serve the brothers at a deal table by the hall fire than to go to all the palaver of setting the mahogany table in the dining-room. Even Walter's formal habits soon took second place to comfort and, inch by inch, his 'Edinburgh' standards were allowed to slip. He no longer insisted that they 'dress' for dinner, by which he meant dickeys, cuff-links and polished black shoes and Austin would turn up minus a cravat, shirt open at the collar, looking, Walter thought, like one of the fish brokers who hung about the piers.

On that particular evening Austin was wrapped in a bulky cardigan, green corduroys and a pair of thick stockings. Only his embroidered Chinese slippers reminded Walter of the civilised joys of Charlotte Square and brought on quite a fit of melancholy.

'No, it's not right,' Walter said sharply. 'Not right at all.'

One of the hounds, Odin, looked up from his position in front of the fire. He might have scrambled to his feet in defence of his master if Austin hadn't instructed him to 'Stay.'

'What isn't right?' Austin said.

'You spend more time with those blessed animals than you do with me.'

'Come with us then. Come out and stretch your legs. Do you more good than skulking indoors.'

'Stretch my legs? Stretch my legs in teeming rain? If you come down with pneumonia, Austin, you will have only yourself to blame.'

'I'm not coming down with anything.'

'And I'm not skulking,' Walter said.

'Who told you that I've met Bridget Campbell? Was it Thrale?'

Austin shrugged. 'Not that I've made any secret of it.'

'I'm sorry we ever encouraged them.'

'Who?'

'With that damned silly luncheon, for a start.'

'Oh, I thought that went down very well.'

'And that dance, that . . .'

'Ceilidh,' Austin said. 'If you had spent less time jawing and more time dancing perhaps you would have enjoyed it as much as I did.'

'You didn't enjoy it.'

'I did.'

'She more or less ignored you all evening.'

'She did not.'

'She had eyes only for the shepherd.'

'She did not.'

Walter was silent. He stared bleakly into the fireplace. Damp logs burned with much smoke but no lustre and the gigantic creel of peat that flanked the hearth gave off an earthy effluvia that, mingled with the smell of dog, made him feel almost nauseous. He pushed away his cheese plate, lifted a glass of port, sank it like a hardened tippler, then got up, plucked a handbell from the sofa table and, taking a pace or two towards the corridor that dived down into the kitchen, rang it forcefully. Then he flung himself down on the sofa and kicked, not viciously, at Thor who, too dozy to distinguish one Baverstock from another perhaps, had tried to lick the toe of his slipper.

'I say, Walter, don't take it out on the dog.'

'The dog! Damn the dog!'

Willy, whistling, appeared out of the gloom. His striped waistcoat was unbuttoned and his collar was improperly fastened. He too sported a pair of the hideous hairy stockings; all very well for tramping the moors but not, in Walter's book, suitable attire for indoors. Willy was accompanied by Margaret Bell, who, Walter had to admit, hadn't gone to the bow-wows like the rest of them.

'Do you wish us to clear away, Mr Baverstock?' Willy asked.

'Yes.'

'Coffee?'

'Yes.'

'Brandy,' Willy said, 'or would you prefer whisky?'

'Brandy.'

'Well, sir, I think whisky's the ticket for a night like this.'

'Whatever you wish.'

'Margaret,' Austin put in from his place at the table, 'are you still here?'

'Just clearing away, sir.'

'Is it not time you were off home?'

'Soon, Mr Baverstock, very soon,' Willy answered for her.

'What time is it, actually?'

'Almost eight o'clock, Mr Austin,' Willy said.

'God, is that all?' Walter threw himself back against the upholstery, stuck his hands behind his head and waggled his house shoes petulantly, as if it were the servants' fault that time hung so heavily upon him.

Austin watched the servants clear the plates and cutlery and, each carrying a tray, vanish down the corridor again. He stared at his fingers for a long moment, then turned and said, 'Walter, why don't you go home?'

'I am home.'

'I mean, why don't you go back to Edinburgh?'

'Can't.'

'Why not? What is there here that demands your attention? The wool crop has been taken and dispatched to Sangster, hasn't it?'

'Long since.'

'Tarrant will cut out the lambs and see to it that the tups are introduced to the ewes – when?'

'Next week.'

'So – what's to keep you here?' said Austin.

'I'm not prepared to leave the house unoccupied.'

'I'll stay.' Austin said. 'I'll stand guard.'

'You?'

'You don't have to sound quite so scathing, old man. I'm quite capable of ensuring that the water pipes don't freeze and that Willy doesn't steal the silver.'

'I can't run off and leave you stuck here. It wouldn't be fair.'

'Walter, I want to stay.'

'Because of this girl, this redhead?'

'I like it here.'

'You're infatuated, that's all.'

'Perhaps I am,' Austin admitted. 'But I see no harm in it. I mean, old man, it's not as if I'm going to turn the house into a drinking-den or carry Bridget Campbell off in the dead of night.'

Walter studied his brother soberly. 'Do you mean that you'd rather stay here than return to Edinburgh with me?'

'I think I probably would.'

'You're not just playing the martyr?'

'Certainly not.'

'Tell you what,' Walter said, 'why don't I go back to Edinburgh for a week or two just to see that everything's ship-shape in Charlotte Square and you can join me for Christmas. Bring Willy and Queenie with you, of course. They'll appreciate a change of scene, I have no doubt.'

'And then?'

'In January or February we'll all travel back together.'

'Well, if that's what suits you, why not?' Austin agreed, amiably. He got up from the table, wandered to the fireplace, stooped and stroked his hand along Odin's broad, brown, muscular back. 'What d'you say, young feller?'

Odin gave a contented little whine by way of reply and flopped over to have his belly scratched.

Frowning again, Walter said, 'Do you really like it here?'

'I think I do, rather.'

Walter leaned forward and extended an uncertain hand towards the hound who gave a little snap of the teeth as if to indicate that he did not allow just anyone to take liberties with his abdomen.

Walter said, 'You're not going to make a fool of yourself when I'm away, are you, Austin?'

'Would I do that, old man?'

'I don't know what you'll do,' Walter told him. 'You've changed so.'

'For the better, I trust.'

'That remains to be seen,' said Walter.

The shed was invisible from the landward side of Pennypol. In fact, you needed a sharp eye to spot it even from the sea, for it was hardly much more than a collection of weathered grey planks leaning against the end of Campbell's jetty. No matter how the wind blew, it let in quantities of air and rain, and that forenoon the wind had heaved to the north-west and the sea was rough. Neil and Donnie had hauled the boat up to the edge of the turf where broken shells, clumps of sea-pinks and cattle slabber marked the division between beach and pasture and Neil, who did not seem to mind the rain, could get on with the work of scraping the keel. Donnie and his father, however, sought what shelter the hut provided and got on with the job of repairing cords and replacing hooks for the final weeks of the line fishing season.

Rain ran in rivulets along the slope of the roof and blew inwards against the men's faces. There was no door. Much of the tackle stored in the hut had rotted away but broken creels, still weighted with stones, made a comfortable couch for father and son. They worked hip to hip, cutting and splicing, threading and knotting with pinched, salt-swollen fingers. Every now and then Ronan would pause, blow on his hands, pick the bottle from the basket at his side, sip from it and offer it to Donnie who, though no warmer than his father, would always shake his head. Donnie was faster and no less thorough than his father. He worked without interest, though, his eyes almost unseeing, as if he had been rendered not only mute but blind by the stultifying nature of the task.

On that dreary October morning, it was Ronan who, by fits and starts, endeavoured to strike up a conversation.

'I am hearing a whisper that one of our gentlemen might be going away to spend the winter attending his business in Edinburgh.'

'Is that a fact now,' Donnie said.

'It will be the other one next. And then, before you know it, it will be absentee landlords we will be having for neighbours.'

'That will do us no harm.'

'Your sisters will be missing them, however.'

'Aye, I suppose that might be the case,' Donnie conceded.

A lengthy silence, then, 'I am wondering if it is just the fine gentlemen from Fetternish who are thinking of leaving us?'

Donnie's eyes lost the glazed look they had had for most of the morning. 'What are you meaning by that, Dada?'

'Oh, just a suspicion I have that one of us might have it in mind to be striking out on his own.'

'If you are meaning me . . .'

'She is a fine sturdy lass, MacNiven's daughter.'

'What has Neil been telling you?' Donnie said.

'I am not needing Neil to tell me anything,' Ronan said. 'I have a pair of eyes in my head. I can see how it is with you and the lass from Leathan. You will soon be for marriage, I'm thinking.'

'Indeed, and I will.'

'I will see to it that there is another room built for you and your bride.'

'Another room? Where?'

'At the back.'

'Here, do you mean?'

'Where else?'

'No.' Donnie shook his head. 'There is no room for us here. And there is not enough coming in from the boat to support us.'

'I am sure she will be willing to work for her keep, this bride of yours.'

'Muriel might be willing to work – but it will not be on Pennypol.'

'Will you be looking for a cottage then?'

'There is no scarcity of cottages,' Donnie said. 'It is paid work that is difficult to find. I might be going on the steamers, like Muriel's brothers.'

'I would not like to see my son selling himself as a wage slave.'

'What would you like to see me do? Work for you?'

Ronan paused once more. 'It is a boat of your own you'll be needing.'

'Aye, and how am I to afford such a thing?'

'Have you no money saved?'

'Well you know that I have not.'

'Well, Donnie, you have never gone hungry, have you?'

'That is the truth.' Donnie knotted a hook to the light line and the line to the rope, six or eight dextrous little motions and a final tug with his teeth to finish with. 'I have never gone hungry.'

'Is that not enough for you?'

'No, Dada, it is not enough for me.'

'She has turned your head, this girl from Leathan, her and her family.'

Donnie sighed. 'It has nothing to do with her family. I am

wanting the best for Muriel and for my children. Is that such a bad thing?'

'It is no bad thing at all,' Ronan said. 'Except that it will take money to get you started and set you up.'

'Are you telling me that you have no money to give me?'

'No, I have no money to give you. And you will get nothing from McIver, neither alive nor after he is dead.'

'Then I will apply to MacBrayne's company for work on the steamers.'

'The steamers!'

'It is better than nothing.'

'It is not better than a boat of your own.'

'I am not going into debt for a boat of my own,' Donnie said.

'I would not be putting you into debt, son.'

'What are you saying to me?'

'I know how there is money to be made.' Ronan let that sink in before he added, 'Enough money to buy you a boat and all the tackle you will be needing. And to pay the rent of a house. And to furnish it.'

'What is this you are telling me?'

'I am telling you that I have been thinking about your situation, Donnie, and I have found an answer to the problem.'

Ronan reached for the bottle but Donnie grabbed it from him. He held the bottle in both hands, hugged into his lap, so that if his father wanted it he would have to wrestle it away. 'What is the answer?' Donnie said.

'You are holding the answer in your hands.'

'What are you saying?' Donnie asked, mystified.

'Whisky is the answer.'

'Whisky? This stuff, Fergus's drippings?'

'Fergus's drippings are going to earn us money before long,' Ronan said. 'The Baverstocks' man-servant has asked me to go into a partnership with him, to transport whisky without the knowledge of the Revenue officers.'

'Smuggling!' Donnie shook his head. 'You can be put into the jail for smuggling, Dada.'

'Nobody has been jailed for whisky smuggling these past twenty years.'

'Because nobody does it any more, not on Mull.'

'Except Fergus,' Ronan said. 'But now the law has been changed there will be a new demand for it. Naismith will be putting up the stake to bring off the first run and we will deliver it to Bucks' Island.'

'Who will pay us?'

'Naismith.'

'And who will be doing the picking up?'

'That is not a matter that need concern us.'

'I am concerned, however,' Donnie said, 'since he will be the man who will be paying Naismith in the first place.'

Ronan chuckled. 'Donald, Donald, it is all taken care of. There will be four pounds the shipment in it for you. Four pounds for skimming down to Loch Buie every two or three weeks.'

'Whatever you say, Dada, smuggling is still illegal.'

'I do not deny that it is against the law. But it is against the Englishman's law, a law for which no Scotsman has respect.'

'Does Neil know of this?'

'He is all for it.'

'How will he be paid?'

'I will pay Neil out of my share.'

'And me?'

'One-third of what I receive.'

'In cash, not promises?'

'In cash,' Ronan promised.

Donnie lifted the bottle from his lap and held it to the light from the doorway. 'Let me be thinking about it.'

'It is the only way of getting what you want.'

'I will think about it.'

'Do not take too long thinking about it, son,' Ronan said. 'If you will not be doing it with me . . .'

'What?'

'I will find someone else who will.'

If it had been left to Biddy to make the running in that raw month she would have flung all caution to the winds, would have ridden roughshod over family objections and strutted out of the cottage as soon as supper was over.

'And where do you think you are going?'

'To my lover's house, to my lover's bed.'

That sort of honesty was impossible, of course. She was supposed to be a lady and ladies did not take lovers until after they were wed. But she had learned too much ever to be a lady now. She had learned the true meaning of the crude words that were bandied about the cattle marts, for instance, and while she refused to utter them aloud they rang in her head as she toiled in the mud of the potato patch or flogged the shirts against the sides of the laundry tub. They were not words of love but of love-making, for Michael Tarrant had unleashed in her a tempest of desire which swept aside thoughts of courtship and marriage. Not even the shepherd could quite satisfy her hunger. She expected more of him, more perhaps than the sexual act itself could ever deliver.

She lived through the late autumn days in a haze of need, trapped in a web of farm work made arduous and unpleasant by the cold, wet weather.

One of the spring calves was sick. It had to be nursed. Though the cows were Innis's responsibility, it was Biddy's task to draft feed and muck out the stall where the poor, coughing creature was housed. In spite of the weather the root crops were gathered in. The potatoes were of poor quality. Some were already blackened, others had that mushy feeling which meant that they would not store well. Meanwhile, it continued to rain, and the sisters said little to each other, for even at night they were too bone-weary to do more than eat supper and loll listlessly by the fire until, with eyelids drooping, they took themselves to bed. Church on Sunday, a walk now and then between squally showers, a trip into Crove to stock up with flour and tea. For the rest it was work and more work and not much else to brighten the dreary days. Biddy alone had energy to spare.

She would steal off in the middle of the night while the rest of the household slept. She would meet Michael in the byre and couple with him, their love-making swift and harsh and urgent. Between times, she could think of little else but his hands upon her, his mouth and the sudden slithering penetration that she always seemed ready to accommodate. She limped from one dangerous assignation to the next and on those occasions when she was delayed and he was gone or when he did not appear at all then she would weep and wring her hands and loathe the state that loving had reduced her to.

Sometimes in the mornings Austin Baverstock came down from the big house and if Innis or Biddy happened to be in the calf park he would lean on the wall at the bottom of the hill and talk to them for five or ten minutes. The dogs were leashed and under control and Mr Baverstock's tweeds and boots had roughened, all the newness gone and even to Biddy he seemed more of a man than he had been when he first turned up on Fetternish. Sometimes too his polite conversation would cause Biddy's self-absorption to lift and she would watch him stride off into the wind and wonder what it would be like to lie with him, if it would be just the same as it was with Michael or if the man made the difference.

Try as she might, though, she could not imagine Austin Baverstock in such a state of arousal that he would take her on a sack on the floor of the byre or a blanket laid out in the heather. It would have to be a bed for Mr Baverstock: a four-poster with spotless sheets and a feather mattress and, probably, so much by way of respect and 'niceness' that she would hardly know that he had been with her at all.

She was thinking of Michael that morning, however, when Austin stumbled upon her. 'Miss Campbell! What a pleasant surprise.'

'What are you doing here?' She had not intended to sound so shrill.

'I trust I'm not intruding?'

She made an effort at politeness. 'No, not at all. As you can see I was doing nothing of any great importance.'

'Anything you do is important, Biddy.'

'Pardon?'

'I mean your work.'

One of the hounds made water against the wall. Biddy watched, unembarrassed. Mr Baverstock looked away. She hoped that Fingal was asleep indoors for she did not want his barking to bring Vassie out to see what was wrong.

'I had hoped to find you alone this morning.'

'Oh, really, Mr Baverstock! Why would that be now?'

'I have something for you – if you will be gracious enough to accept it.'

Biddy brushed a hand over her tangled hair and patted her bodice. She had no need to resort to such tricks to gain Austin Baverstock's attention.

'Something for me?' she said.

'Yes,' he said. 'It just happened to come my way. I mean, when I saw the object I thought at once how pretty it was and how it would suit you.'

Biddy squared her shoulders and tilted back her head to show off her figure. 'What sort of object, Mr Baverstock?'

'I would ap – appreciate it, Biddy, if you would call me Austin.'

'What is it – Austin?'

'Ah, yes, well – it's this.'

He handed her the strap of the leash which Biddy accepted reluctantly. The dogs regarded her balefully and might have tested her mettle if Austin, fumbling beneath his Ulster, hadn't muttered, 'Stay, stay.'

'Ah!' he said again. 'This.'

The brooch was bedded in silk. It was a delicate little object of pure silver scrollwork set with semi-precious stones, in the Celtic manner.

'It is beautiful, Mr Bav – Austin.'

'Take it,' he said. 'It's for you.'

'I cannot go accepting gifts from a gentleman. My mother would not consider it proper.'

'Need you tell her?'

'If I do not tell her I cannot wear it.'

'Keep it then as – as our secret.'

'That would not be right.' Biddy had no intention of letting the brooch slip from her grasp. 'It is very generous of you, Austin, but it is also improper. Do unmarried gentlemen give intimate gifts to ladies in Edinburgh? Is that the custom in the city?'

'No, I can't say it is,' Austin admitted. 'Although it is done, I'm sure.'

'Have you done it?'

'No, never.'

'Then I'm flattered.'

'Take it. Please, Biddy.'

'I am wanting to be sure that you do not think this implies any sort of promise on my part, Mr Baverstock?'

'None whatsoever. I assure you most emphatically that it is given without any strings at all.'

She lifted her arm, cocked her wrist and in the manner of a child selecting a sweetmeat picked the brooch carefully from the silk. She held it between finger and thumb and placed it against her breast.

'It certainly suits you, Biddy.'

'Aye, it is a very pretty thing.'

'Will you accept it, please, in the spirit in which it is given?'

'What sort of spirit *is* that?'

'A spirit of affection and admiration.'

Biddy nodded as if that were the only possible explanation he could give that would satisfy her and pressed the trinket to her dress, a warm but dowdy woollen garment the colour of dried seaweed and for the first time since the night of the Harvest Home felt the burden of desire lift from her shoulders. Mr Baverstock's devotion had restored a sense of power that was missing from her relationship with Michael Tarrant and for that, more than anything, she was grateful to him.

'If that is the case, Austin, then I will accept,' she said. 'I will keep it in a safe place. It will be my secret and will remind me of you when I take it out.'

One of the hounds, Odin, yawned audibly.

'Will it,' Austin said. 'Will it, really?'

'Where did you get it?' Biddy asked.

'In Tobermory.'

That, Biddy reckoned, was a white lie, for she knew every ornament and trinket that was to be found in the town and she had seen nothing so fine as the Celtic brooch in any of the trays.

'I hope you're not offended,' Austin repeated.

'How can I be offended?'

'An unmarried gentleman, an unmarried lady – the act of giving might be subject to misinterpretation.'

'Mr Baverstock – Austin – are you courting me?'

'Well – um – no. If I were to take that liberty, however, would it be anathema to you?'

'Anathema?'

'Objectionable.'

'It would not be objectionable, no,' Biddy told him. 'Provided it was done with discretion. I would not want you to be placed under any sort of obligation.'

'I would not mind that.'

'No, but I would,' Biddy said.

'Do you think your family would resent it?'

'That's it, Austin. That is it in a nutshell.'

'And you, do you resent me?'

'Oh, no,' Biddy said.

'Do you like me, even a little?'

'I do not know you well enough to say.'

'But you don't dislike me?'

'Oh, no,' said Biddy once more.

'So then I do have a chance?'

'Of what, Austin?'

'Of being more than your neighbour?'

'If you mean of being my friend, I would say that you have.'

She took the piece of silk from the palm of his hand, carefully laid the brooch upon it, wrapped it and tucked it into the neck of her dress. Then she offered him her wind-burned cheek to kiss, a gesture that a man less smitten than Austin Baverstock would have been hard pressed to ignore.

'Thank you, Mr Baverstock.'

'Austin.'

'Yes, Austin. Thank you very much.'

'My pleasure, Biddy,' the gentleman assured her, sincerely.

For eight days woman's nature deprived Biddy of Michael's company. It did not occur to her to seek him out for anything as staid as conversation; that, Biddy knew, was not what Michael wanted from her or, to be truthful, what she wanted from him, for conversation would be but a poor substitute for what usually took place between them. She informed him of her condition by placing a message in a whisky bottle which she hid under a rock on the side of Olaf's Hill.

I am unwell and will not see you for a week.

Michael's reply would be equally devoid of romantic fallacy. He would not write, *I will miss you with all my heart and soul and will count the hours until we are together again. Your most humble and obedient servant, Michael Tarrant.* In fact his responses were so brief and telegraphic that there were occasions when Biddy began to wonder if he was even literate: *Monday – Byre. Thursday – Rock.* Biddy knew by experience at what hour a meeting was possible. It did not occur to her simply to scribble *No*, leaving him to ponder the reason or to pen the cryptic question, *Why?* which at least would have been the beginning of a dialogue between them.

When they met by chance during the day they were almost like strangers to each other. Michael would appear upon the hillside accompanied by Thrale or Walter Baverstock and Biddy would glance up, glance away again, ignoring him as pointedly as he ignored her. She would say nothing to Michael and he would acknowledge her existence with nothing more forward than a nod of the head.

'Do you not like him?' Innis would say. 'I thought you liked him?'

'It is obvious that he does not like me.'

'What has happened between you?'

'Get on with your work, Innis, and do not be asking stupid questions.'

Eight days without the satisfaction of being clasped in Michael Tarrant's arms. Eight days with only the recollection of Austin Baverstock's generosity to keep her mind from whirling itself to pieces like an old wicker creel caught in an eddy. Then: *Wednesday – Byre.*

All day long she could think of nothing but what he would do to her, how his skin would feel, how her muscles would tighten, how he would bring her to a climax that was close to pain. How, when he was done, she would start on him again, nuzzling her breasts against him until he either pushed her away or, with an angry little snarl, rammed himself against her and began again.

There was no light in the byre. They did not dare risk a lantern or candle and they spoke only in whispers. She could feel his breath against her ear, though, and smell the odours of the cattle stall, the rank, dank smell of straw, familiar things that increased her pleasure. When it was done she would lie panting for two or three minutes, then he would say, 'You had better go back now, and she would peel herself from him, slip out into the cold night air, hurry round to the cottage door and silently enter the kitchen.

On that Wednesday night, however, Michael did not chase her away. He pinned an arm about her waist, held her to him like a wrestler and whispered, 'What did Baverstock want with you?'

'What?'

'Baverstock. He gave you something. I saw you take it.'

'Michael Tarrant, have you been spying on me?'

'I was on the hill with sheep. I could not help but see what happened. What was it? What did he give you?'

'Nothing. A trinket.'

'He would have you if he could. He would have you as I do.'

She struggled against his arm, her breasts flattened against his hairless chest. 'No,' she hissed. 'There you are wrong. He would *marry me* if he could.'

'So that's it?'

'Let me go. I must get in.'

'Would you not like to marry him?'

'I am not for marrying anyone, Michael.'

'Not even me?'

'No, not even you.'

'Am I not good enough for you?'

'You are fine for me,' Biddy said, struggling again.

'Austin Baverstock would be better, though.'

'I dare say he would.'

'What did he give you?'

Was it jealousy or shame that prompted the question? Michael Tarrant had given her nothing, nothing except pleasure and experience. She rested her hand flat on the stone floor, leaned on an elbow and in a tone as flat and dry as she could make it, answered him. 'He gave me a brooch.'

'Silver?'

'Yes, silver.'

'And you kept it?'

'Of course I kept it.'

'He would be a perfect match for you, Biddy.'

'Only for what he could give me – and that would not be enough.'

'After what you've had from me?' Michael asked.

She misinterpreted the question. 'What is it that I have from you that I could not have from another man?'

He gave her a little shove. 'You had better go back now.'

'Not until you answer me.'

'How can I answer you?'

'If you loved me you would find an answer quick enough.'

'Love,' he said. 'Is that all you want from me, Biddy?'

'I do not think you even like me very much.'

'That's not true,' he said. 'It's just that I cannot marry you.'

'Cannot, or will not?'

'I do not think that you love me, Biddy.'

'Huh!' she said. 'Is it only men who are entitled to take what they want just for the pleasure of it?'

'I thought . . .'

'Why is it that you cannot marry me? What is to prevent it?'

'We are too – too selfish ever to be man and wife.'

'Selfish? Are you telling me that I am selfish?'

'No, no. Keep your voice down.'

'Are you trying to tell me that you are tired of me?'

'Hardly that,' he said.

'Why are you pushing me at Mr Baverstock? Is it because he is your master and you wish to curry favour?'

'That's ridiculous.'

'He gave me a silver brooch. I did not ask for it. He gave it to me out of the goodness of his heart. I would have been foolish to have turned it down.'

'Yes, so you would.'

She got to her feet and skinned the shift down over her thighs. She had lingered too long and the cold had crept into her. She shivered. When she stood above him she could see him more clearly, sprawled on the sacking on the stone floor. She shivered again, almost violently, and hugged her arms to her breasts. There was no anger in her, however, and she felt lost without it.

She said, 'Why do you not just admit that you do not love me?'

'It would make no difference if I did,' he answered. 'Would it stop you meeting with me? Would it stop us doing what we do?'

'No.'

'Biddy,' he said, 'you are no more in love with me than I am with you.'

'Do you think I would give myself to a man I do not love?'

'Yes.'

'Huh!' she said again, like her father.

'You had better go now.'

'Why?'

'Because it's very late and . . .'

'You have had enough of me?' Biddy said.

'For tonight, yes.'

'Well, I have had enough of you too, Michael Tarrant.'

She turned to the door, unloosed the rope and drew the door open. The cloud had gone and the wind swooped across the hill and stars oscillated in the blackness overhead. The night seemed huge and empty. Then he was behind her, hand on her waist and she let him swing her around and kiss her on the mouth with more passion than he had ever kissed her before.

'Saturday?' he asked, quietly.

And Biddy nodded. 'Yes.'

Biddy's first thought, when she pushed open the door, was that she had been found out. Fingal was on his feet, growling. Her mother was in the act of lighting a lamp and all sorts of strange sounds came from the loft at the top of the ladder. Guilt trickled through Biddy like boiling water. She felt her face flush up and her belly turn hot again and she pressed her arms to her breasts as if to hide them.

'Is that you, Biddy?' Vassie glanced over her shoulder as she applied the taper to the lamp-wick. 'Where have you been?'

'I – I – to the outhouse,' Biddy said.

'Oh, God! Are you sick too?'

Biddy realised that she was not the source of her mother's concern and let out a sigh of relief. Her father and brothers were still fast asleep and, Biddy knew, if Vassie had suspected that she had been in the byre with a man then the entire household would have been put on general orders. It was suddenly brought home to her just how dangerous her liaison with Michael Tarrant had become for, if they were discovered together, he would be forced to marry her and she would have no say in the matter.

'No, I am not sick,' Biddy answered. 'I just – just needed to go.'

Vassie capped the lamp and adjusted the wick. The reek of oil was strong in the cool air of the kitchen and coils of black smoke drifted upward. Before Biddy could offer her excuse and ask what had disturbed her mother, Innis's head appeared at the top of the ladder.

'Give me up a cloth, quickly,' Innis said.

'Is she still being sick?' Vassie tossed her daughter a towel. 'Has she got her head in the pot?'

'Yes.'

'Does she have the cramp?'

'No, she is just being sick.'

'Who's sick?' Biddy said. 'Is it Aileen?'

'Aye.'

Innis vanished. Biddy filled the kettle from the water tub, put it on top of the fire. Upstairs, Aileen retched, retched again, and let out a whimpering cry. Lamp in hand, Vassie climbed the steep wooden ladder and looked into the loft just as Donnie, roused by the commotion, stuck his head out of the alcove.

'What is wrong with everybody?'

'Aileen's sick,' Biddy told him.

'Is that all?' he muttered, retreated behind the curtain and, presumably, went back to bed.

Vassie placed the lamp on the floor of the loft and hoisted herself up. Biddy could see nothing but the filter of light through the floorboards and hear nothing except an indistinct murmur of voices. She sat back on her heels by the hearth and looked down at her stomach, at the curve of her belly and the shadow between her thighs. She had no concern for Aileen, could think of nothing but her own precarious situation and how terrified she had been when she had first entered the kitchen.

As she knelt by the fire waiting for the kettle to boil a sudden wave of exhaustion overwhelmed her and she felt angry and resentful at Aileen for causing all this fuss. Fingal sniffed at her, his nose wet against her knees. She lashed out at him with her forearm, sent him skulking away to lie beneath the table, his sullen, yellow eyes upon her. Then, heavy and sluggish, she got to her feet and pulled herself up the ladder to look into the loft.

Aileen was in bed, blanket pulled up to her chin, chamberpot placed conveniently near her head. The oil lamp was balanced on a little driftwood shelf beneath which, in a hole in the roof turf, Biddy had hidden Austin Baverstock's gift.

'Is she all right?' Biddy said.

'Oh, she is fine,' Vassie said softly. 'She is a fine girl and will be as right as the rain in the morning.'

'What is wrong with her?' Biddy asked.

'Something she ate, I expect,' Innis said.

'Can I go to bed yet?' Biddy said.

'No, let her fall asleep first,' Vassie said.

Biddy tutted under her breath but said nothing and, a moment later, stepped down into the kitchen again to brew a pot of tea while Vassie crooned a lullaby to soothe the little one to sleep.

For the first time that Innis could recall she and her sisters were to be left in charge of Pennypol. They would not be entirely without protection, however, for Donnie had volunteered to remain behind when Ronan, Neil and Vassie went off with the cattle to the mainland sales.

In past years Vassie had sold the beasts off the field to Mr Simpkins, a dealer from Perth, who bought all his beef on Mull and paid a price that was fair if not exactly generous. This year, however, Ronan would not countenance paying a middle-man and declared that Neil and he would fall in behind the herd and, with Vassie riding one of the ponies, would accompany the beasts not just to the lading point but all the way to the Oban cattle ring.

Vassie was anything but pleased at the prospect of her husband taking charge of the herd. Ronan had never been much of a farmer and was not considerate of the beasts that she had bred and reared. There had been a bitter argument and Ronan had struck out at Vassie, offering her the back of his hand, but Donnie had caught his father's fist in mid-air and held it tight. Ronan's mood had changed instantly. He had laughed at Donnie's intervention and had ruffled Donnie's hair as if he, Donnie, were still a wilful child.

Vassie diligently arranged grazing along the route and worked out what the drove would cost per head in grass fees. Ronan, she knew, would try to persuade her to feed the cattle on the cheap so that he might have more to spend on drink. To counter this manoeuvre, Vassie fished out a big, black leather bag which she would keep strapped to her body and within which the travelling money would be safe from thieving hands, by which, of course, she meant her husband's. They would be gone, all told, for the best part of a week and would return on the mail boat from Oban which would be a novel experience for Vassie and Neil, not to mention the pony.

Aileen had begged to be allowed to go too but Vassie would not hear of it and Aileen had been left weeping behind.

The girls, and Donnie too, accompanied the herd as far as Crove. They walked behind the cattle while Vassie rode on ahead, scarves flying and her big black leather bag jangling, crying, 'Hey, hey, harry-hup, harry-hup,' to maintain pace and to remind Ronan to keep the stragglers tidy and Neil to steer the calves out of the ditches and away from the unfenced woods. They followed the old track that ran behind Crove's main street past gardens and outbuildings and the back of the Arms. McKinnon himself came out and presented Ronan with a gill of whisky to see him on his way. Shopkeepers, crofters' wives, even children from the babies' school trotted out to see the Campbells off, for the sight of Vassie on a pony was attraction enough, let alone the sight of a cattle herd passing so close to the village.

At the kirk gate Reverend Ewing and his 'daily' waved a red handkerchief and a bristle broom respectively as the kye trotted towards the bridge and the start of the metalled road to Dervaig which was as far as Donnie and the girls would go. Vassie lifted herself up on the canvas stirrups, leaned on the luggage that was roped behind her and waved her hand, and that was all her family had by way of farewell, though they lingered to watch the dry, cold dust fade away and listen to the bellowing of the cattle grow fainter and fainter until at last the herd passed out of sight.

Innis had expected to be thrilled by the sight of the herd on the move, for there was something romantic in Grandfather McIver's tales of the great cattle drives when three or four thousand beasts would mill together on the shore at Grass Point and swim the narrow channels between each of the islands that speckled the firth until they scrambled ashore on the coast of

Argyll. The drovers still came to Mull, of course, and the huge cattle sales on the mainland still took place but as she stood by the hump-backed bridge on the outskirts of Crove on that clear November morning Innis felt as if she were bidding goodbye not only to the Pennypol cattle but to her mother too, as if Vassie were riding backward into the past and would not return on MacBrayne's mail boat in one week's time.

'Are you crying?' Biddy demanded.

'It is the dust that is making my eyes water.'

'It could hardly be your heart breaking to see the back of them.'

Innis dabbed her eyes with her cuff. 'Where is Aileen?'

'Under the bridge.'

'What is she doing there?'

'Making water,' said Biddy. 'She is making more water these days than the rest of us put together.'

'Will you be keeping an eye on her, Biddy, please.'

'Why? Are we not walking back together?'

'I need to have a word with Mr Ewing before we go home.'

'Mr Ewing, is it now? What would you be wanting with him?'

Innis did not answer, for she was already hurrying back towards the kirk gate before the minister vanished down the little path that led to the manse.

'Is this what you wanted, Mr Ewing?' Innis said as soon as the boat had cleared the skerries south-west of Pennypol and had entered the tidal stream.

'It is everything that I wanted, Innis,' the minister answered. 'And more than I expected in respect of the weather.'

'Aye, we could not have been anticipating such a fine day.'

'They say we will suffer for it,' Tom Ewing reminded her.

'Och, they say we will suffer for everything, in this world or in the next.'

'You have not heard that from my pulpit.'

Innis smiled. 'No, not from you, Mr Ewing. There are times when I'm thinking you worship a different God from the rest of us.'

'Just the same God, Innis. But He is more accommodating than folk give Him credit for.' Tom adjusted position in the bow and

leaned an elbow on the gunwhale. 'Look about you. Do you think
that the God who made a world as beautiful as this one would
condemn us to anything less wonderful after we have passed
into paradise?'

'Aye,' Innis said, 'but it is not always as beautiful as this. If we
were here with the rain lashing down upon us and the waves
soaking us through it would not be so easy to believe in God's
beneficence.'

'Beneficence is a different thing from judgement,' Tom said,
then laughed and shook his head vigorously. 'No, no, Miss
Campbell, I'll not be letting you trap me into theological debate,
not this morning.'

'I cannot debate with you, Mr Ewing,' Innis said. 'I haven't
enough knowledge.'

'Then why do you tease me with so many difficult questions?'

'So that I can learn.'

'Well, put your quest for knowledge to one side, please,' Tom
said. 'This is not your day to learn. It's mine.'

He wore his dog-collar under a tweed jacket and a dark blue
woollen pullover. His overcoat and hat were folded away in a
dry creel in the bottom of the boat. He had a fine, free air to
him, with his dark hair fluttering in whatever breeze there was.
He looked at ease, not lordly, and he had been smiling since the
moment he had stepped into the *Kelpie* and Innis had rowed
them away from the jetty. Biddy had come to see them off. She
had stood on the turf waving her red bandanna in a theatrical
manner with Fingal by her side, his tail wagging as if the dog
were as eager as she was to bid them farewell.

Donnie had gone across to Leathan to help with fencing and,
at Biddy's insistence, had taken Aileen with him.

With half the herd gone the pastures of Pennypol were
uncannily quiet in the calm November sunshine. Even the surface
of the sea seemed passive, glassy as a mirror. Only the oily swell
that thrust the boat forward and the shaping of the lugsail that
Innis had set indicated that there was any breeze at all.

Innis worked the sail from the stern. The rudder bar was
tucked under her arm, the big, worn oars temporarily feathered.
She wore a patterned day-dress, a tasselled shawl and a plain felt
hat that reminded Tom of a Spanish beret. He was tempted to

ask who had taught her to sail but he knew what the answer would be – the same answer Innis gave to almost every question concerning her education: 'Grandfather McIver.'

The morning was perfectly clear, the sun warm enough to be pleasant. Tom lifted his face up to its rays as the *Kelpie* progressed towards the flat-topped rocks that marked the rim of the Treshnish Isles, north-west of which lay the isle of Foss, Evander McIver's kingdom.

Over the years Tom had heard many stories about the old man. He had seen him here and there at fairs and shows, a tall, handsome figure with a mane of white hair tied into a pigtail at the back of his head. He was usually dressed in dark tartan trews and a broad leather belt with a sporran hung on it, not to the front but to the side. A quilted brown leather waistcoat added to his bulk and his canvas half-boots, which had gone out of fashion half a century ago, looked, to Tom at least, both practical and snug. He had a piratical swagger and a hard, threatening stare that belied his true character. Hard he might have been in the days of his youth but threatening he never was, not to man or woman or beast.

There were few of McIver's kind left now. They were being replaced by sharp-witted 'eccentrics', mystics and self-anointed sages whose reputations hung on nothing more substantial than a poem here or a ballad there or some act of trickery that had conned money out of an Englishman. Tom had watched them rise up along the fringes of the tourist routes, poseurs whose masculinity was all show and as inauthentic as most Jacobite souvenirs.

Whatever his faults, Evander McIver was no poseur. He had been a dancer, a thrower of weights, a wrestler, a gambler and, latterly, a breeder of fine Highland bulls. He had chosen to live on Foss, out of the public eye, rather than exploit the legend that he had unwittingly created. Tom had been eager to meet the old man face to face for some time now but had never been able to find a suitable opportunity. He felt a strange thrill of excitement and anticipation when Foss appeared, sliding out from behind the island of Groom More.

Innis steered the *Kelpie* down a channel where seals basked in sunlight and seabirds flocked above a steep cliff. Then the saucer-shaped isle lay before them. A blunt summit and a scant line of trees protected both the anchorage and the house. Tom had been in small boats before. He had nosed in and out of sea lochs, had even fished – though the sport was not to his taste – along the shelves off Inch Kenneth and had, of course, visited Staffa several times. But he had never seen anything quite like Foss before.

There were no columns of basalt to impress the visitor, no great caves, or skull-shaped rocks or isolated stacs, only a bright green table not much more than a hundred feet high, a house and, here and there, heavy, tobacco brown cattle, huge-horned and massive, quietly cudding the grass.

The two-storey house was set low against the base of the hill. It was not built of local stone but of imported timber. Even the roof was shingled with wooden tiles. With shutters roped open and a railed verandah at the front it reminded Tom of a plantation house or a residence in India. He had only a minute or two to survey the architecture as the boat swooped across the channel and Innis hauled down the sail and dropped the oars. Four bulls and six or eight cows raised their heads and watched, un-impressed, as the *Kelpie* beached on the shingle sand and two small boys and a woman not much older than Innis, who had appeared out of nowhere, dragged the bow above the tide-line.

The boys were smooth and brown-skinned, with bare legs, brown hair and dark eyes. They were as clean and as tidy as if they too had been cropped down by the cattle.

'Ho, Mairi,' Innis called out.

'Ho, Innis,' the young woman answered and, to Tom's sur-prise, waded through the shallow water by the side of the boat and embraced Innis affectionately. The minister clambered over the bow and jumped to the shingle. He turned to offer a hand to Innis but she had stepped down, bare-legged too, into the shallows. When he looked round Evander McIver was on the verandah, leaning into the rail. He wore nothing but trews and a leather vest, chest, shoulders and feet naked in the slant of November sunshine.

Several other women and children were visible, including a couple of handsome young girls who looked uncannily like Innis and a young man of fourteen or fifteen who stood at the verandah's end. When Tom glanced in his direction he gave a nod and made a gesture of welcome with his closed fist. Tom nodded back. Innis was behind him, carrying gifts for her grandfather and the wrapped parcel that Tom had brought and which contained a leather-bound copy of Horton's *Tractatus*, a book with which he had never been able to make much headway but that, Innis told him, Evander McIver would appreciate.

Innis led him to the house. To his right was a herb garden. Beyond that was the wall of a vegetable garden. Another woman, not so young, stood among the rows with a hoe in her hand. Her hair was tied up in a bright blue bandanna. She too waved to him and Tom waved back.

'Who are they, Innis?' he murmured.

'His children, his family.'

'I thought you were his family?'

'He has another family here.'

'Which one is his wife?'

'Who knows?' Innis said.

Evander McIver swung himself away from the rail as the couple approached. He too was smiling and seemed as friendly as everyone else on the little green island of Foss.

'Well now, Minister, it is good to have you here at last.'

'Thank you, Mr McIver. I am pleased to be here.'

'Have you come to see how best I should be buried?' the old man said, with a twinkle in his eye.

Tom surprised himself by blurting out exactly what was on his mind.

'Standing upright, sir,' he said, 'might seem to be appropriate.'

Evander McIver laughed and with a sweeping motion of his bare arms welcomed Tom Ewing to his house.

Austin brought the dogs and Willy brought the flask and the pair of them headed out in good spirits to walk to Friendship Farm.

For once Willy made no moan about being dragged away from the warm kitchen, for he too had developed a taste for the great outdoors which, if it did not match up to his master's, was certainly novel enough not to be ignored.

Part of his urge to stride across the heather from time to time stemmed from his uncertainty about what to do about Maggie Bell. It wasn't that he didn't know what he wanted from her – that was obvious enough – but that he was wary of the price that he might have to pay for the experience. Fear of consequence had never prevented him having his way with a woman before now and Willy was thoroughly flummoxed as to what had got into him and why he was suffering this sudden attack of doubt. Scruples? he thought. Surely not scruples, not at my age. Every kitchen hand or maid who had ever succumbed to his charms and had fallen, even fleetingly, in love with him had been fair game as far as Willy Naismith was concerned, a victim of her own weakness who had asked for all she got which, to be blunt about it, was plenty.

But not 'shy' Margaret Bell. She doted on him, idolised him, yet she refused to let him take any liberties whatsoever; not a kiss, not a cuddle, not a squeeze in the pantry or a pinch in the hall by way of reward for all Willy had done for her. As for letting Willy escort her to her bedroom now that she had become a full-time servant and didn't go home at nights – well, that was certainly *not* on Maggie's agenda. What was more, Maggie had somehow got Cook on her side and old Queenie was as protective of Maggie's honour as she was of her own, which, given Queenie's chequered past, wasn't saying much. Even so, between the two of them, Willy was getting nowhere at all in the seduction stakes and was suffering all the symptoms of frustration because of it.

In common with Mr Austin, Willy had had a fair taste of what winter would be like on Mull, how foul weather kept one indoors, how gloomy the big house of Fetternish could seem, downstairs as well as up, when the sun set at half past four o'clock and the evenings stretched out like jail sentences, with only three servants, two dogs and one master all rattling about in the empty rooms, and nothing to do by way of diversion except watch Queenie darn stockings or Maggie sew aprons or, if summoned, to play checkers with the gentleman upstairs. Small wonder that he was glad to escape during daylight hours, particularly now that the rain had ceased and the wind had fallen away and the island was bathed in sunshine.

'I think this is a bonus, Willy, don't you?'

A Midnight Courtship

'I do, Mr Austin. I do.'

He had asked for, and had been given, a handout to pay for stalking boots and had bought a fine pair off the shelf in Tobermory. He had also been given permission to borrow the tweed cape and hat that Mr Walter had left behind and there was not much to separate master from man as the pair strode out towards the ruined croft with the hounds, unleashed, lolloping on ahead of them.

It was not until they were seated on the ruined wall, looking out at the sea and the great brooding heights of Ardnamurchan that Austin raised the subject of women and Willy, sensing trouble, produced the silver hip flask which he had filled half and half with moonshine and spring water.

'As you know, William, I have never been one to concern myself with what goes on below stairs, between – I mean – the servants,' Austin began, 'but do I detect a certain affinity between you and our new young lady?'

'You do, Mr Austin – alas.'

'Why do you say "alas", William? Miss Bell seems a pleasant soul.'

'Oh, aye, sir,' Willy agreed. 'She's very pleasant.'

Austin watched the Boots pour a dram from the flask into the silver cup. He took it carefully between finger and thumb, his left hand open under it so as not to spill a drop. In Edinburgh he would have regarded it as decadent to drink spirits before noon but the keen fresh air of the coast had changed his habits and eliminated many of the social niceties.

Austin sipped whisky and gazed out to sea while the hounds snuffled about the ruins as if in search of ancient bones.

'I'm not being impertinent, William, am I?'

'Not at all, Mr Austin.'

Another sip, another observation of the ocean: 'I wish I had your looks, Willy. Truly I do.'

'My looks!' Willy exclaimed.

'I mean, I wish I had your appeal for women.'

'Oh, you're not so bad, sir.' Willy said. 'On a dark night on Princes Street I'm sure you'd pass muster.'

For an instant Willy wondered if he had overstepped the mark. Austin glanced at him, frowning, then laughed. 'Are you trying to tell me that it isn't appearance that matters?'

'That's it, Mr Austin,' Willy said.

'What *do* women want from a man? I mean, what do they look for? What attracts them to one chap in preference to another?'

Willy drank straight from the flask. He wiped his beard with his palm and thought how good the whisky tasted in the open air, how Jack Stratton was getting a bit of a bargain after all. He wished now that he had held out for a better offer but Haggerty's first run would be ready early next week and Campbell would see to its delivery as soon as he returned from Oban.

Willy sighed. 'I know what you're askin' me, Mr Austin, but I'm not sure I'm the right person to tell you.'

'Are you as confused as I am? Surely not.'

'I'm not confused, sir. By which I mean, I know damned well what Margaret Bell sees in me. She sees a husband.'

'She could do a great deal worse, William.'

'Aye, Mr Austin,' Willy agreed. 'But she could do a great deal better. I know it, even if she doesn't.'

'But you're a man of some - well - slight status and you are hardly old.'

'I'm hardly young either,' Willy said. 'The truth of it is, sir, I'm not reliable.'

'My sister has never complained.'

'Your sister!' Willy said with a trace of alarm. 'What's she been—' He snipped the end off the sentence before he gave too much away. Austin Baverstock, innocent as morning sunshine, obviously had no notion as to what had gone on between his sister and his man-servant. 'No, sir. I mean that I'm not reliable when it comes to being a husband.'

'I think I would be "reliable" on all fronts, William, don't you?'

Relieved that his relationship with Agnes Baverstock was no longer to the fore, Willy said, 'Why don't we come down to it, Mr Austin, since we're both men of the world? You've got eyes for Biddy Campbell and you want to find out how you can get her.'

'I want to marry her, William, not just - you know.'

'Do you mean, sir, you wouldn't just - you know, if you got the chance?'

'I – I might.'

'I would, I can tell you,' Willy said.

'William!'

'I mean no disrespect to the lady, Mr Austin, or to you for that matter, but any man of spark would be attracted to her.'

'She seems to offer so much.'

'Uh-huh,' Willy agreed. 'But I do think she'd be a bit of a handful in and out of the bridal suite.'

'Really?'

'Red-haired girls are usually fiery when it comes to – you know.' Willy paused and added, 'At least, that's what I've heard.'

'I am surprised that Miss Campbell has not been taken up already.'

'Taken up,' said Willy. 'Where?'

'To the altar. Not taken in marriage.'

Willy said, 'Does Mr Walter know that you're attracted to the lady?'

'I've made no attempt to hide my feelings for her.'

'I take it he doesn't approve?'

'I think he is of the opinion that Miss Campbell is – well – beneath me.'

'I see,' Willy said. 'I'm afraid I must disagree with Mr Walter, sir. I have the feelin' that, given a wee bit of polish, Biddy Campbell could hold her own in any sort of society.'

Austin raised an eyebrow. He was obviously pleased at Willy's endorsement of Biddy Campbell's worth which was just the effect that Willy had intended his remark to have. Austin shifted his position, leaning conspiratorially towards the servant as if he feared that they might be overheard.

'How do I get her, William?' he muttered. 'Can you tell me that?'

'Patience, Mr Austin. Patience and money.'

'Money?'

'Aye, sir,' Willy said. 'In the end the ladies all come around towards the man with money. They always know how their bread is buttered, and who will best butter it for them.'

'Is that not just a little cynical, perhaps?'

'It's how ladies think, Mr Austin, believe me.'

'All of them?'

'Almost without exception,' Willy told his master. 'Patience and money will do it for you.'

'Well, well, how interesting!' Austin Baverstock said and, cheered by Willy's prediction, held out the silver cup for more moonshine.

During the course of midday dinner Tom Ewing realised that he had not come to Foss of his own volition, that he had been summoned to appear before the old man and that Innis was only her grandfather's emissary. Nothing was said to indicate that he had been expected or that McIver had a motive for treating him as an honoured guest. But even old McIver and his tribe of females would hardly have been able to furnish so lavish a table without a great deal of preparation.

The house had been constructed some thirty years ago out of imported hardwoods. It was double-skinned and cedar-panelled. The ceiling of the broad living-room was low-beamed. The walls were lined with bookshelves filled with weighty volumes on every subject under the sun. The furnishings were simple: canvas-covered sofas, a brass-topped table, two or three oil lamps on sturdy brass stands. The fireplace was hardly taller than Tom's waist and on a prominent shelf above it was displayed a series of marine instruments together with a beautiful brass microscope in a velvet-lined case.

In spite of the remoteness of the isle Evander McIver did not go short of the finer things in life. From the bonded Islay malt that Tom was offered as an appetiser to the claret that accompanied the meal everything was of the best. The minister dined on smoked salmon with mustard sauce, scallops, prime rib of beef, fresh vegetables and a peach tart with clotted cream. A cheese board was laden with ripe Stilton, mature Cheddar and a fine, firm Brie. The dining-room was hardly more than an alcove off the living-room but two small windows looked out on to the cattle pasture and as he ate the minister studied not only the huge-horned beasts from which McIver made his living but also the women who worked the fields: five or six of them, together with half a dozen children, all so brown and lithe and healthy that they had obviously been bred and reared according to the tenets of good husbandry.

All sorts of questions burned on the minister's tongue. Old McIver was aware of his guest's curiosity but teased him by skirting the subject of relationships and the origins of the family of Foss. Tom was not bored by the dinner-table conversation. McIver was certainly no Philistine. Indeed, it was all that Tom could do to keep up with the burl of questions that the old man put to him concerning the problems of contemporary theology, a subject in which Tom was not as well versed as his host, apparently.

Innis listened without saying a word. She left the serving to a handsome young woman by the name of Katrin who, like everyone Tom had so far met, smiled upon him and addressed him in Gaelic. When the meal was concluded Evander led him out into the living-room again where they were joined by Katrin and Mairi and an olive-skinned boy who sat quietly upon one of the sofas and, like Innis, listened to the conversation without intruding.

Evander opened the packet that Tom had brought. He admired the book, thanked him for it; then, standing, he asked the woman, Mairi, to bring him his hat and suggested that they might take a turn out of doors before the air grew too cold and before the minister was obliged to return to his duties on Mull.

Tom followed McIver down the steps on to a little shell-sand path. He expected Innis to accompany them but she stayed behind, leaning on the rail of the verandah flanked by the boy and one of the women. McIver strode out like a chap in his prime, only the steely-grey pigtail and the white down on his bare shoulders to hint at his age.

For no particular reason, Tom glanced back at the house. He felt his breath catch in surprise at what he saw. Innis had a baby in her arms, an infant wrapped in a shawl, a small, brown-skinned, chubby-limbed child who seemed to Tom like a vision of the future rather than of time past.

Evander waited, smiling benignly.

'Is it that you have a question, Mr Ewing?' he said.

'I am curious, yes.'

'Is it about the children?'

'It is.'

'They came into the world in the same way as we all came into the world.'

'Are they your children?'

'My children, my grandchildren and great-grandchildren.'

'Where are the fathers?'

'Gone,' Evander McIver said. 'Gone – or never were.'

'Never were?'

'One was a man from the Long Isle, who spent a winter here some years ago. Another came from Nova Scotia. He was a deep-sea sailor who was called home to attend his dying mother and never came back. Another still was a horse dealer out of Bantry Bay.'

'Were none of the children born in wedlock?'

'I suppose that is a question a minister must ask.'

'I am afraid it is, Mr McIver.'

'Is it not enough that they were born and lived?'

'I am no subscriber to the League of Purity,' said Tom, cautiously, 'but I am ordained by the Church of Scotland and you cannot expect me to condone casual couplings.'

'I assure you they were not casual couplings, Mr Ewing.'

'No matter what opinion you may have of them, Mr McIver, men and women are not beasts of the field to couple and breed as they will.'

'Is the birth of a calf, or a child, not a miracle of God whether or not it is blessed by the Kirk?'

'Sophistry,' Tom said. 'Not argument.'

'Would you not baptise them?'

'Oh, I see. I see.'

'If I brought my children to your church one Sunday morning, would you baptise them in the name of the Lord?'

'No.'

'Because of what your elders would say?'

'I would have to have permission from the Presbytery and the Presbytery would refuse me outright,' Tom said.

'And you would not be one for defying the Presbyters?'

'No,' Tom said again.

'Well now, at least you are an honest man,' Evander McIver told him.

'Is that why you invited me to Foss, Mr McIver? To ask if I would baptise your grandchildren?'

'No, it is not.'

A Midnight Courtship

'Why did you have Innis bring me here?' Tom said. 'I know that you did. There is no point in denying it.'

'I do not deny it. I wanted to show you my island.'

'So it wasn't Innis's idea?'

'It was more my wish than hers.'

Tom was mildly disappointed. 'I suppose I am partly to blame.'

'Blame?'

'Let us say that my nose bothered me."

'Why should it not?' Evander said. 'We are all curious by nature, Mr Ewing, whether about the world or the habits of the folk who dwell in it. It is only when a person, or race, loses their curiosity that the rot sets in.'

'So, there is nothing that I can do for you, Mr McIver?'

'Ah, well now,' Evander told him. 'I would not be saying that. There are things that you could be doing for me, Minister Ewing. It is just a question of whether you will be willing to do them or whether you will not.'

They walked as they talked, Tom matching his shorter stride to Evander's long-legged gait. He had been intent upon the conversation and puzzled as to what the old bull-breeder might want from him.

As they climbed the slope of the little hillock and put the beach and the house behind them, the open sea came swiftly into sight. The sea was the same inky dark blue as the seas around Iona where granite cropped out into the Atlantic. The waters north of Foss had a similar hue with the cold currents curving blue-black along the edge of the roadsteads, like velvet against silk. Tom could feel the breeze against his cheek, the sifting spray that rose from the sea-tumbled boulders below the path. In winter, he thought, the entire island must float like a raft in a haze of spray while McIver and his children and his children's children nestled inside the wooden house and the bulls and bull calves huddled in the rushes with their tails to the wind and the sky roaring over them.

'Here we are then.' Evander McIver pointed at his feet.

At first Tom could see nothing but a depression in the rough pasture, a horseshoe of turf fringed with bracken and heather. So discreet were the markers that he could have searched the isle for a week without finding them. They did not rise up from the ground but lay flat, almost buried in the turf. They were mapped with lichen and almost indistinguishable from the boulders about them except that they bore carvings and two at least had letters carved on them.

'What are they?' Tom asked.

'Graves.'

'Who is buried here?'

The old man lifted his shoulders and spread his hands. 'I cannot read the lettering,' he said. 'It is an ancient script and too weather-worn to be decipherable. If they are no one then they can be everyone.'

Tom stooped, hands on his knees, and peered at the slabs.

Tombstones of slate and schist engraved with a Virgin and child, a galley with furled sails, a bull calf, a sword, a letter here, not Roman; a letter there, not Gaelic. Numerals that made no sense had been driven into the slate by a mallet and cold chisel and when he rubbed away the moss with his fingertip, he could make out the strike of the tool as a clean-cut edge.

The stones of Foss made Tom feel strange, even stranger than the upright stones in the graveyard behind the ruined chapel at Pennygown or stone circles or the pits of ancient forts, or old Caliach standing tall on her headland. Visiting the relics of the time before always imparted a heretical little thrill to some indistinct part of his soul. Nothing so strong, so strange, though, as the discovery of the unrecorded graves on the little green isle of Foss which, looking up and out to sea, he suddenly saw as staging-posts in an inevitable journey westward, out towards the sunset and the rim of the world.

Evander McIver put a hand on his shoulder. 'This way,' he said. 'It is just a step or two, I promise you.' McIver kept a hand on his shoulder, though whether it was to guide him or steady him Tom could not be sure.

The three new stones had been placed side by side on the edge of the bracken; not of slate or schist but pinkish granite from the Tormore quarry on the Ross of Mull. Tom could make out the plug and feather marks where the slabs had been split from the block. They were unpolished and not old, not yet.

'My wives,' Evander McIver said. 'Eillien is here. And here is Vanessa.'

162

'Innis's grandmother?'

'Aye.'

'Has Innis been here?'

'I have shown it to her, yes.'

Tom's mouth was dry. He could taste the salt in the air, though there appeared to be no breeze to drive it inshore. He thought of his own mother, still very much alive, in a tenement in Dundee, that high, surly tombstone of a house overlooking the Tay. He thought of his father, buried in the cemetery at Ninewells on the outskirts of the city; of his brother and his sisters in Glasgow and how they talked of the day when they would all return to the Hebrides together – and never would, not now.

'What did she – what did Innis say when you brought her here?'

'Oh, she is too young yet to understand,' Evander answered. 'But you understand, Mr Ewing, do you not?'

'I cannot explain it.' Tom shook his head. 'But, yes, I understand.'

'There are two children buried there with Eillien, two babies. They took her with them when they went.'

'How long ago was this?'

'Twelve years.'

'And the other?'

'Thirty-five.'

'You have lived a long time without them,' Tom said.

'Too long, I think.' Evander McIver touched his toe to the third stone, the one which already bore his name. 'Will you do it when the time comes? Will you say the words over me, Minister Ewing?'

'I may not be here. On Mull, I mean.'

'I think you will, Mr Ewing. Somehow I think you will.'

'Then, yes, Mr McIver, I will conduct your burial service.'

'In spite of what the Presbytery may have to say about it?'

'What they do not know will do them no harm.'

'I thank you for that, Mr Ewing,' Evander said. 'I have one other thing to ask of you before you take your leave.'

'What might that be?'

'Will you watch out for Innis when I am gone?'

'Innis,' Tom said, cautiously, 'can surely watch out for herself.'

'She is not like the others.'

'I am well aware of that,' Tom admitted. 'She might have a husband of her own to look out for her by then, of course.'

'She might,' the old man said, 'but if not?'

'I will watch out for her,' Tom promised. 'It will be no hardship.'

'Thank you, Mr Ewing.'

Tom hesitated. 'Is that all, Mr McIver? Is that all you want from me?'

'The rest is taken care of.' Evander McIver placed a hand on Tom's shoulder once more. 'I think we should be going back now.'

'Yes,' Tom said, 'before it gets too cold.'

He had her down upon the bed, flat down on her belly. Because they were alone at last she groaned and cried out at the hot, wet slap of his thighs against her buttocks. She could feel his fingers twined in her hair, drawing her head back, his hands tugging at her breasts. The narrow bed creaked. Outside, the collie scraped at the locked door of the shed, and whined continuously. With the sun low in the sky, an angular beam of light slipped down the wall. It dazzled Biddy. It mingled with the blind flashes that ran through her nerves as release came bursting upon her. She thrust back against him then sagged beneath his weight. For an instant she longed to have him touch her with nothing but his lips, to whisper, 'I love you, Biddy. I love you,' before the sensations started up again, but Michael, of course, said nothing.

She was hardly aware of the shadow that passed across the sunlight. A split second before the bolt rattled and the cottage door rattled on its painted hinges, though, she sensed that someone was outside. She stiffened. She braced herself on her elbows on the bed and lifted her head. She felt Michael withdraw. She heard him suck in breath then he too fell still, utterly and completely still.

'Tarrant,' Hector Thrale called out. 'Tarrant, I know you are in there.'

Bolt rattling changed to the thump of fists, angry and urgent.

'What are you doing, man? Open up. I wish to speak with you.'

A Midnight Courtship

Biddy made as if to rise but Michael pressed down on her, his forearms across the small of her back. So softly that Biddy could barely make out the words he murmured, 'Lie still.'

'Open this door, Tarrant, or I will be kicking it down.'

The collie was barking now, a harsh, savage sound accompanied by ferocious scraping on the bottom of the shed door.

Biddy put her brow upon the pillow and closed her eyes. She felt swollen with annoyance that her enjoyment had been spoiled. If Michael had not been so calm, she might even have shouted at Thrale to leave them in peace. She thought of his fat red face and sly eyes, how he would love to do to her what Michael was doing or, failing that, to ogle her as she lay naked on the shepherd's bed.

Silence outside; she wondered if Thrale had gone.

Frowning, she glanced round. Michael shook his head.

A moment later a shadow cut across the band of sunlight and she heard the tap, tap, tapping of Thrale's knuckles upon the window pane.

She whispered, 'Can he see us?'

'Not from there.'

Her skirts, stockings, drawers and shawl were humped on a chair by the fire. Her shoes, kicked off, lay on the stone-flagged floor. The tapping continued. Thrale's voice, cajoling now, seemed to float in the sunlit air. She could not believe that she had no fear. She felt massive and exposed in her nakedness, though. Twisting her head, she glanced over her shoulder at Michael who, to her astonishment, had remained erect. She shifted position, clenched her fists and elbowed herself backwards. Spine arched, she rocked against him teasingly until he entered her again, as smooth and impassive as always.

After a while Hector Thrale went away.

Since wind and tide were against them Tom offered to man one of the oars. Seated side by side on the draft seat the minister and the fisherman's daughter rowed in harmony until the *Kelpie* cleared the little isles and a following wind out of the southwest allowed Innis to sling up the sail.

Tom took more away from Foss than he brought to it: eggs in a straw basket, smoked fish, a cheese the size of a wheel hub and two old books on the early history of the Gaels that Tom had never heard of, let alone read; all this in exchange for promises that would tax neither his time nor his patience.

He was quiet during the trip but not brooding, not solemn. He felt an affinity with Innis that had not been there before. He was no longer afraid of the brush of her skirts against his knee, of the touch of her thigh against his. In the course of the day he had been affected by a kind of innocence that was not innocence at all. But unfortunately the spirit of Foss, Evander McIver's isle, soon diminished once they were inside the line of the Treshnish and the mountains of Mull loomed ahead.

The swell carried the *Kelpie* out of the narrows. The long, polished crests of the open sea thrust the boat forward. In the deep glens of Mull the shadows had already grown long and a white chill in the air reminded him that it was November and that winter would soon come down upon them. Innis was happy, though, happier than he had ever seen her. She sang to herself as she plied the rudder or the oar or trimmed the sail back. He glimpsed the standing stone on the headland, old Caliach for ever looking out to sea. He wondered which it was that represented the true spirit of the isles: the old woman or the old man, legend or history, or was it all just so much nonsense and false romance?

Gulls were dipping in the *Kelpie*'s wake and over the crevasses of the fretted coast he could see ravens circling. He looked at Innis who was smiling as if she knew exactly what was on his mind.

'Do you see who I am now?' she asked.

'I'm beginning to,' Tom told her and, for the time being, let it go.

SIX

Dead of Winter

The autumn sales were profitable for the Campbells. Pennypol calves were reputed to be sturdy and free of disease and to come off the same strain as the famous breeding bulls of Foss which, of course, were beyond the purse of all but the richest landowners, and Vassie came home with her black purse stuffed full.

No less successful was Ronan's meeting with Jack Stratton. Within two days of their return from Oban Ronan and the boys were off for a spot of 'night fishing', an exercise in commerce so unusual that Vassie's suspicions were aroused, particularly when there was neither fish nor cash to show for it.

Before the week was out, though, Ronan sailed off again, without lines or bait, for more of the same. She knew better than to quiz Neil about what was going on. Neil was steadfastly loyal to his father. She had more faith in Donnie's good sense, however. She tackled him for an explanation after the third all-night absence which was undertaken in thick weather and, by the look of it, had taxed her boys considerably. But even Donnie would not be drawn. He grew quite hot-tempered, shouted at his mother to mind her own business and stamped off through the drizzling rain to Leathan where, he claimed, he was better treated than he was at home.

After the fourth trip Vassie went down to the jetty to inspect the *Kelpie.* She leaned on the gunwale, sniffed and ran her hand over the woodwork in search of fish-scales or bait grease. She found nothing except three black bottles, two empty and one not, together with the paraphernalia of bow and stern lanterns, an extra set of oars and, of all things, a spade.

As soon as Ronan rolled out of bed, Vassie tackled him about it.

'What is it that you are up to, Ronan Campbell?'

'I am eating my porridge, woman, that is what I am up to.'

'I am meaning with the boat, at night.'

'Fishing.'

'Without lines, without bait?'

'They have been put away.'

'Without a damned catch either?'

'The catch has been sold.'

'Where?'

'Croig.'

'In darkness, at night?'

'What do you think I am doing, woman?'

'Is it the drink?'

'Aye, it is the drink.'

'Is it a fancy woman?'

'Hah!'

'Is it that you are taking my boys to visit fancy women?'

'We have enough trouble with women at home without putting out in bad weather to find more,' Ronan said. 'If it *was* a woman who had caught my fancy, do you suppose I would take the boys with me? I told you, it is the drink.'

'I do not believe you.'

'There you are then, Vassie,' he said in the patronising tone of voice against which no argument could prevail. 'If you will not believe the truth then why should I go to the bother of lying to you?'

'What are you saying?'

'I am saying no more. I have work to do at the boat.'

'Are you going out again tonight?'

'No, not tonight. Tonight I have some other business to attend to.' Ronan lied with perfect composure. 'Business in Crove.'

'Drinking at the McKinnon Arms?'

'There you are, Vassie,' he said, 'I can hide nothing from you,' and laughed in that sly way of his that made all of them, except Aileen, cringe.

Austin was half asleep in the armchair by the fire in the great hall of Fetternish House. Odin sprawled on the carpet at his feet, Thor had his head in his master's lap and a letter lay loosely in the man's left hand; a letter from his brother, Walter; a dreary account of the escalation and oscillation of share prices on the London exchange interspersed with some light, not-quite-libellous Edinburgh gossip. The contents of Walter's letter were enough to send anyone to sleep, let alone a chap who had been tramping the moors all day, rain or no rain, just for the pleasure of being out of doors with his dogs.

Austin was only dimly aware of the booming sound that rose airily up from the kitchen quarters and put it down to the fact that Willy Naismith had neglected to bolt a door or fasten a window catch. In fact, Willy was playing bezique with Maggie Bell while the cook sewed by the fireplace, a pot of hot chocolate on the fender by the side of her chair. The booming knock upon the yard door caused all three servants to look up if not in alarm at least with some apprehension, for the hour was late and Fetternish far off the beaten track.

'Now who the devil can that be?' Willy said.

'Are we expecting visitors?' Mrs McQueen enquired, licking chocolate from her whiskers and tidying an errant lock of hair.

'At this hour of a winter's night? No.'

Willy tossed his cards upon the table as the big iron horseshoe that hung against the outside door was lifted and dropped once more. 'Someone for you, Margaret?'

Maggie shook her head. Her eyes were round, but she was not afraid, not with Willy to protect her, not with a carving knife and an iron poker well within reach. 'Better answer it, Mr Naismith,' she said and got to her feet too just in case Willy should be felled on the doorstep.

It was no robber who disturbed the peace of the night, however, but only Ronan Campbell. He stood on the threshold, his oilskin cape flapping about him and his great long bill-like hat dripping rainwater.

'Good God, man! Come in, come in,' Willy said.

Ronan stepped into the corridor and let Willy close the outer door behind him. He said, 'I was hoping that I would be finding you at home.'

'Where else would I be on a night like this?'

'I have come for my money,' Ronan said, *sotto voce*, his back to the open door of the kitchen within which Maggie and Queenie waited.

'You shall have it,' Willy promised.

'Four trips, four deliveries.'

'I know.'

'While I am here, however, I would be grateful if I might be having a word with Mr Baverstock, if he is not too busy.'

'What do you want with Mr Baverstock?' said Willy, frowning.

'That is none of your concern.'

'Everything to do with Mr Baverstock is my concern.' Willy tried not to sound too testy. 'It's not about – about our transaction, is it?'

'No,' Ronan said, 'it is another matter altogether.'

'Step into the kitchen,' Willy said. 'I'll go upstairs and enquire if Mr Austin will be gracious enough to see you without an appointment.'

'Will you be fetching my money too?'

'Yes,' Willy said. 'Yes, I will be fetching your money too.'

By the time Willy ushered Ronan into the hall Austin had pulled himself together. He had put on a silk-lined smoking jacket that had not seen the light of day since Walter left for Edinburgh, though why the laird of Fetternish felt compelled to impress a neighbour so far beneath him on the material scale Austin could not be sure – except that the neighbour was also Biddy's father. He adopted a pose before the fire, the jacket draped from his shoulders like a coronation robe, one hand casually inserted in the jacket's big side pocket.

Willy made the introduction and dispensed refreshment. Campbell seated himself gingerly on the sofa with a whisky glass in his hand while the dogs sniffed up and down his trouser-legs until Austin ordered Willy to put the brutes out into the corridor. This Willy did, then, soft-footed as a deer, he returned to the hall, took up position behind Mr Austin's armchair, folded his arms and, in the manner of confidential servants from time immemorial, kept his mouth shut.

Campbell lifted the whisky glass and drank. Austin Baverstock rocked gently from side to side. The wind whistled loudly within the house, almost drowning out the *tock-tack-tock* of the seven-foot-high grandfather clock that lurked beneath the staircase and the whining of the hounds from the corridor.

Ronan cleared his throat.

'Yes?' Austin Baverstock said.

'I have been asked to pass on to you my daughter's regards.'

'Well, well!' Austin beamed. 'That's very – very civil of her. Be sure to return my sincere felicitations. Is she – I mean, is she – well?'

'There is nothing wrong with our Biddy that the finding of a husband would not cure,' Ronan said, in the wheezy, sing-song voice that he adopted when he was pretending to share a confidence.

'Are you – I mean, is Bridget in search of a husband?'

'She is in need of one,' said Ronan.

Willy wondered how Campbell managed to make such a simple statement sound suggestive. He had never treated any of his children, even those born on the wrong side of the sheets, in such a cavalier fashion. It riled him to think that the islander would be so disrespectful to one of his own.

'Ah!' Austin said. 'I understand.'

No, sir, Willy thought. You don't understand This man isn't like one of the marriage brokers of Charlotte Square, those mamas and dadas and maiden aunts who will trade away a fine piece of bridal material in exchange for a favour at Court or a slice of farming land.

'However,' Ronan said, 'it is not to discuss my daughter's future that I have come over to see you tonight, Mr Baverstock. There is another matter that I wish to discuss with you.'

'Another matter? Yes?'

Ronan said, 'If it was to be coming on the market would you be interested in acquiring Pennypol to add to your estate?'

'Pennypol?' said Austin, stupidly. 'You mean your croft?'

'Farm,' said Ronan. 'It is a farm. It has good grazing, ground under crop and' – he glanced up at Willy – 'a jetty.'

'I was led to believe that Pennypol could not be sold,' Austin said.

'The right of sale lies with my wife, that is true,' Ronan admitted, 'but if my sons and daughters are not there to work it

171

for her then she will have no option but to sell it.'

Austin Baverstock was by no means a fool when it came to business. He said, 'Let us assume that Pennypol does come on the market, do you intend to auction the acres or offer them for purchase by negotiation?'

'Private transaction,' Ronan said. 'To you, if you are interested.'

'I would have to consult with my brother, of course.'

'Of course you would,' said Ronan. 'You could be reminding him, however, that Pennypol has the only landing north-west of Croig. If the Fetternish flocks thrive then you will soon be needing a place to load your sheep, will you not?'

'Do you have any sort of price in mind?' said Austin.

'No. There are too many factors to be considered,' said Ronan. 'Not least the finding of husbands for my daughters.'

Don't ask about Biddy, Mr Austin, Willy pleaded silently. Don't mention Biddy, for God's sake. It's a trap. The land doesn't belong to Campbell. He's stringing you along.

'I am looking not for a commitment on your part, Mr Baverstock,' Ronan went on, 'only to find out if you are interested.'

Austin had the good sense to hesitate. He glanced round at Willy and raised an eyebrow before he answered. 'If Pennypol ever does come up for sale, Mr Campbell, you may take it that my brother and I would certainly be interested in acquiring it. You do not, however, appear to have considered the most feasible alternative.'

'Alternative?' Ronan said. 'And what would that be?'

'Leasing,' said Austin Baverstock.

'Uh-huh!' Ronan exclaimed.

'If the deeds inhibit sale why do you not consider leasing the grazings, along with freshwater rights and sea access, by which I mean the jetty.'

'Rent them out?' Ronan said. 'By God, Mr Baverstock, that is a very clever suggestion.'

'If – because of marriage, say – you no longer have the hands to work the land profitably I think I might safely say that my brother and I would make good use of it. And you, Mr Campbell, would not have to do anything but collect the rent every quarter. Leasing could be the answer to all your problems.'

Now you've done it, Willy thought. Now you've put the cat

among the pigeons. All the old devil has to do now is sell his daughters to the highest bidder and he can live a life of ease and idleness for evermore.

He kept his mouth shut, though, for Austin seemed pleased with himself, as if he had done something clever. Further refreshment was offered and refused. Ronan Campbell had more on his mind than drink now, Willy reckoned, and he wore a distant expression, as if he were listening to music that nobody else could hear. A few platitudes, a handshake and the meeting was over. Margaret was summoned to fetch Mr Campbell's oilskins from downstairs and Willy was instructed to see Mr Campbell out by the front door.

He escorted Ronan through the foyer and down the step on to the patch of gravel that was lit by the storm lantern above the arch. The sky was streaked with cloud and the wind contained little spits of sleet and the house soared into the darkness above them like a medieval keep.

Willy slipped the fisherman a wad of banknotes, folded small and tight and bound with a rubber band. In daylight, Ronan would no doubt have counted them but tonight he had too much to think about and simply tucked the wad into his waistcoat pocket and tied his oilskin cape over it.

'Have you heard from Fergus?' Willy asked.

'I have.'

'When is the next run?'

'He will have eighty proof gallons ready by next Monday.'

'I had better see to it that he's paid what's owed to him,' Willy said.

'Yes, you had better be doing that,' Ronan said, 'since I know Jack Stockton has already paid you.'

'I heard that you'd met him in Oban,' Willy said, nodding. 'Listen, can you make the delivery even if the weather turns rough?'

'We will manage somehow.'

Whatever else he thought of Ronan Campbell the man was certainly worth his fee. As Ronan turned to leave, Willy put his hand on his sleeve. 'Tell me something, Ronan,' he said. 'Do you really suppose that Biddy might be persuaded to marry Austin Baverstock?'

'It is possible. I still have some influence over her.'

'And why are you so all-fired keen to be rid of Pennypol?'

Ronan laughed. 'To spite her,' he replied. 'To spite my wife and her damned father. Lease out the grazing rights – aye, I should have thought of that myself. There is nothing McIver can do to stop me trading on a lease. Once I have some money of my own I will be a man again, a man in my own house.'

'And what will you do?' Willy asked.

'I will be a gentleman,' Ronan answered, 'and do nothing.'

'That's what I thought,' said Willy and, releasing his grip on the fisherman's sleeve, shoved him off into the darkness without a word of farewell.

On a dreary, drizzling December afternoon, with precious little doing about the farm, Vassie sent Innis into Crove to buy provisions. Out of boredom Ronan and the boys had put out in the *Kelpie* to do a spot of fishing for the pot.

Behind the veils of rains the sea tossed and heaved and Innis suspected that the boys would navigate no further than Arkle where they would squander the best part of the day drinking with Fergus Haggerty. On Pennypol a wash was on. Tubs steamed, suds foamed, sheets and shirts, drawers and stockings draped the beams like bunting. Fingal, grouching, had slunk off to lie in the byre. Biddy, grouching too, had complained of a cramp and had been sent to lie down for half an hour while Aileen sloshed in the soapy water and beat at the clothes with a spurtle as if they were snakes or sea-serpents that had to be killed.

Innis was relieved to be out of the cottage, even if it was raining. What she hated most about winter was not chilblains and chapped lips, frozen feet and a dripping nose but the long evenings cooped up with the family. After early supper she would perch in a corner with a piece of knitting or a book in front of her and try to ignore her mother's complaints, her father's sarcasm and the bickering arguments between her brothers and sisters.

Vassie needed tea and thread and, if one could be found, a big ham bone to add flavour to soup. Until a year or two ago packmen came round the cottage doors with their baskets to sell tea, bobbins of thread and all sorts of trinkets and necessities. Mr McGonigle, Mr Shaeffer or old Mrs Monoghan would be welcomed and given a bite to eat and, if it was late, even invited to stay for the night and would pay for their supper with gossip from the road. But those days were past now, for Pennypol lay so far off the beaten track that the packmen did not come any more and everything that Vassie needed had to be fetched from Miss Fergusson's shop in Crove, or done without.

Innis carried one of the old fishing bags and a purse containing the coins that her mother had counted out. She draped a shawl over her head and shoulders and fastened it about her waist with a piece of rope and, looking more like a tinker than a lady, set off along the track through the chill, December rain.

It had been weeks since she had seen Michael face to face. She felt sure that he was avoiding her but she did not know why. There was no sign that day of the shepherd on the hillside or on the track that linked Pennypol to the road. In fact, she encountered no one at all until she stepped through the door of the tiny shop at the main street's end and found herself confronted not only by Hector Thrale but also by Michael Tarrant.

There was hardly room for two customers let alone three in the space before the counter but the men and the collie had disposed themselves as best they could. The smell of damp flannel and wet oilskins mingled with the aroma of smoked meats, kippered fish and grain meals and the men seemed as tall as giants crammed under the low-beamed ceiling. Even Roy had had to make himself small. He was folded like a concertina on the sawdust between the sacks, crunching on a biscuit that Michael had thrown down for him. Thrale and the shepherd were drinking ginger beer, drawn from a smooth, blue-glazed bottle that stood like a tombstone at the counter's end. Old Miss Fergusson was wrapping something that looked suspiciously like pig's feet.

'Well now, Michael, if it is not pretty Miss Campbell,' Hector Thrale said, wiping his moustache with his knuckle and putting his pipe back in his mouth. 'Is that not a sight to be cheering a man's heart on a dismal afternoon?'

Innis glanced at Michael, who looked down at the sawdust.

'I will – I will – come back,' Innis stammered.

'Och, no, in you come,' Thrale said. 'As soon as my feet are wrapped up I will be away and will leave you young people to it.'

'Leave us to – to what?' said Innis.

Thrale winked. 'Do not tell me that it is coincidence that you are meeting like this. I expect you will be going back to the Solitudes for a nibble of bread and cheese when you are done here?'

'That's enough,' Michael said.

'I – I do not know what you are talking about, Mr Thrale.'

Another wink, to Miss Fergusson this time. 'Hah, they thought I did not know that they were sparking.' Thrale tapped his nose with the stem of his pipe. 'I am not one to be giving away your secrets, however.' He leaned towards Innis, so close that she could smell the meaty odour of his breath. 'Mum's the word, Innis Campbell. Mum is the word. It is not from me that your father will learn what is going on between you and our shepherd.'

'Nothing is going on between us,' Innis said.

'Is it not you who visits the Solitudes on quiet afternoons? Oh, come now, I am not such an old fuddy-duddy as all that. I have seen you there, Innis, and there is no good denying it.'

Michael growled, 'Enough, Thrale. You've said enough.'

Innis would have stepped out of the shop if Michael hadn't caught her by the hand. She felt herself go cold, cold all through at what Hector Thrale had revealed. She was aware of Miss Fergusson's withered face and beady-bright eyes peeping over the counter, of Michael's pale, pinched cheeks and the expression of abject horror that even he could not disguise.

'We are not so far gone that we cannot remember what it was like to while away the time with courting, are we, Miss Fergusson?' Thrale went on. But the woman had the decency not to answer and went back to stringing the package of pig's trotters as if her life depended upon it.

'It wasn't Innis,' Michael stated.

'If it was not Innis, who were you with that afternoon?'

'Nobody.' Michael's voice was so dead and hopeless that Innis could not bring herself to believe him. 'I don't know what you think you saw, Thrale, or who you imagined was with me but –

but—' He lost the sense of what he was saying. He could not defend the lie, could not deny one truth without uncovering another.

As if to protect the shepherd from further embarrassment, Miss Fergusson cleared her throat and said, 'I have your trotters ready, Mr Thrale. I am thinking that you should be taking them home while they are fresh.'

Thrale reached over the counter and lifted the brown paper parcel, already stained with blood, from her hands while Michael, chalk white, found his voice again. 'Is there *nothing* in this damned village that you don't know about?' he shouted. 'All of you, tattle-tattle-tattling away all the time. God, I tell you, I'm sick of it.' Then, snapping his fingers to the collie, he charged out of the door and leaped up the steps to the street.

'Well, now,' Hector Thrale said, 'if that is not the sign of a guilty conscience then I do not know what is.'

'Never seen the like, never seen the like.' Miss Fergusson shook her head like a gull with a limpet. 'I have never been so insulted in all my born days. He will not be coming into my shop again, I can be telling you.'

'Oh, you must make allowance for the poor fellow,' Thrale said. 'He is just sensitive, sensitive and passionate, a young man in love. Am I not right, Innis Campbell?'

'Why are you asking me?'

'Because you would know better than any of us,' Hector Thrale said, 'since you spend your afternoons with him at his cottage.'

The coldness had taken possession of her completely. She drew herself up. She tightened the rope around her waist, unslung the fishing bag and set it down upon the counter with a thump. 'That is a calumny, Mr Thrale,' she said. 'If I hear you repeat it to anyone then I will be reporting you to Mr Ewing and he will make a pronouncement against you from the pulpit.'

'You would not dare,' said Hector Thrale.

'Would I not now?' said Innis. 'One pound of Marsallis Indian tea, please, Miss Fergusson, and two cards of strong thread.'

'If it was not you who was sparking in the cottage with Tarrant,' Hector Thrale said, 'then who was it?'

'I neither know,' Innis said, 'nor do I care.'

But she did.

She both knew and cared very much.

She sat in the kitchen watching Donnie and Neil, both a little the worse for drink, spar and chuckle. Watching her mother weave restlessly in and out of the clothes that hung from the strings under the rafters. Watching her father, who was seated at the table, glass in hand, with Aileen on his knee. Watching Aileen smirk and wriggle, her eyes blue as kerosene, until Dada could no longer resist her childish pleas and gave her a finger-dab of whisky to moisten her lips. Watching Biddy who was curled up by the side of the fireplace, elbow on a cushion, a blanket under her thighs, exhibiting her long legs, her breasts ripe and heavy under her cotton bodice as she combed her long red hair. She looked, Innis thought, sullen and alluring, and petted and spoiled, her eyelids blue with fatigue and her lips bruised by Michael's kisses. It seemed to Innis that she had been looking at her sister in that same pose for most of her life and she could stand it not one minute longer.

She got to her feet and, ducking her head, walked from the shadowy alcove to the fireplace. Fingal glanced up, lifting his head from his paws but no other soul in the room paid her the slightest attention.

It was as if she did not exist for them, none of them.

She had a book in her hand, a volume of Scott's poems, her thumb stuck into the middle of it to mark her place. It was not her intention to create a scene or betray Biddy's secret in such spectacular fashion. She made for the ladder, would have reached it and gone up to bed without a word if Biddy had not suddenly and deliberately raised her leg to block the way. She, Biddy, did it without looking up, without checking the motion of the comb through her long shiny red hair. She just raised her leg, bent at the knee, to be annoying.

And that was all it took. Innis hit her with the book, a back-handed slap that sent the comb flying from Biddy's grasp.

'You cow,' Biddy screamed. 'You cow, Innis Campbell. What is that for?'

'You know what it is for.'

Innis made no move towards the ladder. She stood over Biddy, the book still hanging in her hand and, when Biddy scrambled

to drag her down, struck out again, slapping Biddy's other cheek.
'Because I won't let you pass?'

'Because you are bedding Michael Tarrant.'

Out of the corner of her eye she saw her mother stiffen, saw
her father slip Aileen from his knee. 'Innis,' Biddy said. 'Oh,
Innis!' and began to cry.

Vassie was first to find her voice. 'Is it true, Biddy?'

Biddy buried her head in her hands. Her hair cascaded over
her shoulders and hid her face. Then Innis was pushed aside,
sent reeling into the wall, as Ronan leaped forward, grabbed
Biddy by the hair and yanked her down on to her knees. 'Is this
true?' he yelled. 'Tell me the truth. Tell me or I will thrash it out
of you. Have you been taken by Michael Tarrant?'

Biddy's cheeks were scarlet, her mouth wide open. She
struggled to tear herself from her father's grasp but his fingers
were knotted in her hair. He crushed his forearm up into her
rib-cage so hard that she could hardly draw breath and he jerked
her head forward and back so violently that it seemed as if her
neck would break. 'Has – he – been – inside – you?'

'Dada, Dada, do not be hitting Biddy any more,' Aileen cried
and might have rushed forward if Neil had not scooped her in
against his knees.

'Did you open your legs for him? Tell me.'

He had been drunk all along, and none of them had noticed.

'Yes,' Biddy shouted. 'Yes, Yes.'

Whipping his arm from about her ribs he flung his weight
upon her, drove her down with such force that her brow and
cheekbone smashed against the hearthstone. He drew back and
kicked her. He steadied himself and drew back his foot and
would have kicked her again if Donnie had not lunged upon
him and, with an arm about his neck, hauled him bodily away.

Bleeding from nose and mouth, Biddy lay still. She seemed
oblivious to pain, however, and before Vassie could come to her
aid, swung herself up on one hand, spat out blood and cried,
'He wants me. Michael wants me. Do you not understand?'

'Aye, well, he had better want you,' Ronan shouted. 'For he
will have to have you for the rest of his damned life.'

He aimed another kick but she was too quick for him.
Maddened by his father's actions, Donnie dropped to the floor

like a wrestler and took Ronan down with him. For half a minute or more father and his son struggled for supremacy while Aileen wailed and Fingal barked and Vassie, her hands up to her head, screamed at them to stop. The fight ended with Donnie astride his father's chest, pinning him down. Ronan's eyes were like coals of fire. Foam flecked the corners of his lips. He looked, Innis thought, more like an animal than a man. She had no pity for him, only loathing.

Biddy was on her feet. She crouched over, blood dripping from her broken lip and nostrils, smearing her face like war-paint. There was no contrition in her, no shame. She swayed and shouted, 'I will go to him tonight. He will take me in and you will never see me again.' She leaned into Vassie, panting, and let her mother lift her up and lead her to a chair at the table. Ronan was yelling incoherently, Aileen screeching and Fingal, denied his place at the hearth, barked and barked until Neil, with Aileen tucked under his arm, flung open the door to let night air flood into the room and the dog rush out.

Innis lowered herself down against the wall. She made herself as small and inconspicuous as possible. She would have wept, except that there were no tears in her. She observed the drama as if she had no part in it at all.

The wind flung pearly spots of rain through the doorway into the lamplight. Neil put Aileen down. The girl-child, still wailing, ran this way and that in a state of distraction until, like Fingal, she found the open door and darted out into the rain. Donnie lifted himself away from his father. 'Touch Biddy again,' he said, 'and I will break both your arms and where will you be then with your boat?'

Ronan hoisted himself to his feet and, without a word, stalked out of the cottage and vanished into the darkness. Vassie nodded, as if this was precisely what she had expected of her husband, and said, 'Innis, fetch me a bowl of warm water and the cotton.'

'I am going to be with Michael. I am going to him tonight,' Biddy said.

'No, you are not,' Donnie said.

'Who are you to tell me . . .'

'Do you want to go to him as you are?' Vassie said. 'Look at you. He will not be taking in a scarecrow to live with him.'

'Michael won't care.'

'Aye, but he will,' said Donnie. 'We will go tomorrow when we have thought about it calmly. I will come with you. We will make an arrangement for your marriage.'

'My – my marriage?' Biddy said.

'You are not carrying his child, are you?' Vassie asked.

Biddy shook her head.

'Are you certain?'

'I am certain,' Biddy told her, then pain gripped her. She winced and groaned and rocked upon the chair, her lips already beginning to swell, a great reddening bruise spreading across her cheekbone. She slumped forward across the table, her head on her arms. 'I did not mean to marry him. I did not mean to do anything. It is not Michael's fault. It is my fault. I do not know what is wrong with me. I cannot . . .'

'Hush now,' Vassie said. 'It is done. It cannot be taken back again. You cannot be as you were, Biddy, so we must make sure that he understands what he must do to make it right.'

'He will marry me.'

'No,' said Vassie. 'What he must do to make it right is promise never to talk of it to anyone, never to be alone with you again.'

'But, Mam, he will want to marry . . .'

'He is only a hired shepherd,' Vassie said. 'He will never amount to anything. No, Biddy, he is not for you.'

'But I want . . .'

Now came anger, a thin, piercing note in Vassie's voice and a restless waving of her arms. 'You have done us enough harm without bringing more down upon us.' She took the cotton that Innis had brought to the table, dipped it in the bowl of clean water and applied it to Biddy's nose. 'The shepherd will be told what is to be done and he will abide by what we tell him.' She removed the swab, wiped Biddy's nostrils with the corner of a towel. 'You are not in love with him, Biddy, are you?'

And, to Innis's astonishment, Biddy answered, 'No.'

That was not the end of that night of trouble, only the beginning.

Shock soon took its toll on Biddy. She sobbed uninhibitedly. Vassie comforted her and said no more about Michael Tarrant or what would happen tomorrow. She gave Biddy tea and a spoonful of powdered valerian and helped her up the ladder to the loft where Innis had placed one of the stone 'pigs' filled with hot water to warm the mattress.

Next Vassie sent Neil and Donnie out to find Aileen and fetch her back indoors. She gave no instruction concerning Ronan, for Vassie did not care where her husband had gone to lick his wounds. Innis did everything that her mother told her to do without comment. She felt guilty at having betrayed Biddy. Tomorrow Vassie would arrange a meeting with Michael in the course of which he would be forced to admit that he had seduced Biddy. Perhaps he would offer to marry her and perhaps Vassie, on Biddy's behalf, would refuse.

Scandal was no novelty in the parish of Crove. Bundlings, seductions, jealous rages, hastily arranged marriages, absconding husbands, unwanted pregnancies had provided the islanders with gossip down through the years. Hector Thrale would soon spread the word of Biddy's downfall and Vassie would have to act swiftly to protect her daughter's reputation.

Innis realised that she too was bound to be affected by the rumours and she worried that Mr Ewing would think ill of her because of it. She would hardly dare to show her face in church for the next few months for she, as well as Biddy, would surely have to put up with snubs and whisperings while the congregation peeped at her belly and counted the weeks on their fingers until it became clear that somehow Michael Tarrant had got away with it. She found that she did not much care. They could think what they liked about her and say whatever came into their empty heads. She had one good thing to hold on to – Biddy's admission that while Michael might be her lover he was not her true love.

She sipped tea and watched her mother wash and put away the bowl and dispose of the bloody cotton. She tried to think rationally about what had happened, to bring her emotions under control. Vassie was stiff with her now. She did not interrogate her but glanced at her out of the side of her eyes, dark, fierce, accusing looks that Innis did her best to ignore.

At length, Vassie said, 'Where are they?' She pulled open the door and called out, 'Donnie, Aileen, where are you?' There was no answer from the darkness. Then Fingal padded into the kitchen and flopped down before the fire. He looked up at Vassie, yawned, lowered his head, tucked his snout between his paws and appeared to fall asleep. 'Aileen, come in now. Aileen?'

Neil was next to appear. He loomed out of the darkness, his shirt clinging to his muscular frame, his fair hair plastered to his skull.

'Did you not find her?' Vassie asked anxiously.

Neil shook his head.

'Is she not in the byre?'

Neil shook his head again.

Innis handed him a cup of hot tea. 'Is she not with Father?'

'No, Dada is in the byre but she is not with him,' Neil said. 'Donnie has taken the storm lantern and gone out to look for her.'

Vassie said, 'Have all the buildings been looked at?'

'Aye,' Neil said. 'That is what has taken us so long.'

'She must be hiding,' said Vassie. 'She would not be running far off on a night like this.'

'Have you been down to the boat?' Innis asked.

'What would she be doing down at the boat?'

'Who knows with Aileen?' Innis said and, tugging a shawl from the drying rope and unhooking one of the lanterns, hurried out into the night.

She went first to the byre, for it occurred to her that it would be typical of her father to hide Aileen there just to add to Vassie's burden of concern. She opened the byre door and, with the lantern held out before her, looked in.

He was lying against a straw bale, grinning, a bottle in his fist.

'Do you think I have her?' he said. 'Well, I tell you I do not.' He beckoned. 'Why do you not come here and keep me company, dearest? I will give you a dram to keep you warm. And if that is not enough for you I will give you a cuddle.'

'Aileen is lost.'

'Let the boys look for her. The boys will find her. Come here, sweetheart. I am in sore need of your company after what has happened tonight.' He beckoned again, lost balance, slipped and sprawled into the shallow stone gutter, saying, 'Oh, Jesus! I am worse than I thought.' Innis pulled back and was on the point of closing the door when he called out, 'Innis, Innis. Here, Innis. See.'

He propped himself up. His jacket was smeared with cattle slitter. His legs stuck out before him like those of a monstrous child who has not yet acquired the ability to walk. 'I – I know – I can tell you where Aileen has gone.'

'Tell me then.'

'A kiss first, my sweetheart. A kiss for your poor old dada.'

Innis stepped back in disgust and closed the door behind her as her father roared, 'She will have gone to find the shepherd, to have a taste of what her sister got. She will have gone to be served by the Baverstocks' ram, that is where she will be, under, under the damned shepherd.' Innis turned and ran.

It was raining heavily now. It hissed on the crown of the storm lantern as she dithered by the new wall, not knowing which way to turn. After a minute or two, however, she saw Donnie's light glimmering through the rain and hurried down the slope of the park to meet him as he came up from the shore.

'Is she not at the boat?' Innis called out.

'No.'

'Perhaps she has gone to Michael's cottage?'

'Why would she go there?'

'To – to tell him what has happened.'

'She would not tell him anything of the sort, Innis.' Donnie stood close to her, the lantern raised. 'If she told anyone it would be the people under the hill.'

'At Dun Fidra, do you mean?'

'Aye.'

The ruins of the old fort were Aileen's summer refuge and Innis felt sure that her sister could find her way there even in the dark.

The fort was not far away. It lay beyond the end of the high shore, just across the burn, and a straggling little path led up to it. As Donnie and she approached they could hear the rush of the burn, swollen with winter rains, the wind howling about the stones and the sea, not far below, pounding on the rocks. Innis's anxiety turned to fear, almost to panic. She could not understand why Aileen had run from the house in the first place. It was not the first quarrel that the girl-child had witnessed. What

particular aspect of Biddy's revelation had thrown Aileen's mind
out of kilter Innis could not begin to imagine.

'She is not here, Donnie. Perhaps she has fallen over . . .'

'Wait, wait,' her brother shouted. 'I will look properly. Hold
both lanterns and light me down.'

The ring of stones glistened in the flickering light. Innis knelt
on the grass and watched her brother slither down the muddy
ramp that led to the trench where once, a thousand years ago or
more, watchmen had cowered round a wood fire and snuggled
under their cloaks. She saw the ledge upon which her sister
placed her summer offerings, withered sprigs of sea-pinks and
heather, shells and fish bones, and wondered if Aileen had
offered herself up to propitiate those ancient spirits who, for
her sister, had taken the place of God.

Holding a lantern at arm's length, Innis peered down into the
pit. She could see Donnie well enough and there, cowering
against the stones, Aileen, her face as tiny and white as a
snowdrop.

'Well, well,' Donnie said, gently. 'What are you doing out here,
wee lass?'

Aileen shrank back from him, drawing herself into a ball as if
she were trying to sink into the earth, as if the earth would
protect her.

'It's me, Aileen. It is Donnie. I have come to take you back.'

He reached down. Aileen did not resist. She went limp at his
touch, her eyes rolling back in her head.

Donnie continued to talk while he braced himself, wriggled
his hands under her and brought her up to him. He sounded like
Grandfather, not Father; a soft-voiced McIver, without guile or
cunning. 'Mam is worried about you. She thought you were lost.
It is time you were in your bed, my wee lass, all warm in your
bed. There is nothing to worry about now, nothing to worry
about.' He lifted her slowly, patiently, supporting her with his
chest and shoulders until Innis, the lantern laid behind her, could
grasp Aileen's waist and hands and ease her out of the hiding
place. She laid her down on the grass and, taking the shawl from
her shoulders, wrapped it around her sister. She put a hand to
Aileen's cheek which was marble cold, another to her brow
which was burning.

'Donnie, she is sick. I think she has a fever.'

'We will get her home soon.' Donnie grunted as he hauled himself out of the trench. 'Vassie will know what to do.' He knelt over Aileen and gave her a little shake. 'Aileen. Aileen? What is wrong with you?'

Her eyes flicked open.

'Baba,' she said, quite distinctly. 'Bab-baba.'

'What?'

She smiled at Donnie, said again, 'Bab-baba,' and went on repeating the meaningless phrase until Donnie gathered her into his arms and, with Innis leading the way, set off through the rain for home.

Willy told them he was dying but nobody seemed to believe him. It was not that the members of the household were unconcerned. They were very concerned. In fact, it was their anxiety that had first alerted Willy to the seriousness of his condition. God knows, he felt bad enough. He would be lucky to make it through the night. He was *even* beginning to think that dying might be preferable to shivering, sweating and aching in every joint and sinew.

The fever had attacked him without warning in the course of an otherwise uneventful afternoon; a roughness in the throat, a tickle in the chest, a bit of a headache, nothing much. He tried to brush it off but within a couple of hours he felt as if he had an axe blade buried in the middle of his forehead and was shaking so violently that he could hardly unbutton his waistcoat let alone his breeks. He would have collapsed upon his bed in the downstairs cubby if Margaret had not insisted that Mr Baverstock be informed and a local boy sent to fetch Dr Kirkhope.

Next thing Willy knew he was being helped up the back stairs, across the great hall and up the main stair to the first floor. He had a vague impression that Mr Austin was stooped under one of his arms and Maggie under the other; a clearer impression of Mrs McQueen's broad bottom preceding him as she carried a clean night-shirt, towels and a big, china chamber-pot upstairs.

'I – I can't put you to . . .' he mumbled.

'Hush, William. Of course you can.'

The genteel Edinburgh voice had been comforting as Willy

had limped up that interminable staircase and along the passage that led off the gallery. He suffered a nightmarish impression of height, of the hall falling away below, the log fire under the stone arch becoming tinier and tinier, of Odin and Thor peering up at him as if they were awaiting a supernatural sign that it was time to set up a mournful howling.

He was ushered into the big guest bedroom where a fire had been lighted. Queenie turned down the bed. Maggie undressed him. He was far too sick to be embarrassed and when she said, 'Hold up your arms,' he obeyed without protest. When he felt the warm flannel night-shirt sheath his nakedness he groaned with relief, rolled on to the feather mattress and lay like a corpse while Maggie tucked the bedclothes up to his chin.

'Poor Willy. Poor, poor Willy,' Mrs McQueen intoned in a teary voice. 'I'll fetch him a hot sock for his throat and an infusion for to break his sweat.'

'Would a hot toddy do him any harm, d'you think?' Mr Austin asked.

The genteel Edinburgh accent reminded him now of healthier times, of strutting down George Street to visit his masters or, as he drifted into hallucination, of Agnes Baverstock Paul's occasional unladylike enquiry into the state of his male member. 'No, no, Mrs Baverstock Paul,' he groaned. 'I shouldn't. I really shouldn't.'

'What?' said Austin.

'Who?' said Margaret Bell.

'Dear me! I believe he's talking to my sister Agnes.'

'The fever must have him confused,' said Mrs McQueen and, because she had heard rumours about Willy and the lady of Sangster, hastily clapped an ice-cold compress to the patient's nose, an action which restored him to full if temporary consciousness. 'I think a hot toddy might be just the ticket, Mr Austin, if you don't mind makin' him one.'

'Yes. Yes, of course.' Austin scampered off downstairs.

Mrs McQueen peeled the cloth from Willy's face and brushed his brow with her fingertips which Willy thought felt oddly floury, as if she were dusting him down to pop into the oven. She whispered, 'Ssshhh, Mr Naismith. Ssshhh. Try no' tae talk in your sleep.'

'Wha – what have I been sayin'?'

'Nothin' much as yet,' said the cook. 'But I think I'll suggest leavin' Margaret here to look after you while I tak' Mr Austin away.'

'Margaret?' said Willy, dreamily. 'Margaret?'

'I'm here, Willy.'

'Maggie, my bonnie Maggie.' His head rolled on the pillow. His yellow eyeballs rolled up under his lids as if he had been possessed of an ecstatic revelation. 'Oh, Maggie, Maggie, let me kiss your bonnie lips, your . . .' His voice trailed off into a mumble and Margaret, thrusting shyness aside, slid past the cook and, on the pretence of checking Willy's breathing, pressed her ear close to his mouth while he sighed and muttered incoherently.

'Oh!' she said, very softly. 'Oh, dear.'

'What did he say?' Queenie asked.

Blushing slightly, shy Margaret shook her head.

Soon after, mercifully, Dr Kirkhope turned up. He pronounced Willy the victim of an ardent fever, replaced the toddy with a bitter concoction and six analgesic powders, advised against aggravating the patient's mind with religious terrors – whatever that meant – and left again.

Maggie held the patient while Austin wielded the spoon.

Willy swallowed the bitter medicines and, soon after, drifted safely off into the Land of Nod.

She took the girl behind the curtain and stripped her to the skin. With Biddy asleep in the loft and Ronan still out in the byre it was the most suitable place for Vassie to make the examination while Donnie and Neil dried themselves in front of the fire. There was nothing to indicate what was going on behind the curtain, except the murmur of voices and, once, just once, Aileen's strange little cry of 'Ba-ba-baba,' as if her nocturnal experiences had transformed her into a ewe.

'Where was she?' Neil said.

'Hiding in the Dun,' Donnie answered.

'Why did she go there?'

'Lord knows.'

'Is she sick?'

'She has always been sick.'

'I do not mean in the head, Donnie. I mean, is she really sick?'

'How the hell would I know?'

'All right. Keep your hair on. After what we heard from Biddy . . .'

'Shut your mouth, Neil,' Donnie said.

' . . . nothing would surprise me.'

'Shut your damned mouth.'

It was as if Donnie had guessed the reason for Aileen's distress. Innis listened to her brothers with acute unease, an inexplicable feeling that what had gone before would count as nothing compared to what might come next. Whatever wilful urges had driven Biddy into Michael Tarrant's bed could be controlled by reason and put behind her. With Aileen, though, there was no reason, no self-control and, as far as Innis could make out, no awareness of past and future, of cause and consequence.

The silence in the kitchen was oppressive. The boys huddled by the fire, sipping lukewarm tea and, for once, not arguing. They too, it seemed, were paralysed by the same uncertainty that gripped Innis.

All three waited, mute and brooding, for Vassie to reappear. Five minutes passed, then ten before Vassie parted the curtain and came out into the kitchen. She carried Aileen's wet clothes in her arms. Saying not a word, she shook them out and hung them, one item at a time, on the drying rope. She carried the girl-child's shoes, pathetically small, pinched by the heels and, stooping between Donnie and Neil, laid them carefully up the edge of the hearthstone.

In a voice so low as to be barely audible, Donnie asked, 'How is she?'

'I have put her into my bed. She will sleep with me.'

'Is she fevered?'

'No.'

'Is she not sick then?' Neil asked.

'She's with child,' Vassie said.

'No,' Donnie said, shaking his head in denial. 'No, no. She cannot be.'

'With child?' Neil said stupidly.

'Are you sure, Mother?' Innis whispered.

'I think she is about five months gone.'

'Hold on,' said Neil. 'I thought Biddy said . . .'

'Not Biddy, you idiot,' Donnie said.

'You don't mean – Jesus! Aileen? She's only – I mean . . .' Neil shot to his feet. 'I will kill that damned, filthy shepherd with my own bare hands.'

'Be quiet, Neil,' Vassie said, in a small, cold voice. 'You will be doing nothing. It is not your concern.'

'She is my sister – and if that shepherd . . .'

'It is not the shepherd,' Vassie said.

'Did she tell you who it was?' Donnie said.

'She does not know who it was.'

'Oh, God! God in heaven! She *must* know who it was,' Neil protested. 'She is not so far gone in the head as all that. I mean, who would be doing such a thing to a half-wit?'

'There is no father,' Vassie told him.

'What are you saying?'

'Aileen's child has no father. Do you understand?'

'And there is no baby either, I suppose,' Neil said.

'Yes, there is a baby,' Vassie said. 'But there is no father, none that we need to be knowing about. Do you understand me?'

'What is this?' Neil said, suspiciously.

Donnie had clasped his brother's thigh and squeezed it hard. 'Listen to what Mother is telling you.'

'The baby will be born when its time comes,' Vassie stated, 'and then we will take them both away.'

'To Foss?' Innis said.

'Yes,' Vassie said. 'To Foss.'

'So nobody will know of it,' Neil said. 'Well, that is all fine and well but what of the man who did it to her? Surely, he must be made to pay.'

'Oh, he will pay,' Vassie promised.

'Then you do know who it is?' Neil said.

Vassie hesitated.

'Whoever it is,' she said, 'he'll pay.'

In summer it would have been dawn but in mid-winter it was still the dead heart of the night when Vassie left her children and, with a blanket thrown over her shoulders, slipped out of the cottage and around to the byre. She was moved by no sense of irony that two of her daughters were suffering at precisely the same time. Deep within her, perhaps, she felt that she was receiving no more than she deserved for capitulating to Ronan Campbell all those years ago. She had known from the outset that he was after a share of her father's land and that what he did to her on the sands on a bright, cloud-scudding afternoon was done less out of love than for the gain that might accrue to him because of it.

She had been in love with him, though, madly in love with him. She had listened to no one, not to her stepmother, not to her father, not to her sister, Stella, who had still been on the island in those days. She had listened to nobody except Ronan Campbell who told her all the things she had longed to hear and did all the things that she wanted a man to do, even though she knew that more than half of what he said was lies.

She had never been a beauty like her mother, never a beauty like Biddy was now. She had been leathery and stick-thin, too ugly to have choice in anything she did or to be loved by anyone but her father, who loved everything. She had been pregnant with Donnie before marriage and her wedding had been a sad and furtive affair because Ronan had squabbled with her father by that time and she had sided with the fisherman.

She had lived with that wrong choice ever since. She had been compensated by the birth of her children and the flourishing of Pennypol but punished by her husband's idleness, his wickedness. She had watched him beat her children and had put up with his demands upon her. She had become the scapegoat for his rage, had been blamed because she could not perform the miracle that would make him not only rich but important. But now, by God, he had gone too far and in future he would live in fear of her, of what she might know and what she might tell. Her rage was cold and violent. She would have murdered him there and then without a qualm of conscience if it had not been for her children, who needed her more than ever.

She lit the candle in the lantern with a match from the box. The light brought the calf to the rail. It still was too young to be wintered out, too young to be roped or chained. It stuck its moist black nose through the gap between the rail and the floor and stared at her out of liquid brown eyes. It lowed softly when

Vassie, hip pressed against the rail, let it nuzzle the palm of her hand.

Ronan lay at her feet, unmoving. He had rolled out of the straw into the gutter. His head rested on his forearm which was crooked against the gutter's shallow rim. Thin trickles of calf dung and urine had wetted more than his jacket. In the chill air his breath hung in a frosty cloud.

She might have smothered him with a fistful of straw, stuffing it down his throat until he choked. She might have rolled him over and pressed his face into the slitter until he drowned. The magistrates or the constable from Tobermory or whoever was sent to inspect the remains would reckon that he had died in a drunken stupor, had reaped no more than he had sown.

The calf, silent now, watched her, its jaw moving softly on the cud, its glossy brown eyes uncomprehending.

The sack was damp and stank of sour meal. She kneaded the sack in both fists, moulded it into a pad. Ronan stank too. He reeked of whisky and urine and he had been sick, a little, down the lapel of his jacket. She bent closer and, with the calf as her only witness, whispered her husband's name.

He opened his eyes. There was no comprehension, no recognition. They were as brown as the calf's eyes and, Vassie thought, just as vacant. He rolled on to his side and, groaning, closed his eyes again. She sat back on her haunches and, crying out in anger at her own weakness, tore the blanket from her shoulders and draped it over him to keep him warm.

Then, still trembling with anger, she blew out the candle and went back to lie with Aileen in the narrow alcove bed next door.

He had no idea what time it was or what day. He opened his eyes cautiously and discovered that the axe-blade headache had gone. He felt weak, very weak, but lucid. He stirred, eased himself on to his hip and looked out into the strange bedroom which, lit only by firelight and a solitary wax candle, seemed vast. Conscious of rain beating on the window panes and of darkness outside, he stirred again, and blinked. She was seated on an upright chair close to the bed, a small floral cushion supporting her spine. She was dozing, hands folded in her lap, her white bonnet prim and trim on her head. Dreamily, he watched her bosom rise and fall and when she gave a little sigh Willy involuntarily matched it.

She opened her eyes instantly. 'Oh, Willy.' She reached out and touched his brow with the back of her hand. 'Oh, Willy, how do you feel now?'

'Not so bad.'

'I'm thinking that your fever's down.'

'Aye.'

'I'll be making up your medicine.'

'What time is it?'

'After two.'

'Have you been sitting up with me all this while?'

'How could I sleep when you were so ill?'

'Maggie . . .'

Whatever had been in the brown concoction that Dr Kirkhope had prescribed had not rendered him muzzy. He had never been so lucid in his life. Everything seemed magnified. Every detail of the grand guest bedroom, every fold on the sheet, every tiny stitch of Maggie's dress was thrown into sharp relief. Even the teardrops that clung to her lashes.

She wiped her eyes with her knuckles. 'I'll get your medicine now.'

'No,' he said. 'No, just - just hold my hand, Margaret, please.' And she did.

Dear God! Willy thought. What's happening to me? I'm falling in love with shy Margaret Bell? I really must be sick after all.

'What is it, Willy?'

'Nothing,' he said, sinking back against the pillow.

'What? Tell me.'

'Maggie, don't leave me. Please don't leave me.'

And Maggie, brushing away another tear, promised that she never would.

SEVEN

The Parting of the Ways

The boys had gone to the boat, the girls were in the dairy and Vassie and Ronan were alone in the cottage.

The cold in the byre had eventually roused Ronan from his stupor and he had crawled into the cottage more dead than alive. Finding Aileen in his bed space he had lacked the strength to oust her. He had dragged a blanket from the bed and had wrapped himself in it and, still wet and stinking, had lain on the floor of the alcove and had fallen asleep again.

He had slept through breakfast, a sullen meal, and had not wakened until after ten o'clock. Vassie was standing over him. She was braced against the bed-end with a half-glass of whisky in her hand.

Ronan sat up, peered at her bleakly, took the glass and emptied it.

Vassie said, 'You will wash yourself. You will come and eat your breakfast and then I will talk to you.'

'Will you?' he croaked. 'I have work to . . .'

'Aileen is pregnant.'

A pause: 'Do you not mean Biddy?'

'I mean Aileen.'

'I see,' he said.

'You will wash yourself and you will eat your breakfast.'

He pushed himself up from the floor. He crouched between the bed-end and the wall and stripped to the skin. He went under the curtain into the kitchen and stepped into the tub that Vassie had placed before the fire. He washed himself with soap and a rough cloth, turning this way and that, an arm raised and then

195

a leg as if he were proud of his physique. He showed no sign of whisky sickness – but then he seldom did.

He did not ask where the children were and said not a word about Aileen. He caught the towel that Vassie threw at him. He dried himself down and put on the clean clothing that Vassie had draped across a chair while she lifted the tub, staggered outside with it and emptied its contents into the weeds. By the time she returned he was seated at the table, bottle and glass to hand.

Still he said nothing. He watched her, though, following her with his gaze as she gathered his soiled garments and stuffed them into a basket in the corner. He watched her ladle porridge into a bowl and set it before him. Still watching her, he ate the porridge and bread dipped in hot ham fat with two eggs broken over it and drank a cup of strong black tea. He watched her lift crockery and put it on the stones by the hearth. Watched her wipe her hands on her apron, smooth her dress and adjust the little cotton cap that she wore indoors. Watched her step to the door and drop the latch. She seated herself opposite him. She was still now, devoid of her usual restless energy. That worried him. He reached for the whisky bottle. She pulled it from him. He did not protest.

'It would seem,' Vassie said, 'that we have not done well by our children.'

'*Is* Aileen pregnant?'

'Aye.'

'Who else knows of it?'

'Nobody outside of the family.'

'Do you think it is my fault?' Ronan said.

'I do not know whose fault it is.'

'There is nothing to be done about it, I suppose.'

'Aye, but there is,' Vassie said. 'In a week or two I will send Innis to tell my father what has happened.'

'Oh, so you will be packing Aileen off to Foss, will you?'

'No, not until after the baby is born. She will be needing me with her.'

'McIver can surely take care of her. God knows, he has women enough on his island who can midwife a birth.'

'I intend to keep Aileen here,' Vassie stated. 'Afterwards she will go to stay with my dada out of harm's way, if he will accept her.'

Ronan hesitated. 'Who does Aileen say that the father is?'

'She says that she does not know.'

'I see.'

Vassie said, 'I will keep her here by me until she is delivered in the hope that she might remember who fathered her child.'

'Does she even know and, if she does, will she tell?'

'If she tells anyone she will tell me.'

'And what will you do with the knowledge?'

'I will keep it to myself.'

'Aye, that is the sensible thing to be doing,' Ronan said.

'That is how it will be.'

'So, before the summer's out, Aileen will be gone from us too?'

'Yes.'

'What about Biddy?'

Vassie drew the whisky glass across the table, poured from the bottle and pushed the half-filled glass towards him. He wrapped his fingers round it but did not drink. 'What about Biddy?' Vassie said.

'I am thinking I will take Neil and Donnie and we will be visiting Mr Tarrant and will make him understand where his responsibilities lie.'

'You will be doing nothing of the sort,' Vassie said.

'Is it your intention to let Tarrant off with it?'

Vassie stared straight at him.

He opened his mouth to protest, thought better of it, lowered his gaze to the glass and swirled the liquid around in silence.

Vassie said, 'I will call on Michael Tarrant this afternoon. I will be taking Donnie with me. Just Donnie.'

'Is it not a father's right to protect his children?'

'Donnie will speak for his sister.'

'Am I not to be given my place in this, Vassie?'

It was so unnaturally quiet in the kitchen that Ronan could almost hear his heart beat.

'Do you know where your place is now?' Vassie said at length.

'It is to stand up for my children.'

'Your place is in hell, Ronan Campbell.'

The Island Wife

He took in a long breath.

'Do you hear me?' she said.

'I hear you, Vassie. I hear you,' Ronan said and then, at last, tossed off the whisky in his glass, down to the dregs.

He was too drunk to use the spear-shaped blade. Wisely, Neil took it from him and hid it under a tangle of old rope. In any case, the bucket of clams was almost cleaned out. Even the gulls had had their fill. They had swooped in on the south-west wind to pick at the empty shells and devour the small slippery shellfish that Neil had tossed to them.

Father and son were huddled in the bottom of the boat. She tossed up and down on the mooring rope that linked her to the jetty, her planking protected by great knots of coconut matting draped over the gunwale. The tide was full now and the waves formed a slick pale green coating over the top of the jetty and broke, booming, along the line of the beach.

Neil's hands were raw with salt water.

Working the knife for so long had damaged even his callus-hardened fingers and they bled a little. Between whiles he would suck them, tasting shell-grit and blood, sucking and spitting, working the knife until there was nothing left to do and he slumped forward, the oilskin tight across his broad back. He was angry that his mother had taken Donnie with her to visit the shepherd. He did not care what his father had done, or what the women said he had done, Dada should be given his rightful place.

Neil did not want to be here, tethered within sight of the cottage that smelled of women. He wanted to be out beyond the skerries, sail stiff and ropes singing, his father at the rudder, his brother feeding out the long lines from the tubs. He wanted to have heard none of what he had heard, the woman thing, and to have to imagine what it might mean. But he could not escape its consequences, not here on the shore or, he guessed, out there on the sea.

He sucked on his fist and spat.

He watched a herring-gull come swooping in, broad wings spread, its eyes beady with greed, its beak wide open so that he could see the pink within. It jeered at him, lifted again and soared away on the wind.

'Neil?'

'What is it that you want?'

'Neil?'

'What?'

'Did Aileen say anything?'

'About what?'

'About me?'

'I have not spoken to her. She has been hanging on to Mam all day.'

'What did she tell you last night?'

'She told us nothing.'

'Has she not said who fathered her child?'

Neil snorted. 'She says it was the fairy king.'

'Maybe she means the devil?' Ronan said. 'If she says any-thing . . .'

'You will be the first to know,' Neil promised and, sticking the knife into the seat, fished a clam from the bucket and tossed it up for the herring-gulls to pluck cleverly out of the air.

'Do you know why we have come to call on you, Mr Tarrant?' Vassie asked, a second after the shepherd had admitted them.

Michael took Vassie's shawl and Donnie's oilskin and hung them neatly on pegs behind the door. 'I think I might be able to guess.'

Although it was only five in the afternoon the fire in the grate burned brightly and the room shone like a new pin. Even the collie lay tidily in a shallow basket by the side of the fireplace, nose resting on the rim, eyes bright and alert.

Michael had been about to start his evening meal when the Campbells had arrived at his door. He had set the table with a cloth folded in half, a water glass and a jug of milk. He had put out a bowl of boiled potatoes and an oval plate with a two haddock upon it.

The savoury smell reminded Donnie how hungry he was. He longed to have this embarrassing ordeal over and go home for his supper.

Tarrant wore a clean striped shirt and a leather waistcoat and looked, Donnie thought, too thin to be healthy.

'Will you take a seat by the fire, Mrs Campbell?' Michael

Tarrant said. 'I will make us all tea as soon as the kettle boils.'

'I'm thinking that tea will not be necessary, Mr Tarrant.'

'Perhaps I should put my supper into the oven.'

'Aye, perhaps you should.'

Mother and son watched as the shepherd covered the dishes with cheesecloth, tugged open the door of the oven that stood in against the iron grate and slipped the dishes inside. He closed the door not with his foot but with a forefinger, quickly and neatly.

Vassie said, 'Biddy has told us what has taken place between you.'

'I thought that would be it,' Michael Tarrant said.

He returned to his place behind the table, pulled out a chair and seated himself upon it.

He looked, Donnie thought, far too calm and cool for a man who had just been accused of fornication. If he had been confronted by the MacNivens and charged with such a thing he would have been squirming like a crab on a griddle. But then he would never have got himself into such a mess. Muriel and he had too much sense to do what Biddy and the shepherd had done. He swallowed the hard lump in his throat that was neither anger nor pity, and let his mother make the running.

'Do you not deny it?' Vassie said.

'I will deny it if you wish,' Michael Tarrant said. 'But what would be the point? I assume that Biddy was discovered returning from one of our meetings. It was always a risk.'

'A risk?' said Vassie. 'Do you not think that it was wrong of you to take advantage of a young and innocent girl?'

'Biddy is hardly a girl and she certainly isn't . . .' He frowned slightly. 'Biddy was not unwilling, Mrs Campbell.'

'How many times?'

'Several,' the shepherd admitted.

'Do you not realise that you might have made her pregnant?'

'She isn't pregnant,' Michael said. 'If you tell me that she is I won't believe you.'

'It is not my intention to trick you, Mr Tarrant,' Vassie said. 'I am not going to tell you falsehoods like those you have told to my daughter.'

'Falsehoods? What do you mean?'

'Biddy says that you will not marry her.'

'No, no,' Michael Tarrant said sharply. '*She* won't marry *me*.'

'Have you asked her?' Donnie heard himself say.

'I did not have to ask her.'

'So you *will* marry her?' Donnie said.

'What does it have to do with you?' Michael Tarrant said. 'Can Biddy not be trusted to speak for herself?'

'Biddy is too much under your influence, Mr Tarrant,' Vassie said. 'We have not come here to threaten you. It is our intention to thrash things out in a calm and rational manner.'

'Without consulting Biddy's wishes in the matter?'

'Biddy wants no more to do with you.'

'Did Biddy say that?'

'Biddy will do as she's told,' Donnie blurted out. 'We are here to see that you do right by her.'

'Right? What's that?'

'Marriage,' Donnie said.

'Very well,' Michael said. 'If Biddy will have me, I will marry her.'

Vassie stiffened and glanced at her son. It seemed as if the argument was over and that Michael Tarrant had shown himself to be more honourable than Biddy anticipated he would be.

'But,' Michael went on, 'I'll have to hear Biddy say it before I make any promises.'

'Say what?' Donnie asked.

'That she wants to marry me.'

'Do you think that she will refuse?' Donnie said.

'I don't think that Biddy's in love with me, if that's what you mean.'

'Are you not in love with her?' Donnie said, his voice rising.

'No – and I never have been.'

'But you will marry her,' Donnie said, more statement than question.

'If she will have me,' Michael Tarrant repeated.

'She will have you if we tell her that there is no other choice.'

'No,' Vassie said. 'I will not be encouraging my daughter to marry a man who despises her.'

'I don't despise her,' Michael said. 'I just do not love her.'

'And yet you would – would lie with her?' Donnie said.

'Look,' Michael said, 'even if Biddy was in love with me, I doubt if you would be willing to accept me as a suitable husband for her.'

'Why not?' Donnie said. 'What's wrong with you? For God's sake, man, do not be telling me that you are diseased.'

'No, I'm not diseased.'

'Then you have a wife?'

'No wife.'

'What is it then?' Donnie shouted.

Vassie sat up very straight, the tip of her tongue showing on her nether lip. In the basket by her side Roy growled faintly and pricked up his ears as Michael Tarrant reached beneath the table, pulled open a drawer and brought out a string of beads. He threw them down upon the tablecloth.

'This,' he said.

Donnie said, 'What does a necklace have to do with . . .'

'Not enough for you?'

Michael tugged at his collar stud and unbuttoned his shirt to expose his hairless chest. The silver chain was so delicate as to be almost invisible, the ornament so small and fine that it snuggled undetected against his breastbone. He treated it more gently than he had done the rosary. With the ball of his thumb against the shaft he held out the crucifix.

'How about this then, Donnie?' he said. 'Even you know what this is.'

'My God!' Donnie exclaimed, recoiling. 'You're a Papist.'

'A Roman Catholic,' Michael said, 'and proud of it.'

'I might have known it!' Donnie said. 'Only a stinking Papist would have had the gall to rob my sister of her innocence and not be sorry for what he had done. Did some bloody priest tell you it was all right? Did the Pope forgive you because Biddy's a Protestant?' He was on his feet, shouting. 'I hope you rot in hell, Tarrant, you and your whole Papist crew.'

'I take it that you no longer wish me to marry Biddy? I will, you know,' Michael said. 'I will marry her. But only if she converts.'

'Converts?'

'To Catholicism,' Michael said.

'I'll see her dead first,' Donnie cried.

* * *

'Well, that is that then, is it not?' Neil said. 'If Tarrant is a Pape then he cannot come into our family and he cannot be marrying Biddy.'

'Oh, so it is for you to say, is it?' Biddy snapped. 'All of a sudden, it is for you to be telling me what I cannot do.'

'You would not marry him now, Biddy, surely?' Donnie said.

'Not if he was the last man on God's earth, I would not marry him now.' Biddy had circles of exhaustion under her eyes and, Innis noted with a certain satisfaction, seemed suddenly to have lost her lustre. 'I know what you think I am. But I was taken in. I never did love him. If he had told me what he was I would have had nothing to do with him in the first place. I certainly will not be putting myself into the hands of the anti-Christ just for the sake of becoming Michael Tarrant's bride.'

'It is a bit late to say that now,' Ronan put in, 'since he has had what he wanted from you and will get away without paying for it.'

'A Catholic,' Biddy said, shuddering. 'Inside me.'

'Biddy, that's enough,' Vassie told her.

'My old father, rest his soul, must be turning in his grave,' Ronan said. 'He was a fine upstanding Ulsterman who pledged his blood to fight the Papes. And he did, he did, until his dying day. My father would have known what to do with your precious shepherd. He would have slit his throat from ear to ear.'

'For God's sake!' Donnie said. 'Don't talk like that in front of Aileen.'

'I would do as much myself.' Ronan squinted at his youngest who, far from being frightened by talk of bloodshed, sat on her high stool with an eager little smile on her face. 'I would. I would be slitting the bastard's throat myself if I was not a law-abiding citizen and a true Christian.'

'Are there not better ways to be rid of him?' Neil said.

'Better than slitting his throat?'

'Tell his employers. Tell the Baverstocks what he is.'

'It seems they already know,' Donnie said.

'What? About Biddy?'

'No, about his religion.'

'And they dared to employ him?'

203

'They are different from us,' Ronan said. 'It would not be to Hector Thrale's liking to have a Catholic idolater on the books, though.'

'Why did he come here?' Biddy said. 'To Mull, I mean. Surely, he could have found work on Barra or Eriskay with his own kind.' Nobody seemed willing to answer her question. She continued, 'I think he used his alliance with the devils in Rome to put a spell on me. Catholics do that, you know.'

'Och, yes,' Ronan agreed, 'it is part of their game to spawn with God-fearing Christians like ourselves and they are praised for it by their masters in Rome. That was why they invented absolution. It is to reward them for luring true Christians into the arms of Satan.'

Neil nodded.

With a patient little sigh, Aileen murmured, 'Aye,' as if she were privy to the secrets of the Vatican or, more likely, believed every word her father said.

Biddy put her arm about her sister and, to Innis's disgust, kissed her on the brow. It was as if the Campbells had evolved their own system for the forgiveness of sin and, not for the first time, intolerance drew them together and bigotry restored harmony to the household. The fact remained, however, that Biddy had yielded not only to Michael Tarrant's charm but to her own desires and that whatever forces they chose to believe in, Aileen was still carrying a child that had no father or whose father could not be named.

Innis could stomach it no longer. She got up quietly, took her shawl and the lantern from the peg by the door and slipped outside.

It was a relief to be out of the cottage. She walked along the grass in darkness, cold, clean air swirling about her, the stars whirling among the clouds overhead, a little shard of moon hanging over Olaf's Hill. She could hear the sea sounding on the shore below, as rhythmical as a heartbeat now that the wind had changed. She lit the lantern in the shelter of the wall and walked in the direction of the calf park, thinking of the turmoil that had come upon them since the wall had been dug out of the earth; thinking how no wall was high enough or thick enough to keep out the troubles that lay within.

Eventually the anger passed out of her and she leaned on the gate of the calf park with the lantern at her feet.

She looked up at the swaying pines and wondered what she would see if she climbed to the top of the ridge: a candle in the window of Michael's cottage, a signal that Biddy had not been good enough for him and that he was still waiting for someone else? With that thought in mind, she placed a kiss in the cup of her hands and blew it like thistledown into the starlight night for, sinner or sinned-against, Michael Tarrant was still the man she loved.

'I want my money, Dada,' Donnie said.

'I will be giving it to you soon, after we get back.'

'Is this your way of telling me that you have not been paid?'

'Of course I have been paid. Do you think I would be setting foot in the *Kelpie* in this sort of weather if I had not been paid? Your money is safe in my hands, Donnie. You will be getting it as soon as we return to Pennypol.'

'Donnie is afraid, that is what it is,' Neil said. 'He is not wanting to go with us because of the rough weather.'

'Is that a fact, son?' Ronan Campbell said. 'Are you frightened of a wee bit of a blow?'

'Oh, I will make your damned run with you, Dada, never fear. But it will be the last. I am collecting what is due to me and striking out on my own just as soon as I can. I am not waiting until the spring. I have had enough of you and your smuggling,' Donnie said. 'How much is due to me?'

'I have not counted—'

'How much?'

'Twelve pounds.'

'Twelve pounds!' said Neil. 'Is it the same for me?'

'It is.'

'By God, at this rate I will soon be a rich man.'

'And will you be leaving me too?' Ronan asked.

'Not I,' said Neil, then to Donnie, 'Twelve pounds will not be buying you a boat, though.'

'It will furnish a cottage.'

'With your sweetheart from Leathan, I suppose.'

'She will not be my sweetheart. She will be my wife.'

'And will you and your sweetheart live on love alone?' Ronan said.

'I will take work with the mail boats, with MacBrayne's.'

'That is no life for a man,' Ronan said.

'Do you think this is?' said Donnie.

'Is it because of what has happened with the women that you are so anxious to be leaving?' Ronan said.

'The women have nothing to do with it.'

'He is wanting to sleep with his sweetheart,' said Neil, grinning.

'And what is wrong with that?' said Donnie. 'Do you think I want to share a bed with you for the rest of my days? As soon as I have my money and can find a cottage to rent, I will be away. Whatever happens, I will be making no more whisky sailings after this one.'

Ronan nodded. He seemed unperturbed by his son's announcement.

He sniffed at the bottle in his hand, took a sip from the neck and looked out of the shed at the fretful sea. In the half-light of the winter's afternoon the mountains of Ardnamurchan were almost invisible and the shelf of Canna had vanished altogether as if the sea – or the sky – had absorbed it.

He took another small sip from the bottle, corked it and stowed it in the pocket of his oilskin jacket. He knew that he must remain sober, for it would be a hazardous trip to Bucks' Isle and if the wind held from its present quarter an even more hazardous run back.

He got up, stoop-shouldered under the sagging roof.

'We will be going now,' he said.

'I will tell Mother that we are leaving,' said Donnie.

'No, son,' Ronan said. 'It will be better for all of us if we just slip away.'

The roar of breakers and a great organ-pipe drone from Haggerty's cave filled Arkle bay with deafening sound and spray created a strange phosphorescence against which the static shapes of landmarks were defined.

Fergus Haggerty, a scarf wrapped around his head and a garment of coarse wool flapping about his thighs, emerged from the cave carrying a storm lantern lashed to an ash pole. Even in sheltered Arkle bay the surge was considerable, though, and the glimmer of Haggerty's guiding light came and went, appearing and disappearing as the *Kelpie* swooped inshore and Donnie and Neil, already soaked to the skin, leaped from the bow to drag the boat ashore.

Donnie's canvas thigh boots were as heavy as lead. His oilskins floated on pockets of air as the breakers dashed against him. Only brute strength kept him upright. Hauling on the *Kelpie*'s bow rope, he waded out of the water on to the sand. He cupped a hand to his mouth and shouted to the Irishman to come and help but Haggerty would not leave the shelter of the rocks. Ronan and Neil stayed with the boat while Donnie, crouched low, zigzagged up the sand on to the sward where Haggerty cowered.

'I did not think that you would be comin',' the Irishman shouted. 'You can't be makin' a boat journey on a night like this.'

'My father thinks we can,' Donnie shouted back. 'Where's the load, Fergus? Is the load not ready?'

'Aye, it is ready. It's there behind the rocks. Eight casks.'

'Eight, is that all?'

'Surely Ronan willnae be riskin' his boat for just eight casks?'

'He would do it for one,' Donnie shouted.

'Is he after drownin' you, and himself too? Tell him to pull the boat up an' come into my house. I'll seal the door, build up the fire an' we will drink all eight casks ourselves.'

'My father says that the man from Oban will be expecting us.'

'That's pish. The whole country is sufferin' from the gales. Even MacBrayne's mail boats have been ordered to harbour. I tell you, Donald, I've not had a London newspaper for four days.'

If Donnie had not been drenched, frozen to the marrow and filled with apprehension about the trip ahead he might have laughed at Haggerty's definition of hardship.

There was a strange, hot core in him that wanted to make the sail to Bucks' Isle, though, to get it over and done with and to be under no further obligation to his father. He had survived a couple of raging storms before now. He had hung on the *Kelpie*'s mast with the wet sail wrapped around him, baling, baling with a battered iron bucket while Neil and his father steered with the oars and the waves came marching out of the sky like mountains on the move. When the boat had finally been beached, however, when he had crawled away from her and had heard his father laugh and had seen him pump his fist defiantly towards the sky then Donnie had known what it meant to throw caution to the winds and risk everything on the whim of fate and your strength of will, that survival was part of his heritage.

'You'll make no headweigh against the tide, Donnie,' Haggerty said. 'It's madness even to try.'

'If it proves to be too much for us then we will put in at Croig.'

'With the cargo on board?'

'Is that what it is that worries you, Fergus, your precious cargo?'

'What worries me is that you'd consider going out on a night like this at all. How will he navigate?'

'By instinct, the way he always does.'

''B' God, Donnie, you're as mad as he is. And you don't even have the excuse of the drink to save you.'

'It's my last run, Fergus,' Donnie said. 'I will be getting married soon and I will not be seeing you again.'

'Married, is it? Well, I wish you well,' Fergus Haggerty said. 'I tell you what, why do we not all go into my house for to toast your nuptials?'

'No, Fergus. I owe my father this much,' Donnie shouted. 'The wind may not be so bad once we get round Caliach Point.'

'Aye, it may be worse,' said Haggerty.

It took the best part of a half-hour to load the consignment. The casks were awkward to handle and had to be fastened under a sheet in the stern to balance the *Kelpie*'s bow and prevent wallowing. Only Ronan's stubborn insistence kept Donnie and Neil from quitting. Fergus Haggerty could not bear to watch. He left the lantern stuck in the sand, retreated to his cottage and let the Campbells get on with it.

When the cargo was on board at last the boat sat low in the water, battered by waves that roamed in from the mouth of the cove, rolling on the backlash from the rocks. It was all Donnie and Neil could do to make any headweigh at all after they left the shore. Seated side by side they strained at the oars together but could find no rhythm or cohesion for, in spite of the load,

The Parting of the Ways

the *Kelpie* bobbed like a cork in the big sea. By then Donnie realised that there was no hope of reaching Bucks' Isle that night. His strength was almost used up even before the boat crept out of Arkle into the tidal stream that washed the reefs.

Ronan was crouched in the stern, ankles locked under the ribs that braced the casks, his head barely visible above the canvas. Surely even he knew that what they were attempting was impossible. Under sail the journey was long and arduous but tonight in the teeth of a south-westerly with the *Kelpie* already shipping water Bucks' Isle might have been a million miles away. Something more than stubborn pride was driving his father now, Donnie realised; not blind ignorance but anger, as if his father were seeking revenge on them for their disloyalty. He was suddenly filled by fear that he would become a victim not of courage but of pettiness and if he had not been chained to the oar by a need to keep the boat upright he would have rounded on his father there and then.

Neil too was aware that their situation was hopeless but if either of them stopped rowing even for a moment the *Kelpie* would be left at the mercy of the sea which, Donnie knew only too well, was indifferent to what it did with them. He tried to think of Muriel, her soft lips against his lips, the feel of her breasts against his chest. He tried to bring to mind the smell of her hair. But there was something too harsh and elemental tangled round his soul to admit remembrance of the girl and how he loved her, for the sea in this mood took everything from you and it left you empty, so empty that not even despair remained.

He released the oar.

It swivelled on the rowlock and struck him on the chest. He ducked down and clawed his way through the water that swamped the bottom of the boat until he reached his father's knees.

'Put her in,' Donnie cried. 'For Christ's sake, Dada, put her in.'

He could not see his father's face but he could sense his rejection and envisage the crooked little smile that was meant to assure him that all was well when nothing was well, nothing ever had been well.

Donnie was still on his knees when the *Kelpie* capsized.

She did not go under suddenly. She heeled against the breakers so that the sea ripped over the port side and Donnie found himself waist deep in water. Then she righted and for a moment hung poised on the side of the sea. As in a dream, Donnie saw the mast collapse, the oars fly away, the sheet that covered the casks inflate like a gigantic lung.

He reached out for his father but Ronan, panicking at last, kicked him away and sent him hurling overboard into the darkness of the sea.

It was three days before the body was washed ashore, by which time it was almost unrecognisable. Ronan was summoned to make identification.

The body was laid out on a trestle in a shed behind a croft on the shore of Loch na Keal, a quarter-mile from the spot where it had been discovered. It did not take long for the Depute Procurator to conclude that the loss of the *Kelpie* and Donald James Campbell's death were acts of God and to release the corpse into the care of his next of kin.

Things were not quite so cut and dried as all that, however. Bobbing among the flotsam from the *Kelpie* were several casks of raw whisky that had led to Ronan being questioned as to what he was doing offshore on a night when every vessel for fifty miles around had sought shelter. Ronan declared that he had been fishing and had no knowledge of the casks of illicit spirits that the sea had thrown up along with the remains of his fishing boat.

If it had not been for the loss of life Ronan Campbell might not have been let off so lightly. The death of a son was a tragedy, though, whatever act of enterprise or folly lay at the back of it and after a brief meeting in the courtroom in Tobermory the Depute Procurator decided that it was best to take no further action, at least against Campbell, and to let grief stand in lieu of punishment.

Ronan travelled alone to Loch na Keal.

Neil was too broken in body as well as spirit to accompany his father and Ronan refused to allow any of the women to leave Pennypol.

The Parting of the Ways

Out of respect for Vassie and sympathy for Biddy and Innis, Tom Ewing volunteered to support the fisherman but Ronan would have none of that pious nonsense either and rode off on the pony with a fresh shirt and a pair of clean shoes in a bag on the saddle and Vassie's leather purse strapped to his waist.

It was a grey, cold, cloud-scudding morning when he left, a bright, calm afternoon when he returned, seated in the back of a hired wagon with the pony tied behind and Donnie, what was left of him, sealed in a coffin. Ronan sat with his back to the boy, his legs dangling over the board, and looked back down the dreary miles, his eyes not bleak or tear-rimmed but with that hard, sly glint to them that never seemed to change.

When the wagon reached Crove, Ronan helped carry the coffin into the Wingard, though he had no permission to use the village hall as a resting place. He paid the carrier and sent him away, then he rode up the main street, tethered the pony outside the McKinnon Arms and went in.

He ordered and drank a whisky, ordered and drank another then, without a word to anyone, walked down the length of the main street to the manse to inform Tom Ewing that the burial would be tomorrow at eleven in the morning in the plot behind the kirk. He placed the certificate that the Examiner had signed and the Depute Procurator had counter-signed on the minister's desk, nodded curtly and said, 'It is all right, you see. Everything is all right.'

'Where is the – where is Donnie now?' Tom Ewing said.

'I have laid him out in the Wingard.'

'Do you want him put on view?'

'No. No one must see him.'

'His mother may wish to . . .'

'Not his mother. No one.'

'Does he look bad, Ronan? Is he that bad?'

'He does, aye.'

'Would you like me to visit him?'

'For what reason? He is dead.'

'To pray, perhaps.'

'Praying will do him no good now.' Ronan took in a breath. 'Eleven o'clock tomorrow. All right?'

'All right, Mr Campbell,' Tom Ewing said.

The Island Wife

* * *

The little cutter with the bright blue paintwork and gilded lettering appeared at the slipway at Croig at high water. It carried three Protection officers and four crewmen. They had made record time from Oban in spite of the scarcity of wind. It had been many years since the last raid on Mull and none of the officers was familiar with the island. One of the crewmen had an aunt on Gometra, however, and knew where Haggerty's hideout was situated. He led the officers round the back of the hill and down to the jumble of rocks at the base of the cliff and, with lanterns lit, along the perilous little path that overhung the cove.

It was a still, clear winter's night, the air so sharp that every sound, even the scrape of a shoe on a pebble, carried across the mirrored waters of the cove and rose in ringing echo up the cliff-face.

The officers carried no weapons except painted batons, for they had no legal authorisation for the raid upon Fergus Haggerty's stronghold. At the corner of the cliff they halted and blew out all but one of the lanterns. They could see the cave, dark against the faint frosty sheen of the rock. They whispered together, hands cupped over their mouths, then, leaving the crewman behind, slipped down on to the sand and darted over the grass to Haggerty's cottage.

There were no windows. Sifting smoke from the chimney hole outlined the ramshackle building, though, and the glow of a fire or a lamp defined the door. They listened for the gurgle of a kettle but heard nothing. They sniffed the air and smelled – yes, the unmistakable odour of mashed grain.

'Are we ready, lads?' in a whisper.

'Aye, sir.'

'Then here we go.'

The door was held shut by nothing more substantial than a hitch of twine which, such was the enthusiasm of the officers, broke before their onslaught so that they tumbled, not quite in a heap, straight into Fergus Haggerty's living-room. Fergus was seated in an old wicker chair before the fire. He was smoking a cheroot, sipping whisky and browsing through a week-old copy of *The Times*. He did not seem to be surprised at the officers' intrusion. He frowned at them, blew smoke, and said, 'Faith, an' is the Queen not teachin' ye enough manners to be knockin' on a fella's door before ye go breakin' in?'

'What's that you're drinking?'

'Whisky,' Fergus said.

'Is it now?'

Fergus put down the newspaper and held the cheroot away from his face. The officers ringed the chair. Fergus sniffed the glass in his hand, touched his tongue to the liquid's surface. 'Aye,' he said. 'It's whisky right enough.'

'Do you admit it?'

'Why should I not admit it?' Fergus reached down and from a nook between a potato sack and a bag of dried peas produced a tall clear-glass bottle elegantly labelled *Old Highland* which bore across its lower edge those stamps and recommendations which the law of the land required. 'Has imbibin' a dram o' our nat'nal drink in yer ain hame been declared a crime?'

The bottle was snatched from his hand, uncorked, the contents sniffed, sampled, swirled about the mouth and softly swallowed.

The tester scowled.

'Glenlivet,' he said. 'Probably a Dufftown malt.'

'Where did you get this, Haggerty?'

'I bo'cht it,' Fergus said, 'in Salen.' He dipped into the pocket of his waistcoat and produced a scrap of paper which he held up between finger and thumb, 'I even have a recipe for it if ye'd care tae tak' a look.'

A pause, then, 'What's back there?"

'Ma gairden.'

'In a cave? A garden in a cave?'

'Ca' it what ye like, it's mine an' ye've nae provocation for goin' in there.' Fergus scrambled to his feet and hurried to the canvas curtain that divided the cottage from the buildings in the cave. 'Ye've nae right tae gang pokin' and pryin' aboot ma property.'

'Have we not? I say we have.'

'Naw, naw, ye canna gang back there.'

'What is back there, Haggerty? Could it be a still, an unlicensed still on which no tax has been paid?'

'Naw, it's just – just my livelihood.'

Fergus stretched out his arms but the officers were eager now and, sensing victory, brushed past him, ripped the curtain from its rings and hastened down the passageway into the cavern beyond.

'Smell it?'

'I smell it, sir.'

There was a rush, a charge, and a sudden bumping of knees and buttocks as first one officer and then the next came to an abrupt halt.

The stink of mash overwhelmed them, along with a whiff of something that none of them cared to define. Holding up the lamp they peered past scattered straw, past a driftwood paling to troughs and hay-pits and found their scrutiny returned by angry yellow eyes as the animals from which Fergus claimed to earn a living glowered at them.

'Goats, gentlemen.' Fergus leaned on the cavern wall, blew out tobacco smoke and silently thanked God that Ronan Campbell had had the gumption to warn him that the Protection officers might be on their way. 'Just goats.'

'Is he not with you?' Vassie held the door and, after Ronan had entered, peered into the darkness outside. 'Where is he? Why is he not with you?' She swung round. 'Was it not him? Was it not Donnie?'

'It was Donnie.' He seated himself at the table and took off his hat and, fumbling, unstrapped the purse from about his waist. 'Aileen, I have put the garron in the byre. See to it that it is given water, fodder and a good rub down.'

The girl seemed disinclined to lift herself up from her place by the fire where she lay, thumb in mouth, side by side with the dog.

'Do it.'

Still with her thumb in her mouth, she got up and went outside.

Ronan put the purse on the table and pushed it towards his wife. 'It is all there and accounted for,' he said. 'I have noted the cost of everything.'

'Where is he?' Vassie said.

She stood before him, separated only by the breadth of the

table. Her hands were raised to her shoulders. She closed her fingers upon the straps of her apron, tugging and tugging at them as if she might strip herself in her grief. Her voice was shrill but not loud.

'He is in Crove.'

'Why did you not bring him home?'

'I had paid the carrier enough.'

'Where did you leave him – in the street?'

'He is in the coffin which Laidlaw of Salen made for him. He is resting in the Wingard Hall.'

'I want to see him

'No, Vassie. You cannot see him. The coffin is sealed.'

'I do not believe you, Ronan Campbell. I want to see him for myself.'

'You will see the box tomorrow.'

'Tomorrow?'

'We will go to the church at eleven o'clock and he will be buried after that in the graveyard behind the kirk.'

'Has Mr Ewing been told?' Innis asked.

'I have spoken with Mr Ewing. He has the papers, all signed. He will attend to the service and to the committal. And that will be the end of it.'

'I want Donnie here with me,' Vassie said.

'I have been on the road since the crack of dawn,' Ronan said, 'and I am wanting my supper.'

'Your supper?' Biddy shouted but Innis stayed her, a hand clasped to her sister's shoulder.

Innis said, 'Is the coffin really sealed, Dada?'

'It is.'

'Was it the carpenter from Salen who sealed it?'

'It was.'

'On whose instruction?'

'Mine.'

'Because Donnie was – it was . . . ?'

'Yes,' Ronan said.

Vassie sat down. She looked from Innis to Biddy and then towards Neil who had dragged himself from the alcove bed and was huddled against the wall by the dresser. His face was white with the pain of his cracked ribs and the huge, empurpled bruise

215

that spread across his cheek and down the line of his jaw. Three broken fingers on his left hand were bound together with plaster bandage and he held the hand to his chest and breathed shallowly.

'Who will carry him?' Neil said.

'Oh, we will find folk willing enough to do that,' Ronan said.

'I will take a corner,' Neil said.

'How can you?' Biddy said. 'In your state?'

'I will take a corner.'

'Well, we will see,' Ronan said. 'We will see how it is in the morning.'

'Has Muriel MacNiven been told?' Innis said. '

'Told what?'

'That he – that Donnie is dead.'

'What business is it of hers?' Ronan said.

'She was to have been his wife, Dada.'

'Aye, well, she will not be his wife now,' Ronan said.

'I will go to Leathan first thing and tell her,' Innis said.

'I expect you will be wanting to tell McIver too?' Ronan said.

'He knows,' Vassie said. 'He is here on Mull already.'

'What? Where?'

'He is staying in Dervaig with Mr McColl.'

'Is he now?' Ronan said. 'Well, I am hoping that he is receiving better attention from Mr McColl's wife than I am from mine.'

Vassie rose, stalked to the dresser and brought down a bowl, stalked to the fire and tipped the lid off the black pot, ladled soup into the bowl and brought it back to the table. She held the dish in both hands eighteen inches above the table top and dropped it before him.

Ronan did not look at her, did not wipe at the mess that splashed his breast and sleeves. He lifted a spoon in his fist and began to eat.

After a moment, Innis said, 'I think I will be going out now.'

'Going where?' said Biddy.

'I am going to walk over to Leathan to talk to Muriel.'

'I will come with you,' Neil said, trying to struggle to his feet.

'You are going nowhere,' Vassie told him and then, with a glance at Innis, nodded and said, 'Go if you wish, dear. Go if you feel you must.'

216

'I think I should, Mam,' Innis said.

'Aye, I think you should.'

It seemed odd for a Protestant minister to light two candles and place one at each end of the coffin. If Tom was aware of the significance of those slender columns of light at the head and foot of a corpse he managed to put it out of his mind and did not let it trouble his conscience. He needed light, just a little light and candles were less intrusive than oil lamps.

It was cold in the Wingard, a hazy sort of cold. Tom was glad that he had had the foresight to put on an overcoat and scarf. He pulled a chair close to the coffin and with one hand on the lid prayed to God to administer to the soul of the deceased and bestow upon him the blessing of life eternal. He prayed for the lad's mother and sisters and Neil, the brother, and requested that their faith might be strengthened and their understanding increased by their loss.

He prayed with a sincerity that needed no outward show. He had learned how to communicate with God many years ago and did not think of it as a trick, a knack, but as a talent that he cherished above all the other gifts that God had showered upon him. He had no particular expectation that the Lord would do as he asked. He was sure, though, absolutely sure that God would listen and, having heard, would make His judgements according to Divine plan. And if he, Thomas Ewing, could not understand why the life of a young fisherman had been cut off so abruptly and his promise left unfulfilled that only went to prove that God was mightier than mortal man and that His purposes were fathomless.

Tom prayed for ten or fifteen minutes, during which time he was conscious of the creak of the chair beneath him, of the faint groaning of the hall's wooden walls as the night frost tightened its grip. He was also aware of the odour of the corpse, not dusty, not decaying but somehow fresh, as if a trace of the salt sea and sea breeze had been distilled out of Donald's flesh and he would be buried with its fragrance around him.

Tom did not hear Innis come into the hall.

When she spoke his name he was startled and, for an instant, afraid.

217

'I am sorry, Mr Ewing. I did not mean to disturb you.'

She looked much as she always did, with the shawl over her head and coarse woollen mittens covering her hands. It was as if she had come straight from the byre or the hayfield, stealing time to mourn her brother.

Tom got up.

'Innis,' he said. 'Are you alone? I mean, is your mother not with you?'

'My father would not let her come.'

'I think he is afraid that she will ask for the coffin to be opened.'

Innis came forward and moved past him.

She stood by the unpolished pine box that the carpenter-undertaker had knocked together and looked at the brass screw-nails that held the lid in place. She put out a mittened hand and rubbed the tip of her forefinger on one of the screws as if it were in her mind to demand that her brother be exposed to the air again, so that she might look into his face for the last time.

She shook her head. 'I cannot believe that it is so small.'

Tom said, 'Would you like to be left alone?'

'I would rather that you stayed with me. I will not wait long. I felt I had to come, just to see where he was.'

'I will pray with you, if you like.'

'I would rather not pray, not tonight. I will pray for him tomorrow.'

'He's at peace now, Innis, at peace with God.'

'Yes,' she said. 'I see that now.' She turned and, to Tom's surprise, leaned an elbow on the coffin lid. 'There should be more to it, though, should there not? It does not seem right for Donnie to be buried in the ground of the kirkyard. He should be put in a boat and it should be pushed out towards the skerries and, when it was far from land, it should burst into flames.'

'Well, he was hardly a warrior, your brother,' Tom said. 'Perhaps it is as well that he is laid out peacefully.'

'Perhaps.'

He wanted to put his arms about her, draw her head to his chest, to encourage her to release the tears that were in her, to comfort, console and protect her. He had not forgotten his promise to McIver of Foss, a promise upon which he would never renege. It was not time yet, though, neither the time nor the place. He said, 'I took the liberty of informing Mr Patterson of the letting committee that the hall was being used for this – ah – purpose. I told him that it was my suggestion that Donald be put here.'

'That was kind of you.' Innis hesitated, head held to one side, the shawl slipping so that he could see her face in the candlelight. 'I cannot think that I will not see Donnie again.'

'You will see him again, Innis, when God calls you too.'

'It was my father's fault, you know.'

'Now, Innis, you must not blame anyone.'

'All Donnie wanted was a boat of his own. He wanted a boat and roof over his head and Muriel MacNiven for his wife. He would have been happy enough with these things and would have sought nothing better,' Innis said. 'Now there is no boat, and in time Muriel will marry another man; it will be just as if Donnie had never been here at all.'

'I do not understand why these things happen any more than you do, Innis,' Tom said. 'But God is not so cruel as to take away life without reason.'

'Reason,' she said, not bitterly. 'The reason was that my father took them out to help him smuggle whisky.'

'Oh!'

'That is the truth of it, Mr Ewing. That is the reason why Donnie is dead.'

'I do not think you should be telling me this, Innis.'

'Why not?'

'It is not my business.'

'*He* took them out. *He* came back. Donnie did not.'

'Innis, I wish I could explain but – but I cannot.'

'Donnie paid the price for my father's greed,' Innis said. 'He is an evil man, my father, but he was not the one who was asked to pay the price.'

Tom was oddly unmoved by her confession. It was as if he had known all along that Ronan Campbell was behind the tragedy. It took no leap of the imagination to deduce that something other than long-line fishing had kept the *Kelpie* at sea in the teeth of last week's gale. He glanced behind him, then seated himself on the chair again and reached for her hand.

She yielded it to him without reluctance.

'Haggerty?' he said. 'Fergus Haggerty supplied the whisky, I suppose?'

'Yes.'

'Where did they take it?'

'To Bucks' Isle, on the shore of the firth.'

'As good a place as any, I suppose. What happened to the boat, Innis?'

'It capsized just off Quinish.'

'It is fortunate that your father and Neil were not drowned too.'

'Fortunate?' Innis said. 'Our Donnie is dead. Neil has broken bones. Only my father got away without a scratch upon him. Neil saved him. Neil dragged him to the shore. But there was no hope for Donnie.'

And she began to weep.

Tom drew her to him. He could not help himself. He was filled with compassion for her suffering and shared her anguish willingly. He let her rest her brow against his shoulder and weep, weep as if her heart would break.

It was to be the last bright day of the year and it would be remembered, by those who did not attend as well as those who did, as the day of Donnie Campbell's funeral. The fact that there was no vigil and no wake and that Vassie Campbell would flout tradition by going to the kirkyard, at least as far as the wall of the graveyard, may have kept some of Donnie's friends from turning up. There were other reasons for the scarcity of mourners, however. What kept many away was a turn in the tide of sentiment against feckless Ronan Campbell coupled to an awareness that some outlaw element had been at work and that it might be better not to appear at the graveside in case some blame rubbed off.

Better excuses were offered round the fire in the McKinnon Arms: stubble begging to be ploughed, wheat to be sown, stock to be let out to breathe and, so calm and fine was it, a last fling at the fishing before the end of the year. Ronan would understand. Donnie would have done just the same thing himself if Donnie had not been drowned. So, few men appeared at the

Wingard where Reverend Ewing had held service, fewer still at the graveyard. But there were women in plenty in the street, girls and young women who had once dreamed of marrying the boy from Pennypol, who had known him at school, who had yearned for him vaguely or, the bolder ones among them, had made sheep's-eyes at him whenever he came to town. They had come down from the hill farms, begging time off from dairies and crofts, even up from Tobermory, two of them, to bid goodbye to the son of the sea who, without reason, they had once admired.

The Campbells arrived in Crove early.

The women and Neil rode in on the farm cart.

Neil was hunched, his big, fair face swollen and the colour of a turnip, the pain in him so bad that he could not sit upright in a chair but had to lean upon the back, his head down and his tears flowing like water, though whether for himself or for his departed brother no one could properly say.

Vassie shed not a tear, not at the service, not on the road to the graveyard, not at the wall where the women gathered while Reverend Ewing read the words of the committal in a strong voice and the coffin was lowered into the ground. Vassie remained as dry as an old corn husk, her visage grim, her brows knitted fiercely so that the dart of flesh between her brown eyes was almost black, her teeth showed against her lip, except when she was offered condolences when she would snap her head and say impatiently, 'Aye, aye, aye,' as if she would not entertain such niceties.

Evander McIver walked in from Dervaig. He was a rare enough sight these days to fetch to their doors those to whom Donnie Campbell had meant nothing. They hoped only to catch a glimpse of a great man whose deeds had been passed down from fathers long dead to sons who were old themselves now but who still remembered everything that they had heard about the Hebridean Hercules who had licked the best throwers and best wrestlers that the duke could find to match against him and how he had won not just money but land from the old duke and had gone to live with only women for company out beyond the Dutchman's Hat.

Evander wore a kilt and a black jacket, a pure white stock and a cocked hat with a black feather in it. He stood head and shoulders above the other mourners and supported his grandson, Neil, at the graveside. But it was noticed that he said not a word to Ronan Campbell, who had never been half the man his father-in-law was and was hardly fit to lace McIver's shoes.

Biddy wore black, Innis dark brown. The little one, Aileen, clung to her mother's hand, with her glittering, acquisitive eyes that you could not bring yourself to look at, her thumb in her mouth, her mouth all wet and slabbery and her nose running. Some thought that Aileen did not know what was going on, others that she did not care. But when she glanced over at poor, tearful Muriel MacNiven, who had come in from Leathan with her mother, the scornful wee smile on Aileen's face would have made your blood run cold.

Mr Austin Baverstock turned up in the gig along with Margaret Bell. His full black suit, black alpaca overcoat and a top hat with crape ribbons added more dignity and distinction to the occasion than Dr Kirkhope and Mr Leggat could muster between them. Willy Naismith, whose acquaintance with the deceased had been slight, was not well enough to venture out of doors yet and sent his apologies and condolences via Mr Baverstock.

Of Michael Tarrant there was no sign, though both Biddy and Innis took time off from their grieving now and then to scan the gathering.

It was not until the burial service was over and the menfolk left the kirkyard that Hector Thrale sought them out and, standing before them, fat and glossy in solemn Sunday black, shook each by the hand, then, leaning forward, murmured into Biddy's ear, 'Your sweetheart will not be coming.'

'My sweetheart?'

'Tarrant. He has taken leave.'

'Leave?' said Innis.

'Gone away.'

'Where?' said Biddy.

Thrale shrugged. 'He says he will be back on Sunday evening.'

'Who is looking after the sheep?'

'Barrett,' Thrale said. 'There is little enough to do now since the rams are with the ewes until January and there is still nourishment in the grass.' Without pause, he went on. 'I hear that your brother was ferrying whisky for Haggerty when he met his untimely end. Is that true?'

'My brother was fishing,' Innis said while Biddy, already wrung out, began to weep again. 'That is all Donnie was doing, Mr Thrale. Fishing.'

'Uh-huh.' Thrale patted Biddy on the shoulder in a mockery of consolation. 'Uh-huh,' he said and, when Biddy pulled away, smiled knowingly, as if the Campbells' secrets were all one and the same to him.

Evander McIver would not go back to Pennypol, not even when Vassie begged him. He waited by the kirk gate while the men drained away in the direction of the McKinnon Arms. He had spoken with his granddaughters, with Reverend Ewing and had lent Neil his arm to lean on throughout the proceedings but he would not put himself in a position where he might have to speak face to face with Ronan Campbell.

He stayed where he was on the edge of the village, back to the kirk wall, arms folded and waited until they had all gone, all except Vassie and Neil.

'Mr McColl is sending the wagon for me. Mairi will have the boat at the slipway at Croig by half past one o'clock,' Evander said. 'I would like to be home before dark.'

Vassie said, 'You should not have come at all.'

'I did not come for your sake, Vassie. I came for Donald. And for Neil.'

Neil glanced up, wincing. 'You did not have to be bothering with me.'

'I do have to be bothering with you,' Evander said. 'I want to know what you will do now that there is no boat and no future for you without one?'

'Will you not buy us a boat?'

'You know that I will not.'

'Neil will work on the farm with me,' Vassie said.

Evander put his hand on Neil's back and leaned close to him. They were so large, the pair of them, that Vassie seemed dwarfed. She stood back, watching, the furrow between her brows darker than ever.

'You must not stay on Mull, Neil,' Evander said. 'It will destroy you, son, and you must not let it do that. It was not your fault, what happened to Donnie, but it will be your fault if you stay here and let it pull you down too.'

'I will look after him,' Vassie said. 'I can look after my own.'

'Come back to Foss with me,' Evander said. 'Now, just as you are. Come back on the boat with me and I will see to it that you are taken care of until your wounds heal and you are fit again.'

'Aye, and what then?' said Neil.

'I will give you money, not much but enough, and a letter to my sister Hetty in Glasgow. She will give you board and lodging and help you find work.'

'I have no wish to go to Glasgow.'

'Do you wish to stay here, to go down too?'

'I will – I will not go down.'

'In Glasgow, there are good jobs with good wages.'

'I will think about it,' Neil said.

'I am making you an offer now, Neil. You must come with me now.'

Neil frowned. 'Why is there so much hurry?'

'Because it is a new life you are needing, Neil, and I am offering it to you.'

'I will have to be asking my father what he thinks.'

'No,' Vassie said, suddenly. 'Go with your grandfather.'

Wide-eyed, Neil swung round. The pain in his ribs struck hard. He thrust his fist into his side to numb it. 'What is this you are telling me, Mam, that you want to be rid of me too?'

'Go with him.'

'My clothes are all at home.'

'I will send them to you. Just go, son, for God's sake go.'

'But Dada needs me for – for the fishing.'

She caught him by the jacket and he brought up his bandaged hand and covered her fist with it as if to make her swear that he could trust her.

'For nothing,' Vassie said. 'Think, Neil, think what has happened to Donnie and what will happen to you because of him. Is that what you want to cling to when you can have a new life all to yourself?'

'Away from Mull, away from you?'

'Yes,' Vassie said. 'Yes, yes.'

'I'm sore,' Neil said. 'I am hurting. I am sick.'

'I will make you well again,' Evander promised.

'But what can I do? What can I do in Glasgow?'

'Start again,' Evander said.

'I need to talk to my dada,' Neil said, plaintively.

'Talk to him then,' Vassie said, her hand still pressed to her son's breast. 'Find him and talk to him. Do you know where he is?'

'Aye,' Neil blurted out. 'He is . . .'

He looked down towards the little town with its curls of smoke rising passively in the still morning air. The sky above the roofs was pale blue and the sense of the sea behind the hillocks of heather and rough pasture was strong. In the main street the women came and went and, up by the Wingard, his sisters waited by the cart. Looking down on Crove from the little rise that led to the church and the bridge and the road out of there, Neil could see how small it all was, how empty and, in its way, how uncaring.

'Where, son?' Vassie said. 'Where is your father?'

He hesitated then said, 'Drinking.'

A quarter of an hour later Mr McColl's wagon arrived from Dervaig.

Neil was helped on board and, with only the clothes on his back and his grandfather by his side, rode out of Crove without looking back.

Willy was making the most of his convalescence. He was still shaky on his pins and had a tendency to fall asleep at awkward times but was otherwise well enough to enjoy being cosseted.

He had been in the full grip of the fever, however, when Mr Austin had brought him the tragic news from Pennypol and, to Margaret's considerable alarm, he had fallen into a fit of grief far in excess of anything that seemed appropriate. He had wept and lashed about in bed as if somehow poor Donnie Campbell's drowning had been all his fault. He had not quieted down until she had taken him in her arms and hugged him to her bosom while Mrs McQueen hurried off to make up a soothing dose of laudanum and warm milk.

After grief, however, came fear; a babbling, gabbling, half-awake, half-asleep nightmare in which he, William Naismith, was being tried for murder and kept calling out for Maggie to save him.

Throughout the following day Willy slept fitfully and when he wakened on the morning of the third day after the shipwreck he was in full command of his faculties and sensible enough to joke about his frenzied behaviour and claim that the only thing he remembered about it was being held in the arms of a beautiful woman. None the less, he asked Margaret to discover what she could about the loss of the *Kelpie* and what, if anything, the Board of Inquiry had come up with now that poor Donnie Campbell's body had been found.

Margaret did what was asked of her. It wasn't difficult. Her father, staid though he might seem, was an inveterate tattle-tale and much local gossip circulated around the stables. Austin Baverstock too was interested in the outcome of the tragic event and regretted that he did not have his able confidant, Willy, on hand to advise him whether or not he should call personally upon the Campbells and offer them – Biddy in particular – his condolences. He raised the issue with Hector Thrale, who knew perfectly well what was in the wind and warned his employer to steer clear of Pennypol, at least for the time being.

When the Protection officers or county constables or someone else in authority did not descend upon Fetternish House, snatch him from his bed of sickness and lead him away in chains, Willy began to feel better. He should have known that Ronan Campbell, let alone Haggerty and Jack Stockton, were far too downy to be caught out and while the smuggling escapade might be over there would be no repercussions. Sympathy for Donnie was tempered by dislike of Ronan and, within a day or two, he had even managed to absolve himself from guilt and self-recrimination.

He returned to his own small room at the end of the kitchen corridor, for while he had enjoyed a taste of life upstairs he had felt too cut off up there. He liked being closer to the kitchens, to Margaret and the casual informality which nursing brought out in her.

Margaret was no longer half so shy as she had been. She would frequently interrupt her work to slip into his cubby bearing warm, sustaining drinks, pieces of fruit or a newspaper or journal that Mr Austin had sent down for him. Now and then she would even give him a kiss on the brow or a cuddle to warm his weary old bones and if Willy had been just a shade less experienced in seduction he might have attempted to persuade her to slip beneath the sheets and let him pamper her for a change. But he did not, for – a disquieting paradox – the more he longed for her, the more he respected her.

Margaret was upset when she came back from Donnie Campbell's funeral and, on Willy's instruction, was given a snifter of brandy to steady her. The sight of one so young being put into the ground, she said, had brought home how temporary, and how precious, life really can be. Mr Austin had also been affected by the ceremony and by seeing Biddy in tears. Soon after he got home he gathered the dogs and set out for a long walk 'to contemplate the eternal sea' from the vantage point of An Fhearann Cáirdeil.

Soon after that, Willy extricated himself from bed, donned a pair of thick stockings, slippers and one of Mr Walter's woollen bathrobes and tottered into the kitchen to join the ladies for mid-afternoon tea.

The kitchen was filled with slanting winter light, brilliant but somehow melancholy, and when Willy knelt on the box seat and looked out at the sea he experienced a prickle of sadness at the thought that he would not be around to enjoy the beauty of the earth for very much longer since, come what may, his days were numbered. Shakily, he went back to the tea and hot buttered scones and the comforting attentions of the women.

Ten minutes later Ronan Campbell turned up at the back door.

Margaret's protest that Willy was still ill and could not receive visitors was mingled with expressions of sympathy that went unheeded by the fisherman and before Willy knew what was happening he was alone with the grieving father in the privacy of the cubby at the corridor's end.

'I'm sorry I couldn't attend,' Willy began. 'As you can see I've not—'

Ronan interrupted him. 'I have not come to hear about your health.'

'What have you come for then?'

'I am needing the money you owe me.'

'But I don't owe you money.'

'For the last shipment.'

'But the last consignment was lost, wasn't it?'

'Aye, and my boat with it.'

Willy studied the fisherman cautiously, wondering if Campbell's brain had been softened by grief. But nothing in Ronan Campbell's expression indicated irrationality. He looked exactly the same as always and Willy found it hard to believe that less than four hours ago he had been standing in the kirkyard at Crove watching his son being put to the sod.

'How much do you think I owe you?' Willy said.

'Payment for the final shipment.'

'I haven't been paid for the last shipment. Stockton will not pay me now, since the casks were lost.'

'My boat was also lost.'

'I'm sorry about it but that, surely, was your fault.'

'Was it my fault that my sons were lost?'

'Sons?' said Willy. 'I thought only Donnie was drowned?'

'I have lost Neil too, it seems.'

'Dead?' said Willy, shocked.

'Sent away to Foss. Never a word, never a by-your-leave. Just packed into McIver's wagon and spirited away from me.'

'But he'll be back, though, won't he? After he's recovered?'

'I will not have him back. He has made his bed and he must lie on it. She tells me that he will be going to Glasgow to find work. Neil is as dead to me as Donnie. It would be better, I tell you, if they both lay together side by side rather than have him turn against me in my hour of need.' He spoke without inflexion, his voice as smooth as spun flax, anger and bitterness hidden by matter-of-factness. 'I have lost my boat and my boys,' he went on. 'And you are to blame.'

'I see.'

'You must compensate me for what has happened.'

'How much?' Willy said.

'The price of a new boat.'

'Is that how you calculate the loss of a son?'

Ronan did not answer. Perhaps he expected Willy simply to buckle, for guilt to overcome common sense. Even if Willy was groggy after fever, however, he was not so muddled as to surrender to blackmail.

'I do not have any more money to give you,' Willy said. 'I have kept my end of the bargain. You were paid for the cargo in advance, as promised.'

'I refused to tell them your name even when they threatened me with jail.'

'I assume you didn't tell them about Fergus Haggerty either?'

'Fergus has been visited by the Customs officers. They found nothing with which to charge him.'

Willy said, 'I suppose you'll be telling me that if you don't get a new boat you might be inclined to remember a few things you'd previously forgotten.'

'I might.'

'If you follow that course of action,' Willy said, 'instead of having a nice new boat to call your own you'll just be scratching about to pay a fine, like the rest of us.'

'It would be the jail . . .'

'It would not be the jail.'

'You would be sacked from your employment.'

'I doubt it,' Willy said.

'How much will you pay me?'

'Not a penny.'

'What about the whisky?' Ronan said.

'What about it?'

'If I had a new boat I could run more whisky for you and Mr Stockton.'

'Dear God!' said Willy. 'I can't go back to how it was before. A life's been lost just for the sake of a few pounds' profit and I can't square that with my conscience even if you can.'

'How much *will* you give me?'

'Nothing,' Willy said. 'I told you – nothing.'

'Do you not care what happens to me?'

'You have a wife, three daughters and fifty acres of land, man. You are a long way from being destitute.'

'Land! What can I be doing with land?'

'Work it,' Willy told him. 'Work it and make it pay.'

The farmhouse stood square-shouldered and whitewashed a mile or so north of Craignure. It emanated the kind of solidity that reminded Michael of the farmsteads of the Border country, so much so that it occasioned a twinge of homesickness. He also felt a little lost without the presence of sheep and the companionship of his collie whom he had left with Barrett back on Fetternish.

Broom House, as the farm was called, had a large, fenced front garden. Running alongside the fence was a pebble path that led to the stone barn where a visiting priest held early mass on the fourth Sunday of the month. Mull was not a Catholic island like Barra or Eriskay. It had no permanent chapel and the duty priest would scamper on to Salen and Tobermory to administer the sacraments in 'borrowed' halls and residences before returning to Morven on the Monday morning mail boat.

The back side of Broom House was as neat as the front, free of the trash that often accumulated around Mull's farms. The path led to the cobbled yard and the barn was guarded by a row of junipers and, though it was still very early, the barn door stood open.

The sky was slaty. The hills across the Sound of Mull were large and ominous and Michael could smell the approach of rain. By noon, when the tide changed, it would come in from the north-east, coiling across the water. The clouds that wisped Ben More and draped the saddle of Ben Talla would thicken and roll down to obscure the glens and his tramp back to Fetternish, the best part of thirty miles, would be a wet one.

Michael had asked for three days' leave to be sure that he was out of Crove when Innis's brother was buried. He hadn't the guts, or the gall, to show himself at the graveside and face up to the girl and her family. He had frittered away the day in Tobermory and had put up in a lodging house on Friday night. On Saturday, a cold grey day, he had walked the coast road to Craignure and lodged in the inn there to be close to the place where the priest would perform the rites first thing on Sunday. It had been seven months since he had last been to mass and had participated in the intimate solitude of the confessional.

He looked into the barn and saw to his relief that the benches had already been set out, the floor swept and the table that would serve as an altar furnished. An old woman and an old man were kneeling on the stone, praying towards the altar while a young man – hardly more than a boy – in a robe that was too short for him, guarded the casket in which, Michael guessed, the Elements of the Sacrament were conveyed about the islands.

The barn smelled of straw. The wall behind the altar was a wall of straw, as tidily baled as any Michael had ever seen, and the little side aisle was a chamber made out of straw too. When he dropped his knee in supplication and the young man beckoned he felt within himself a strange alarm, a quickening that was both exciting and demanding.

'Will you be wishing to see the father?' the boy asked, in English.

'Yes, I am here for confession.'

'If you will be going in there. The father is ready to hear you.'

Michael had been brought up in a devout Catholic household but the surroundings were so novel that, for a moment, he felt quite lost in the little straw room. There were none of the trappings of an anonymous confessional, no box or grid or curtain, only a crucifix on a shelf and the priest kneeling before it, his back to the penitent. The priest did not, of course, turn round.

He asked a general question which Michael answered.

Their voices were muffled by the straw. He could see nothing of the father's face, could not judge his age or disposition from the stoop of his broad, black-clad back or his worn heels. One bale had been separated and set apart from the others. Michael hesitated, not knowing whether to seat himself upon it or to kneel. He knelt. He rested his elbows upon the bale, clasped one hand in the other and lowered his eyes.

He was asked if he wished to make his confession in the Gaelic tongue and answered that he would prefer English.

He paused, then began.

He confessed that he had committed a carnal sin with a young woman of his acquaintance on several occasions. He confessed that he had been carried away by lust and that he had pursued the young woman and persuaded her to submit to him simply to gratify his sexual desires.

He was asked if he wished to marry the young woman.

He answered that he could not marry her because she was

not of the true faith and that her family would be opposed to such a marriage.

He was asked if he did not love the young woman.

He answered that he did not.

He was asked if he was in love with anyone else.

Michael answered that he thought perhaps he might be.

'Is she of the true faith?' the priest said. 'Is *she* a Catholic girl?'

'She is the sister of the girl with whom I committed the carnal sin.'

'She is not for you either, my son,' the priest told him, 'You must have no more to do with her. In future you must avoid such temptations.'

'Is that to be my penance, Father?' Michael said.

'Certainly not,' the priest answered, 'that is not penance enough.'

'It is for me,' Michael whispered in a voice so low that the father did not hear him and went sternly on with his reprimand.

EIGHT

Redwater Fever

Spring on Mull was supposed to begin on St Bride's Day on 2nd February but anyone who had ever stood up to their ankles in sleet with the north wind pinning their ears back and the cold eating at their fingers and toes knew that this was a nonsense. March 17th, St Patrick's Day, was a more acceptable date, especially if the weather was fine. But for Innis the first signal that winter was well and truly over came in April with the crying of new lambs, the sowing of barley and the locking away of grassland which would later be cut for hay.

The cattle survived the winter by growing rough coats and adopting a stance towards the scant months that was more stubborn than stoical, hiding themselves away for days on end in hollows on the moor where they sulked and snorted and nibbled whatever green stuff they could find. Vassie showed no great concern for them. Hardy stock, stiffened by the blood of the famous Foss highlanders, a rake or two of hay poked into a hedge or a cartwheel of cattle cake staked to the turf near the burn did them well enough by way of supplement even in the lean spell.

Cows in calf were a different matter. They were given much attention, more attention than Vassie appeared to give to Aileen, though by mid-April, the bump on the girl's belly could not be disguised and she walked about in a proud, daft way with it stuck out before her, her hands planted on her buttocks, so that anyone who saw her would know at once that her time was not far off. Vassie kept her confined to Pennypol and spirited her quickly away if Thrale appeared on the hill or Michael Tarrant showed his nose over the ridge. No church for Aileen. No New Year visit to Tobermory to buy presents. No trips to Crove for candy. It was as if Vassie Campbell and what remained of her family had gone to ground and only the two grown girls were to be seen out and about in the tail of the long winter season.

Vassie had an excuse for seeking solitude, of course: Donnie's death and the sudden departure of Neil who, it was rumoured, had gone to Glasgow and had found work as a caulker in a shipyard. Few folk were interested in Vassie Campbell's problems, however. When Ronan came rolling into Crove to seek solace in the McKinnon Arms he was more or less shunned, as if the loss of his boat, let alone the loss of his sons, had somehow made him less of a man.

Some fishermen on the coast might have hired him if he had not been drunk most of the time. The *Kelpie* had not been insured. It was generally assumed that old McIver would stump up for a new boat and that come February or March a vessel of sorts would appear by the jetty at Pennypol and that Ronan would go drifting off with his lines and pots to breathe whisky fumes over the creatures of the deep and pretend to busy at the fishing. But February came and went and March followed and to judge by Ronan's alcoholic mutterings old Evander McIver had learned sense at last. If Ronan wanted another boat it seemed that he would have to find somebody else to pay for it or, God forbid, earn the money himself.

Meanwhile Vassie kept him supplied with money for drink. Although she treated him now with undisguised hostility when it came to tossing him a half-crown to replenish his stock of Old Caledonia she was never less than generous. Ronan was so far gone that he mistook charity for sympathy and could not understand why she would not allow him to share her bed. He slept in the alcove on the mattress that his sons had once used. Most nights, he went to bed soon after supper and if his dreams were troubled by recollections of happier days he gave no sign of it and would be snoring only seconds after his head hit the pillow.

Aileen slept with her mother. Come bedtime Vassie would fasten a string between her wrist and that of her daughter as if she feared that the fairies, or some other nocturnal entity, might try to steal Aileen away. In the hours of darkness whatever tenderness remained in Vassie came to the surface. She would hug her daughter, place a hand on the swelling stomach, stroke her hair and try vainly to cajole out of her that which she, Vassie, already knew – the identity of the man who had seduced her.

On Sundays Innis went to kirk alone. When Reverend Ewing enquired where her mother and sisters were Innis would tell him a little white lie – always the same little white lie – that they did not feel up to it yet. And when Reverend Ewing would suggest that he might call upon the family to offer support, Innis somehow managed to put him off.

In the first quarter of the New Year the only person with whom Innis and Biddy came into regular contact was Mr Austin Baverstock. He still came tramping over the hill with the dogs from time to time and if he spotted Biddy or Innis in the calf park he would raise his hand in greeting in the hope that they would indulge in a few minutes' conversation, which they usually did. Mr Austin was far too much of a gentleman to ask impertinent questions about Neil or Ronan but Innis suspected that he was less naïve than he pretended to be.

If Biddy pined for Michael Tarrant she kept her suffering hidden. She missed Donnie and Neil, as they all did, but even that loss was tempered by selfishness. It was left to Innis to mourn for the brother who was gone, to think of him not less but more as the wet, cold weather of the winter eased into spring and the sea around the coast was once more dotted with the sails of fishing boats, large and small.

Neil's letters from Glasgow cheered her. They were written in pencil on penny paper, never more than one sheet at a time. He was all healed up, he said, and happy enough with his job which paid more than he had ever earned at the fishing. He lodged in a tenement in the Greenfield district with Hetty Philp, Grandfather McIver's youngest sister, who had been recently widowed. He paid two shillings a week for his bed and another three shillings for board which left him a half-crown a week to spend on himself. Mrs Philp had two daughters at home. One was called Benita, which had been Mr Philp's sister's name. Neil admitted that he thought Benita was very nice. He sent his best wishes to his sisters and said that he missed them all, even Fingal.

Innis's letters to her brother were filled with all the petty little obsessions that made up news in Pennypol: weather and crops and the health of cattle. She did not mention Donnie or how their father squandered his days by lounging in bed or huddled in the rain-lashed shed at the jetty, peering blearily out to sea. She did not mention Aileen's swollen belly or Biddy's 'shame' or how much Mother missed her sons, the one who had gone away no less than the one who would never return; nothing of that, nothing of the inner life or the emotions that tormented them as if Neil, in exile, had become a stranger too.

Lambing began on the last day of April. As soon as Innis put her nose out of the door she heard bleating drift down from Olaf's Hill, not the throaty complaints of gravid ewes but the light, lingering blether of new-born lambs. She had already heard the pee-wits' cries and seen hares congregating above the burn and pheasants racing about in sexual frenzy. She had remarked these signs of spring as if she had been trapped in a shell but when she heard the call of the lambs in the misty white morning she lifted her head and let out a little 'Huh' of pleasure as if all the woes of winter had suddenly been shed.

Michael wore a bloody apron and had rolled his shirt sleeves up to his shoulders. His arms were thin and white and his small, delicate hands, ideal for midwifing, were stained with ewe spatter. He was crouched on his knees in wet bracken with the ridge rock above him and a ewe tottering before him. Three other ewes, each with a lamb, nosed about on the ledges but the new lamb, freshly delivered, had only just staggered to its feet, the placental mess still steaming on the grass and the umbilical cord still dragging.

Michael had spent the previous month gathering in the sheep, dosing them for intestinal parasites and separating out the weaklings. He had prepared warm straw beds in the shed for sickly orphans and had fenced off a section of sheltered pasture for twins. He had done everything that a shepherd could do but, nature being thrawn, the first drop had come thick and fast and he had hardly had a wink of sleep in the past three days.

'What do you want, Innis?'

'I came to see the lambs.'

'Have you not seen lambs before?'

'Many a time. But it is not something I get tired of.'

'I do.'

'Have you nobody to help you?'

'The Barretts. They are over in the Solitudes trying to untangle a stray.'

He wiped his hands on the apron but did not rise from his knees. He watched the lamb stagger on its little black hoofs while the ewe sniffed it warily. Then she did a little dance around it while the lamb, all ruched and rickle-backed, cried out piteously, its tiny blue-black tongue vibrating.

Michael sat back on his heels. 'I hope you are not going to offer to help.'

Innis shook her head.

'Then you had better go home,' he told her.

'I am not frightened of you,' Innis said.

'Frightened? Frightened of what?'

'Of what you are.'

'What I am,' he said. 'What's that?'

'A Catholic.'

'Oh, how kind of you, Innis Campbell, how forgiving. You'll be telling me next that I don't look much different from other human beings.'

'I'm not frightened of you because of what you did to Biddy.'

'Hoh!' he exclaimed, taken aback.

'Is that sort of thing not a sin, though, a mortal sin?'

'For God's sake, Innis!' Michael leaped to his feet fast enough to startle the ewe. 'Will you kindly just go away.'

'Did you have to confess what you did with my sister?'

'Yes.'

'And accept a punishment?'

'What are you doing here?' he asked. 'You didn't turn up just to watch me lambing a few Cheviots, did you?'

'What did you tell the priest – about Biddy, I mean?'

'That's none of your business.'

'A secret of the confessional?'

'You know nothing about my religion.'

'That's true,' Innis said. She paused. 'But I *am* prepared to learn.'

'To learn – to learn what?'

'What it means.'

Michael stepped cautiously around the ewe as the lamb, driven by instinct, began its search for the teat. 'I can't tell you what it means. I don't know what it means, only what it does.'

'And what's that?'

He shook his head as if to indicate that she could not tempt him with words or promises, or with that direct, intelligent gaze of hers.

'Can you not be telling me, Michael?'

He shook his head again, scowling.

'Then I will be finding someone who can,' Innis said and, before he could ask her just what she meant by that, turned on her heel and was gone.

She could see him in the distance, down at the end of the jetty where the boat used to be. The sea looked empty without the boat. It was as if a piece of the sky had been taken away. She thought she could see Donnie sometimes. He was always in the same place, coming up the path from the shore, bent into the slope, one hand on his thigh, thrusting where the grass became steep. She could not see Donnie now, though, for Dada was there. Donnie never came when Dada was there. She wondered if it would be better if the boat came back and Donnie came back and Dada went away. Then the people under the hill might talk to her again and send again the man who made her lie down and who put his hand over her mouth and touched her, the man who smelled like her house, her bed and like the fish that came out of the sea.

She lay with her shoulders against the wall that Mam had built to keep the sheep out. She stretched her legs out in front of her. She could feel the sun on her belly, her round belly that contained the thing that the people under the hill had put there. She could not imagine what it would be like, if it would be all wet and slippery and the way a mackerel is or the way an otter is when its fur is slicked down, in the pool that the tide left below Dun Fidra.

She had a sun hat. Biddy had given her a sun hat. It was made of soft stuff and it had flowers on it. She had had a straw hat once that Neil had found on the shore but it had smelled like gulls' droppings and she had only worn it once. The hat that Biddy had given her was Biddy's hat. It had come out of Biddy's chest. Biddy had worn it long ago before she had so much hair. Biddy had given her the hat, throwing it at her and saying, 'Here. This might keep your brains from boiling over.' She did not know what Biddy meant but she had snatched up the hat and put it on her head.

It felt cool. She could look out from under the brim and see the shadow of the flowers that were printed on the hat and the sea and Dada, down there.

She did not know what he was doing. He was wading into the water and wading out again. He was carrying stones in both hands the way Mam and Innis and Biddy had carried stones a long time ago. He was carrying stones out of the sea and putting them all together in a heap. He would stop and take out his bottle and throw his shoulders back, his elbow crooked against the sky, then he would wade into the sea again and stoop and come up with another stone and wade out and put it on the pile. She did not know what Dada was doing.

She knew what Mam was doing. Mam was working in the earth of the potato patch where they had planted in the seedlings on dry days. She thought of the way the potatoes grew. She wondered if the thing inside her was green and smooth and if what she felt inside herself were the shoots of the thing reaching down into her belly. It was quiet now, though, sleeping, with the sun on it.

She was sleepy too. She closed her eyes.

He said, 'Aileen? Is that you, Aileen?'

She opened her eyes.

He had on a hard shell collar and a black hat and the black jacket with braid sewn round the lapels. She could see the silver watch chain across his waistcoat. She knew it was the minister because of the watch chain.

He hissed under his breath the way Dada did when he took a mouthful from the bottle, hissing and narrowing his eyes.

He said, 'So it is true.'

Aileen looked up at him and smiled.

* * *

239

'Oh, come now, Mrs Campbell,' Tom Ewing said, 'I cannot believe that the child is so silly that she does not even know who the father is?'

'Since it was Hector Thrale who told you about Aileen's condition—'

'Mr Thrale did *not* tell me,' Tom interjected. 'Mr Thrale merely suggested that all was not as it should be with your family.'

'Then perhaps Hector Thrale can also tell you who fathered her child.'

'I hope you're not suggesting that it was Mr Thrale?' Tom said.

'I am suggesting nothing of the sort,' said Vassie. 'I am saying that it is none of Hector Thrale's business – and none of yours either.'

'My elders . . .'

'Have no authority over me and mine,' said Vassie, curtly. 'Oh, yes, Mr Ewing, I know how it would have been in the old days when Aileen would have been made to stand before the Session and be questioned like a criminal.'

'Appearance and rebuke,' Tom said, 'went out of the window along with discipline. Although I am a man of liberal principles, on occasions like this I am inclined to think that it was a bad thing that they did.'

'Will you be taking sugar?' Vassie asked.

'Pardon?'

'In your tea – sugar?'

'If you please.'

If he had been less concerned about Aileen Campbell and the effect of the girl-child's pregnancy on Innis, he might even have found Vassie's tea-making amusing. She clattered the ewer, rattled the kettle, raked the iron poker through the peats, thumped down the caddie and sugar canister as if she were loading cannon and buttered the coarse slices of oat bread as if she were cutting throats.

Tom sat on the bench at the table, his hat before him and one leg extended just in case he had to make a run for it.

Aileen had come straggling in after him and Biddy had appeared from the byre but Vassie had sent her daughters packing, her command so shrill and snappish that there was no standing up to it.

No doubt the girls were loitering outside, eavesdropping on a conversation that was hardly a conversation at all but more of a shouting match. There was no sign of Innis. Tom did not know whether to be relieved or disappointed, for Innis might have been able to persuade her mother that it *was* a minister's business what happened to one of his flock. On the other hand, he was disappointed that Innis had not seen fit to take him into her confidence. Sunday after Sunday she had lied about the reason for the family's non-appearance, had, in effect, traded on his sympathy and, to some extent, betrayed his faith in her.

Vassie poured a stream of pale tea into a cup, clacked cup on to saucer, flung a spoon into the saucer and dumped the lot unceremoniously before him.

'Sugar it to suit yourself,' she told him.

'Are you not joining me?' Tom asked.

'No, I am not joining you.'

Tom said, 'It is not as if this were a Godless family.'

'What does God have to do with it?'

'I mean, it is not as if you have not been received into full membership.'

'Are you telling me that you will have to report this to the Presbytery?'

'That,' Tom said, swallowing, 'is my duty.'

'Your duty be damned, Mr Ewing.'

'Aileen is only a child.'

'She's old enough to marry.'

'Will she marry? I mean, will the father of the child not marry her?'

'You are no better than the rest of them,' Vassie told him. 'It is scandal you are after spreading, like your friend Thrale. Who else has he told?'

'Thrale did not tell me. Not in so many words.'

Vassie paused. She was breathing like a mare, a war-horse more like, Tom thought. She strove to contain herself by clenching her fists and thrusting them down, stiff-armed, into the folds of her apron.

'What sort of words did he use?' Vassie asked.

'He thought – he suggested, well, that Biddy might be pregnant.'

'That pig! That foul-mouthed, foul-minded pig of a man!'

'All right, all right, Mrs Campbell.' Tom held up his hand to placate her. 'I am too sensible to believe everything I hear in the village, especially when it emanates from a fellow like Thrale. I have no more respect for that gentleman than you have. However . . .'

'Aileen does not know who it is.'

'Pardon?'

'She is not right in the head. She does not know who the father is.'

'Do you mean to tell me that there's more than one candidate?'

'One what?' said Vassie, puzzled.

'That Aileen has lain with – has known more than one man.'

'What?'

'That, Mrs Campbell, is what you have just implied.'

'I implied nothing of the sort.'

'If there was only one man then he must be the father.'

'A drover,' Vassie said suddenly. 'It was a drover.'

'Oh?'

'Last summer. Last fair time. She told me it was a drover, a drover from Perthshire. Yes, that is what she told me.'

'What was his name?'

'She does not know his name.'

'Did he take her by force?'

Vassie hesitated. 'Yes.'

'Did Aileen tell you that she struggled against his attentions?'

'She – yes, she told me just that.'

'When?'

'Then. At the time.'

'And you did not see fit to make report of it?'

'Report it to who?' said Vassie.

'The constable, the fiscal. Me.'

'Who would have believed her?'

'Dr Kirkhope could have ascertained if she was telling the truth.'

'No.' Vassie shook her head violently. 'No doctors.'

'Has Kirkhope examined her?'

'Why should he examine her?'

'In her condition it would surely be prudent to seek medical advice.'

'I am not in need of medical advice.'

'She is pregnant, Mrs Campbell.'

'That is not an illness, Mr Ewing,' Vassie said. 'I am not in need of Kirkhope's service or the services of the midwife from Dervaig. I have delivered enough babies in my time to know what to do. I will be with her when the child is born.'

'That is no longer the issue.'

'What is the issue then? The drover has gone on his way long since. We will never be finding him now and I doubt if he will dare come back to Mull.'

'Can you be sure?'

'I am sure.'

'Because there never was a drover from Perthshire, was there?'

He knew that she would see the question that lay behind the question. If she answered him truthfully then he would ask her next who the father really was. He could think of only four or five men who might have gained enough of the girl-child's trust to persuade her to lie with them but he could not believe that any of those men would do such a thing.

Quietly, he said, 'Was there, Vassie?'

'No.'

She glanced out of the half-open door, down towards the shore. From his position at the table Tom could not see what she was looking at. She lifted her shoulders like a shag or a cormorant, tucked her head to her breast and stepped to the door and closed it. She did not look at him. She stood by the table's end, head hanging as if she were ashamed of herself.

Then she said, 'It was her brother.'

Tom felt the hairs rise on the nape of his neck.

'Oh, God!' he whispered. 'God help him. Is that why he was sent away?'

'Not Neil,' Vassie said. 'Donnie.'

Tom reached out, caught her hand and brought her down on to the bench by his side. Now that she had finally confessed all resistance had gone out of her.

'Did Aileen tell you that it was her brother?'

She was shaking now and there were tears in her eyes.

'It – happened when – when he was drunk.'

'Do Aileen's sisters know?'

'I kept it from them.'

'And your husband?'

Vassie shook her head.

'So Donnie has taken his guilt to the grave with him?' Tom said.

'Aye.' She looked up at him, her eyes enlarged by tears. 'Promise me that you will not tell the Presbytery?'

'Since Donnie is dead what is to be gained from telling anyone?' Tom said. 'I doubt if what he did was done with evil intent. If he had not been drunk then it would never have happened.' He let the platitudes die on his lips. 'What will become of the child?'

'As soon as it is born Aileen will be sent to Foss. My father will take care of her and the baby.'

Tom was distressed by what he had learned but not sceptical. He knew how foolish even decent young men could become when lust took control of their senses. At least the baby, and Aileen too, would be protected from malicious gossip on McIver's remote, green isle.

'I will say nothing.' Tom got to his feet. 'You have my promise. God will forgive him all his sins, great as well as small.'

'Aye, I am sure that He will,' Vassie said. 'May He also forgive me mine.'

The girls were lurking by the peat stack when Vassie finally emerged from the cottage door. Biddy and Aileen had been joined by Innis who would have gone in to the house to talk to Mr Ewing if Biddy hadn't stopped her with a few whispered words. When Reverend Ewing emerged looking white about the gills he was certainly in no mood to linger. Without so much as glancing at the girls he headed straight for the path that led up by the burn to the end of the track where he had left his horse. Even at this stage Innis was inclined to run after him, to discover how the news of her sister's condition had affected him and what he intended to do about it. But before she could free herself from Biddy's grasp, he was gone. Any notion that the girls might have had that things had gone well was dispelled a moment later when Vassie, wiping her eyes on her apron, came out into the sunlight

Aileen turned her head.

'Mam is crying. Mr Ewing has been bad to Mam and made her cry.'

'What has he been saying to her?' Biddy whispered. 'Perhaps he has forced her to tell him who the father is.'

'We do not know who the father is,' Innis reminded her.

'It does not take much brain to guess who might be responsible.'

Innis shook her head. 'I cannot believe he would go that far.'

They looked down at Aileen as if, miraculously, they expected her to blurt out the truth, but the girl remained entirely unaffected by their attention and, smiling to herself, laid her head back and closed her eyes again.

'If Mam has been forced to tell the minister the truth,' Biddy said, 'then they will both be taken away.'

'What do you mean?'

Biddy shrugged. 'One into the care of the parish, the other one to jail.'

'How do you know that? Did Michael tell you?'

'Michael! Hah!' Biddy said.

'Where is Mam going now?' Innis said, as Vassie marched down the path by the potato patch towards the jetty.

'Perhaps she is going to tell him that he is going to jail,' Biddy answered with a malicious little chuckle that made Innis's blood run cold.

It was only the cold water and the effort required to carry out his task that kept him from falling down. He was already on to his second bottle of Old Caledonia and he had better remain sober enough to tramp into Crove later or he would be faced with the prospect of running out of consolation before nightfall.

The curious fact, the thing that none of them understood, was just how good whisky made him feel. He could not say that he was aware of every mouthful or that every drop ran rich in his bloodstream. But he loved the brisk, indefinable sensation on his tongue and the feeling of it as it went down his throat into his chest. He loved the wave of unreality that came upon him after he had consumed enough of it. How he could hold the flavour of unreality in his mind the way he held the liquid in his mouth. How, after a while, a numbness stole over him so that nothing mattered but obeying the demands of his body for more of the stuff, that craving that those who were not as he was dismissed as mere thirst.

By God, he was working hard today, though. In and out of the water. Up and down the shore. Seawater soaking his clothes. Seawater seeping through his pores so that he could feel it inside, mingled with whisky, his organs floating light as cork or clumps of bladderwrack. Big, slippery lumps of stone secure in his hands as he staggered for balance. The sun lay about him, flakes and flecks and cuticles of light that slithered when he moved through them. He groped in the pea green water.

When he stood upright he could see the bottom, sand trickling away under his boots, fragments of weed and shell and the decayed entrails of shellfish. The waves lapped against his buttocks and around his thighs and broke before him in a frill of brown froth. He stooped until the water lapped his chest, groped and found a stone, tested it and lifted it, dragging it up out of the water as if he were pulling up a piece of the sea bed. He hugged the stone to his chest and paddled inshore. And then she was there. He was waist deep. He had the rock against his chest. And she was there, waiting on the shore. And she was angry. She was always angry.

'Vassie!' he called out, cheerfully. 'Vassie, my love.'

She was as still as a post or a standing stone.

'Do you see what it is that I am doing?' He stood with seawater lapping about his thighs, the big rock held against him. 'Do you see how I am going to repair the shed? We will be needing it as soon as I have my boat back, as soon as Neil comes back. We will be needing a dry place for the lines and nets as soon as the boys come home.'

Sunlight danced around him. Brown froth fringed the shore. Beyond that he had only a vague impression of grass and cattle, the cottage squat against the long ellipse of the moor, and Vassie McIver propped against it like a stone or a post, watching. It did not occur to him that she could make out hardly a word, that he did not stand tall and strong in the sea with the rock in his arms but swayed and staggered, that his smile was a leer and the rock nothing but weed.

The movement was sudden. She stepped back, stepped to one side, bent and picked one stone from the untidy little heap that his industry had produced.

She drew her hand back and threw the stone at him.

It struck him a glancing blow on the cheek. He flinched and the world fell away and the fine haze of unreality was dispersed. He felt his feet sink in the sand, the slithering eels of weed drag him down. He fell sideways. Water closed over him. Brine rushed into his mouth. He tried to shout but could not. He was drowning. Drowning like Donnie. He had commandeered not Donnie's youth but Donnie's death and now he wanted none of it. He came up, thrashing in the shallows, and looked to his wife to rescue him.

'Vassie,' he cried. 'Vassie.'

She was already halfway back to the house.

They had spent the morning out with the dogs looking at grass on the north quarter where cropping had been intense and bracken had begun to encroach upon the pastureland. Thrale had suggested that the ground be cleared, ploughed and reseeded before the Fetternish flock was increased in size. He had presented a costing to Mr Austin and was eager that the work be started before the month was out. Whatever his other faults – and they were many – Hector Thrale was an efficient manager and Austin was inclined to give him the nod to put the work in hand before peat cutting claimed the attention of the tenants.

It was after two o'clock before Willy and Austin took leave of Thrale and climbed through the alders to the house. They were both famished and eager to attack whatever dish Queenie had prepared for lunch but, it seemed, lunch would have to wait, for when they emerged from the shrubs they saw two flatbed carts laden with crates and one large, roofed wagonette pulled up on the gravel.

'What in heaven's name is going on?' Austin asked.

'Looks to me like Greeks bearing gifts,' Willy said. 'Or, to put it another way, I think Mr Walter's arrived.'

'He's early,' said Austin, tutting again. 'A whole week early.'

He called the dogs to him, leashed them and walked briskly towards the convocation of vehicles just as the side door of the wagonette opened and Walter stepped down into the courtyard. He looked much the same, trim and tidy, but by comparison with Austin he seemed pale and puffy as if wintering in Edinburgh had imposed a strain on his system.

Austin hugged his brother, clapped his back, then pulled away.

'Why didn't you let me know you were arriving today?'

'Did you not receive my telegraph message?'

'Of course I didn't or I would have been here to greet you,' Austin said, a little piqued at the disruption to his routine. 'What is all this, Walter? What have you brought with you?'

'Luggage for the summer. Necessary goods.'

'What do you mean?'

'Oh, clothes and furnishings, an ornament or two – and a pianoforte.'

'A piano? What do I want with a piano?'

'It's not for you, Austin.'

'Oh, dear God!' Austin exclaimed. 'Don't tell me!' At which point the back door of the wagonette swung open and Mrs Agnes Baverstock Paul, in a promenade dress with a plastron front and a bustle as big as a boulder, descended the three little wooden steps to the gravel.

'Agnes!' Austin said, remembering his manners. 'What a marvellous surprise. How – how good to see you.'

Two Sangster maids, Doreen and Ellen, followed their mistress, fussing and primping at her rear as if this were George Street or St Andrew Square and not the Fetternish peninsula where nobody would adjudicate your appearance or be impressed by the cut of your jib. Austin and Agnes embraced stiffly, her enormous gable hat shadowing his face as well as her own.

Then she turned towards Willy who, with the dog leash taut in his fist, had been staring at her in dismay.

'William,' she cooed. 'How well you look.'

She offered her gloved hand which Willy took.

He did not kiss it, of course, but let it rest on his palm while he bowed as graciously as he possibly could with two hounds hauling on his arm.

'Are you fit, William?'

'Aye, Mrs Paul, fit enough.'

'I am pleased to hear it,' the woman said and, with the gentlest pressure imaginable, squeezed his horny hand in hers.

It was Biddy who stumbled upon the beast. The bullock had apparently wintered well and had been gaining weight with the best of them. Now he was lying on his side in the heather three or four hundred yards on to the moor. Even when Biddy almost trampled on him he did no more than coil his head, roll his eyes and emit a hoarse moan. She did not touch him. She was not shy of handling cattle but unlike Innis she was afraid of contagion and was still inclined to believe the old wives' tale that the breath of a sick animal could bring down blood in an unmarried woman. She hurried from the moor to the calf park, a distance of half a mile, and brought Innis back to examine the bullock.

He had risen unsteadily to his feet but all natural aggressiveness had gone out of him. He swung his head from side to side and uttered pathetic moans as Innis walked around him. She could tell at once that he was unlikely to see out the day. His bones stuck out and his skin was so rough and thin as to seem almost transparent. She looked to the tail and just before the animal collapsed once more caught a glimpse of the puddling.

'Moor-ill?' Biddy asked.

'I think so,' Innis said. 'He must have been wandering about for days in this condition. Why did we not notice him before?'

Tending cattle on Pennypol was not haphazard. On the other hand, the herd was left much to itself in the fat part of the year. Innis stepped back from the stricken animal. All the manuals agreed that the disease was confined to cattle and did not communicate itself to humans but she could not shake off the fear that the entire herd might be affected by the pollution that had come down upon the moor.

She shaded her eyes and looked anxiously towards the straggle of stirks that grazed the grass above the foreshore.

Biddy said, 'It does not *always* go through a herd, Innis, does it?'

'Not always.'

'Do you think it really is moor-ill?'

'There is only one way to find out.' Innis unbuttoned her sleeves and rolled them up to her elbows. 'Hold on to his horns, sit across his neck and keep him close to the ground.'

'What are you going to do?'

'Look at his tongue and gums.'

'He will breathe on you.'

'It is his blood that is affected, not his lungs.'

'He has passed the red water.'

'I know. I saw it. Sit on him, Biddy. He is in no state to do you harm.'

Gingerly Biddy approached the animal from the tail end. He glowered at her balefully, neck coiled, flesh wrinkled in ugly folds but when she grabbed his horns and straddled his neck with her knees he did not have the strength to resist. Kneeling, Innis gripped his jaw, forced his mouth open and peered at his parched pinkish tongue and near-white gums.

'Insanguination,' she said, nodding.

'What?'

'Redwater fever has caused his blood to decay.'

'Can I let him go now?'

'Aye,' Innis said. 'There is nothing we can be doing for this poor chap. It is the rest of the herd we must attend to.'

'What is the treatment?'

'There is none that I know of. We must watch them carefully, though, to see how many have it.'

'We lost some beasts before, I remember.' Biddy disentangled her skirts from the nub of the horn and eased herself to her feet. 'Mother was very upset.'

'Yes, I was about eight when it happened,' said Innis. 'We lost five or six that summer, I think, but we did not graze as many then as we do now.'

'Will Mam not know what to do about it?'

Innis sighed. 'There is nothing to be done about it, Biddy.'

'Can we not nurse them through it?'

'Most will survive,' Innis said. 'One or two will die, I expect.'

'Is it the poison that does it?'

'No,' Innis said. 'Nobody seems to know how it gets into a herd. I have read that some veterinarians in America are beginning to think it is ticks that cause it but there is no proof yet.'

'That is ridiculous,' Biddy said. 'Ticks!'

'Well,' Innis said, 'it seems to me that there is some sense in the theory.'

'If the Americans are so sure of themselves why is there no cure?'

'I do not know,' Innis said. 'The only remedy is to scour the pasture land and leave it ungrazed for a year or two.'

'A year or two?' said Biddy. 'We cannot afford to be doing that.'

'I know,' said Innis.

'Does it affect sheep as well as cattle?'

'It seems that it does not,' said Innis.

'Even so, should we not be warning Fetternish?'

'Michael, do you mean?'

'Or Mr Baverstock.'

'Mother would not be standing for that.'

Biddy said, 'Perhaps Grandfather knows of a cure.'

'Perhaps,' Innis said, dubiously. 'I will write to him tonight, just in case.'

'In case?'

'It gets worse,' said Innis.

Austin was exceedingly uncomfortable in an evening-dress coat and corkscrew trousers that had not been out of the wardrobe since Walter had left in the autumn. There had been a time when the donning of full regalia for dinner had been a matter not just of habit but of pride and he had relished the feel of silk-lined materials, starched breastplates and tight winged collars. Those days were now in the past and he resented the necessity of having to wear a formal suit just to eat his evening meal. He was mannerly enough to hide his discomfort, however, to pretend that he was delighted to welcome not only his brother but his sister too to the big windy house on the cliff top.

The dining-room was lit by candelabra that Willy, working like a Trojan, had unpacked from one of the crates that had accompanied Mrs Baverstock Paul from Edinburgh. He had polished up the silver sticks and placed them according to Mrs Baverstock Paul's exact instructions about the huge, wood-panelled room. It was still broad daylight when the Baverstocks sat down to dine. The western sky was tinted with subtle shades

251

of salmon pink and delicate iris blue and, far out towards the horizon, the red-gold of an impending sunset against which candlelight seemed pallid and artificial.

Austin had to admit that Agnes looked handsome in the rather equine way that distinguished his mother's branch of the family. Her elongated features, sharpened by evening light, were saved from severity by a proud, high-bridged nose that – as Willy had once impertinently pointed out – did tend to make you think of Euripides. Not that Agnes was inclined to poison her children. On the contrary, she was fond of her two daughters and doted on her son Harry.

Walter had always been a wee bit under Agnes's thumb. Having endured two days of travel across land and sea in her company he was temporarily cowed, a punishment that was no more than he deserved, Austin thought, since he had invited Agnes to Fetternish without so much as a by-your-leave.

The omission made Austin suspect that there was more to the visit than fraternal obligation. He cleared his throat and said, 'I must apologise for the paucity of the fare, Agnes. If you had given me even a day's notice I would have seen to it that the fatted calf was killed and something a little more elaborate than grilled fish and mutton stew came up from the kitchens. I promise I will make amends for the duration of your stay. Which will be – what – a week?'

Agnes smiled thinly. 'I am not averse to fish, Austin, so long as it does not come swimming towards me in a sea of boiled milk. As it happens I have brought one or two little delicacies from home and first thing tomorrow I will instruct Mrs McQueen on how best to utilise them.'

'How long, I mean, are we going to have the pleasure of your company?'

'That rather depends.'

'Oh! On what, my dear?'

'On you, Austin.'

'On me? Well, of course you are welcome to stay as long as you wish.'

'So Walter told me.'

'Walter?'

Walter tapped his soup spoon lightly on the edge of his plate.

'In case you've forgotten, Austin, may I remind you that half the estate is mine, even if you have rather laid claim to it in the past half year.'

'No, no. I had not forgotten,' Austin said. 'It is just that . . .'

'If I might have permission to speak, ma'am?' said Willy with a bow towards the head of the table.

'By all means, William.'

'I believe Mr Austin is worried about domestic arrangements. Your bedroom has been prepared, Mrs Paul, but the maids – well, the maids present a wee bit of a problem.'

'Do they? What manner of problem?'

'In havin' them on the same floor as you.' Willy wore a green striped vest and a heavy formal shirt that, according to Agnes, made him look like a publican. 'If you are intendin' to stay for a while, ma'am,' Willy went on, 'then I'll see to it that rooms adjacent to your own are opened and aired for the maids' convenience.'

She studied him intently, brows drawn, her eyes a little flinty.

'What is the alternative, William?'

'To bed them down below,' Willy said.

'Is there accommodation down below?'

'Aye, ma'am. Plenty of it.'

'I do not wish them to be uncomfortable.'

'They'll be as snug as they are at home.'

'I will leave the arrangements to you, William.'

'Aye, ma'am. Thank you,' said Willy. 'For how long will that be?'

'That, Willy,' Walter Baverstock put in, 'is a matter between my sister, my brother and myself.'

In other circumstances it might have given Innis pleasure to watch her grandfather work cattle. It had been years since she had seen him stroll through a herd, stroking a flank here, a hock there or lifting up a foreleg to inspect a hoof. Age might have stiffened his joints but he had lost none of his gentleness and even the mad, bad bullocks of Pennypol responded to his authority and rubbed against him, grunting and slavering, as soon as he entered the pen.

As a rule Pennypol cattle were brought in only two or three

times in the course of a year, usually for dosing against ringworm or prior to being sold. Consequently they had no patience with Fingal's darting little runs and snappings and would have had him up on the horns if they could have got at him fast enough. But Fingal had been stirred by the sight of the big-horned crossbreeds milling down from the hillside. He was quick into the fray, streaking through the young bracken to round up a straggler or nipping at the heels of some rebel who had failed to realise that fate had him marked for a butcher's hook no matter how hard he dug in his hooves and roared.

The cattle were penned overnight. They were fed from a hay rack and watered by a canvas hose that ran from the burn to a galvanised iron trough that Biddy and Innis carried from the byre. Even before Evander McIver gave his expert opinion it was clear that a dozen bullocks were ailing. Dark red urine dripping from their parts was too obvious a sign to ignore, along with a faint, seedy smell like rotting turnips.

Grandfather had arrived from Foss on board an Oban fishing smack that moored at high tide at the jetty's end. He did not come alone but brought along the woman, Mairi, and a boy who Innis knew as Quig. There was a certain urgency in the manner in which Evander led them up the shore to the pen, for the smack would have to put out again before half water. Besides, his loathing of Ronan was palpable and he made no attempt to disguise it. He brushed past his son-in-law with Mairi and the boy following Indian-file. He headed straight for the spot where Vassie, Biddy and Innis waited while Ronan, pretending that he hadn't noticed the slight, ambled down the jetty to pass the time of day with the boatman and offer him a dram.

Grandfather McIver began by asking Innis six or eight questions. Who had found the first beast? Had it recovered? It had not. It had died last night. What had been done with the corpse? It had been left where it was, so far. Where had the herd been pastured? On the moor and on the grass steps above the shore. Which beasts had been pastured on the moor? All of them had ranged there at some time during the past three or four weeks.

'Innis, what do you think it is?'

'Redwater fever, Grandfather. I am sure of it.'

'It is not the first time we have had it here,' Vassie added.

'No, and I fear it may not be the last,' Evander McIver said. 'Once it gets into the ground there is no getting rid of it.'

He leaned on the temporary fence and studied the cattle for a minute or so then he signalled Quig to come to him and with the boy's help hoisted himself over the gate into the pen. Nimble as a hare, the boy leaped after him and together they moved among the herd, examining each animal in turn. Mairi leaned on the fence close to Innis but Vassie and Biddy stood off to one side and Aileen, who had appeared from the cottage, sat on the ground like a doll, braced on her elbows, her stomach thrust out.

When Evander came back to the fence the beasts followed him. It was all Quig could do to hold them back. He leaned upon them, shoulders and buttocks pressing their muzzles and brows.

'Was I right, Grandfather?' Innis asked.

'Yes. Redwater is not difficult to diagnose.'

'I am sorry if I brought you here for no reason,' Innis said.

'You were correct to send for me,' her grandfather said.

'How many have it?' Vassie called out.

'Twenty-one of them.'

'Twenty-one?'

'You will not be losing any more, though, not if you nurse them properly.'

'I will do that,' Vassie said. 'The last time it happened there were only six affected and they were not so bad as to die of it.'

'That was the last time, Vassie,' the old man said. 'Once it is in the ground then it is there for ever unless you scour out the grazing and leave it free of cattle for two full years.'

'I cannot do that,' Vassie said. 'I do not have enough grass to keep the herd off the moor.'

'Then you will be risking having sickly beasts year after year.'

'Are you telling me that we are ruined?'

'I did not say that, Vassie,' her father told her. 'They will recover. They will be lean and will not fill out in time for the autumn sales but there is nothing in the Prevention Act to prohibit you selling them for beef.'

'Do I not have to notify the Board?'

Evander shook his head. 'There is nothing in the listing of

notifiable diseases that obliges you to report cases of redwater. It is not the cattle that are polluted but the ground upon which they feed.'

'Innis says it is the ticks that cause it,' Biddy said, sceptically.

'It may be that it is,' her grandfather told her. 'I know no more than anyone how the disease originates or how it is transmitted into the cattle. All I can tell you is that it is bad for the condition of bullocks and worse still for cows.'

'Have you had it on Foss?' said Innis.

'Never. Foss is a clean island.'

The boy was having trouble holding the animals off now. They were nudging and nuzzling with increasing excitement and Evander prudently decided to quit the pen. He climbed unaided over the fence and Quig followed him. Biddy and Vassie came around the corner of the pen and joined the old man near the gate. There was no communication between Mairi and Vassie and it was not just concern over the health of the cattle herd that prevented it.

The old man wiped his hands carefully on his trousers. He looked older now, Innis thought, much older than he had done back in November, as if at long last the years were catching up with him.

'I have brought you something to give them,' he said. 'Four sacks of it. It is nothing special but it will restore their appetites and help them to be putting on weight. Dose them with it once each day with water or mixed into feed.'

'I have not enough feed to keep them penned for long,' Vassie said.

'Enclose those who are sick or who become sick. Keep them penned for a week or so. The others you can let out. But,' the old man said, 'do not let your cows or calves graze with the herd. How soon until you are making hay?'

'Five or six weeks, with the weather,' Vassie answered.

He nodded. 'That will have to do.' He signalled to the boy and took Mairi's hand in his. 'That is all I can be doing for you, Vassie, in the matter of the cattle. What of Aileen? When is she due?'

'Before the month is out.'

'And then you will be bringing her to Foss?' Evander McIver said.

'I will.'

He glanced at the girl-child who gave him a coy smile as if to convince him that she was sweet-natured and innocent and the thing that grew inside her was none of her doing.

'We could take her back with us today,' Mairi suggested.

'No,' Vassie snapped. 'She is my daughter. I will be there with her when her time comes.'

Evander nodded again. 'I will leave the sacks on the shore. You can bring them up as you need them,' he said, then, still holding the woman's hand, bade the family goodbye and set off down the path towards the jetty.

On impulse Innis ran after him and caught up with him.

'Are you angry with me for sending for you?' she asked.

'It was the sensible thing to do.'

'What is it then? You do not seem yourself.'

'I do not like leaving Foss at this time of year, that is all.'

Innis said, 'Have you told us everything, Grandfather?'

'Concerning the cattle?'

'Aye.'

'No, not everything,' he said.

'It is serious, is it not?' Innis said.

'It is not the disease that might destroy Pennypol,' he said, choosing his words carefully. 'It is everything else.'

'Aileen, do you mean?'

'And Donnie's passing. There will not be enough of you left to work the place,' her grandfather said. 'There is no money coming in from fishing now, I expect. Does he help on the farm?'

'My father? No, not often.'

Evander released Mairi's hand, looked into Innis's face and touched her hair gently. 'You should be marrying that minister fellow, you know.'

'Mr Ewing?' said Innis, astonished. 'He is far too old for me.'

'He is hardly in his dotage.'

'Mr Ewing does not think of me – that way.'

'He would take care of you and treat you with respect.'

'I do not love him.'

'I see,' Evander McIver said. 'Well, there is no more to be said.'

'Wait,' Innis said. 'Tell me the truth, Grandfather. What will happen if the fever lingers in the ground, if we have not enough grass left to fatten the cattle for market?'

'The herd will become weak,' the old man told her. 'In a year or two the grazings will be so polluted that every beast put out upon them will come down with some degree of fever. Soon it will affect the cows as well as the beef and when that happens you will be having low milk yields and your calves, some of them, will be born dead or puling. From then on it will be a struggle to sell anything or to earn enough cash to purchase fresh stock.'

'Is there nothing we can do to make the ground clean again?'

'Yes, Innis, there is.'

'What?'

'Stock it with sheep,' Evander McIver said.

It took less than a week for Agnes to make her mark on Fetternish. Austin was not the only person to find her tiresome. Even Willy, who thought he knew how to handle women, found himself slinking about the corridors waiting for the clang of the handbell with which she summoned attention. Quite the little campanologist was Agnes Baverstock Paul. Never any confusion as to who she wanted or when she wanted them. Three rings for a maid, two rings for Willy, one ring for a brother. From garden or larder, from kitchen or water-closet she reeled them in with the bell.

Thanking God that he was still fit enough to take the stairs two at a time, Willy would gallop up to find Agnes in the drawing-room or hall, bell in hand and a peevish expression on her face that seemed to say, 'Well, what kept you?' She was prudent enough not to complain aloud, though, at least not to the man who had once given her pleasure in bed and who, she sincerely hoped, might soon be moved to do so again.

Austin was less intimidated by the handbell than by Agnes's snide remarks concerning his moral worth. She had always been a bit of a termagant, which was one of the reasons that Walter and he had surrendered both the mill and the family mansion and established themselves in Edinburgh. How her poor husband put up with her was more than Austin could imagine, for it did not occur to him – why should it? – that the energy his sister expended in getting things done to her satisfaction might be a challenge to a certain type of man and that perhaps there were compensations to be had in the bedroom after her handbell had been hung up for the night.

'Austin?'

'Yes, my dear.'

'Have you been meeting with that girl again?'

'Certainly not.'

'Where were you this morning?'

'I took the dogs for a walk.'

'To Pennypol? Is that what it's called?'

'No. I walked to An Fhearann Cáirdeil.'

'I beg your pardon!'

'It's a very pretty spot where sometimes, if I'm lucky, I see deer.'

'Is this "pretty spot" where you meet *her*?'

'It is in entirely the opposite direction from the Campbells' farm,' Austin said. 'Besides which I do not have meetings with Bridget, apart from a rare encounter purely by chance when I am over at Na h-Vaignich on business.'

'Nah – what?'

'Where our shepherd lives.'

'Is that where you meet her?'

'Agnes!' Austin said in exasperation. 'I do not contrive to liaise with Biddy Campbell at the Solitudes or anywhere else. I do wish you would take my word for it.'

'Walter tells me that you are infatuated with this girl.'

'Nothing of the kind. Biddy is a pleasant young woman, that's all.'

'That's not what Walter tells me.'

'Oh, and what does Walter tell you?'

'That she is a vampire, a rough, countrified vampire.'

'Walter didn't say that?'

'Not in so many words, no, but that was the implication.'

'Walter hardly knows her.'

'He knows her type.'

'Her type?' said Austin, bridling. 'How can he know her type when he has spent almost no time at all on Fetternish. Bridget Campbell is not, I confess, a dainty Edinburgh *fille* but she is certainly no primitive. She is the daughter of a property holder, I'll have you know.'

'She is a glorified fieldhand.'

'Well, it matters not what she is, Agnes, since I have no designs upon her.'

'Perhaps not – though I doubt if you're telling me the truth – but did it not occur to you that she may have designs upon you?'

'Absolute nonsense.'

'You're not a very prepossessing chap, Austin, but you do have attributes that make you attractive to a certain type of woman. It is my opinion, and Walter's too, that your age renders you particularly vulnerable. This Campbell girl is a redhead, is she not?'

'Yes.'

'You see.'

'What? *What?*'

'You're thinking about her even as we speak.'

'Of course I'm thinking about her. We are discussing her, after all. If we weren't discussing her I would be thinking of – of – other things.'

'I appreciate that a man has certain desires, certain needs and that in a place as remote as Fetternish those needs are, of necessity, given more weight and prominence than would be the case in Edinburgh where there are diversions to take your mind off things.'

'Agnes, what are you talking about?'

Agnes raised a forefinger. 'We both know what I'm talking about, Austin. It is not that Walter isn't grateful to you for remaining in residence over the winter but he is as concerned as I am that tedium might lead you into error.'

'For heaven's sake, Agnes. I do not find Mull in the least tedious. It's a dashed sight less tedious than swanning up and down George Street. I like it here. I am free here.'

'Free to succumb to this girl's blandishments?'

'What blandishments?'

'If you allow yourself to be caught in a weak moment then it will cost us dearly to be rid of her.'

'Is that why you've travelled to Mull, to save me from Biddy Campbell?'

'A word to the wise, my dear,' said Agnes, tapping the side of her high-bridged nose, 'a word to the wise.'

* * *

He walked with a long, loping stride that had the dogs, and Willy too, straining to keep up. Willy crashed through the new bracken with the silver flask bouncing against his hip and sweat beading the brim of his cap. He did not resent the pace his master set, for he knew that Mr Austin was angry. And he knew why. He straggled on to the green patch by the ruins of the old croft to find Mr Austin already standing out on the point, hands on his hips, inhaling the salt air in great gulps and still seething with annoyance and frustration.

Willy uncapped the flask, approached cautiously, and handed it to his master. Austin glanced at him, took the flask, knocked back a mouthful of whisky and wiped his mouth on his sleeve.

'She thinks I'm – I'm . . .'

'Dandling?' Willy suggested

'Yes – dandling Biddy Campbell.'

'Tut-tut-tut,' Willy said sympathetically. 'What does Mr Walter think?'

'I gather that he's of approximately the same opinion.'

'Tut-tut-tut.'

Austin swigged again and passed the flask to Willy who also took a taste. Austin stared bleakly out to sea.

'Willy,' he said, 'what do you think I should do?'

'Well, sir,' Willy Naismith paused. 'Well, Mr Austin . . .'

'Out with it, William.'

'In my opinion, if that's what she thinks you're up to, sir, you may as well be hung for a sheep as a lamb.'

'Where is she?' Austin peered around the office as if he expected Agnes to pounce on him from behind a sack of grass seed.

'In the kitchen, I think,' Walter answered, 'instructing Mrs McQueen on how to prepare trout.'

'Trout?'

'One of our workers brought us a basketful. Fine fish, if small. Caught in the Mishnish lochs last evening, I believe.'

'Probably poached.'

'Probably.'

Walter was seated behind the desk. He had loosened his collar and unbuttoned his vest but the embroidered cuffs that protected his sleeves were still too 'Edinburgh' for Austin's liking. In time, he thought, Mull might claim Walter too, but Walter was not yet prepared to yield himself up to the island's spell. He was poring over three large drawings that Thrale had prepared at his request. Acreages were neatly pencilled in the margins and little arrows and topographical cartouches gave the sheets something of the quality of art. Walter had a notebook to hand and a slim little volume, *The Agriculturist's Calculator*, pressed open on the desk before him.

Fearing that he might lose the impetus that had driven him to seek out his brother, Austin pulled out a chair, seated himself and resolutely planted both fists upon the desk.

'How much for your share of Fetternish?' he said.

Walter looked up, surprised. 'Beg pardon?'

'How much would it cost me to buy you out?'

'Oh, come, Austin! That's a ridiculous question.'

'I've never been more serious. Name your price, Walter, and I'll see if I have sufficient capital to cover it or, failing that, if I can obtain a loan.'

'You don't really want to buy me out, do you?'

'You loathe the place. I love it.'

'I don't loathe it. I just find it – different.'

'Are you refusing to set a figure?'

'Of course I'm refusing to set a figure. In your present frame of mind,' Walter said, 'I could demand twice what it's worth and you would agree to it.'

'I would have it valued, of course,' said Austin, slightly nonplussed, 'before I actually signed anything.'

'At least you haven't entirely lost your reason.'

'Agnes is enough to make anyone lose their reason,' Austin said. 'Why did you have to bring her here?'

'She was keen to inspect our new estate.'

'Did you tell her that I'd seduced Biddy Campbell?'

'I am not in the least concerned who you've seduced, Austin,' Walter said. 'What does concern me – and Agnes too – is that you may be trapped into marrying someone who is entirely unsuitable.'

'I am not sure that is any of your business, Walter.'

'Perhaps not. But Fetternish *is* my business. And a very lucrative business it is turning out to be. In case you haven't realised it, the cost per head of raising a sheep on Mull is half that of any Border farm.'

'Thrale said as much.'

'Even after deducting the cost of transportation we can crop wool for our manufactory at forty per cent less than buying out of the market,' Walter explained. 'I've talked it over with Alister and he's willing to invest some of his profits into increasing the size of the flock.'

'By how many head?'

'Two or three hundred.' Walter shrugged. 'Indeed, if we could secure a safe water supply and reduce our shipping costs we might take on twice that number.'

'Buy out the Campbells, do you mean?'

'Hmmm. Or lease pasture from them, as Ronan Campbell suggested.'

'I doubt if Vassie Campbell will ever give ground to Fetternish.'

'Thrale has indicated that all is not well with the Campbells. Losing a son cannot have strengthened their hold on the farm. Has the girl, Biddy, said anything to you about their current financial state?'

'Of course not,' said Austin. 'Whatever you might think to the contrary, I'm not her confidant.'

'Perhaps you might do a little fishing – and not for trout.'

'Come now, Walter,' Austin said, his temper rising. 'On one hand Agnes is warning me not even to pass the time of day with Biddy, on the other you're telling me to prise information from her.'

Walter lifted a pencil and tapped it thoughtfully against his teeth. 'Why have you come storming in here demanding that I sell you my half share in Fetternish. I mean, what prompted this outburst?'

'I want to settle down.'

'Do you mean marry?'

'I'm not getting any younger, Walter, and unlike you . . .'

'I would prefer it if you would leave me out of the argument,' Walter said. 'Do you really like the island life, Austin, or are you just carried away with the notion of wedding the redhead?'

'I must have something to offer her.'

'Half of Fetternish is not enough?'

'Something of my own. Something that's mine, not the family's.'

'Hmmm. Agnes is right to be concerned.'

Austin planted his fists on the table top again. 'I'm not a child, Walter. Your assumption that what I feel for Biddy Campbell is plain and simple lust does me no credit.'

'She is a very desirable woman.'

'I know that.'

'But, in all conscience, how can you contemplate having that disreputable little fisherman for a father-in-law?'

Austin had the decency to pause. 'I would not be marrying her father.'

'Ah, but you would. You would be taking on not just the wife but the family. Do you suppose blood is any less thick among Mull crofters than it is with us? Once they have a foot in the door of Fetternish there's no telling what the Campbells would do to ruin it as they have ruined their own holding.'

'And yet you would have me approach Biddy?'

'Only to find out if they are straitened enough to sell us ground.'

'There's something dishonest about that arrangement.'

'Not at all. It's business, Austin, just business.'

'In my book it smacks of exploitation.'

'None the less,' Walter said, quietly, 'will you do it?'

'What will Agnes say?'

'Agnes will understand,' said Walter. 'Will you do it?'

'Yes.'

Whatever devious approach to the leasing of Pennypol Walter Baverstock had in mind was rendered not just superfluous but ridiculous by what occurred next. If Thrale had been on better terms with Michael Tarrant, or if Tarrant had not been so reclusive, news of the redwater outbreak would surely have reached Fetternish much sooner than it did and Austin would not have been thrown together with Biddy. Observation would have made the cattle herd's distress obvious to the outside world. But for the Campbells in that late spring season there was no outside world. Even Ronan on his jaunts into Crove was cautious enough to say nothing about the trouble that had come down upon them.

Three beasts died. Innis wept over them, grieved by the fact that she could do nothing to relieve their distress. The carcasses might have been sold to the knacker for a few precious shillings but Vassie would have none of it. Each calamity that was visited upon her now was measured against the tragedy of Donnie's drowning and, by comparison, found wanting. Aided by Innis and Biddy she buried the bodies on the moor and sprinkled ammonia on the graves to deter any predators that might be tempted to scrape up the bones.

Disposing of the wasted carcasses was a simple task compared with the effort of nursing sick bullocks back to health. Even when they were well again the animals had to be kept from moor grazing and with not enough grass to satisfy them the rebel stirks, starved for a green bite, broke through the fence, invaded the hayfield and had to be rounded up and chased back to the pen.

After supper Innis pored over her collection of agricultural journals in search of a clue to the fever's origins. It appeared that her grandfather had told her all there was to know, however, and correspondence between veterinarians, farmers and scholars became vague and confusing after a while. Tending the herd took its toll on her temper and not even a spell of fine summery weather could bring cheer to Innis and give her hope that in the end all would be well.

As the weeks went by Aileen grew more swollen and more impatient. Her tiny body seemed warped by pregnancy, her belly of such size that it was all she could do to walk let alone work. She girned constantly and would wake Vassie in the night with her restless cries. She would have sought comfort from her father but Vassie would not let Ronan come near and Ronan would rebuff her with a little push or whisking motion, saying, 'Your mam is not wanting you to bother me, my sweetheart, since she is wanting you all for herself,' and would laugh when Aileen squealed and turned on Vassie in blind rage and struck at her with her fists.

Austin Baverstock was blissfully unaware of the dramas that were taking place on Pennypol. His encounters with Biddy had ceased with his brother's return and, thanks to Agnes's warnings, he could not bring himself to think of Biddy Campbell without longing. The more Agnes nagged him about Biddy's mercenary nature, the more he desired the girl. With Willy Naismith's suggestion and Walter's instruction still ringing in his ears he set off one fine May morning not just to converse with Biddy Campbell but to court her.

In one pocket, wrapped in tissue paper, he carried a nice little necklace of pearl and white coral that he had bought in Tobermory. In another pocket was a half bottle of Dufftown malt whisky and in a third, slightly crushed, a packet of Gunpowder, an expensive tea that he reckoned might appeal to Mrs Campbell and soften her attitude towards him. He was not so blinded by love, however, that he missed the irony involved in bearing gifts to the natives and he strode over the hill towards Pennypol feeling just a wee bit foolish.

The pastures were crowded with mothering ewes and lambs that were already growing sturdy and adventurous. Austin had left the exact count of live births to Thrale but he had kept an eye on the tally. Tarrant had done his job well and, despite predictions to the contrary, the Cheviots appeared to be thriving. He had seen little of the shepherd since the start of lambing, though, for Tarrant preferred to keep himself to himself and Austin had no wish to behave like a heavy-handed employer.

He was surprised to find Tarrant lying by the back of the broken wall that overlooked Pennypol, the collie snoozing in the grass by his side.

The shepherd had a bottle of cold tea and a chequered cloth with cheese and bread upon it was spread between his knees. There were no sheep in sight except one untidy-looking ewe with a big brown lamb bleating at her tail who seemed even more chagrined at Austin's appearance than did the shepherd.

'Good morning, Tarrant.'

'Good morning, Mr Baverstock.'

'Good weather for the flock.'

'Fair, Mr Baverstock. Fair. We could do with a wee drop of rain, though.'

'Oh, I thought we had had enough of that to last us all summer.'

'The grass is growing patchy in the west quarter,' Michael Tarrant said.

Austin hesitated. He was eager to be on his way to see Biddy but he did not wish to seem rude or perfunctory. Over the top of the wall he could make out Campbell's cottage and a portion of the grazing and beyond it, stretched out like an exercise in perspective, the contours of the land folding away into the distant hills. The sea was a peculiar shade of green this morning, like mottled jade.

'Now I have you here,' Austin said, 'tell me what you think of Pennypol.'

'What?' said Tarrant, frowning.

'As a property, I mean. How many sheep would it support, for instance?'

'Oh!' For some odd reason the shepherd seemed relieved. 'Hard to say, sir. Three head per acre, four at the very most.'

'From what you have seen of it, would it graze well?'

'With or without cattle?'

'Without.'

'That would be just as well, Mr Baverstock,' Michael Tarrant said.

'What do you mean?'

'The Campbells' herd is not in the best of trim.'

'I have heard nothing of this,' Austin said. 'Thrale said nothing of it.'

'I think they are trying to keep it dark, Mr Baverstock.'

'What's wrong with them, the cattle I mean?'

'At a guess – redwater fever.'

'Are our sheep at risk?'

Tarrant shook his head. 'If it is the fever then, no, it will not affect our sheep. Indeed, there's a theory that grazing sheep on polluted pasture is the only way to be rid of redwater.'

'What makes you think it is redwater?'

'By the way they have been nursing them.'

'Are they keeping them off the moor grass?' Austin asked.

'They are. And a hard time they are having doing it.'

'Dear God!' Austin exclaimed. 'I wonder if they need help.'

'Not them. Not the Campbells,' the shepherd said. 'They are a hard lot, well able to take care of themselves.'

'I was on my way down there. Do you think I should not go?'

Michael Tarrant hesitated. By his side the collie opened both eyes and, without stirring, stared into the leaves of grass. The shepherd looked at Austin, a faint smile upon his lips, a sour little wrinkle by the corner of one eye.

'Aye, go, Mr Baverstock. Go and make sure.'

'Sure?'

'That what I've said is true.'

Labour began before the coming of dawn. In spite of all that Vassie had told her Aileen was caught out by the breaking of the waters and it was only dampness spreading across the mattress that alerted Vassie to the imminence of the infant's arrival. She had prepared for it, of course. Clean towels and pans of fresh water had been kept to hand for days, the peat fire stoked and ready for a boiling. Linen strips, napkins and an assortment of baby clothes had also been laid out and, preparing for the worst, Vassie had rummaged in her stock of remedies and had mixed infusions of Colombo root and Peruvian bark in case child-bed fever should take hold in the aftermath.

She also had a jar of lambing jelly and six stout unbleached ribbons, though what she intended to do with the latter items she did not quite know since Aileen's anatomy was in no way similar to that of a cow's and the baby was unlikely to arrive forehoofs first.

Vassie was caught out by the rapidity with which Aileen's labour progressed. Given her daughter's slightness Vassie had anticipated a prolonged and difficult labour with much pain and screaming. She had instructed Innis and Biddy what they would be required to do and had presented them with such a picture of agony and effort that they felt almost disappointed when, only four hours after her first contraction, Aileen involuntarily arched her back, flung her knees wide apart and with a yelp rather than a scream thrust out into the world a hefty, pinkish male child, already capped with fair hair and already extremely voluble.

Far from collapsing in weakness and confusion, Aileen lugged herself up on to her elbows, peered down at the squalling boy and in the same sweet, sinister tone that she used when she prayed to the gods of wind and weather, said, 'Mine.'

* * *

'I say,' Austin called out. 'I say, is there anyone about?'

He had approached by way of the calf park. From that vantage point he had been able to see most of Pennypol spread out before him and no sign of anyone in the fields or upon the shore.

Twenty or thirty head of cattle were corralled in a pen that backed the east side of the new wall. Straw litter, a water trough and two wooden hay-racks kept them comfortable. The rest of the herd browsed the sward above the foreshore. He noticed that the fence around the hayfield had been repaired with wire and brushwood, that the pony had been let loose and the sled upon which peats were carried had been up-ended to plug a gap in the dike. He no longer doubted Tarrant's conclusion that the Pennypol herd had been smitten by redwater and as he passed the fence he peered at the cattle with an interest which, unfortunately, was backed by very little experience.

The beasts' restless grunting hid other sounds and it was not until he reached the byre that Austin began to suspect that he had picked quite the wrong time to call upon his neighbours.

He raised his voice. 'I say.'

Noises from within the cottage were audible but unintelligible: a woman shouting, and something else, something strange – a fretful wailing like that of a new-born infant.

'Bridget? Are you there?'

The door of the cottage opened abruptly.

Biddy stepped forth.

She was hardly out of the door before it closed behind her.

'I'm sorry,' Austin said. 'I – I did not mean to intrude.'

The young woman sucked in a deep breath that lifted her shoulders and thrust her breasts against her cotton bodice. 'It is quite all right, Mr Baverstock. We are having our dinner indoors today.'

'I thought I heard . . .'

She took in another deep breath and allowed her shoulders to slacken. She tossed her head, her hair flying like a mane. Then she smiled so winningly that Austin felt his knees go weak.

Barefoot and bare-legged, she stepped towards him and extended her arm. The arm was bare almost to the shoulder. He could see the shape of her shoulder and bosom, the hair beneath her armpit not tufty but curled by perspiration as if each strand had been delicately painted on her white flesh.

'Since you have been kind enough to call on us,' Biddy said, 'shall we be walking a wee way together, Mr Baverstock?'

Austin took her arm, warm, firm and so strong that he could not have resisted even if he wished to do so. She locked him to her side like a George Street *boulevardière* and led him away from the cottage towards the burn before he quite knew what was happening. He was lost in admiration for the country girl who, caught in her shift and bodice, ungroomed and ungirdled, still managed to demonstrate a degree of aplomb that would have put a Morningside dowager to shame. If he had not been in love with Biddy before he was most assuredly in love with her now.

'No doubt you have been hearing that we have had a spot of trouble with our cattle?' Biddy said, casually.

'Yes,' said Austin, dazed. 'I believe I did hear something of the sort.'

'It is nothing serious.'

'The rumour is that it's redwater fever?'

'Moor-ill,' Biddy told him.

'Ah!'

'In a week or two everything will be as right as the rain.'

'If there is anything that I – that Fetternish can do to assist . . .'

She shook her head, her hair flying. Her underlip was wet and her tongue lay between her teeth as if she were holding back a question.

Austin did not press. Remembering Willy Naismith's advice, however, he slipped his arm from hers and tentatively put it about her waist.

'Mr Baverstock! Austin! Please.'

Thinking that he had overstepped the mark he was on the point of jerking his arm away again when Biddy stopped and swung against him.

She leaned heavily into him. He had dreamed of having Biddy Campbell in his arms so often that he could not believe that it was finally happening. Her solidity, her tangibility frightened him. He might even have drawn away if she had not clung to him and with a wriggling motion of shoulders and hips pressed each point of contact between them in turn.

'Oh, Austin,' she said in a broken voice, 'I am so glad that you are here,' and pulled him down on top of her into the soft green fern.

NINE

The Wedding March

In the not so dim and distant past Willy Naismith would undoubtedly have worked his charm on one or other of the sweet little maids that Agnes Paul had imported from Sangster. The trouble was that neither of the girls was all that sweet and, in combination, displayed a cynicism that was far too caustic for a man of Willy's generation. They were scathing in their criticism of Mull, of Fetternish and of Mr Austin Baverstock who, it seemed, they regarded as a buffoon. Willy was under no illusions as to his master's lack of wit but it galled him to hear two lassies who were hardly old enough to wipe their own noses sneering at a gentleman whose age and position demanded a modicum of respect.

The arrogance of the young maids irritated him, that and their inexplicable allegiance to Agnes Paul, who treated them abominably. Beneath his antipathy, though, was the realisation that he did not find the buxom little creatures physically attractive and that his days as the scourge of the servants' hall were probably over. In fact, he was beginning to wonder if he was worthy enough to be Margaret's friend, let alone her protector, or if he might be too old for her as well. He was not, it seemed, too old for Mrs Baverstock Paul, however.

Now that she had settled in, the handbell summoned him at all sorts of odd hours or, smirking, Doreen or Ellen would come tripping downstairs from the lady's 'suite' to inform him that Mrs Baverstock Paul would like a word with him. Willy was no fool. He could read the signals with perfect clarity. He knew that the masters' sister – his mistress-that-was – was endeavouring to lure him into making advances that would not be rebuffed.

The first time such a thing had happened was all of fifteen years ago. Agnes Paul had been fresh out of the marriage bed and Willy had been excited by the perverse nature of her demands upon him. He had been much more of a man then, not merely more vigorous but daring too and had thought that he had nothing to lose. He had swept the almost-new bride off her feet, had thrown her across the big four-poster and had shown her what legions of servant lassies had found so irresistible about him. After that, two or three times in the year, when Alister Paul was away, William had been called upon to 'comfort' the lady of the house, a chore that he had never regarded as distasteful – until now.

In many ways Agnes Paul was more attractive than she had ever been. The bearing of children had reduced the angularity of her limbs and plumped up her bosom and the years had mellowed her imperiousness so that when she had him alone she could seem almost coy. Here on Mull, however, her allure was much diminished and when she made up to him, which she did with increasing frequency, Willy found himself drawing back as if he were the master and she a winsome maid who did not know her place.

'Ma'am?'

'Ah, William. Yes, now what did I want from you?' She would be seated at the pianoforte in the drawing-room, candles lighted, dress folded around her long legs, her long, teasing fingers laid on the keys. 'I'm sure there was something I wanted you to do. Come closer, William, while I try to remember.' He would be buttoned up tightly in his striped vest, protected by the chamois apron that he used when he cleaned the silver.

'Are you familiar with music, William? I seem to recall that you were something of a singer in your younger days.'

'I never learned to read the notes.'

'That is unfortunate. Nevertheless, you may turn the page for me when I tell you to. Will you do that for me, William?'

'If that's what you want, Mrs Paul.'

Once she had him up close she would bend forward so that he could see the shape of her breasts under the boning. She would stroke a ripple of notes from the ivory keys and would look up at him, slanting her eyes and lowering her lashes and would cover his hand with hers while she guided it to the music page on the rack before her and would wait for Willy to do what he had always done, sweep her into his arms and kiss her with his great, rough, bearded face, his great, rough tongue thrust into her mouth.

Willy did nothing of the sort. He knew that she would not command that he took her into his arms, for she was still his superior, his mistress, and she would not lower herself by giving him such an order. It might seem churlish not to indulge her, particularly as he had indulged her before, but for Margaret's sake Willy was determined not to succumb.

Margaret soon realised that something was going on between the masters' sister and Mr Naismith and watched apprehensively for signs that Mrs Paul had had her way and that Willy Naismith was no longer fit to be her friend let alone – one day – her husband. She blocked her ears to the sniggering of the Sangster maids and Queenie's warnings about what a devil with women Willy had been and prayed that Mrs Baverstock Paul would soon go back to where she came from and leave them all to get on with their lives.

Then, on a drizzly night late in May, matters reached a climax.

The Baverstocks and Agnes had been out to dine with Mr Clark. Willy had been commissioned to drive them there and back again and it was after midnight before Maggie, tucked up in her closet in the basement, heard the crunch of the wagonette's wheels on the gravel and, a minute or two later, the front door opening.

At that hour of the night the house had a peculiarly resonant quality so that Maggie, sitting up, could hear voices in the hall above; in particular, Agnes Paul's angry complaints. She could also make out Mr Walter's voice, slurred and soothing, and now and then Mr Austin's apologetic interjections. She remained upright against the pillow and, after two or three minutes, heard the door at the top of the stairs open and someone, Willy, descend. He came padding along the corridor on stocking feet, his shoes in his hand. Maggie heard him enter the kitchen itself and then the faint creak of the boards as he returned.

She could not contain her curiosity. She got up, opened the

door a little and peeped around it. Willy was almost opposite her. He carried a large pitcher of milk in one hand and a drinking glass in the other.

'Willy, what is it that is going on?' Maggie hissed.

'All kinds of things,' Willy said. 'Did they wake you with their ruckus?'

'What is the milk for?'

'Her ladyship claims she has a headache that only cold milk will cure.'

'Has she been at the drink?'

'Aye, they've all been at the drink.' Willy sighed. He hesitated, seemed about to move on and then, with a wry little grunt, said, 'Mr Austin has just announced that he's going to marry Biddy Campbell.'

'What?'

'He came right out with it at Mr Clark's dinner table, apparently, so that Agnes has had to contain herself all evenin' and pretend she knew about it.'

'Has Biddy accepted him?'

'Not yet. It seems she's been – um – dandling him.'

'Dandlin' Mr Austin?'

'Hard to credit, ain't it?' Willy said. 'Agnes is furious. The masters are as drunk as pigs. They'll be rollin' off to their beds immediately but – well – her ladyship wants me to take her milk to soothe her sore head.'

'Is that all she wants soothed?'

Willy said, 'Go back to bed, Maggie, and keep out of it.'

'Willy?'

'What?'

'Be careful.'

The dress lay on the rug where she had tossed it and her hairpiece hung like a bird's nest on a candle bracket. Her stays were draped over a chair and her shoes had danced away into a corner. The lady herself lay on top of the bed clad only in a chemise and a pair of lace-edged drawers. She had unpinned her hair and her anger was naked enough to give her a blaze that Willy could not help but find arousing.

'Your milk, Mrs Paul.'

'Why did he do it? Why did he have to announce it to the Clarks before he told me?' Agnes demanded. 'By tomorrow the whole island will know that he wants the Campbell girl for his bride.'

'Perhaps that's why he did it,' Willy suggested.

He poured milk from the pitcher and carried the glass to the bed. He had forgotten how thrusting she could be. He had not had a woman for the best part of a year and dislike added spice to his desire. He watched her hold the cold glass against her brow and then against her breast.

'Made his promise public, do you mean?' Agnes said.

'Aye, ma'am, that's about the size of it.'

'Tell me, William, what does he see in her?'

'If you'd met her I think you might understand.' Willy leaned against the dresser, one knee crossed lightly over the other. 'She might be a country lass with not much culture or refinement but she is a looker, Mrs Paul, a real looker.'

'Austin claims he has already cohabited with her?'

'Mr Austin is not the sort of man to make up lies.'

'So, has she a claim on him?'

'I would say that she has.'

Agnes showed no sign of wishing to drink the milk and continued to rub the glass across her chest, shivering slightly. 'Do you not have a fancy for this country girl, William?'

'No, ma'am, she is not the sort for me.'

'If Austin is determined to stay on Mull then I've no doubt that a position could be found for her in the household – if only she could be persuaded to marry you instead of my brother.'

That, Willy thought, is the most idiotic suggestion I've ever heard. Does she suppose that Biddy Campbell has no more feelings than a mare that can be traded back and forth without consent?

'That might be a bit awkward, ma'am.'

'Awkward?' Agnes Paul raised an eyebrow. 'For whom?'

'For everyone concerned. If Biddy chose me over Mr Austin and came to live in the house as a servant – well, it would be a slap in the eye for the master.'

'But it would also be very convenient, wouldn't it?'

'You mean he could have my wife whenever he wanted her,'

said Willy, 'without having to marry her? Biddy would never accept such an arrangement.'

'I suppose she sees herself as lady of the manor.'

'That's right,' Willy said. 'And she would make a good lady of the manor. Aye, and a good wife besides.'

'He could never bring her home.'

'Fetternish is Mr Austin's home.'

'Nonsense! Fetternish is just a fad. In due course Austin will tire of Mull and come trotting back to Edinburgh. Then, then he'll learn what sort of coarse creature he's married to and will live to regret his impetuosity.'

'I doubt it,' Willy said. 'For one thing, Biddy will turn every head in Princes Street and that's always flatterin' to a husband.'

'Is she much better looking than I am?'

Willy took a deep breath. 'She's a redhead.'

'Oh, that's the attraction, is it?'

'It's not her only attribute.'

'Do you not find her attractive?'

'Well, I – that's not really for me to say.'

'Why not?'

'If she's to become Mr Austin's wife.'

'And what about Mr Austin's sister?'

'Pardon?'

'Do you not find *me* attractive?' Agnes edged forward and put the glass of milk down upon the bedside cabinet. Then she leaned back on both elbows and looked up at him, smiling. 'Lord knows, William, you used to.'

'That was – was before,' Willy said.

'Before what?'

'Before I became engaged to Margaret Bell.'

She sat bolt upright from the waist then, realising that he was entirely serious, rolled from the bed and reached for her robe. Out of habit Willy dived to fetch it for her and for a moment he was so close to her that he could feel the heat from her body pass like a wave across his skin. She snatched the robe away and, turning her back, wrapped it around her.

When she swung round to face him again she was all covered up.

'And you would have her in preference to me?'

'Aye, Mrs Paul. I would,' said Willy.

Margaret had not been asleep. She had been dozing, though, and it gave her quite a start when the door suddenly opened and Willy stepped into her room. He looked grizzled and huge, like a bear. She felt a thrill of fear and admiration shoot through her at the sight of him and, hoisting herself up, clutched the bedsheet in both hands.

'Maggie,' he said in a throaty whisper, 'will you marry me?'

'Wh – what do – do you mean, Willy?'

He came forward. She backed away, swaying against the bedhead.

He got down on his knees, grunting a little, and clasped his hands together as if he were praying.

'I mean, dear Maggie, will you consent to become my wife?'

She stared at him for several seconds and then, quite rationally and deliberately, lowered the sheet from her breast and with a gentle motion turned back the bedclothes.

'Get in,' shy Margaret said.

He was comparatively sober that morning. He had no inclination to celebrate. He felt cold and just a touch sick, though, as he watched the infant being put into a napkin and a little gown. He wanted to take the baby in his arms as once he had taken Donnie, to carry the new-born infant down to the beach and, kneeling, do that thing that his father had done to him, kneel at the water's edge, touch salt water to the infant's brow and by that gesture bind his life to the sea.

Vassie would not let him near the baby. Vassie kept the baby, and Aileen, to herself. Aileen was the only one of them who had loved him without stint. She sat on a chair where her mother had put her in her best shawl and dress, her shoes sticking out from under the hem, the little bonnet tied tight beneath her chin. He wanted to hold her and take her on his knee and have her kiss him. But Vassie let him come no nearer than the door while she packed into a canvas bag Aileen's belongings and the clothes they had gathered for the child.

He had nothing to give Aileen. He would have given her money from the jar in the shed where he kept what savings he had left, the shilling or two not spent on drink. He would have put it into a paper wrapper and pressed it into her hand as a hansel for the baby, a reminder that whatever he had done he was still her father and still loved her. Vassie would have none of that either. Vassie gave the girl money out of the black purse, more than he could have done. What use money would be to Aileen on the isle of Foss he could not imagine since McIver and his women would see to her every need.

'Baba,' he said. 'Let me be holding the baba for a minute or two.'

'Touch him, Ronan Campbell, and I will kill you where you stand.'

'Aileen, sweetheart, let me . . .'

Aileen looked up at him. He saw love in her eyes and felt the warmth that she had brought to him before he had learned that she was not right in the head. Then he saw that Aileen was not looking at him at all but at the baby in Vassie's arms, at the spill of the white shawl and the two tiny pink-purple fists that showed within it and the closed eyelids, shaded fair like damp sand.

Aileen reached out, keening. Vassie put the baby down in her lap and she kissed the baby's brow and would have nuzzled her face into the shawl if Vassie had not taken him away again and cradled him in the crook of one wiry arm while she finished packing the bag.

If the baby had been older, Ronan thought, Vassie would have hung him on her hip as she had done with Donnie and Neil, would have worked with the boy clinging to her like part of her body. He would not see that happen now. Aileen would go to Foss and the child with her and McIver would teach them to despise him and would never let them return to Pennypol as long as he was alive.

It was not as he had planned it. In truth, he had planned nothing. He had drifted through the years without effort. He had replaced labour with pride and had settled for less when he might have had more. He would not smell a penny of McIver's money now, though he had taken care of McIver's daughter for almost thirty years and had got nothing else out of the marriage.

Only Aileen had ever loved him and Aileen was not right in the head.

'What will you be calling him, sweetheart?' he asked from his position by the door. 'Will you be calling him Ronan?'

'Mine,' Aileen said, without force. 'He sucks my teat.'

'Aye, dearest. I have seen him,' Ronan said. 'What will you call him?'

'Leave her alone, Dada,' Innis said. 'Can you not see she is confused?'

'But she is happy, is she not? Happy with her wee new lamb.'

'My lamb.' Aileen reached out for her baby as if for a doll. 'I will be takin' him to see the people soon.'

'Aye, so you will,' said Ronan.

At the jetty below he could see the boat from Foss manned by two brown-haired boys and a woman, not Mairi but the older one with the grey in her hair. The sail was furled neatly against the mast and oars were shipped. He wondered where the boat had come from, for it was a sound and solid vessel and one that he could have made use of, even without the boys to help him.

Vassie gave the baby to Aileen who held him up high against her throat so that she could push her nose down against his little face.

There was nothing in Aileen's pale blue eyes now but love.

Love had washed everything else away.

Ronan wondered if love would be enough to see the infant through or if, in three years or four or five, he would one day blink and stare at his mother and realise that she had no brain worth speaking of, and if her son would come to feel disgust for being less than perfect as he, her father, had done.

He stood to one side to let them pass. He did not offer to carry the canvas bag down to the boat. He would have offered to carry the baby but he did not want to be hurt again. He knew what Vassie was about, what she thought it meant. But he was sick in his stomach and his head had begun to ache again.

They filed silently past him, four women and the child that he would have raised as his own if only there had been money and he had had a boat. He took a step to the right and slid down against the wall of the cottage, sick and sweating with the cold. He watched them go down the path by the potato quarter and, squinting against the silvery light, saw Vassie get into the boat and Innis hand Aileen down to her, then Biddy hand down the baby.

He stared at his shaking hands. He counted the black flies that flickered before his eyeballs. He knew that he would have to drink soon. The thirst that was more than thirst was killing him. He could feel the pain inside, eating at him, the little hard, stabbing *pock* of it like cod coming to the bait. He put his head into his hands, closed his eyes and wept, not for Aileen, not for Vassie but only out of pity for himself.

When the boat passed out of sight around the headland the sisters walked up towards the calf park arm-in-arm. There were four calves from the spring drop. Thanks to the redwater outbreak they had received only a minimum of care but seemed, nevertheless, to be thriving. It was a bright airy morning with hawthorn beginning to flower and the smell of the grass strong in the air and in Innis there were feelings of both regret and release as if the departure of Aileen and her baby had represented both an ending and a beginning.

The Pennypol herd had been weakened. Any cattle dealer worth his salt would be able to tell at a glance that the stock was worth little in its present state. Still, they had three able hands, a roof that did not have to be paid for, ground under cultivation and enough clean grass to feed half a dozen cows. It might be enough to see them through, though it was a far cry from the sort of farm that Pennypol had once been with a bit of money coming in from the fishing and five or six hands to ensure that the pasture was kept in good heart.

It was only when they reached the fence, a safe distance from the cottage, that Biddy released Innis's arm. 'Mr Austin Baverstock has asked me to marry him,' she said. 'I am going to accept his offer.'

Innis hid her shock. 'If he means what he says.'

'Oh, he is meaning it,' Biddy assured her. 'He wants me.'

'Do you – I mean, do you love him?'

'He is not so bad.'

'Biddy!'

'What is there here for us?' Biddy said. 'It is not just the animals that are sick. Father will never work again and I am not willing to slave in the fields for the rest of my life just to keep him in drink.'

'Mother will see to it that he lends a hand.'

'No, she will not. Mother will give in to him. She always gives in to him,' Biddy said. 'Look how she got rid of Neil and Aileen. She is depending on us to do the dirty work and I will not do it any longer.'

'She won't let Pennypol go.'

'She may have no choice,' said Biddy. 'Austin says that he is willing to offer for the grazing rights. If that happens we will be little better than crofters. I have no intention of scratching out a living from three acres of vegetable plot while waiting for some man to come along and take me off to work his ground instead. I have my chance, Innis, and I am going to take it.'

'What about Michael?'

'How can I marry him, him being what he is?'

'Do you not still love him?'

'I told you. I never loved him.'

'Why did you give in to him then?'

'Because I thought that he might love me.'

'Perhaps he did. Perhaps he still does.'

'You are a right fool sometimes, Innis Campbell.'

'What do you mean?'

'Even if Michael was not a Roman Catholic, he is only a shepherd.'

'I see nothing wrong with marrying a shepherd.'

'Well, I do. I can do better than Michael Tarrant, a great deal better.'

'If you marry Austin Baverstock you will be the mistress of Fetternish.'

'Of course I will.' Biddy tossed back her hair and smiled. There was no regret in the smile, no wistfulness or even uncertainty. 'Austin is a fine strong man. He will suit me very well. I will live in the big house and have a room of my own and servants. I will make sure that Austin makes provision for you.'

'I do not need to be taken care of,' Innis said. 'What about Father? Do you think the Baverstocks will make provision for him too?'

'Austin says he will buy Father a boat. Mam will have the

cottage and a few acres of ground and Dada will have a boat to keep him happy.'

'He's buying you, Biddy. That's all he is doing.'

'What if he is? I do not mind being bought.'

'What about his brother and the sister who is staying here for the summer, do you think they will let Mr Austin marry just anyone?'

'If you mean I am not good enough for Austin Baverstock then let me tell you that he thinks I am. He thinks I will make him a perfect wife. I am not going to be stopped,' Biddy went on, 'not by them, not by you.'

'Why would I wish to stop you?'

'Because after I marry Austin you will be the last one left.'

'Perhaps not for long,' said Innis.

'What do you mean?' said Biddy, suspiciously.

'I might get married too before long.'

'To whom?' Biddy said.

'Michael Tarrant,' Innis said, airily.

'Michael? Michael would never marry the likes of you. He will only marry a Roman Catholic and you are not one of those.'

'Not yet,' said Innis.

Willy had lived on his nerves many times in the past but in those days he had been so arrogant and assured that he had enjoyed flirting with the threat of ruin almost as much as he had enjoyed the fruits of his seductions. Island life had changed him, however. Age might have something to do with it too but, whatever the reason, he could not blink the fact that he had fallen in love with Margaret Bell and that being in love made him very, very nervous.

He had married Prudence Hardisty only because she was pregnant and her father and brothers would have lynched him if he hadn't done the right thing by her. He had stood by Pru for twenty-four years, had endured her nagging recriminations until the day she died but he could say, hand on his heart, that he had never felt for Pru what he felt for Maggie Bell.

Ironically, nervousness had affected his performance. In fact their first love-making had been a near disaster and Margaret was lucky - if that was the word - not still to be a maid. Only her ingenuity and effort had saved the day, but afterwards she had been so full of gratitude and admiration that Willy had felt almost heroic and had realised that he could not live without her and that to evade Agnes Paul's clutches he had better act quickly.

'Mr Austin, sir? Are you awake?'

'Yes, Willy, I am.'

'Will I open the curtain?'

'Please do.'

He put down the tea-tray, pulled the cord that opened the drapes in his master's bedroom and admitted the brilliant gleam of a summer's morning.

Mr Austin was lying against the pillow with his hands behind his head and a beatific smile upon his face. 'What time is it, William?'

'Em – quite early, Mr Austin.' Mr Austin showed no sign of stirring himself from his reverie. 'If I might have a word, sir, on a personal matter.'

'Concerning my sister?'

'What? No, not about – about that, Mr Austin. Somethin' else.' Willy cleared his throat. 'I wish to marry Margaret Bell.'

Austin sat up and took his hands from behind his head. 'You, Willy? Marry, Willy?'

'Aye, Mr Austin. Maggie – Miss Bell – has consented to be my wife.'

'Well, well, well. I must say I'm delighted.' Stretching out, Austin offered his hand which Willy, somewhat embarrassed, shook. 'Surprised, but delighted. It's about time that someone made an honest man of you. Must be the sea air, what, that encourages us to matrimony? Do you intend to beat me to the post, William? When's the happy day?'

'I still have to ask her father.'

'That should not be an impediment, should it?'

'I'm not so sure about that, Mr Austin. I'm not a Gael, you see, not of the true blood, not related to the barons of Lewis or the earls of Eriskay or whatever gives you standing in this part of the world. There's also the matter of position.'

'Position?' Austin said. 'I say, you're not thinking of leaving us, are you?'

'I'd rather not, sir, if my – my wife can be accommodated too.'

'Of course she can, of course. We'll make her our housekeeper.'

'That's very kind, Mr Austin, but Mrs Baverstock Paul might not . . .'

'Agnes will have no say in the matter. Agnes will not be here. Once my sister realises that I am determined to marry Miss Campbell and that neither she nor my brother can stop me then Agnes will take herself back to Sangster with her tail between – well, you know what I mean.'

'Miss Biddy might not like havin' one of her own kind as housekeeper.'

'Bridget's not like that. She will probably be glad to have a friendly face about the place.'

Willy was not so sure. But negotiating minor details could be left until after he had confronted Maggie's relatives.

'I take it then that you have no objection, sir, if I go forward with the arrangements for a quiet wedding.'

'On the contrary, William. Congratulations.'

'Thank you, sir,' said Willy and, heaving a sigh of relief, hurried away to tell Margaret the news.

Father Gunnion was more conscious than most priests of the legacy he had inherited from the Bishops of the Highland Mission. He was also conscious of the vagaries of wind and weather and had stored in his head not only tide tables but the sailing schedules of all MacBrayne's mail boats. Brother Franciscans had once likened him to the White Rabbit in *Alice's Adventures* for his habit of scuttling around, muttering under his breath and constantly consulting his watch. None of this harassment showed, of course, for whatever else Father Gunnion might be he was not a figure of fun, not even to those Protestants who thought that all priests were either comical or sinister.

Fifty-five years old, with a craggy, perpendicular face and an expression that bordered on the lugubrious, the island priest emanated patience, wisdom and a sense of being so thoroughly filled with knowledge that nothing could shake his faith in his calling. To Mull's scattered Catholics Father Gunnion's visits were as much part of the cycle of the year as seed time and harvest.

No matter how late the steamer or how long he had to hang about the pier they were ready and waiting, barns swept and halls cleaned, suppers cooked and beds turned down, gigs and horses at his disposal. It was how they served not just Father Gunnion but their Church, how they held together on an island and in a society that did not entirely favour them.

At Craignure mass was held in a stone-built barn. At Salen in a whitewashed laundry room at the back of the schoolhouse. At Coyle, at the eastern end of the long valley of Glenarray, however, fifteen of Father Gunnion's parishioners assembled at half past one o'clock in the comparative splendour of a public hall, a wooden building a mile off the coast road and a good nine miles by hill track from Tom Ewing's kirk in Crove.

Hemmed in by hills, Coyle in winter was a gloomy place. But on that warm May afternoon it was pretty enough and if he had not been dashing off to Tobermory Father Gunnion might have been tempted to borrow a rod and cast a fly or two into the river that swept in a broad curve around the knoll on which the hall was situated. He had never fished the Array. Common sense told him he probably never would. But while he waited for Mr O'Connel to return for him in the dogcart, he stole a few minutes of leisure to admire the pools where the sea trout lay. So intent was he on studying the river that he did not notice the girl on the pony until she was almost upon him.

She came out from behind the wooden building as if she had deliberately kept out of sight while the little congregation had dispersed and Mr O'Connel had ridden off in the dogcart to drive the elderly McLeish sisters back to their farm on the top side of the hill. She was about eighteen years of age, Father Gunnion reckoned, better dressed than most crofters in a plaid day-dress and a light summer cape and a hat that had 'Sunday-best' written all over it. She wore grey gloves and a pair of boots that would do both for walking and for riding. She was very polite, a little hesitant but not bashful. And he knew at once that she was not one of his.

He watched her dismount, tether the pony and come towards him.

'Are you the priest, sir?'

'I am. I am Father Gunnion.'

287

'I wonder if you would be sparing me a few minutes of your time?'

He looked up at the sheep path where O'Connel had steered the dogcart and felt a little wave of temporal panic as the timepiece within him began to tick frantically. He was familiar enough with the sensation to control it, though. He even managed to smile.

'Certainly, young lady,' he said. 'Are you of this parish?'

'I am from Crove, from Mr Ewing's parish.'

'And what is it you want with me?' said Father Gunnion.

'I need to ask your advice.'

'Do you go to church?'

'Aye, sir, almost every Sunday.'

'To Reverend Ewing's church?'

'That is where I have come from today.'

'So you already believe in God?'

'I do.'

'Why then are you seeking advice from me and not Mr Ewing?'

'Because I do not think Mr Ewing would be sympathetic to the kind of questions I wish to have answered.'

She was by no means ingenuous, Father Gunnion realised. What was more, he suspected that she had just told him a white lie or, to give her the benefit of the doubt, had not told him the whole truth.

He said, 'Do your family know that you have come to see me?'

'No, sir. They would be angry if they knew I was speaking to a priest.'

He studied her long, sun-dusted, intelligent face and found no hint of rebellion in her eyes, only a determination that caused his initial doubt about her motives to waver. He scratched the underside of his chin with his forefinger. 'Are you from Crove itself or from further beyond?'

'I am from Pennypol which is near Fetternish. Have you heard of it?'

'Oh, yes,' said Father Gunnion. 'I have heard of it.'

He remembered the young shepherd's confession of sexual coupling and his confusion about the nature of love and, putting two and two together, guessed that this was one of the girls who had lured the young fellow from the straight and narrow.

But which one? Father Gunnion wondered. Was this the girl whose favours the young man had already enjoyed, or the one with whom he was half inclined to fall in love?

Cautiously, he said, 'What is your question?'

'If I were contemplating becoming a Catholic, how would I go about it?'

'You would receive instruction in the foundations of our faith.'

'From whom would I receive such instruction?'

'From me,' said Father Gunnion. 'There is a lot more to it than that, however. It is not like a school examination, Miss . . .'

'Campbell.'

'Well, Miss Campbell, conversion is not something that is undertaken lightly. It is a decision that will alter the whole tenor of your life.'

'I hope that it will, sir.'

Father Gunnion glanced towards the hill as O'Connel's dogcart appeared in the distance. The timepiece inside his head had stopped ticking. His parishioners in Tobermory could wait a while. No harm it would do them, no harm at all. He was unsure about the girl. He suspected that her motive for discovering more about the Church of Rome might rest on nothing more solid than wilfulness or fancy, an affair of the heart not the head. Even so, she would not be the first to be won over by love not logic.

He place his hand gently upon her arm and steered her towards the wooden building.

'Come, lass,' he said. 'I think it might be better if we talked inside.'

The Bells were not great ones for attending kirk, for they considered Tom Ewing's mastery of Gaelic to be less than perfect and his moral stance liberal to the point of laxity. Once in a blue moon they would dust off their musty suits, brush their dresses, prop Granny McLeod on top of a horse and trail into the village to partake of communion but, as a rule, they preferred to worship in private by reading from the great black-bound Gaelic Bible that reposed in Granny McLeod's room though she was too old and frail to open it let alone lift it down from the high shelf.

Where the family stood on the subject of marriage to an

incomer and widower not even Margaret could be sure. For this reason, and without mentioning the word 'betrothal', she had managed to convey to her relatives the purpose of Mr Naismith's up-and-coming visit, to allow them time to consult grizzled great-aunts and long-lost female cousins who were scattered hither and yon across the waters of the Hebrides. Most of the great-aunts and long-lost cousins could not have cared less who Margaret married but they made a great song and dance out of it none the less to alleviate the tedium of ploughing, sowing and milking kye and for a fortnight letters darted back and forth between the isles like gulls after a herring shoal.

As it happened, Willy need not have worried. The Bells were only too glad to have Margaret taken off their hands and when Willy put his question to the elders of the tribe in the cool, shadowy, horse-smelling kitchen of the stable house the response was astonishingly crisp.

'Fine.'

'What?'

'Fine, fine,' said Margaret's father.

'You mean I have your permission to marry your daughter?'

'Aye, you are having our permission,' the old man said. 'I have just the one question to be putting to you.'

'And what is that?' said Willy.

'How soon will you be taking her away?'

There was no such amenability towards matrimony in the big house of Fetternish. Agnes Baverstock Paul was furious with her brothers and discarded all decorum in trying to persuade Austin to change his mind before it was too late and the honourable name of Baverstock was dragged in the mud of the barnyard and besmirched by the stench of the cowshed. She telegraphed her husband who, far from rushing north to her aid, sent back the cryptic message, '*Congratulations. Good luck to him,*' which declaration of masculine solidarity caused Austin to whoop with glee and Walter, who was more sympathetic to his brother's cause than he let on, to hide a smile behind his hand.

'It may not be so bad, Agnes,' Walter told his sister. 'After all, Austin seems determined to make Fetternish his home and this girl knows how the land lies. She won't squeal to be taken shopping in Princes Street every ten minutes, like so many Baverstock wives have done before.'

'Whose side are you on, Walter?' Agnes demanded.

'It isn't a question of sides,' Walter said. 'I do not imagine that you would be creating such a fuss if he had become engaged to some long-stemmed rose from Corstorphine.'

'First Naismith and now Austin.'

'What?'

'Marching to the altar.'

'What's Willy got to do with it?'

'Everything,' Agnes snapped. 'I would not be surprised if that scoundrel Naismith had put Austin up to it.'

'That's ridiculous. Why, you haven't even met the girl yet.'

'I do not intend to meet her, or her loathsome family.'

'Oh, are you leaving then?' said Walter.

'I will leave only when Austin comes to his senses.'

'In that case you may be here for many a long day.'

'It's infatuation.'

'I know it's infatuation,' Walter said. 'On the other hand, Austin is happier than I have ever known him to be. Why do you resent this girl so much?'

'She has no breeding.'

'Her grandfather . . .'

'Oh, yes, the wrestler, the cattle-dealer, who lives on some rock with a harem of women. I do not call that breeding.'

'Who told you about McIver?'

'I have been making certain enquiries about the family.'

'Thrale told you, of course.'

'Mr Thrale is one man whose judgement I trust.'

'Thrale is an excellent manager, that I can't deny,' said Walter, 'but he is mean-spirited and certainly not someone whose word I'd take at face value.'

'Austin is not the first man this girl has tried to ensnare,' Agnes said. 'She set her cap at your shepherd.'

Walter sighed. 'Something else you heard from Thrale, I suppose. Thrale's jealous, that's all. Besides, Biddy Campbell could never have married Tarrant.'

'Why not?'

'He's a Roman Catholic and Biddy Campbell would hardly be

trying to trap Tarrant into marriage when marriage would mean forsaking her religious principles.'

'I doubt if principles have anything to do with it,' Agnes said.

Walter paused, thinking of what Agnes had said about Willy Naismith. Willy had certainly been changed by Mull. He wondered if he had been wrong to take himself off to winter in the capital, if Edinburgh's diversions were really sufficient compensation for the unadventurous life he had led until now. He thought, too, of the red-haired woman who had caught Austin's eye and how incomprehensible that relationship was once desire had been extracted from it. How unfathomable all this roughness must be to Agnes, a far cry from the brittle gentility of the Border society in which she had been reared. He could not imagine Agnes ever wading bare-legged through a barley field or stroking milk from an udder.

'No,' he said. 'I expect you're right. Principles have nothing to do with it.'

'And yet you will not try to prevent Austin's marriage to this trollop?'

'I may not have to,' Walter said.

'What do you mean?'

'The Campbells may not want her to marry Austin.'

However much Vassie wanted to disapprove of her father, of his women and his unbaptised children – the family that had usurped her – she could not help but covet the air of contentment and serenity that pervaded the tiny green isle on the rim of the open Atlantic where nothing ever seemed to change.

She had endured too much to evade her responsibilities, however. She stayed on Foss no longer than was necessary to ensure that Aileen and the baby were settled. She left them there to be fussed over by the women without regret. After all, she, Vassie Campbell, was not a stone, like Caliach, that would stand mute and motionless for a thousand years. She had broken her back with the work of the farm in the belief that she could make amends for what she had done all those years ago. She had saddled herself with Pennypol and Ronan Campbell as punishment for the hurt she had caused her father – and to teach him a lesson. But the gesture had gone unrecognised for he, Evander

James McIver, had always loved her and always would just as she, come what may, loved her children no matter how sorely they tried her with their foibles and follies.

Ronan had not shown himself upon her arrival back from Foss. He had not come into the cottage to welcome her. She had not expected it. She no longer cared what her husband did. What she cared for were her girls, her cattle and the quarters of good ground that she had dug and seeded, raked and hoed and which, in a week or two, would flush green again.

It was a calm, calm evening about half past five o'clock. Milking was done, the calves fed. The last parcel of penned cattle had been dosed and watered. Before long they would be let out to graze the meagre pickings along the shore or, as her father had suggested, turned into the hayfield to fatten before the first of the autumn sales. Vassie looked to the line of the moor grazing, to the wall she had reclaimed from the turf, that high, solid wall of old stones that had, after all, kept nothing out and nothing in and had been, like so many things she had done or had tried to do, a waste of precious time.

Their work done, the girls came to her, Innis and Biddy together.

'Is Aileen all right?' Biddy asked.

'She is fine,' Vassie answered.

'And the baby?' said Innis.

'The baby is well. She will be for calling him Donald.'

'Oh!' Biddy said. 'Who put that idea into her head?'

Vassie sighed. 'It was her own notion.'

'Is the baby' – Biddy hesitated – 'like her?'

'He is like himself,' said Vassie.

'I mean, is he right in the head?' said Biddy.

'We will see what sort of intelligence he has when he is older.'

Vassie was reluctant to discuss Aileen and the baby. She had put them as far from her as possible and did not want to have to contemplate what the cross-child might be like when he grew up. She would not have had him named after Donnie, would not have put that particular name into Aileen's head. But it seemed somehow fair that her lie to the minister had come back to haunt her and that, through her grandson, she would have to live with the sorry secret for the rest of her days.

She said, 'Where is your father?'

'He has gone into Crove, I think,' Innis replied.

Biddy smoothed her skirts. 'I have something to tell you, Mam,' she said. 'Something important.'

'And what might that be?' Vassie said, quietly.

'Mr Austin Baverstock has asked me to be his wife.'

The moment Agnes laid eyes on Bridget Campbell she realised that she had no hope of saving her brother.

In fact, she was so taken aback by the young woman's striking good looks that she even began to wonder if Austin's infatuation *was* folly or if he had not captured something that he did not really deserve. It was not just Biddy's flame-red hair, the curve of the hips and swell of the bosom that caused Agnes to retreat but a glint in the girl's eye, a certain calculation. She also caught the exchange of glances between Austin and the Campbell girl and, being experienced in such matters, knew at once that they were already lovers.

She had learned a great deal about the Campbells from Hector Thrale, with whom she had formed a guarded relationship. When they were ushered into the drawing-room she was careful to hide her dislike, to offer her hand to the brown-skinned little wife, to the man with the bland smile and sly eyes and, last of all, to the flame-haired young woman whose modesty could not quite hide her passion and her greed.

Austin bounced about the room making his beloved and her parents comfortable while Walter poured sherry which, to Agnes's surprise, Ronan Campbell refused.

He sat square on the gilded chair – one of five that Agnes had brought from Sangster – and looked not at Austin or at Walter but at her, straight at her, as if he were sizing her up. He was, or had been, a very handsome man. When she smiled at him he smiled back as if to acknowledge that she would deal with him as honestly as he would with her.

'I see, Mr Campbell, that you did not bring all the family with you?'

'I am called by the name of Ronan, Mrs Paul. Under the circumstances in which we are meeting it would seem to me not to be too forward if you would be calling me by my first name.'

He spoke English slowly and softly, with pedantic correctness.

'You have, I believe, two other daughters,' Agnes said.

'My middle daughter is called by the name of Innis. She is at home attending to the work of the farm.'

'Is that where Innis is,' Austin put in. 'I must say, I do like Innis. I'm sorry that you won't meet her today, Agnes. She's an excellent conversationalist.'

'And the other one?' Agnes said, not smiling now.

'Ah, well, Aileen has not been herself lately,' Ronan Campbell explained. 'She is a weak child and she has gone to stay for a while with her grandfather, Evander McIver, of whom you maybe have heard.'

'Weak?' said Agnes. 'In the head, do you mean?'

'Agnes, I say! What sort of a question is that?'

'It is a reasonable enough question,' Vassie Campbell put in. 'It is the sort of question I would be asking myself if there was to be a marriage and children coming afterwards.'

'And the answer?' Agnes said.

'She is weak-minded,' Vassie said before Ronan could stop her.

'I see,' Agnes said. 'Thank you for your honesty.'

'Will you be as honest with me, Mrs Baverstock Paul?' Vassie Campbell said. 'What of your family? Is there no feebleness in your family?'

'Certainly not.'

'There's Uncle Trevor,' Austin put in.

'Uncle Trevor is eccentric, that's all,' said Agnes.

'You always said he was as mad as a hatter.'

Walter intervened. 'It isn't quite the same thing, Austin.'

'As what?' said Austin, bewildered.

'What we're talking about,' said Walter.

'Which is?'

'Children,' Walter whispered.

'Bit early for that, isn't it?' said Austin. 'But since Bridget and I are – ah – sound in wind and limb, I'm sure it won't be long before the patter of tiny feet sounds in Fetternish House.'

'Austin, for God's sake!' Walter sighed.

Ronan said, 'There will be no marriage.'

Austin Baverstock reared back as if he had taken a bullet in the chest. 'But Biddy has already agreed to – I mean, you do want to marry me, don't you, dearest?'

Biddy answered timidly, 'Yes.'

'There will be no marriage,' Ronan went on, 'if there is no agreement.'

Agnes said, 'What sort of agreement?'

'An agreement about the disposition of land,' Ronan said.

'Do you mean that you intend to dower your daughter with a portion of the Pennypol estate?' said Agnes.

'I mean,' said Ronan, 'that you will be taking away not just my daughter but one of my hands.'

'Hands?' said Austin.

'Austin, please be quiet,' Walter said. Then to Ronan, 'I must say that I did not expect this afternoon's meeting to be other than social. I'm not sure that we are prepared to discuss such settlements off-the-cuff.'

Ronan, still smiling, got to his feet. 'Perhaps you would be good enough to let us know when you are, and we will return another day.'

'Sit down, Mr Campbell,' Agnes told him.

Ronan defied her for a moment then seated himself on the gilded chair once more, hands clasped over his knees.

Agnes said, 'I gather that we are doing business in the island way and that you speak both for yourself and your daughter in this matter.'

'That is how it is,' Ronan agreed.

'What is your proposition?'

'I will agree to let my daughter marry only if there is a settlement.'

'Precisely what do you want from us, Mr Campbell?' said Walter.

'I want you to rent Pennypol.'

'All of it?' said Walter.

'All except the cottage and the vegetable gardens.'

'What about grazing for your cows?'

'Three acres, measured from the wall to the burn,' said Ronan.

'Not including the water?' said Walter.

'You may have the water rights too,' said Vassie.

The young woman, Biddy, kept silent. Agnes wondered what

her contribution to the proposal had been and why Vassie Campbell was suddenly prepared to give up her farm when, according to Thrale, she had clung to it tenaciously through thick and thin. The answer, Agnes supposed, was obvious: to get a hold, somehow, on Fetternish.

'I'm not at all sure what we are negotiating here, Mr Campbell,' Agnes said. 'In fact, I'm not at all sure that you are in a position to prevent your daughter marrying my brother if she chooses to do so. She is, I assume, past the age when the law demands parental consent.'

'That is quite true.' Ronan allowed the statement to hang in the air for a moment. 'Indeed, there is nothing to prevent your brother marrying my daughter in front of the registrar in Oban whenever he chooses.'

'And you would not raise a hand to prevent it?' said Agnes.

'I am not in a position to prevent it,' Ronan said.

'He means, Agnes,' Walter put in, 'no more are we.'

'I say, I never thought of that,' Austin said.

'It is not the fact of the marriage but its convenience that we are discussing, Mrs Paul,' Ronan said. 'It would not be fair if your brother's marriage to my daughter deprived me of my living, would it now?'

'If that's the only problem,' Austin said, 'it's easily solved. I'll look after you. I mean to say, in-laws and all that.'

'I do not wished to be "looked after", Mr Baverstock,' said Ronan. 'I do not wish to be succoured by another man or to depend upon him for my bread.'

'What *do* you want?' said Walter.

Vassie answered. 'I want my daughter to be married here on Fetternish where everyone can see her.'

'Of course, of course,' said Austin, eagerly. 'That was always our plan.'

'And what else?' said Walter.

'For Fetternish and Pennypol to merge.'

'Merge?' said Agnes.

'For you to take over Pennypol, all but the cottage,' Vassie said.

'Where you will continue to live?' said Walter.

'Yes.'

'And what will be the term of the lease and the cost per acre?'

'Whatever the land surveyor says it is worth,' Ronan answered.

'Without the cattle?'

'Without the cattle.'

Agnes opened her mouth to protest but Walter held up his hand to silence her. He came forward across the drawing-room and stood before the young woman who looked up at him out of cold, sea green eyes.

'Is this what you want, Bridget?' Walter asked.

'It is,' said Biddy.

'If we agree to lease Pennypol from your parents will you give yourself in marriage to my brother without any other terms or conditions?'

'Yes, I will.'

'Austin?'

'That's absolutely fine by me.'

'So be it,' Walter Baverstock said, nodding, and rang the bell for Willy to bring in the champagne that had already been put on ice.

The Campbells were invited to stay for dinner. Ronan would have none of it. He excused himself and, soon after five, Vassie and he left the big house to walk down by the shore path to Pennypol. At Austin's insistence Biddy remained behind, however, and just before she stepped out of the drawing-room Vassie caught her daughter's eye and received a little arrogant wink as if to indicate that Biddy supposed that everything had worked out according to plan and that their troubles were now over.

As she picked her way down to the soft sandy path that was the short-cut to Pennypol and less strenuous than the climb over Olaf's Hill, Vassie felt no resentment but she did not share her daughter's sense of triumph. She had no fear for Biddy's future. Her daughter was strong-willed and would not allow herself to be humbled by the likes of Agnes Paul or other Baverstock relatives who might try to put her down. She felt flat inside, though, flat and almost indifferent to Biddy's good fortune, for she knew only too well that it was not scheming, and certainly not industry, that had netted Biddy such a worthwhile husband but chance, pure chance.

The Wedding March

On the hillside above the shore she could see Tarrant, the shepherd, his dog and a cluster of ewes that had been cut out of the flock. The sheep were running in a bunch then stopping, bewildered, as if they did not know which way to turn, lost without the shepherd's whistle and the menacing attentions of the dog to direct them. She felt a little like a ewe herself right now, a bit lost and bemused. She wondered how Michael Tarrant would react when he learned of the engagement, if he would be hurt by the loss of a woman he had loved or if he would be rendered angry and anxious by the fact that the woman would soon become his employer's wife.

Ronan, almost running, was ahead of her on the path. The ambling gait that had been part of his attraction twenty-odd years ago had changed to a bent-kneed shuffle, for drink and laziness had aged him prematurely. When she called out to him to wait for her he answered her with a snarl that seemed at odds not just with the man she had married but with the plausible islander who had done his best to win over the Baverstocks' sister. She could not bring herself to hate him in spite of his wickedness, for he was like the island itself, two-faced and moody. When he snarled she answered him with a smile of sorts, for she knew where he was going and what his needs were.

The bottle of Old Caledonia was hidden beside a huge grey boulder that rose out of tall weeds and young bracken. He was on to it instantly, urgently, and had the cork out and the neck clicking against his teeth before Vassie reached him. He drank whisky as another man might drink fresh water or cold tea, gulping it down, gasping between each mouthful. He drank half a pint of spirits in half a minute then sank back against the boulder and closed his eyes.

'Dear Christ,' he said. 'I was needing that.'

'Aye, you must be worn out being pleasant for a whole hour at a stretch.'

'What is wrong with you? Did I not do as you asked?'

'You did,' Vassie said. 'You did.'

Still leaning on the rock, he drank again, slowly this time, sipping.

He said, 'Are you ashamed of me, is that it?'

'Are you not ashamed of yourself?' Vassie said.

'I did nothing to embarrass you. You got what you wanted, did you not?'

'What is it you think I wanted?' Vassie asked.

'A fine husband for your precious daughter.'

'Our daughter, Ronan.'

'Uh-huh. Our daughter then.' He squinted at her. He was calmer now, sly now that the whisky was in him and taking effect. 'Was it not a good idea of mine to talk them into renting Pennypol? It is not as if we could be running the place profitably ourselves, not after what has happened. You will still be having your cottage and your garden and you will be having a fine island wedding to show off what a lady you have made out of Biddy.'

'It was all I had,' Vassie said. 'Pennypol.'

'It is still yours.'

'No, it is not. It is gone from me, like everything.'

'You will have made tenants of the Baverstocks. Does that not please you?'

'Sheep,' Vassie said, shaking her head. 'Sheep everywhere.'

'You will be able to call into the big house whenever it suits you and all our neighbours will be treating you like a fine lady.' He was not trying to console her, though his voice was soft and furry as a thistlehead. He was sneering at her and toasting her with sarcastic little gestures of the hand that held the bottle, for he knew that he had won the day. 'Even your father will be proud of you, Vassie. Your daughter will have a claim to more land than McIver ever dreamed of owning. We will not be starving now, not even when we are old. We have done well between us, I am thinking.'

'Is that what you are thinking?' Vassie said.

'It is, it is,' Ronan said, smiling broadly.

'Well, it is not what I am thinking. I am thinking of Donnie.'

'Donnie?'

'And Neil. And Aileen too.'

'They are gone,' Ronan said. 'Let them go, woman. You still have me to look after.'

'Aye,' Vassie said, grimly, 'I still have you.' And moved on down the path to the shore.

They lay together in the loft in the darkness listening to the sound of the waves on the sand, the rhythmic *pah-dah* that echoed the sound of their heartbeat.

Innis was elated by Biddy's announcement of an official engagement to Austin Baverstock, for Michael would surely welcome the news that he had been relieved of an obligation to pay for his sins and the divide between Michael and she would consequently be closed. She would be the neighbour now, the girl on the farm next door and he would not be able to ignore her in favour of her gorgeous sister.

She thought of him in the cottage above the Solitudes, all alone, tormented by his need for female companionship. Thought how she would lie with him, not in sin but out of compassion, how he would soon come around to loving her simply because she loved him. There was no reason to it, no rhyme or reason to loving that she could see and all the novels that Grandfather McIver had thrown her way told her nothing that she did not already know, or thought she did.

In the past few weeks she had grown more and more sure of what she wanted. She had convinced herself that she would be lacking intelligence if she did not go after the one man who would make her happy. Behind her self-assurance, however, lay a blank, a hollow, for she knew little or nothing of the character of the man she loved, except that he was sensual by nature and had a streak of arrogance in him that needed to be tamed. She was also intrigued by his Catholicism for she had teased enough out of her conversations with Father Gunnion to believe that Mr Michael Tarrant, though emphatically no saint, was a man of conscience and that his fling with Biddy had been an unfortunate accident, no more.

She lay listening to the waves. She could not imagine living far from the sea, in Edinburgh or, like Neil, in the city of Glasgow. When Biddy talked of Edinburgh Innis experienced a patronising kind of pity for her sister as if she, Biddy, would be taken from Mull reluctantly and shown the sights of the capital against her will.

Biddy was saying, 'I will be chaperoned by Austin's cousin, who is a wee bit older than me but still young. Her name is Caroline. Austin tells me that we will get along famously. I will be staying at Caroline's mother's house in a place called

Morningside, because it would not be proper for me to stay with
Austin in Austin's house which, by the by, is in Charlotte Square
which, I gather, is a very wealthy part of the town.'

'Yes,' Innis said. 'I suppose it would be.'

'You could come with me if you wished,' said Biddy, half-
heartedly.

'I have to stay here to look after the calves.'

'They will be sold soon, will they not?'

'We will be keeping one cow with calf and a heifer which
will be put out to Mr Clark's bull as soon as she comes into
season.'

'And I will be in Edinburgh,' Biddy said, with a throaty
chuckle. 'I can hardly imagine what it will be like. Oh, remind
me, I must take your measurements. You will be my maid at the
wedding and I will bring you back a suitable length of material
for your dress. Miss Crabb, in Aros, will make it up for you and
do a fitting.'

'Who will be paying for all of this?'

'Austin, of course.'

'What about Father?'

'He has no money. Austin has plenty. I know it is not the way
things are supposed to be done for a wedding but I do not care
about the conventions. And neither does Austin. He wants a
stylish wedding here on Mull. I thought we might be married in
Edinburgh or in Sangster but Austin says that would not be right.
He says that we will be islanders for the rest of our lives and that
our children and our children's children will be the lairds of
Fetternish and that it would only be right for us to start them off
by marrying here, as they will when their time comes. It is also
what Mam wants, of course.'

'Will you wear white?'

'Certainly. Ivory white, with silk lace on the bodice and yards
of tulle.'

'Will Mr Baverstock's sister help you prepare?'

'No. She will go home to Sangster soon. I know she does not
like me. But why should I care about her?'

Biddy's voice was beginning to sound strident. Innis wished
that she would shut up and allow them both to sleep. Tomorrow
there would be the rounds to make, as always, and in less than

a week Biddy would depart on her mainland trip and there would be even more work to do. Soon, too soon, the cattle would be gone, though, and there would be no livestock, except two cows, the garron and the hens, to keep her busy.

As if she had picked up her sister's thoughts Biddy fell silent. She lay on her back, arms above her head, so still now that the straw in the bolster did not so much as rustle.

Innis could feel the excitement pass out of the air, replaced – she thought – by wistfulness. Was this, she wondered, her mood or her sister's? The first sign of regret that she, Biddy, would be swept away and that everything she had known would be gone? It seemed to Innis that Biddy and she were at last united, linked not only by blood but also by their sex, that there was – must be – in Biddy a new tenderness and new understanding.

Innis said, 'I thought it would always be here but now I know it will not.'

'What are you talking about?'

'Home. Pennypol.'

'Oh, that,' Biddy said. 'Of course Pennypol will not always be here.' She stirred, making the bolster rustle then crackle. 'But Fetternish will. Fetternish will always be here. I will make sure of that.'

'With Austin's help,' said Innis.

'With Austin's money,' Biddy answered, then, drawing her elbows to her sides, burrowed deep beneath the blanket, down into the mattress straw, to sleep.

'What sort of an hour is this to come calling?' Michael said, grouchily. 'It is hardly even daylight yet.'

'I thought all shepherds were early risers?' Innis said.

'Aye, but not this early. What time is it?'

'About half past five,' Innis said. 'Are you not going to ask me in?'

'No, I am not,' Michael said.

Nevertheless, he pulled the door open another few inches and peered out into the pearly grey light of dawn. He scowled as if he expected to see Hector Thrale or some other gossip already positioned upon the hillside, spying on them.

He had probably been up out of bed, Innis thought, but had

not begun dressing. He wore trousers, no stockings or shirt, and had hoisted his braces over bare shoulders. He had been building up the fire to boil a kettle and warm a frying pan and she could see upon his narrow, hairless chest smudges of peat dust and, like some ceremonial mark, an accidental vee of brown ash.

She had a sudden desire to lick her fingers and wipe the mark away, buff him up with the heel of her hand to make him clean and smart.

'I am not going to be biting you,' Innis said. 'And there is nobody up yet to see us and accuse you of taking one sister after another.'

He winced visibly. 'What do you want, Innis?'

'I have news,' she said, 'information that might interest you.'

'And will it not keep?'

'No, it will not keep. I want to be the first to tell you, if you must know.'

He had stopped scowling. He regarded her in silence for ten or twenty seconds while somewhere in the kitchen behind him Roy yawned and let out a little whine.

'What sort of news?' he said. 'Good or bad?'

'Good for some,' Innis said. 'Bad for others.'

'Is it about Biddy?'

'It is.'

'Come in,' Michael said and stepped back to let her enter.

The kitchen was much cleaner than the last time she had seen it. It smelled of smoke and carbolic soap and, the rumpled bed notwithstanding, had a tidiness to it that suggested that, early though it was, Michael had already set about his housekeeping. A polished plate and a cup and saucer were on the table, together with a bowl of brown eggs and a jug of milk. Four slices of bacon lay on a strip of newspaper and the frying pan on the stone by the hearth had already been greased. The fire itself had flame in it, licking brightly along the sticks of kindling under a pyramid of peat and small coals. Roy, just wakened, stepped out of his basket in the corner, shook himself then trotted past Innis and out of the door, no doubt to relieve himself against the gable wall.

Michael and Innis watched the dog go, then, for no reason that seemed logical, Michael quietly shut the door behind him.

'I would ask you to take tea,' Michael said. 'But it will be ten minutes before there is steam in the kettle and you will not be waiting that long.'

Innis said, 'Biddy's getting married.'

'Hmmm.'

'Is that all you have to say to it?'

'What do you want me to say? Do you want me to writhe upon the floor in a paroxysm of grief?'

'I would not be expecting that, no.'

'My heart is not broken.'

'Biddy will be disappointed to hear it.'

'Did Biddy send you here?'

'Of course she did not. She is still snoring in her bed, in fact.'

'Why did you come, Innis?'

'To see for myself how you would react to the news,' Innis admitted. 'And you are behaving much as I thought you would.'

'It's Baverstock, I suppose,' Michael said.

'It is.'

'Austin?'

'Yes.'

Michael was silent again, one eyebrow raised. Then he said, 'Do you expect me to say "Lucky fellow," or some such thing? Is that what you are waiting for, a revealing comment?'

'I am waiting for you to tell me if it is good news or bad.'

'Good for Biddy, certainly.'

'And for Austin Baverstock?'

'That remains to be seen.' He glanced at the shiny black kettle perched on an iron grid over the peats and frowned as if he were willing it to boil quickly. 'Are you asking about me, Innis? How I feel?'

'That is about the size of it, yes.'

'Why? What concern is it of yours?'

'I am curious, that is all.'

'Oh, no, that is not all, not by a long chalk.'

She had determined to remain unflustered but when he raised his eyes and looked at her directly she felt her self-control begin to slide. She could not match him for opaqueness, for inscrutability, and had no wish to fall into speculation about what that long look might mean or what he was thinking at that moment. She gave a sudden little whirl, turning her hips and shoulders and, affecting cheerfulness, said, 'Do you not wish that you had a woman here?'

'*What?*'

She felt her cheeks redden. 'I mean, to – to take care of you.'

'I take care of myself perfectly well.'

She swung again, searching for something that would allow her to round out her proposition. There was only the bed, the clean, patched sheet turned down and the pillow still with the impress of his head upon it. He slept, she saw, with only a single thin blanket to cover him as if he generated enough heat to keep him comfortable even in the chilly hours of the night. She had said quite the wrong thing and suffered for it inwardly. It was all too obvious that Michael was entirely self-sufficient and not in need of a housekeeper.

'So you would not want to take care of a wife?' Innis said.

He laughed, a little bark with more bewilderment than amusement in it.

'Do you think that I wanted Biddy as a wife, is that it?'

'No, I do not . . .'

'And now that she is spoken for the way is wide open for another candidate? No, no.' Michael shook his head. 'I made a mistake. I will not make the same mistake again.'

'A different mistake then,' Innis heard herself say.

Another little bark of laughter, without so much edge. 'Are you offering yourself to me, Innis Campbell?'

'Offering . . .'

'Do you think I am the sort of man who will take any girl?'

'You took Biddy quick enough,' Innis snapped.

'That was weakness.'

'Whatever you are, Michael, you are not weak. You knew what you wanted and you took it without a qualm. That is not weakness. That is selfishness.'

'Biddy was wil . . . not reluctant.'

'I will believe it,' Innis said. 'But I am not here to talk about Biddy.'

'Are you not? I thought you were.'

'She will be married and gone in eight weeks' time.'

'That's hasty.'

The Wedding March

'Mr Baverstock does not wish to wait.'

'I'll wager he doesn't,' Michael said. 'It seems he is not the only one.'

Innis cocked her head questioningly. 'If you mean . . .'

'I mean nothing.' Michael sighed and seated himself on one of the kitchen's three wooden chairs. 'What will happen to Pennypol? Will your mother rent the ground to Fetternish?'

'How did you know that?'

He shrugged. 'It is the only sensible thing to do with the grazing, especially when there's redwater fever in the ground. It will not affect my sheep, not in the slightest, and it will give me charge of a flock worth tending.'

'Is that your ambition, to be a flockmaster and nothing else?'

'What else is there for me, Innis? It is what I do, what I am.'

'What if my sister has you dismissed?'

He glanced up sharply. 'Biddy wouldn't do that, would she?'

'She might. She might think that it is an embarrassment to keep her former sweetheart as an estate employee.'

'The Baverstocks will not let me go.'

'Mr Austin will be running the estate on his own before the year is out,' Innis said, 'and he will be Biddy's husband and, I suspect, will do whatever she tells him to.'

'Sack me, do you mean?'

'Possibly,' Innis said.

'I knew that Biddy was wilful but I did not think she was malicious.'

He was concerned now, a faint cloud of anxiety in his eyes. He tapped his bare feet upon the stone floor and clapped his hands upon his knees. He glanced up at Innis and then, doubtful as to whether or not she would choose to reassure him, stared down at the floor again.

On the hob the kettle began to boil and from the hill outside, like a waking call, came the demanding bleat of a half-grown lamb.

'Biddy is not malicious,' Innis said. 'But she might get rid of you to protect herself and her marriage. You cannot blame her for that.'

'I suppose not,' Michael said.

'You will find another post quite easily.'

'I do not want another post,' he said. 'I like it here.'

'Mull has put its spell on you, has it?'

'I would not go so far as that,' Michael said. 'But I have three seasons' work invested in the Fetternish flock and I would not like to see it wasted.'

'There is one way to make sure.'

'Sure of what?'

'That you are not dismissed,' Innis said.

'What way?'

'Marry someone. If you are married then the tongues will cease to wag and there will no longer be a cause for scandal and gossip.'

'That's drastic,' Michael said. 'Too drastic. Besides . . .'

'It would have to be someone of the Catholic faith,' Innis stated.

He stopped tapping his feet and, putting an elbow on the table's edge to steady himself, leaned forward. He was, Innis thought, even more handsome and provocative when the pride in him was tinted by anxiety. She felt a strange glow of satisfaction at having finally put him in a position where a sense of equality could be restored.

'You've been taking instruction, haven't you?' he said.

'I have talked to Father Gunnion.'

'I knew it.'

'Did Father Gunnion tell you?'

'Of course not. I heard a whisper from O'Connel, if you must know.'

'There you are then,' Innis said.

'There I am, what?'

'You will soon have a candidate on your doorstep.'

'You?'

'I am not averse to marrying a Roman Catholic.'

'Innis, I have lain with your sister.'

'But you did not love her, did you?'

He answered without hesitation. 'No.'

It was on the tip of Innis's tongue to ask outright if he loved her but she could not bring herself to take the risk that he would tell her the truth.

She said, 'Even my sister Biddy would never dare sack a man who had married into the family.'

'You're blackmailing me.'

'I am not,' Innis said. 'I am warning you.'

'Against Biddy?'

'Against me.'

'Good God!' Michael exclaimed. 'What sort of a family are you?'

'It is probably our Irish blood that makes us different.'

'Would you really convert to Catholicism if I ask it of you?'

'I would.'

'Do you know what that means, Innis?'

'That we would be stuck together for life with no possibility of parting,' she said. 'Is that such a terrible prospect?'

'You would be ostracised, cut off, cut dead in the street.'

'But you would not be sacked.'

'No, the Baverstocks have no prejudice of that sort.'

'And I have nothing against sheep,' Innis said.

'Why are you doing this? To be out of Pennypol, to shake off your family? I mean, I cannot think of any sane reason why you would choose me after what has happened here.'

She leaned forward and kissed him on the brow. He was not warm but quite cold and he tasted not of smoke or perspiration as she might have expected but of carbolic soap as if he had scrubbed himself clean just prior to her arrival.

'Then you must ponder the matter,' Innis said. 'Think about it. And when you arrive at a satisfactory answer I will be where I always am, just over Olaf's Hill, waiting for you.'

He puffed out his cheeks and shook his head. 'What if I do not arrive at a satisfactory answer?'

'Oh, you will,' Innis said. 'Given enough time, I am sure you will.'

Michael leaned in the cottage doorway and watched her pass among the sheep on the cropped edge of the hill pasture. Roy had skulked into the shed and would be snuffling about his empty dish waiting for breakfast. From within the house came the hiss of the kettle full on the boil. He could not tear himself away from the door, though, for Innis Campbell would surely turn at the top of the ridge and wave to him and it would be heartless of him to disappoint her. Somehow he already felt committed to obeying her wishes, that indefinable edict that he suspected might be a variety of love with which he was unfamiliar.

Until now he had loved only with his loins. Biddy was not the first girl that he had hungered for and who had lain with him willingly; Ettrick villages were no more moral in that respect than any other rural community. He had never lacked attraction for the lassies but he had been circumspect in satisfying his hunger, restrained by both caution and conscience and, deep within himself, a longing for love-making to mean more than it ever seemed to do.

Only Biddy Campbell had lifted him out of himself and by her responsiveness had carried him too close for comfort to the sinful edge of obsession. For the weeks that their affair had lasted, he had found himself thinking of her constantly but in a manner that, at root, was demeaning. He had been drawn to Biddy as a ram is drawn to a ewe, by blind sexual instinct. He coupled with her without compassion or regard for consequences.

Innis's judgement of his character was wrong. He was not strong at all. He was weak, too weak to resist Biddy. He would have gone on with their furtive meetings if it had not been for Thrale and the fact that he had been exposed not as a lover but as a sham, a deceiver who, though he had never promised marriage to get his way, had been all along in love with another. In love he was. He could not deny it. He was in love with Innis Campbell. The mystery that he could not solve, however, was that he did not want her as he wanted Biddy. There was something soft and debilitating in his feeling for Innis: admiration, respect, a pleasing, smiling sort of thing that made him long to be near her. But not heat in the groin, the hardness that, until now, had been a sure sign of a girl's attractiveness.

From talk of men in the fank, from chat at markets and laughter in public houses he had learned that what he felt was natural and that whatever the priests said to the contrary, it was something that no man could ignore when it came to picking a wife. But it was not there with Innis and, lacking it, he felt more of a cheat than ever. He did not know how it was possible to love a woman whom he did not passionately and selfishly desire. He could not imagine himself breaking her trust by doing to her all the things that he had done to Biddy. It made him shudder even to think of it. He was split, divided between a longing to cosset and protect Innis and fear of what might be lost in the marriage bed.

He had no words to explain the distressing phenomenon of love without longing, only an instinct that if he married Innis he would harm her, that the binding of their souls before God would end in bitterness.

Even as watched her, lithe and young and slender, climb up to the knob of Olaf's Hill he felt not one tweak of desire.

She turned and waved eagerly.

And Michael, unsmiling, waved back.

TEN

The Duties of a Wife

Austin Baverstock's wedding gift to his trusted man-servant, William Naismith, took the form of domestic improvement. Two pairs of brothers from Tobermory, tradesmen not tenants, were hired to renovate the servants' quarters and provide Willy and his bride with a neat little suite of rooms at the quiet end of the basement corridor.

With characteristic patience the tradesmen dismantled the wall of an old 'hanging larder' and linked it to what had once been a laundry room. A fireplace was discovered, the chimney line explored and an iron grate and modern cooking range were purchased and installed. Finally, wallpaper, paint and several layers of varnish were applied to various surfaces, and a bed, armchairs, a table and a dresser were unearthed from the basement in Sangster and, courtesy of Alister Paul, shipped north to Fetternish. Thus, when Willy and Margaret returned from the bibulous two-day wedding celebration that the Bells had laid on there was a pleasant place for the couple to put their feet up and, later, flop wearily into bed.

If ever a man felt well and truly married it was Mr William Naismith. The brevity of the declarations before the minister was balanced by prolonged and strident festivities, for not all Bells were as dour and cheerless as Margaret's immediate family. Far, far too much whisky and not nearly enough sleep resulted in amnesia not only among the guests but also in the groom. Waking in an unfamiliar bed in a freshly varnished cubicle at the corridor's end Willy could recall little of what had taken place and had nothing to cling to for support but the sight of his wife

Margaret smiling at him and offering him a tall glass of Seltzer
water and two Abdine powders.

'Death or matrimony, dearest,' Margaret said, 'which is it to
be?'

'Matrimony, I suppose,' Willy croaked, and bravely reached
for the glass.

When his hangover had departed and the skirl of bagpipes
and fiddle music had faded at last from his ears Willy found
remarriage to be a very pleasant state indeed and had no reason
to suppose that his brand-new wife thought any differently. They
were united in love and in service and while Margaret might
bow to her husband's rank in the servants' hall, once the door
of their apartment was closed upon them she was quite definitely
his equal.

All in all that summer was a pleasant time in Fetternish House.
Agnes Paul and her maids had departed much sooner than either
Walter or Austin had anticipated. She left the piano behind,
however, declaring that it would be her wedding gift to her
brother and his bride and that she was sure it would take the
Campbell girl no time at all to learn to play upon it since she,
the Campbell girl, was obviously a marvellous study and a
paragon of wifely virtues.

Sarcasm might be Agnes's style but it was not Walter's.
Whatever doubts he harboured as to the suitability of his
brother's intended he was polite enough to keep to himself. In
fact he did not really object to having Bridget Campbell for a
sister-in-law. Now that he knew her better he realised that she
would be good for Austin and good for Fetternish and, unless he
missed his guess, would produce a fine healthy brood of little
Baverstocks to ensure the future of the name and – sacrilege, oh
sacrilege! – to prevent Agnes's children from inheriting more
than their fair share.

Austin's marriage also meant that he would not have to spend
four or five months a year on Mull, for if Biddy was even half the
woman her mother was then the overall supervision of the estate
might safely be left in her hands, for he was sure that Biddy
would not be tempted to abandon Mull for the social whirl of
Edinburgh. Correspondence with Aunt Beatrice and Cousin
Caroline indicated that Biddy's first visit to the capital had not

been without its tribulations and that, however much she had enjoyed shopping, she was very much a fish out of water in the drawing-rooms and salons of the Baverstocks' friends and had wept more than once into Austin's lapels at the realisation that what constituted a lady in Crove fell far short of the Edinburgh ideal.

In other words, poor Biddy had been patronised, cold-shouldered and generally looked down upon by all but a handful of the Baverstocks' circle and even those who had no particular prejudice against Gaels had been swayed by Agnes Paul's slanders.

Biddy was well aware that her shortcomings had been exposed and that she had been made a laughing-stock and the butt of jokes. She hid her hurt well, however, and returned to Mull like an empress, dispensing little gifts of trinket tartan here, there and everywhere and exuding a confidence and gaiety that fooled everyone except Innis.

'Will you not be going back again before the wedding?' Innis asked.

'No,' Biddy answered. 'I have made my impression and I will not impose upon the hospitality of Austin's aunt – although she is very eager for us to spend part of the winter as her guests, to partake of the operatic season.'

'I see,' Innis said. 'Will you not have Austin's house to stay in by then?'

'Austin's house? Oh, in Charlotte Square. Yes.'

'I mean, you will be his wife,' Innis said. 'If you felt you wanted to attend the operatic season or whatever it is that goes on in the city during the winter then I am sure he will take you.'

'Are you being comical?'

'No,' Innis said. 'I just thought you had forgotten that you will have a town-house as well as a country estate at your disposal.'

'We will have to be thinking about it,' Biddy said. 'There will be a lot to do at Fetternish. Besides, the town-house is really Walter's and I doubt if it is quite large enough for three.'

'I thought it was a mansion?'

'It is, it is. But . . .'

'You did not like Edinburgh, did you?'

Biddy had a lace shawl draped across her forearms, an object of such exquisite workmanship that Innis thought that it deserved to be put in a glass case and not worn at all.

Innis watched her sister crumple the shawl and knead it to her breast and regretted the directness of her question. She was not in the least jealous of Biddy's trip to the south or of the lavish gifts that Austin had showered upon her. But she had sensed her sister's anger and was curious as to what had caused it, curious and a little bit fearful in case Biddy had lost her desire to marry a Baverstock and even at this late stage might call off her engagement to Mr Austin and grab instead at Michael.

'Yes,' Biddy said. 'Yes, I liked Edinburgh.' She hesitated. 'Not all of it, though. It is a noisy place, very crowded and dirty in certain parts and there is a smell in the air . . .'

'What sort of smell?'

'A smell – I cannot tell you what it is like, Innis.'

'But you would not smell this smell in Austin's house, would you?'

'It is everywhere.' Biddy had abandoned the pretence of gaiety now and the glitter in her eyes was both angry and puzzled. 'It is the smell of the people themselves. Fusty, nasty, stuffy like old sacking.'

'Oh, Biddy! Surely not?'

'There are lamps on all the street corners in the New Town that turn night into day. And the carriages are enormous and are driven by coachmen in blue coats with gold buttons and tall hats, and by boys . . .' She stopped her harangue, twisted the shawl into a knot and shook her head. 'I will not go there again, Innis. It is not my place. Mull is my place. I hope that Austin will not hold it against me. I hope he will not force me to go back to Edinburgh.'

'He will do as you ask, Biddy.'

'And the wedding . . .'

'What about the wedding?'

'I have a fear in me that nobody will come.'

'Nobody from Edinburgh, do you mean?'

'Aye,' Biddy answered her. 'Nobody that really matters.'

'Do we not matter? Mr Leggat, Mr Ewing, Mr Clark? Mam and I?'

'I mean,' Biddy said, 'really matters. I tell you this, though, if

316

they do not come to my wedding they will live to regret it. I will make them *beg* for an invitation to visit Fetternish.'

'How will you do that?'

'I do not know,' Biddy told her, with a little, almost vicious shrug. 'I do not know just yet. But I will. I promise you, if they snub Austin because of me, I will make them pay for it somehow.'

The weather was pretty enough and the bride looked beautiful but the wedding of Austin Anderson Baverstock to Bridget Norah Campbell was not by any means an unqualified success.

Biddy's prediction that the 'Edinburgh crowd' would boycott the occasion proved correct. Not only Austin's friends from the capital but also his relatives from Sangster somehow contrived excuses – or made no excuse at all – for refusing to undertake the trip. Agnes was behind it, of course. Even desperate persuasion by Walter and Aunt Beatrice could not undo Agnes's calumnies and it was a slender party indeed that arrived at Fetternish House the day before the ceremony.

Every room in the place had been cleaned and set up to lodge the guests. Walter had ordered vast quantities of food and drink and had even employed singers from Tobermory and pipers from the Ross to provide entertainment upon the lawn and with the ladies – Beatrice and Caroline among them – in their finery Fetternish assumed an air of elegance that quite took Biddy's breath away and caused Vassie to shed quiet tears of pride.

If guests from the south were few – a dozen couples, no more – local citizens more than made up for the lack. Doctor, school-teacher, minister and all the landowners from round about were only too pleased to dickey themselves up and attend the overture to the union between Vassie Campbell's daughter and the laird of Fetternish, to consort with the capital folk on equal footing and display the friendliness and hospitality for which the isles were famous.

On the slopes of the lawn and terraces tenants and employees of the estate gathered too – though at a respectful distance – to hear the sweet voices of the singers and the skirl of the pipes in the long evening twilight.

The following morning, early, Biddy, her mother and sister were fetched from the road-end in a hired coach and conveyed to Fetternish where, in an apartment on the top floor set aside for the purpose, the earnest business of dressing the bride began. Skilful planning ensured that Austin and Biddy did not meet face to face and that the bride's father, Ronan Campbell, was kept sober throughout the morning, or at least sober enough to do his duty.

On Pennypol a skeleton crew of Quig and Mairi attended to the cattle and the milking. Grandfather McIver lodged overnight with the Clarks. He made his first appearance, in full Highland pelt, at the door of the kirk in Crove. Even today, when carts and carriages were rolling in from all directions, the sight of the old man caused a ripple of interest. There was a dignity about him that not even the expensive gentlemen from Edinburgh could match and he carried in his bearing a remembrance of the days when, before the withering, all the men of the isles were like him, handsome and proud and independent. He moved away from the door of the church only when the first of the carriages arrived from Fetternish and Vassie and Innis stepped down. Waited while they fussed with their skirts, smoothed their hair and tidied their new bonnets then he offered his daughter his arm and led her up the gravel towards the door.

Soft-voiced, he said, 'Is your husband in command of himself?'

Vassie nodded dumbly. She was beside herself with tension, fearing, perhaps, that the mischievous little demons that Aileen believed in would cast a final spell that would stop the wedding in its tracks and turn triumph to ashes.

When she clung to her father's arm, though, she felt his strength ooze into her and when he asked again, more directly, 'Is Campbell sober?' she managed to murmur, 'Yes.'

Not when vows were exchanged, not when her sister and her proud new husband rode off towards the reception in a lacquered coach, not the moment when Austin Baverstock raised his glass at the dining-table and pronounced the words 'my wife', to laughter and applause, none of these things greatly impressed Innis. What did bring tears to her eyes was the departure of bride and groom on their honeymoon.

It was Austin's surprise, a gesture so romantic and out-rageously expensive that nobody could have guessed what he had in store. Even Biddy had been led to believe that they were off to pass their wedding night in a Tobermory hotel and would be leaving on the ferry next morning for a short sojourn in Oban. Love of Bridget had fired the bachelor's imagination, however, and prompted an extravagance that a lesser man might have regarded as unwarranted. There would be no dank hotel bedroom for the first night of his marriage, no fish-smelling trip on a common ferryboat on the morning after.

Mr Austin Baverstock had hired a steamer from MacBrayne's.

Vessel and crew were at the Baverstocks' command for twenty-four hours, for if Biddy and he were setting off on the voyage of life together, so Austin believed, they must do so with a flourish and all the style that money could buy.

Fortunately for Austin it was a dry, windless evening with a sky the colour of oyster-shell. The SS *Iona*, her rigging ornamented with coloured lanterns, stole out of the Sound of Mull and lay out of sight off Fetternish Point. The longboat was rowed inshore and moored to the ring at the rock below the house while Willy and Margaret, parties to Austin's secret, brought down the luggage to be stowed on board.

At Willy's signal that all was ready, the *Iona* steamed around the headland and, a few minutes later, Austin appeared on the terrace with his bride in her going-away outfit and pointed down at the steamer, beautiful in every way, lying just off the Point, her little funnels purling brown smoke across the bay. He whispered in Biddy's ear and she threw her hands to her face and wept with happiness while Walter and Tom Ewing herded the guests round by the gardens and down the path to the rock where the longboat waited to spirit the happy couple away.

To many it was an idyll of romance but to others, Ronan Campbell among them, it seemed like a sheer waste of cash.

But that was not the end of it. As bride and groom were rowed off across the silky waters a great bonfire was lighted on the promontory of An Fhearann Cáirdeil as if to signal Austin's joy to every fisherman and cottager as far as the far horizon. Then there was singing and the shouting of fond farewells from the guests on the shore. The piper played the Bridegroom's Rant. Thor and Odin, who had been brought out on the leash from the gunroom, howled and the skipper of the *Iona* sounded her steam whistle and, ten or fifteen minutes later, just as the sun slipped behind the Treshnish Isles, the paddles churned and the vessel swung away and carved across the fiery sea into the blue shadows of the Sound, with Biddy and Austin, still just visible, waving and waving.

'Why are you crying, Innis?' Tom Ewing said. 'Is it because you are happy for Biddy?'

'Yes, I am happy for her.'

'Do you not wish that it was you?'

'I am not in love with Mr Baverstock.'

'That is not what I meant,' Tom said.

'No.' Innis wiped her eyes on the handkerchief that the minister had given her. 'No, I know fine what you mean. I would not need to have a steamship all to myself to be happy with the man I loved.'

'Who would that be?' Tom said.

He had come up to her quietly on the edge of the gathering and, when the guests began to drift back towards the house, lingered with her on the rocks above the shore.

Innis did not answer.

'Did he not come tonight?' Tom asked.

'Who?'

She looked up at him. He was not severe. He did not carry with him the odour of sanctity that she expected of a minister of the Church, nor was he cautious with her as Father Gunnion was, talking to her from a distance.

She had known Tom Ewing all her adult life, such as it was, and he had never seemed at all remote.

It was Michael she wanted but for no reason that she could explain at that moment she longed to have Tom Ewing's arms about her. She wanted him to hold her, not as he would hold a child, not to comfort her but to demonstrate that he too was aware of the significance of Biddy's wedding night and what it meant, not just to Biddy and Austin Baverstock but to all of them.

They were alone at the crumbling edge of the path above the ring-rock. Even Willy had gone back up towards the house with the dogs on the leash, and the laughter of the women from Edinburgh hung lightly in the darkening air.

Innis glanced across the bay towards Olaf's Ridge and let

out a little sound that was half sob, half sigh.

'Do you not know who it is?' she said.

'I know it is not me,' Tom Ewing told her.

'I wish . . .' she said. 'I wish . . .'

He put his forefinger gently against her lips.

'Hush, Innis,' he said. 'Hush. You must not wish your life away.'

'You would not know what it is like,' she said, brushing his finger aside.

'Why would I not?' Tom said.

'Because you're a minister, a man of God.'

'I am that by choice,' Tom said. 'But as for not knowing about love . . .'

Innis frowned as she recalled what Grandfather McIver had told her not so very long ago. She had dismissed it then and she must dismiss it now. It pained her to realise that she did not have Biddy's strength of will in this matter either, that she could not bring herself to love a man just because he might believe himself to be in love with her. And yet that, she saw, was exactly what she expected of Michael.

She put her arm down by her side, searched for Tom's hand and held it discreetly and not for long, a little gesture of sympathy which, in its way, was almost worse than indifference. His fingers were smooth, not rough like Michael's or like her own. She could not make herself love him, no more than she could make herself not love Michael.

I wish, she thought, I wish, I wish, I wish . . . But she did not know what she wished for any more, except Michael, who had stayed away.

Fetternish slipped away behind the stern, Glengorm, Mishnish and Ardmore. Then Biddy saw the Sound of Mull stretching ahead like a great grey road, set round with the barns and anchorages and spires that hunched timidly beneath the inhospitable hills. She leaned on the rail forward of the painted paddle-floats, the lights of the deck saloon behind her, three crewmen still softly playing a waltz on two violins and an out-of-tune cornet. She could smell the deep sea in the fine spray from the cowling and coal-smoke from the funnels and feel all through her body the shudder of the machinery that drove the paddle-wheels.

Skipper and crew were nowhere to be seen, for Austin had paid for privacy and privacy was what he and his bride would get. Even the navigation bridge, Biddy thought, looking round, was apparently deserted. Austin leaned against her, an arm firmly about her waist as if he feared that she, for all her solidity, might be lifted up by the light sea breeze and carried away like thistledown.

'Did you like it, dearest?' he whispered in her ear. 'Did you like my little surprise?'

'Of course I did,' Biddy said. 'I am just wondering what it cost.'

'Oh, hang the cost!' Austin said.

'How much, Austin?'

'Three hundred, give or take.'

'Pounds? Three hundred pounds? I can think of other things to be doing with three hundred pounds.'

'I've given us a day to remember, though, have I not?'

'Yes,' she said. 'Yes, I suppose you have.'

She felt his knee against her, pressing her skirts. In spite of her mood, she had sense enough not to push him away, not even when she felt his hand stray to her breast and, almost apologetically, caress it.

'Why didn't they come?' Biddy said. 'Why did your friends not come to see you married?'

'I am not in the least concerned, dearest.'

'I am – on your behalf.'

'Please, don't let it spoil . . .'

'Three hundred pounds, Austin, would have gone a long way towards buying more sheep or refurbishing the house.'

'Is that what you want? New furniture?'

'Not just new furniture. I want Fetternish to be so grand that those so-called friends of yours will beg to be invited to visit us.'

'I don't care if I never see them again.'

'But I do, Austin. Three hundred pounds would have . . .' She bit her lip, paused then said, less sharply, 'I appreciate what you've done to make our marriage day memorable. But in future we must be more careful with our money.'

'In future, yes – but let's not dwell on that tonight.'

'No,' Biddy said, 'not tonight.'

Then, because she knew precisely why he had married her and what her obligations were, she turned from the rail, nuzzled against him and let him kiss her hair, her mouth and put his hand down into the hollow of her thighs.

Then she took him by the arm and led him down to the cabin below.

There had been times when Innis could have seen her brothers and sisters far enough but with the last of them gone and the farm lying empty in the summer heat loneliness and melancholy soon stole over her.

It was an end to struggle, her father said – when he was sober enough to make any utterance at all – for if two women and a man could not look after a vegetable garden, a few hens and a couple of milking cows then there was something wrong with the system.

Innis knew what was wrong with 'the system'. Sometimes, when he sprawled against the base of the new wall, crooning drunkenly to himself in the morning sunlight, she was tempted to shout aloud that it wasn't his so-called system that was at fault but himself, his laziness, his selfishness, the sly and scummy appetites that had reduced them to little better than crofters, even if the land still belonged to Vassie and she drew rent for it from Fetternish.

Vassie, Walter and Hector Thrale had argued out the exact terms of the lease. Had measured with string and stakes the precise acreage that the Campbells could still call their own. Certain rights and entitlements had been retained, of course: burn water, access to the road, use of the jetty and boat shed and the right to graze two cows and three calves in the park under Olaf's Hill. The rest of it was effectively gone. And when the last of the cattle were driven away, sold cheaply to Mr Pritchard of Aros, and the hay crop and barley were sold in the ground to Mr Clark, there was nothing left to be done. Nothing except wait for the arrival of the sheep that Michael had been sent to the mainland to buy and that would soon come bleating over the moor to fill up the vacancy.

The arrival of new flocks would not bring Donnie back, though. Would not restore Neil or Aileen or shake Biddy loose from her marriage to the incomer, make everything settled and secure the way it had been a year ago before Michael Tarrant first came toddling over the hill - which, Innis knew in her head if not her heart, was absolute nonsense. The Campbells had never been settled, had never been happy. The seeds of change had taken root even here on the remote west coast of the beautiful Isle of Mull. The land and people who lived from the land were not immutable. They must change too, must bend and yield not just to wind and weather but to steam lighters and motor vessels, to the telegraph, the railway and the rumbustious spread of progress.

It was not the burnings that threatened them - the burnings were a thing of the past - but change, gradual and ineffable, would surely continue until all that was left of Pennypol and of McIver's kingdom out to sea were memories and ruins, the white ash of history for tourists to gawk at or, more probably, ignore.

'By God, that's a right torn face you have on you today, Innis Campbell,' Willy Naismith said. 'What are reading then - a tragedy by Seneca or some woolly tract that the priest gave you?'

'How do you know about the priest?'

'Everybody knows that you've been to see Father Gunnion.'

'Do they know why?'

'The reason isn't hard to guess.'

'Does Biddy know?'

Innis put her book - a novel by 'Ouida', as it happened - to one side and hoisted herself to her feet. She had been lying up by the old wall under the pines at the top end of the calf park waiting for a glimpse of Michael and the first of the market sheep when Willy had stumbled upon her. He had the hounds with him, not leashed, but the dogs were wise in the ways of the country now and snuffled quietly through the bracken in the hope of taking a rabbit by surprise.

'Does Biddy know what?' Willy said.

'That I have been talking with Father Gunnion?'

'I told you, everybody knows.'

'And what do they have to say to it?'

'Some of them are shocked but most of them couldn't care less.'

'And Biddy?'

'She has more to occupy her attention these days than making eyes at a skinny shepherd.' Willy leaned on the wall and when Odin appeared beside him stroked the dog's ears fondly. 'Has she not been down to visit you since she got back from her honeymoon?'

'No, she has not.'

'Come up to the house then.'

'Not without a proper invitation.'

'By God, but you are a proud lot. It isn't as if you wouldn't be made welcome, you know.'

'My mother is thinking that Biddy is best left to get on with her marriage without the family hanging round her neck.'

'Is that what your mother thinks?' Willy said. 'Or is it you?'

'Me? Why should it be me?'

'I thought you might still be afraid of her.'

'Afraid of my own sister? That is ridiculous.'

'Anyway, you are safe for a while yet,' Willy said. 'Young Mr Tarrant will not be back until a week on Monday. He has gone home to Ettrick to visit his mother who is unwell. He will travel back via Perth to pick up breeding stock. So you may as well abandon your vigil until then.'

Anger as well as embarrassment took hold of Innis. It had not occurred to her that she had become the subject of gossip and, it seemed, of ridicule. She cursed herself for having made quite so many trips to consult Father Gunnion. She had supposed that her love for Michael Tarrant was secret, not obvious. She might have known that few things on Mull could remain secret for long. Now that she thought of it, Mr Ewing had been cool towards her last Sunday and Mr Clark, a Protestant die-hard who went off every July to march with a lodge in Glasgow, had practically cut her dead.

'If you suppose I'm throwing myself at Michael Tarrant—'

'Aren't you?' Willy interrupted. 'If you're not and you're contemplating converting to Catholicism for some other reason then you'd better make plans to enter a convent because few in these parts will forgive you.'

'Is that why Michael keeps himself to himself?'

'I've no idea,' Willy said. 'Perhaps he keeps himself to himself because he hopes to have his fun with you the way he had with your sister, without anyone knowing about it and without having to pay the price.'

'Price? What price?'

'Marriage.'

'How can you say that? How can you?' Innis snapped. 'You know nothing about Michael, and nothing about me.'

'That may very well be true,' Willy said. 'But I have been in this world a lot longer than you have, Innis, and I know that there's naught so queer as young folk in love.'

'Michael is not in love with me.'

'Perhaps he is and just doesn't know it yet.'

Innis frowned. 'Has he said as much?'

'Of course not,' Willy said. 'Do you think that men talk of these matters among themselves the way women do? Besides, Michael Tarrant is a law unto himself. If you want to know about Michael Tarrant then surely the person to ask is your sister Biddy.'

'She will tell me nothing. She hates him.'

Willy scratched his beard with his knuckle and, head cocked, looked out towards the islands that floated passively on the surface of the sea. Casually, he said, 'What will your father have to say when he discovers you have it in mind to marry a Roman Catholic?'

'He will not care. He cares about nothing.'

'And your grandfather?'

'He thinks I should be marrying Mr Ewing.'

'The minister?' Willy said, surprised. 'Well, that would certainly be a step in an upward direction.'

'I am not in love with Mr Ewing.'

'No, I don't suppose you are.' Willy said. 'And, of course, you wouldn't contemplate marrying a man you didn't love, would you?'

'I am not like my sister.'

'Don't be too sure.' Willy said. 'You may not have red hair and a figure like a – well, you know what I mean – but you're not so very different from Biddy as all that.'

'I think you have said enough to be going on with, Mr Naismith.'

'Ooooh, I've insulted you. I didn't mean to.'

'Whether you did or whether you did not, I am not in need of advice about what to do with my life.'

The Duties of a Wife

Willy would have put an arm about her shoulder and offered her his lapel to cry on if he had not been a happily married man. He did not dare touch her, though, not even in a paternal way, for Miss Innis Campbell, just like her sister, was stubborn and prickly and would get what she wanted in the end whether it was right for her or not.

He said, 'Come up to the house and talk to Biddy.'

'Why should I?'

He shrugged. 'You never know, Innis, perhaps she can help you.'

'Help me to do what?'

'Find out what you really want?'

'I know what I want,' Innis said.

'Michael Tarrant?' Willy said. 'Well, come anyway.'

'What for?'

'Afternoon tea,' he said.

Biddy showed no reluctance to accompany him to An Fhearann Cáirdeil, though she mocked his pronunciation and did not agree that the name was best translated as Friendship Farm. Austin was not put out by his wife's criticism. He intended to devote the winter evenings to learning Gaelic via an excellent course of home study put out by the Highland Institute. He had also thought of taking instruction in the art of playing the bagpipes but when he raised this possibility with Biddy she laughed so loudly that he decided that perhaps he was a little too breathless, at his age, to make a go of it.

Unlike Agnes, Biddy enjoyed being out of doors. She liked nothing better than to dress up in her new shooting boots and tweed skirt and strike out over the back roads and across the patchwork fields to explore an estate that had been, Austin supposed, *terra incognita* to a little lass from Pennypol.

What, if anything, he found disappointing was that Biddy seemed oblivious to the island's natural beauty. She looked on every chain and furlong as property and condemned as useless those parts that would not yield to cultivation. He was also surprised to learn that she did not know the names of any of the small birds that flocked in to feed on the stalks of wild barley that grew among the ruins of Friendship Farm, that she could not tell one species of gull from another and would not even lift her head to observe the sleek roe deer that grazed among the bramble bushes.

'What are they eating? Is that barley?'

'I believe it is, dear,' Austin said.

'So barley will grow here, will it?'

'It did once, by the look of it.'

'So there must be fresh water in the vicinity.'

'Yes, I suppose so,' Austin said, 'though nothing is marked on the plans.'

'It will be a spring, I am thinking. Tell Thrale to find it.'

'I will,' Austin said. 'Look, aren't the little birds pretty?'

Ignoring the feathered flock, Biddy turned to stare inland at the impenetrable wall of undergrowth that spilled out of the tree line.

'What is back there, Austin?'

'I have no idea.'

'Mature trees?'

'No, probably not.'

'Nothing worth felling?'

'I doubt it.'

'If we burned back the bracken we could have quite a tidy wee piece of ground here.'

She put her hands on her hips, thumbs fanned over the broad leather belt that kept her skirt riding on her hips and her white blouse tucked stiffly into her waist. She looked, Austin thought, his heart thick in his chest, like a beautiful conqueror, red hair wisping from under her bonnet, the curve of her spine and the rise of her buttocks so strong and fecund that he thought that she might plough and seed the ground herself and that, just by her order, might command the rough old rocky headland to sprout green again.

'Spring would be the time for that,' Biddy said, speaking more to herself than for her husband's benefit. 'March, before the lambing starts, before the peat-cutting.'

'I'm not sure we have the labour for such an undertaking.'

'Labour can be hired,' Biddy said. 'There are casuals all over the north island who will be working for not much more than a shilling a day. One good crop of turnips or potatoes would repay the cost of reclamation. You should be thinking about these things, Austin,' she told him then, pointing, asked, 'How far is it to the boundary with Glengorm?'

'I have no idea, really,' he admitted.

'Half a mile?'

'No, not so far. It's very rough in the gully, dearest, a jungle in fact.'

'Come on,' Biddy said, starting forward. 'Let us see if there is anything we can be doing with it.'

The evening sky had turned slate grey and the islands were lost in a haar that would soon thicken into rain. The day had been muggy and Innis had worked with her mother in the potato quarter and the carrot rows, weeding by hoe and by hand. The earth itself seemed sticky as if sullen weather had congealed the sandy soil.

The air about the cottage was ripe with the smell of boiling fish, for her father had brought back a cod, a skinny, snake-like specimen that McKinnon had thrown to him and which, by the look of it, had been dropped in the dirt once too often on the trail back home from Crove. Vassie had cut the bone from its back, had washed the fish in salted water and put it into the deep black pan on top of the peats covered with clean water and a handful of herbs and had left it to simmer and soften, and whether supper would be a soup or a stew was now in the lap of the gods.

It was not the gods that drew Innis to the standing stone but the hope of catching a breeze from the sea. There was no breeze, though, not a breath. Even the ebbing tide on the rocks below old Caliach had a numb lethargic quality and the wavelets broke with a fine, sad hiss like the tearing of calico. She could not bear the sweat – or the memories – and left quickly, walking back towards the burn with the layer of rain thickening behind her and the dark mountains of Ardnamurchan swelling up ahead.

She was sticky with perspiration. Her petticoat clung to her hips and her bodice, stained with earth, was pasted to her breasts. At least she would have the mattress to herself tonight, she thought, with no Biddy and no Aileen to generate an insufferable heat between them.

She reached the burn, removed her bodice and outer skirt and, clad only in her shift, felt for the edge of the pool with bare feet. The water was cool but somehow fetid as if the moor ground too had turned sour. Sighing, she stooped, cupped her hands, brought water up to her throat and let it trickle over her breasts and wet her belly and thighs.

When she straightened she saw him.

He was crouched on all fours like a dog, as if he had tried to hide. His backside was deep in the fern and if it had been darker or if he had not moved, weaving his head from side to side, perhaps she would not have noticed him at all. When she started and called out he did not back away but came forward, still on all fours. Then, sitting back on his heels, he showed himself to her.

Nausea rose within her along with a surge of guilt at the thought that perhaps she had lured him into indecency or had intentionally taunted him. Then that silliness passed and the sickness with it, leaving embarrassment, gaunt and cringing within her. Shame that this man had fathered her and that she must drag him with her like a chain through all her days with no redeeming memories but only as he was now, drunk and leering and exposed.

She picked up her clothes and ran.

'He was there, was he not, waiting for you?' Vassie said.

'Yes.'

'Did he touch you?'

'No.'

'He would be too drunk to touch you.'

'Yes.'

'Are you hurt?'

'No.'

'Are you hungry?'

'No.'

'Go up to your bed then.'

'What are you going to do?'

'Nothing,' Vassie said. 'I am going to do nothing.'

'You have always done nothing.'

'Is that what you are thinking?'

'I am thinking of Aileen and the lies you have told to protect him.'

'I lied to protect you, not him.'

'Me?'

'All of you,' Vassie said.

'You should have sent us away from here.'

'I could not be doing that,' Vassie said. 'I had to have something.'

'Were we what you had, your children?'

'Aye.'

'What do you intend to do now that you no longer have us?'

'I will have him,' Vassie said.

'Is that all it has been for?' said Innis. 'To have him for yourself?'

'And he,' Vassie said, steadily, 'will have me.'

The air was fresh after two days of rain. A light blue breeze came up from the ocean and on the terrace the lawn had been mown only that morning and the odour of cut grass was strong. From the front of the house drifted the sounds of horse-drawn machinery as Mr Bell and two gardeners wrestled with the fancy new equipment that Biddy had persuaded her husband to buy from an agricultural agent who, as luck would have it, just happened to call in at Fetternish three days after the happy couple returned from their pleasure cruise.

Walter had balked at the expense, of course, but Austin had been adamant and new grass-cutting machinery, suitable also for light crops, had been delivered by carrier within a fortnight, all painted and prim with stainless steel blades so sharp and poised that, according to Austin, you could have shaved your chin with them. Since then the lawns had been mown every five or six days even when the ground was soft. In the moist warmth of the summer afternoon the sounds of industry were soothing, as if mowing was something that occurred naturally without any effort at all.

Biddy's tinkling little tricks with the silver tea service and dainty bone-china cups only served to increase the feeling that all was right with the world and that she, Mrs Bridget Campbell Baverstock, was perfectly capable of ensuring that it remained so.

In a light cotton dress and her best shoes and stockings, Innis leaned back in the stout canvas-backed chair that Willy had carried out for her and sipped tea as politely as possible. She ate a slice of the crustless bread that was piled up in little diamonds upon the silver plate and, in spite of her seriousness, eyed a fluffy yellow sponge cake with anticipation.

'Now,' Biddy said, 'let me see if I understand you. He exposed himself to you but did not attempt to - well - do anything.'

'You know what he is like,' Innis said. 'He was too drunk to do anything.'

'He was not too drunk when it came to Aileen.'

'No, but she - she loved him.'

'Lord, yes, I suppose that's the truth of it.' Biddy sighed and rolled her sea green eyes as if the subject of the conversation referred only to a chance acquaintance. 'What did he have to say for himself when he came in for supper?'

'Not a word.'

'No apology, no excuse?'

'Nothing,' Innis answered.

'She would not be challenging him with it, I suppose?'

'No, she made no mention of what had happened.'

'Just - what was it? - that she would have him?'

'And that he would have her,' Innis added.

'I wonder what she means by that?'

'I think,' Innis said, 'she means that she will see him out.'

'Is that what she calls revenge?' Biddy said. 'Outliving him? It is hardly my idea of revenge.'

'She gave him drink,' Innis said. 'Whisky. She keeps six or eight bottles of Old Caledonia hidden away in your chest in the loft. I do not know who buys it for her or if she buys it herself when she is down in Crove but she is at pains to ensure that he never goes short.'

'And he thinks that she is just being a good wife to him, I suppose?'

'By his lights, she is,' Innis said. 'That - that night, two nights ago, she had a bottle on the table just waiting for him to come in. He was far gone already but she poured glass after glass for him and, what is more, ate her supper sitting at the table with him.'

'Was he sick?'

'No, he is never sick,' Innis said. 'He fell across the table after a while.'

'Did she leave him there?'

'She dragged him to his bed.'

'What did you do?' Biddy asked.

'I stayed in the loft where she had told me to go.'

Biddy reached for the silver teapot and poured a stream of pale liquid into her cup and then, with a gesture more hospitable than ladylike, shook the pot in her sister's direction and filled her cup too to the brim.

She said, 'What if he had not been drunk? What if he had done to you what he did to Aileen? It does not bear thinking about.'

'I know,' Innis said. 'That is why I have to get away.'

Biddy sipped tea, head cocked to one side. She wore a gigantic hat, neither sun hat nor bonnet but a hybrid version of each that contained her hair and shaded her face more than adequately. The brim had lost its shop-window stiffness in the moist sea-coast air, however, and flopped over one eye so that Biddy appeared slightly less than immaculate and had, Innis thought, a raffish, almost buccaneering look to her.

'Well, I suppose I could find a place for you here,' Biddy said. 'I mean, I could ask Austin if he would take you on as an extra housekeeper.'

'I am thinking that I would not like that,' Innis said.

'It is not as if you were an orphan,' Biddy said. 'If you were an orphan then Austin would be obligated to look after you, since you are my sister and that is how it is done. He cannot just take you in, you know, without a reason.'

'I know,' Innis said.

Biddy put the teacup down and sat back. The breeze from the sea fluttered the hat's brim irritatingly and she suddenly lost patience with it and peeled the hat from her head and tossed it to the grass by the side of her chair. She shook out her hair and fluffed it up with her fingers.

'You could be going to Foss,' Biddy said, 'and stay with Grandfather?'

'He will not take me.'

'Of course he will. If he took Aileen and her baby then he will surely take you. One more mouth to feed will make no difference to Grandfather McIver. Besides, you have always been his favourite.'

'I – I want to be married.'

'Ah!'

'I want to be married to Michael Tarrant.'

Biddy glanced round at the house, the tall windows sheened with afternoon sunlight. She continued to stare in that direction as if she could not bring herself to meet her sister's eye. 'He is a deceiver, a Pape and a vile deceiver,' she hissèd. 'I cannot tell you how he hurt me.'

'In that case,' Innis said, 'why do you not dismiss him?'

'Because he is too good a shepherd,' Biddy said.

'There must be other good shepherds on Mull.'

'Use your common sense, Innis,' Biddy snapped. 'How can I ask Austin to dismiss an employee who is in every way satisfactory? I would have to explain why I want rid of him and I cannot do that.'

'You want to keep him for yourself.'

'Do not be ridiculous!' Biddy wriggled on the chair and almost lost balance. She gripped the wooden arms tightly with both fists and scowled. 'I am a happily married woman. I have no need to "keep" Michael Tarrant on Fetternish for any reason other than that he is an excellent tender of sheep. If you think that I would sully myself by consorting with an employee, a servant, then you are more ignorant than I thought you were.'

'You liked him once.'

'Before I discovered what he was.'

'Catholic or not, would he not have made a good husband?'

'If that is your way of asking if he was a good lover then I can tell you that he was, though what you would know about it and how you would judge I cannot possibly imagine.'

'I do not mean to pry,' Innis said, 'or to upset you.'

'Well, you *are* prying,' Biddy said, 'and you *have* upset me. Do you think I would not be rid of Michael Tarrant if I could? I tell you, I cannot bear to look at him now, even to see him far across the fields. It makes me burn red with embarrassment to think how I was cheated – yes, cheated – and how he must smirk at me behind my back. Dismiss him? Oh, yes, Innis, I would be delighted to see him sacked.'

'Or married off?'

'No.'

'Because your sister would be married to a shepherd and that would not be seemly for the mistress of Fetternish?'

'That has nothing to do with it,' Biddy said. 'He is not the man for you, Innis, take my word for it. He is vile and wicked and he will betray you just as casually as he betrayed me.'

'Not if I am his wife.'

'Do you think Catholics are better than we are, that they are all such fine, God-fearing people that they can do no wrong?' Biddy said, her voice shrill. 'He had no thought of what sort of sin he was committing when he . . .'

'When you gave in to him,' Innis said. 'If I do marry Michael, will your husband dismiss him then?'

'How could he?'

'And you would be safe from harm, from temptation?'

Biddy straightened. She lifted her shoulders and expanded her chest and then, as an afterthought, whipped up her hat from the grass and placed it firmly on her head. She looked daunting again, almost imperial.

Innis felt her confidence ebb. She could not imagine what Michael had done with and to her sister, how that aspect of marriage, or loving, functioned. It was not the physical aspects of love-making that bewildered her, for she had often witnessed the cockerel cover the hen, the bull go into the cow, the clumsy mating of ram with ewe. What puzzled her was how it could be undertaken without love, without trust. How Biddy could so easily put one man from her and replace him with another. She looked at her sister's scarlet cheeks and pursed lips and suddenly found that she envied Biddy nothing, nothing except her beauty and her experience.

Biddy said, 'You do not know what you are letting yourself in for, Innis. Be assured of this, however, you will receive no help from me if it works out badly, no help and no sympathy. Do I make myself clear?'

'Abundantly,' Innis said.

'Now – do you want a piece of that sponge cake?'

The Island Wife

And Innis said, 'Why not?'

Innis made no bones about the fact that she was going to Foss to seek her grandfather's advice. Vassie did not try to dissuade her but gave her three new shillings to pay to the boatman at Croig and two jars of Aros honey, bought from Miss Fergusson's store at Crove. Vassie would have sent more gifts but Pennypol's vegetables were not quite ready for unearthing in spite of the spell of fine growing weather and she did not have the energy to hunt for and pick a bowlful of the small, sweet raspberries that that were hidden in the bramble tangle by the Fetternish wall.

There was nothing to prevent Vassie accompanying Innis to Foss to see Aileen and hold her grandson in her arms. Except that Ronan had blighted those natural relationships, had tainted them with fear and guilt and a kind of loathing that Vassie tried to pass off as indifference.

She sent no greeting to Aileen, no presents for the baby and wrung from Innis a promise that she would say nothing to Grandfather McIver about Ronan's latest 'indiscretion'.

Innis left immediately after morning milking.

It was a long walk to Croig. She took the coastal track over the headland, around the edge of Mr Clark's property and along the shore of the long loch that bit into the Ards. She wore her everyday dress, brushed clean, and carried her boots about her neck, fastened by the laces, for the ground was soft as far as the Dervaig road that led past Loch Cuan to the mill and past the mill to Croig. She was happy with her boots around her neck and her legs bare, able to delude herself that she was just a simple farm lass whose life was without depth or complications.

To her relief Mr McKendrick's boat was moored at the stone pier and Mr McKendrick was seated on the bench outside the tiny post office, waiting for customers. He was an old man, grizzled and cheerful. He raised his hand in greeting when he saw Innis, for he knew that the appearance of the Campbell girl on his doorstep could mean only one thing – a day's hire.

Rheumatism of the fingers, not drink, had put paid to Mr McKendrick's career as a fisherman. But his wife received a fee for managing the post office and he was content not to have to

336

wrestle with knives and bait, hooks and creels and soaking ropes every day but to put himself and his boat at the disposal of visitors who wanted a sail among the little islands.

'Grand day, is it not now?' The boatman pulled on the oars and eased the boat away from the pier.

'It is all that, Mr McKendrick,' Innis said. 'Will we be having the sun to warm us, do you think?'

'Aye, soon, very soon.'

There was no sun yet, though, and by turning her head a little she could see the stark outline of the Arkle peninsula off which her brother had drowned.

'He is not with us any longer,' Mr McKendrick said.

'Who is not with us?'

'Is it not Haggerty you are thinking about?'

'Yes,' Innis admitted. 'Where has he gone?'

'He has gone away back to Ireland.'

'When did this happen?'

'In the New Year. After,' Mr McKendrick said. 'He was making nothing of it, so Haggerty told me. He sold all his goats to Mr Laurieston and took everything he could be putting into a bundle and just went away.'

'I do not think my father knows this.'

'We have seen nothing much of your daddy since he lost the boat.'

Innis turned on the stern seat and looked back at the face of the cliff. She could not see the bay, though, only the black current swooping against the guard rocks.

'What happened to Haggerty's cottage? Who lives there now?'

'No one. He burned it.'

'Burned it? Why?'

Mr McKendrick shrugged and seemed, Innis thought, to dig deeper into the water with the oars as if the reason for Fergus Haggerty's sudden departure was not inexplicable but merely something that he did not wish to discuss.

It surprised Willy to find his master on the lawn at such a comparatively early hour. The exertions of marriage, of satisfying his youthful bride, had taken their toll on Austin Baverstock. He spent more than his fair share of the morning fast asleep in bed and, after lunch, another hour or so drowsing in the armchair before the empty hearth or oscillating in the hammock that Willy had strung up between the evergreens that guarded the gate of the kitchen garden.

Willy's own nocturnal activities were probably no less vigorous than his master's but he was well used to playing the part of lover or loving husband and had, he supposed, become adjusted to it.

Whatever took place in the big four-poster bed in the bedroom upstairs there could be no doubt that the mistress thrived on it. Unlike her husband, marriage had imbued Biddy with new vitality. It was all Willy and Margaret could do to keep up with her. She was not like Agnes, however. She had no fondness for the handbell, for throwing her weight around. If she wanted something she would fetch it herself or, failing that, would shout out for it, adding 'Please' or 'Thank you' to soften the request.

Austin was on the lawn below the terrace before the sun had burned off the sea mist, shooting jacket thrown over his shoulders and one of Willy's big enamel mugs cupped in both hands. He drank coffee and stared so bleakly out to where the sea should be that Willy wondered if master and missus had had their first squabble and, if so, what had occasioned it.

He arrived on the lawn, cool and casual, with coffee pot in hand.

'A wee drop more, Mr Austin?'

'Ah, William! The very chap.'

Willy poured coffee then placed the pot snugly between the paws of a stone lion. He folded his arms and watched Mr Austin drink.

'It's Bridget, my wife,' Austin said.

'Uh-huh,' Willy murmured.

'She appears to have developed an antipathy to one of our employees and - ah - wishes me to serve him notice of dismissal.'

'Which employee, if I might ask?' Willy said, though he had a fair notion what the answer would be.

'Tarrant, our shepherd.'

'Did Mrs Baverstock provide a reason why she wishes Tarrant sacked?'

'None.' Another mouthful of hot coffee. 'In fact, I'm not altogether sure that she did ask me to sack him.'

'What did she say, exactly?' Willy enquired.

'That I should warn him.'

'About what?'

'I've no idea.'

Willy chose his words with care. 'Has Tarrant been bothering Mrs Baverstock, by any chance?'

'What do you mean – bothering?'

'Has he been, let's say, impertinent?'

'I doubt it. Tarrant's a decent sort of fellow. In any case, we've seen nothing of him for weeks. He's been away, has he not?'

'Aye, I believe he has.' Willy leaned an elbow on the stonework, gazed out to sea for several seconds then said, 'I believe the shepherd was quite sweet on Mrs Baverstock before she got engaged to you. Perhaps she's too embarrassed to tell you herself.'

'Was he? Was he, indeed?'

'Did you not know?'

'I think I did. Something of the sort, yes.' Austin put the coffee mug down, frowned and said, 'Is he still sweet on her, d'you think?'

'I doubt it,' Willy said. 'It would be one of those passing fancies that young men have. I'm certain Tarrant knows his place and that he'll do nothing to embarrass you or your wife.'

'I sincerely hope not,' Austin said. 'Perhaps I should be rid of him.'

'No, no,' Willy put in, hastily. 'I don't think that's what Mrs Baverstock really has in mind.'

'What *does* she have in mind?'

In full, smooth flow now, Willy said, 'It was a little ruse to save you being offended. The sort of thing that women do all the time.'

'Do you mean she wants him sacked only to protect my feelings?'

'That's it,' said Willy.

'What do I do about it? I mean, what should I do? I'm not offended and I certainly don't want to lose a valuable hand.'

'Leave it to me,' Willy said. 'With your permission, I'll have a wee quiet word with Michael Tarrant.'

'Will that be enough, William?'
'Oh, aye, Mr Austin,' Willy said. 'That will be quite enough.'

To Innis's surprise it was Quig who came down to meet the boat.
There was no sign of her grandfather who, Quig informed her,
had gone out to the meadow to dose one of the bulls that had
been showing signs of temper.

Quig was not alone. Aileen was with him, hanging on to his
hand like a child. In the crook of one brown arm the lad cradled
Aileen's baby, quite brown-skinned too now as if sea air and
sunshine had already begun to transform young Donald into one
of McIver's tribe. He held the infant casually and when he moved
the baby moved with him, floppy, not yet firm-limbed. It was
all Innis could do not to reach out, take the child and peer into
the little round, brown face in search of that feyness that
possessed his mother or, and the thought made her wince, for a
likeness to her father.

Aileen was dressed in a clean, patched cotton dress and a faded
shawl. Her hair was lighter, bleached by the sun and her eyes so
clear and blue that they seemed almost transparent, like little
shards of glass. There was none of the sort of conversation that
should have taken place between sisters who had been parted
for a while, no questions about their mother's health or the state
of the farm, nothing that related to Aileen's 'old life' across the
water on Pennypol. It was as if all that had gone from her, wiped
away, and she dwelled safely in time present with no memory
of what had gone before.

A necklace of shells strung on a loop of fishing line dangled
about her neck and a bracelet of shells, like a manacle, hung
from one wrist. She grinned at Innis then lifted her wrist and
shook it, shook her head too, to show off the ornaments that
Quig had made for her

She said, 'Mine, mine,' then, before Innis could even begin to
admire the sea-shells, leaned into Quig, poked a forefinger into
the baby's chest and, gleefully, said, 'Mine too, mine too.'

'What is your baby's name, Aileen?' Innis asked.
'Don-nie. I ca' him Don-nie.'

Behind her Mr McKendrick was hauling the boat ashore. She
could hear him grunting with the effort but she could not help

him. She was trapped in a little triangle of Aileen, Quig and the child and could not have broken free of their spell even if she had wished to do so.

She glanced at Quig and said softly, 'Is she worse?'

'Och, no. She is not so bad,' Quig said. 'Sure, she is not so bad at all.'

'Does she know whose child it is?'

'Mine,' Aileen said. 'Quig's an' mine.'

'Is that what she thinks?' said Innis.

'Let her think what she likes,' Quig said. 'It matters not to me.'

Innis nodded and glanced up towards the house which was unnaturally quiet in the hazy noon sunshine.

'Where is everyone?' she asked.

'They have gone to Grass Point to deliver cattle.'

'What? The children too?'

'All of them,' Quig told her. 'It is an adventure for them, even for Mairi. Two bulls for the duke's agent, four heifers for Drumore estates. They rafted the beasts across to Ulva yesterday and they will be on the drove today, tomorrow and the next day, for they will be taking it slow.'

'Why did you not go with them?'

'He asked me to stay here.'

'Why did he did not go himself?'

'He is not so much himself these days,' Quig said. 'He has not been away from the island since your sister's wedding and he says he will not leave again.'

'Is he ill?'

'No – but he is old, and prefers to be at home.'

Innis had never seen cattle rafted off Foss. But she had heard so much about it from her mother that, in her mind's eye, she could imagine the great square-shaped litter of pine wood and rope with the cattle bracketed on it, bellowing with the strangeness of the sea. The women and children, wet through, clinging to the rail while the boys on the long oar kept the clumsy craft straight in the currents that swirled them from islet to islet across each of the channels and across to Gometra and the sheltering arm of Loch Tuath. She could see them in perspective, like fugitives from another time, coming in from the sea with the sun behind them and the sea itself calm and accommodating all along the rocky and inhospitable coast.

It would not be the same without her grandfather at the oar or leading the drove. He had taken fifty head south in his time and before that, so she had heard, had driven herds of three or four hundred wild stirks across half the islands of the west, down the spine of Mull and away into the Scottish heartland where she had never been. He would not go again. He had sent the boys and the women, even the children, on the raft in his stead.

Quig did not have to tell her that next summer or the summer after, the fine-bred cattle of Foss would be loaded on to a steam-lighter and shipped south to Oban. And that that would be an end of the old ways that her grandfather had lived through and through which he had thrived.

Sadness touched her, a sadness tinged with relief.

Perhaps it was as well that she had not come to live here, for Foss was a fading paradise that, like a dream or a rainbow, would soon pass away.

'You will be needing a bite to eat, I am thinking, Mr McKendrick,' Quig said to the boatman. 'If you will be coming with me I will find something tasty in the house for your dinner.'

'Oh, anything you have will be doing me fine,' Mr McKendrick said. 'But I would be glad of a dish of tea if there is one going.'

'There is indeed one going,' Quig said. 'I can even hear the kettle boiling.' He turned to Innis. 'Evander is out to the west in the sea-meadow. Go and find him and tell him his dinner will be ready in half an hour.'

'Aileen, will you not be coming with me?' Innis said.

Aileen shook her head, scowled, gripped Quig's hand tightly.

'Go by yourself, Innis,' Quig told her. 'He will be fair pleased to see you.'

He was a year, possibly two years, younger than she was and she had never known, and had never dared enquire, how exactly they were related. She had always assumed that he was her grandfather's child, bred off one of the women of the island – if not Mairi, another – but she had never been sure if Quig was her uncle or any blood relative at all.

She responded to his authority without question, though, for he was the one who lived here and who, in course of time, would inherit the little green isle.

Quig smiled and, hoisting the baby up against his shoulder, led the boatman and the girl-child up the sand towards the wooden house that stood so quiet and empty in the summer sun.

He was not dosing cattle at all. There were no bulls in the sea-meadow, though Innis could see the huge heads and great curved horns of the highlanders protruding from the russet grasses over by the knoll that crowned the isle. Fladda, Lunga and the Dutchman's Cap were visible now that the sun had lifted the haze from the sea. The water ran blue-black and, though there was no breath of wind on Foss, whitecaps marked the line of the outer skerries and made the herring drifters, far out towards the horizon, dip and snort.

Her grandfather was seated on a boulder by the shore. He wore a heavy knitted garment over his vest and a muffler was wrapped about his neck as if the day were wintry, not warm. He stared out to sea, eyes glassy and mouth open in a manner that made him look vacant. He did not notice Innis even when she came up behind him.

'I will be giving you a penny for them, Grandfather,' she said softly.

He seemed to come back reluctantly from some distant place. It took him two or three seconds to register who she was.

'They did not tell me that you were coming today. I would have been to meet the boat if they had told that you were coming.' He said, crossly, 'Why did they not tell me?'

'They did not know.'

Innis knelt by him. In the short space of time since Biddy's wedding he seemed to have aged by years not weeks. She realised that she had caught him with his guard down and saw the frailty in him all too clearly.

He stared past her, still not himself.

'Where are they?'

'They have gone to Grass Point with the bulls, Grandfather.'

'Why have they left me behind?'

'They were only obeying your instructions.'

The Island Wife

'Did I tell them to go without me?' He shook his head, bewildered. 'Where is Vassie? Why did your mother not come with you?'

'She is at home on Pennypol.'

'Did she let you sail on the sea alone?'

'Grandfather, I am not a child any more.'

She reached for his hand. For an instant she thought that he would reject her, fling himself away, huddle his arms about his chest as Aileen did when she was hurt or sulking. But then he smiled, placed his hand in hers and let her stroke her thumb across the bones and tendons that lay beneath the skin. His fingers were cold, cold as the sea itself.

He smiled. 'No more you are, Innis, no more you are. Did you bring your minister with you to tease me with his talk?'

'Not today,' Innis said. 'Mr Ewing had other things to do.'

The old man leaned on her shoulder and hoisted himself to his feet. She had never felt the weight of him before. Even now, in old age, it was considerable. She had to brace herself to support him until he found his balance.

'Will you be bringing him to see me soon?' her grandfather asked.

'Yes,' Innis lied. 'Yes, I will bring him with me next time I come.'

'He is the man for you,' her grandfather said, nodding. 'He is a better man than the one that your sister married, though he does not have so much money. I would be seeing you wed to the minister before I die.'

She had come to Foss to seek his advice but he was too intent on telling her what he wanted her to do even to listen to her questions. She felt the sadness intensify and, out of it, come a strange new kind of strength. She must do as she wanted to do, must depend upon no one, not even her grandfather, to make decisions – and mistakes – on her behalf.

Watched by the big highland bulls, they moved along the edge of the grasslands. As his wits had come back to him so did the strength in his legs and before they had gone fifty yards on to the shingle path he let go her arm and walked with the upright gait that she had always thought of as being dignified and proud. Now she was not so sure.

She was impatient with his stubborn refusal to listen, with his weakness, his pride, his slowness. He would send her into the future, if he could, as he had sent his wives and children into the past.

She realised now why her mother had married Ronan Campbell, why she, Vassie, had chosen dispossession over the slow, sure, insidious withering of a life lived in the shadow of another man's past.

Quig was not the future, nor Aileen, nor Tom Ewing, nor her father, drunk and lazy and wicked. Her children, if she had any, might be farmers or shepherds but they would not be the inheritors of Foss or Pennypol or the old, backward-looking traditions, the histories that were no better than romance. The future lay with Biddy, ambitious and self-willed, with Austin Baverstock and all those who would wring from the land as much as it would yield.

When she took her grandfather's arm for the little climb across the knoll to the wooden house by the shore it was to support not to be supported by a man whom she would always love but upon whom she could no longer depend.

'What did you come for, Innis?' he asked her.

'To see you, Grandfather,' she said.

'Is that all?'

'Aye,' Innis answered him. 'That's all.'

It was some time in the mid-afternoon. Michael lay on his back on the bed in the cottage in the Solitudes, worn out by the worry of the journey.

He had gone first to Ettrick to visit his mother.

Steamer and horse-omnibus and several railway trains had brought him at last to the long, low, whitewashed farmhouse that his father rented from Lord Ormond along with grazing rights to several hundred acres of rich grassland. An odd, disconcerting experience, coming home to the Ettrick Pen with its gentle vistas of long, green, rounded hills, wave upon wave, haughs feathered with hazel and alder and oak, and enormous flocks of fat Cheviots wherever he turned his eye, for the parish in which he had been born was nothing now but one almighty sheepwalk from stem to stern.

Whatever had ailed his mother had left her none the worse. She was up and about, hale and hearty as ever, before he got there. He was relieved, of course, that he was not obliged to play out a deathbed scene, for he loved the moon-faced, floury woman who had given him birth. He loved his father, bow-legged and reeking of tobacco. And his sister Sadie and her husband, Georgie, and her three small sons. And he loved his brother, Peter, who had gone into the seminary at Coates and would, in due course, become a priest and perhaps make a reputation for himself in the Church of Rome.

And he still loved, in a way, the girl he had left in Ettrick, Rose Garrity, who had been warned off him – rather late in the day – by Father McLeod and whose family had wedded her quick to a widower from Hawick before some other venal beggar came along to lead her astray with his promises. Rose was gone, of course, and Michael did not think it would be prudent to visit her in her stone house in Hawick, no matter how ardently he longed for her when he passed the hollows where they had lain together. He did not meet his brother Peter either, but that omission was cause for plain regret, untrammelled by anything out of the past or any of the longings that he had lugged along with him from the Isle of Mull.

He had stayed at home for five days. Then he had gone up to Edinburgh and spent a night in a lodging in the Grassmarket and had picked up a street girl with frizzy red hair, and had taken her back with him to the cot in the lodging and had paid her more than she was worth to let him enter her. Even as he had lain upon her, though, and had heard her grunting in fake passion, he had known that he would never find release in that easy manner again.

Next day, Sunday, he had gone to early mass and made a full confession.

And the day after, Monday, he had travelled up to Perth by train to buy a parcel of Cheviots to accompany him on the long, long walk back to Fetternish.

Only the dog seemed pleased to see him.

Roy had been boarded out with the Barretts and did not care for the mush they'd fed him or the fact that he'd had to sleep in an outhouse with only rats for company. Roy had wagged his tail and would have barked a welcome if the dusty, hoof-sore flock of breeding ewes had not been milling around the yard, braying impatiently and waiting to be driven out to grass.

Now, with that done and the new flock settled, the dog was curled up in his basket by the cold fireplace, snoring peacefully with, Michael thought, a contented little smile on his chops.

Exhausted though he was, Michael could not sleep.

He had slept hardly at all in the farmhouses and outbuildings that had given him shelter during the drive, though most nights he had been so weary that every bone in his body ached. He had even wondered if he was coming down with a sickness. It was not his body that was the real source of torment, though. It was his mind. He could not put the Campbell girls out of his thoughts for more than a few minutes at a time and during the long, lonely hours on the sheeptracks and roads that wended across the hills and through the glens he had chafed away at the problems that beset him, trying desperately to separate his desire for one unattainable sister from his affection for the other.

Under the hot summer sun there had been times when he seemed to be accompanied by both young women, to see them, like mirages, wavering in the dust or, as dusk came down, standing beneath the trees in the gloaming. First one and then the other, Biddy and Innis, beckoning. In the dark of the night, cowering in the musty bedding that was a drover's lot, he had been strung tight with desire for Biddy one minute and a minute later would be filled with a need for Innis's loving kindness.

Now that he was home again things were no easier. He closed his eyes and tried to sleep. But he could hear the ewes bleating in the pasture. Fresh grass had been locked away for them and they would soon recover the weight that they had lost on the drive. They were stout Cheviots, hand-picked, and he would be empowered to buy more, another two or three parcels, before winter came.

Lying there on the bed, hungry and exhausted, he tried to concentrate on shepherding, on tallying the tasks he must complete before the cold came down and gales howled up the glen and rain lashed across the headlands. But he could focus on nothing, other than Bridget Campbell Baverstock's auburn hair, her strong white thighs, the curve of her belly, the swell of her breasts; on nothing but Innis Campbell's solemn, brown eyes filled with speculation and with love.

He lay there paralysed by indecision, pole-axed by sixteen days on the road, burning with the shame of what he had done with the whore in Edinburgh and how he had longed for little Rose Garrity when he was home on the Ettrick Pen and how, even there, he had wanted to be back where he was now, lying on his bed in the cottage at Pennymain, waiting for something to happen.

A moment before the door opened Roy lifted his head from his paws and growled. Michael sat up, bleary-eyed and blinking.

'Biddy?' he said. 'Innis?'

'Sorry to disappoint you, old chap,' Willy Naismith said. 'It's only me.'

'What do you want? Is Thrale with you?'

'No, I'm entirely on my own.' He came forward from the door and sniffed. 'By God, Tarrant, you don't half pong.'

'What do you expect?' Michael said. 'I've been living with sheep for the best part of ten days.'

'Fine-looking collection you came back with, though.'

'What do you know about sheep?'

'Not much, I'll admit,' Willy said. 'However, I didn't come down here to admire the muttons.'

'What did you come for?'

'I came to put a word in your ear, as it happens.'

'A word? From Bid – from Mrs Baverstock?'

'Don't be so daft,' Willy said. 'If even half of what I've heard about you and the missus is true then the only word you're liable to receive from her in future is Farewell.'

'What's that supposed to mean?'

'Goodbye. Ta-Ta. Pack your bags and leave.'

Michael swung his legs from the bed, thumped his feet to the floor and shot upright. 'Are you telling me I've been sacked?'

'No,' Willy said. 'I am, however, telling you she's thinking about it.'

'How do you know what Biddy's thinking?'

'I eavesdrop,' Willy said.

'Is that the kind of man you are?' Michael said, sourly.

'All servants do it,' Willy said. 'Now are you interested in what

I have to say or do you want me to go away?'

Michael hesitated. He had no more than a passing acquaintance with the Baverstocks' servant and no reason at all to trust him, yet he could not ignore the implication of what Naismith had told him, even if it was only kitchen gossip.

'I'm interested,' Michael said. 'Tell me.'

'I overheard the missus talking to Mr Austin. She was trying to persuade him to dismiss you.'

'What did he say?'

'He was' – Willy paused – 'non-committal.'

'He has no cause to be rid of me,' Michael said.

'He doesn't need a cause. He's the owner of Fetternish. If he chooses to get rid of you then that's his affair. I dare say he'll give you a good character when you leave.'

'I don't want a good character. I want to stay on Fetternish.'

'You should have thought of that before,' Willy Naismith said. 'Still, how were you to know that your master would fall for the very lassie that you were dandlin'?'

'I'm not dandlin' her now. I'm not dandlin' anyone.'

'I should hope not,' said Willy. 'I would have thought you might have learned your lesson.'

'I don't have to listen to sermons from you.'

'It isn't a sermon,' Willy said. 'God knows, I'm not one to go preachin'. I just thought you should be warned what's in the wind. So you can do something about it.'

Michael threw up his hands in exasperation. 'What can I do about it?'

'Well, you could do what I did,' Willy said. 'Find a nice girl, marry her and settle down.'

Michael squinted suspiciously. 'Biddy did send you, didn't she?'

'No, no,' Willy said. 'No, no, no.'

'You're lying, Naismith. This is just Biddy's way of getting me wed to her sister and take the responsibility off her hands.'

'I doubt that,' Willy said.

'And you're in it with them.'

Willy sighed. 'God, but you're stubborn. I can't fathom what either of them see in you.'

'Either of them?'

'Both of them then.'

'Are you telling me . . .'

'Tarrant, I'm saying no more.'

'Look, I can't just marry anyone. I'm a Roman Catholic.'

'I don't care if you're the Flying Dutchman,' Willy said. 'I've done my bit for fair play.'

'There would have to be an arrangement, an agreement about the raising of the children.'

'That's not my concern,' Willy said. 'Anyhow, I think your religion's only an excuse.' He turned towards the door. 'I told my wife you wouldn't listen, that you're not the marrying sort.'

'Your wife?'

'Yes, coming here was her suggestion.'

'Oh!'

'She felt it was only decent to give you some sort of warning.'

'Oh, I see.'

'There you are then.' Willy nodded. 'I've kept my promise and done the decent thing. The rest is up to you.'

'Yes,' Michael said. 'I suppose it is. Naismith?'

'What?'

'Thank you.'

'My pleasure,' Willy said and, with another nod, left the arrogant young shepherd alone to nibble his nails and fret.

Mr Austin was waiting for him down in the glen by the water pipe. He had the hounds with him but they had been given a good run and had drunk their fill from the freshet and were lying quietly in the grass and did not stir even when Willy came scrambling down the path.

Austin got to his feet. 'Did you talk to him?'

'I did, sir. I did.'

'What did he have to say for himself?'

'Not much. He's a surly young devil but I think he took the point.'

'What point?'

'That if he wants to keep his job then he'd better find a wife.'

'Is that what you told him?' Austin said. 'Well, I dare say that's given him food for thought. Who will have him, though? I mean, who will take him on?'

'I thought that was obvious, Mr Austin.'

'Not to me it's not. Who, William, who is the unfortunate girl?'
'Your sister-in-law, sir.'
'Innis?' Austin said in astonishment. 'Innis Campbell?'
'The very same,' said Willy.

From the study window at the back of the manse Tom looked out upon the moor. It was bathed by a hazy late summer sun and he could see distant peat stacks, cut for the season and erected in pyramids to dry before each household carried off its share. Even in the placid light of a weekday forenoon the fuel seemed ominously dark against the subtle tints of heather and the green of bracken that, in just a week or two, would begin to turn golden.

It had not been much of a summer, Tom thought, not much of a summer at all. Admittedly the past few weeks had brought a settled spell, windless and warm, but there had been an absence of the strong sunshine that would cause the crops to ripen to the full or the cattle, what was left of them now that Vassie Campbell had sold her herd, to lie down and laze and grow fat before the agents came to cream them off to transport to the fall sales. He had never resented the passage of the seasons before, had never dreaded cold weather or even rain. But now he did, suddenly he did, for on that morning, with summer dwindling gently away, he knew that he had no hope, however faint, of making Innis his wife.

She was perched on the study's one padded chair, an old item with a faded plush seat and a carved back that had been imperfectly repaired. Behind her a glazed bookcase reflected his own image, dark and indistinct, slanted across the image of the girl. He looked at the twin reflections with the same gravity as he had stared from the window and, with seconds accumulating into minutes, tried to think of something to say that would not sound too harsh.

'Am I to understand that you would abandon the tenets of the faith in which you have been raised and allow yourself to be ruled by the dictates of the Pope of Rome just' – Tom cleared his throat – 'just because this man demands it?'

'Michael has not demanded anything of me, Mr Ewing,' Innis said.

'Do you mean that he has not asked you to marry him?'

'No.'

'Has he even mentioned the possibility?'

'Not yet.'

Tom felt a little lift of the spirits, a warming in his heart. He took two or three paces to his left, turned on his heel and took two or three paces back again. Innis watched him warily. He wondered if she had come here to hurt him deliberately or if this infatuation of hers for the shepherd was no more than fantasy or an attempt to take revenge on her beautiful sister.

'If that is the case, Innis, why are you here, asking me these questions?'

'I wish to be prepared.'

'For what?'

'Christian marriage.'

Tom swallowed his pride. 'There are plenty in the Kirk who would be telling you that marriage to a Roman Catholic is not Christian marriage at all but a pact with the devil, that what you feel for this man is not love but temptation.'

She was very steady, clear-eyed, apparently ready for him.

She said, 'Is that what you think, Mr Ewing?'

'I think you should be waiting until Tarrant decides that you are the one for him.'

'If I wait for that to happen,' Innis said, 'I will wait for ever.'

'If he is so uncertain then perhaps he is not the man for you.'

'He is the man for me,' Innis said.

If she had been older he might have argued with her but he recalled, with a certain amount of embarrassment, how dour and opinionated he had been at Innis's age. She was not dour, however. She was light in her approach, not casual but rueful, as if she expected not to be taken seriously and was prepared to make allowances for other folks' prejudices.

'Aye, but are you the woman for him, Innis?'

'I am,' she said. 'It is just that he does not know it yet.'

'Good Lord! How can you be doing this to yourself, Innis? Throwing yourself at a man who is an incomer and a shepherd – yes, and a Catholic.'

'I am in love with him.'

'You are obsessed with him,' Tom said more aggressively than he had intended. He was still a minister, a counsellor and dared not allow his heart to rule his head. 'For that reason, I am of the opinion that you should wait.'

'For what, Mr Ewing? Until I am old enough to know my own mind? I know my own mind now. I know it better than anyone else.' Innis paused then, tilting her head, said, 'I do not wish to put off and put off and put off, waiting for the right man to come along and then to find myself left on the shelf.'

'Like me, is that what you mean?'

'Like some folk.'

'It is not the same for a man as it is for a woman.'

'Oh, am I not the one who knows that?' Innis said. 'I have seen how it has been with my mother. I will not be lured down that empty road, Mr Ewing.'

'Are you throwing yourself at Tarrant simply to get out of your father's house and away off Pennypol?'

'No and I am not doing it to spite my sister,' Innis said. 'I am doing it because I love Michael. Why will no one believe me?'

Tom sighed. He stepped back to the window and, facing into the room, leaned his buttocks against the ledge. He had never encountered a situation like this one before, when he must balance his intimate feelings against the great weight of tradition that lay behind his ministry. It was his duty to rage and put the fear of death into her. Many in his Church – honest men and fine pastors – would turn purple with fury at the very suggestion that one of their lambs would be sacrificed to the wolves of Rome. But they were theologians and theology, Tom knew, was not a rational science no matter how its practitioners might contrive to make it seem so.

That he loved Innis Campbell was something that he could not deny. That he wanted her in the manner in which a man wants a woman was also undeniable. How could he blink the fact that sexual attraction might also be at the root of Innis's determination to be Tarrant's wife; the thin red thread of physical desire that coloured everything else and against which the broadcloth of rationalism seemed so grey and glum?

He took a deep breath. 'I believe you.'

'Then will you help me?'

When he had made his promise to Evander McIver that he

would look after Innis it had not occurred to him then that in doing so he would be putting her beyond reach. Once she married a Catholic and committed her children to baptism in the Roman Church then she would be lost to him for ever. Even if Innis did not convert, he owed too much to his parishioners not to respect their prejudices. He would be betraying his vocation if he even remained her friend.

He studied her for a long minute: a solemn, oval face framed by brown hair, intelligent eyes with just a spark of cunning in them or, if not cunning, at least artifice. She was slender-waisted and, unlike her sister, small-bosomed. He could see the shape of her legs beneath her skirt, her ankles above her shoes. He desired her then as he had desired no other woman and, for a moment, let lust rush through him unchecked.

'Will you, Mr Ewing?' Innis said.

'What is it that you want from me, Innis?'

'I want you to tell me what to do.'

'I have told you . . .'

'What is the exact procedure for marrying a Roman Catholic?'

'Oh,' he said. 'That!'

'What did you think I meant, Mr Ewing?'

'Nothing,' Tom said. 'Nothing,' and, stepping quickly past her, flung open the doors of the bookcase and yanked out the appropriate tome.

ELEVEN

The Broken Heart

For the best part of a month clipping and dipping distracted Michael from his problem with the Campbell girl. In the interim three more parcels of Cheviots were purchased off the Morven hills and delivered to Oban for shipping to Mull. The flocks, numbering in all one hundred and sixty head, were collected on common pasture on the Ross and brought north by young Barrett and an experienced old shepherd whom Hector Thrale had hired to accompany the boy while Michael and Barrett senior completed dipping on Fetternish.

As soon as the dip was finished Michael saddled up one of the Fetternish ponies and went out to meet the new arrivals who were coming up by the traditional route through Glen Forsa. En route he managed to attend mass at Glenarray and afterwards to have words with Father Gunnion who by now was the only person he was willing to trust. With Father Gunnion's admonitions ringing in his ears he then set off for the high pass in miserable autumnal drizzle. He was wrapped up like a tinker, the pony snorting and quivering under him, and had nothing to look forward to when he got back to Fetternish but another ten days of back-breaking labour.

The trip, however, gave him time to ponder on what he should do to secure his position on Fetternish, to wonder if marrying Innis would put Biddy out of reach for ever. By the time he arrived in lonely Glen Forsa he had worried himself into a state of near depression and felt as if he had become the victim or, worse, the prey of not one but two predatory females.

Thinking of Biddy, he neglected to take into account the other parts of marriage, no less important than what went on in bed: cooking, cleaning, management of the domestic economy, a willingness to put his comfort above and beyond every other duty, except possibly that of raising the children. He was still so stuffed with masculine conceit that he even managed to ignore the plain, hard fact that Biddy Campbell would not have married him, a Catholic, for all the tea in China.

It did not come upon him in a sudden flash of revelation. In fact, he almost failed to realise that he had reached a decision to marry Innis Campbell or, to put it another way, that he would not be averse to marrying Innis Campbell. The advantages were too obvious to ignore. He would secure his position as head shepherd, would have a loving wife to look after him and would be close enough to Biddy to answer her call if and when she ever tired of Austin Baverstock. Yes, he thought, as he rode up the hillside in drizzling rain with the stags roaring in the mist around him. Yes, if it comes to the bit where I have no other option, I will marry little Innis Campbell and, all things considered, be happy enough with my choice.

Biddy was used to wet weather. She knew by experience that it was not too late for a long spell of warm sunshine to arrive before winter finally set in. She was not surprised, though, when Walter announced his intention to return to cosy old Edinburgh and within twelve hours of making the declaration had his bags packed, the dogcart brought up to the house and was off to the capital, leaving the love-birds, as he put it, to get on with it.

Biddy did not object to being left 'to get on with it'. She had plenty with which to occupy herself during the dreary rain-washed days.

She had begun to tinker with the pianoforte in the drawing-room and had discovered that even if she had no singing voice she certainly had an ear for music and could pick out a simple tune with two or three fingers. Enamoured of his wife's talent as a pianist, as he was enamoured of most of the things that Biddy did, Austin promised to employ a musical teacher to give her proper instruction. He also promised to teach her cribbage and bezique or to have Willy do so, for Willy, Austin confessed, was a far superior player to him.

The Baverstocks had the Clarks to dine. Also the doctor and schoolteacher. They would have invited the minister too but for some reason that Austin could not fathom Biddy had put a damper on that suggestion. Nor did the Baverstocks entertain the Campbells, not to lunch, not to dinner, not even to afternoon tea. Austin was relieved that his wife was disinclined to cling to her family and preferred to leave her parents to their own devices.

Rain did not deter Biddy from completing her tour of the estate. Within six weeks of marriage she knew more about Fetternish than Austin. She personally visited each tenant and employee to enquire what they might require by way of repairs and improvements and, without making rash promises, took careful note of their complaints. She still looked like Vassie Campbell's daughter, still had the sharp manner that had put off so many suitors, but there was no denying that becoming the wife of the incomer had altered Biddy for the better.

Only Thrale detested her. He detested her because she was a woman and because she challenged his authority. It was all he could do to bite his tongue when she instructed him to do things that he had never been asked to do before, like keeping accurate records, measuring acreage, digging up wells and seeing to it that tenants' roofs and fences were repaired without delay. If the factor had known that Biddy was also up to unravelling the mysteries of book-keeping and farm accounts, however, he would have been even more concerned.

On those wet grey late-summer afternoons when Austin snoozed by the fire Biddy would settle in the office, apply herself to understanding profit and loss and struggle to make sense of the large returns netted by the wool sales.

Eventually she sent for Willy.

Seated at Walter's desk, she opened a massive ledger and, beckoning Willy to come closer, tapped her finger on the page.

'Am I wrong, William, or do we – I mean my husband – does he make a double profit on our wool crop?'

'I'm not sure I know what you mean, Mrs Baverstock.'

'It seems to me that we sell Fetternish wool to the Sangster manufactory at a price below what the fleeces would fetch at auction, then we take a share of the profits that the mill makes by converting the wool into tweed cloth.'

'I think you'd have to be asking Mr Baverstock about that,' Willy said, cautiously. 'I have no head for business affairs.'

'Nonsense, Willy,' Biddy said. 'There is nothing about the Baverstocks and their affairs that you are not knowing.' She looked up at him, giving him the benefit of her sea green eyes. 'How much of the Sangster manufactory does my husband own?'

'I couldn't possibly say.'

'Is it a partnership?'

'Aye.'

'Who has control of it?' Biddy said. 'Is it Agnes Paul?'

'No, no.' Willy hesitated. 'Mr Walter and Mr Austin each own twenty-six per cent of the stock. Alister Paul and his family – that is, Agnes – own the other forty-eight per cent among them.'

'I see,' said Biddy. 'Therefore, twenty-six per cent of the profit of the tweed mill comes to my husband by way of a – what is the word, Willy?'

'Dividend,' Willy said, nodding.

'Paid annually?'

'Twice a year,' Willy said.

'Is the increase in breeding stock – I mean the sheep – being paid for out of the profits of the Sangster manufactory?'

'I believe it is,' said Willy.

'How very interesting!' Biddy said, and dismissed him with a polite little wave of the hand.

Though neither of them knew it, it was to be the last close and intimate conversation that Innis and Vassie would ever have. It was not a need for conciliation that occasioned it but, rather, the working out of a destiny that was too subtle for either to comprehend.

Obedient daughter and protective mother were at last revealed to each other. Obedience was shown to be nothing but rebellion in another guise and protectiveness no more than a harbouring of old grievances.

Innis began it. 'If I were to marry Michael Tarrant then, when you are gone, all the land from the boundary of Glengorm to the far side of the burn would belong to us.'

Vassie had not been taught to spin or weave and there was no wheel or treadle on Pennypol. She sat idly on a stool by the hearth listening to the sound of the sea and the hiss of the peats while Ronan lay insensible behind the curtain, too drunk to utter any sound at all.

Vassie looked up. 'What does marriage to the shepherd have to do with land?' she said. 'He is owning no ground and probably never will.'

'I am just thinking that it would a fine thing to have all the ground from the Point to the bay for your children's children to play on.'

'After I am gone?' Vassie said.

'It will not be for a long while yet, I hope,' Innis said. 'But would it not be a fine thing, Mam, to look about you and know that your daughters had done well and that your grandchildren would be doing even better?'

'It would not matter to me.'

'Oh, it would. Surely, it would.'

'Sheep,' Vassie said, 'sheep and snobs and Papists. I would hardly be recognising the place. It would not be the Pennypol that my father bought for me. Why do you want to marry this man, this shepherd, after what he did?'

'In spite of what he has done, I am in love with him.'

'It is Biddy who has put this into your head,' Vassie said. 'What did she tell you? That he has a long thing?'

'*Mam!*'

'That is all it comes down to,' Vassie said, 'that, and how well he uses it.'

'Mam!' Innis was shocked. 'I do not think of Michael like – like that.'

'Do you not? Then you are not natural. It was all I thought of when I encouraged *him* to take me. I thought it was me he wanted. Me, ugly Vassie McIver, who had never had so much as a kiss from a man before,' Vassie said. 'Do you not think that your dada was as handsome as your damned shepherd? Do you not think that I wanted him as badly as you want Michael Tarrant? I could not stand straight in the field for thinking of Ronan Campbell and what he would do to me. Aye, and he was not my sister's cast-off either.'

'Is that why you are so bitter?' Innis snapped. 'Because Dada did not live up to your expectations of him?'

'He did not deceive me. I deceived myself.' Vassie pursed her lips. 'And if I am as bitter as you say I am then why do you think I am still with him? It was never my love he wanted, never my body. He took that because he thought it was the key to an easy life; an easy life and my father's money.'

'How can you possibly think that Michael is just after Pennypol?'

'Pennypol will not be worth owning even if it does come down to you.'

'Grandfather promised . . .'

'Such a grand old man, Evander McIver, with his bulls and his women and his patch of green grass in the middle of the sea,' Vassie sneered. 'I do not trust his promises any more. Once he has gone it will be a scramble for who can grab what, believe me.'

'What is wrong with you?' Innis snapped, then, lowering her voice, whispered, 'What is all this talk you have in you? Are you telling me that I will have nothing from Grandfather and nothing from you? I do not care about what I will inherit. I never thought that Pennypol would come down to me. I thought it would go to Donnie.'

'Donnie, my dear wee Donnie,' Vassie said. 'Christ the Lord, what did my poor innocent Donnie ever know about it?'

'Donnie was not innocent.'

'At least he was honest.'

'Are you saying that I am not honest?'

Vassie put on a sweet, sickly little voice that Innis did not at first recognise as a parody of her own. 'I will be marrying my shepherd and he will be loving me and we will have angels for children, blessed by the priest, and all the land will belong to our descendants. And will that not be grand?'

Innis shook her head. 'I did not mean . . .'

'You have your heart set on becoming the wife of a Catholic fornicator,' Vassie said. 'So I know what you are asking. You are asking if I will stand by you. Is that not it?'

Innis sucked in breath. She should have known better than to try to deceive her mother. She squared her shoulders. 'That is exactly what I am asking, yes.'

The Broken Heart

'If I do stand in your way, Innis, what will you do?'
'Marry him, regardless.'
'You see,' Vassie said. 'You do not need my approval.'
'I will not have to leave the Kirk to do it,' Innis blurted out. 'I can remain what I am and worship how and where I choose.'
'Who told you that? Some priest?'
'No, Mr Ewing told me.'
'Will you not be taking your vows before a priest, though?'
'What is wrong with that?'
'Nothing,' Vassie said. 'And the children?'
Innis paused. 'I would be under an obligation to have them raised in their father's faith.'
Vassie rested her elbows on her knees. She sniffed the wafting smoke from the peat fire, coughed and, to Innis's bewilderment, laughed. 'Papish grandchildren,' she said. 'Oh, how my Ronan will love that.'
'Will he try to stop me?'
'He will rant and he will rave. He will call you all manner of filthy names. But he will do nothing effective. How can he? After all the wickedness that he has done he has no leg to stand upon.'
'What he did to me on the moor . . . ?'
'He did to Aileen too.'
'And more?'
'And more, yes.'
'Why, in God's name, did you not stop him?' Innis whispered.
'I could not be stopping him because I did not know what he was doing until it was too late.' Vassie uttered a wry little grunt. 'Now if I had been a Catholic like your shepherd I might have put the matter before the priest and he would have lifted the burden from me. I did nothing because there was nothing I could do, nothing that would make it as it was before. If Aileen had been right in the head, it would have been different. Aileen was my punishment.'
'Punishment for what, Mam?'
'For needing him to love me.'
'It will not be the same for me.'
'No, you will have your shepherd – if he will have you – and I will have my husband to look after.'
'And the farm?'

361

'That!' Vassie said, scathingly. 'Do you think the farm is anything without you and your brothers? I do not care about the farm now.'

'If Dada dies . . .'

'What is it you are going to say? That Biddy will take care of me?' Vassie said. 'I am proud of her, aye, but I will not be accepting her charity.'

'Will you accept charity from me?'

Vassie glanced up. 'You and your shepherd?'

'I am not his wife yet,' Innis said, almost apologetically. 'But, yes, me and my shepherd.'

'What is it you want from me, Innis?'

'I need to know that you will not think less of me if I marry Michael Tarrant, that you will not think me wilful and foolish.'

'Not foolish, no,' Vassie said. 'Are you asking my permission?'

'I suppose that I am.'

'If he will have you . . .' Vassie began, then paused. 'Marry him, yes, marry him. If he will not have you, Innis, then he is a fool and does not deserve you.'

'And will you stand by me?' Innis asked.

'Have I not always?' said Vassie.

'In your own way,' said Innis.

'Aye,' Vassie agreed, smiling softly. 'In my own particular way.'

It was late in the year for shearing. He had already bundled off the bulk of the fleeces, however, and had been told by Thrale that the weight and quality were all that had been hoped for. He was less sure about the crop from the Morven flocks but he could not be held responsible for another man's rearing and did as good a job as he could in the spells of dry weather that marked the tail of the month.

He was sore at the end of it, though. Everything ached, fingers and forearms, shoulders and neck. Even his thighs felt strained with the effort of straddling the bulky ewes who did not know or trust him and struggled like demons until he had them over on their backs and the shears in the undercoat along the line between udder and hind leg. They quieted then, clattering their hoofs into stillness as if they sensed that he meant them no harm, staring at him out of round, rolling eyes as he snipped the wool cleanly from their flanks.

He stank of sheep and his body was studded with ticks. Every evening he would gather himself and walk down to the crescent of sand that hung on the end of the beach. He would strip to the skin, wade out into the cold sea, dip himself in the ocean and let the salt water shrivel the devilish little monsters that buried their heads in his flesh. Then he would knot a towel about his waist and throw his coat over his shoulders and, carrying his clothing and his boots, would pad back up the track above the rim of the glen to his cottage at Pennymain. There he would dump his clothing into the big wooden wash tub that stood at the door and go indoors, shivering and bleak, to stir up the peat fire and warm himself with a single dram of whisky before he set about preparing Roy's supper and his own.

It was the last day of the clip. Between them the Barretts had managed the dip and he would have nothing to do tomorrow but bundle and rope the fleeces and send the boy up to Fetternish to ask Thrale to bring down the cart. Then he could turn his attention to feeding up the rams that in five or six weeks would be introduced to the ewes. He was pleased with himself, pleased to be done with the worst job on the calendar. He was also chilled to the bone, though, and desperate to be snug indoors with the fire blazing and hot food inside him.

Somehow he was not surprised to find Innis at the cottage door.

It seemed natural that she should be there to help him celebrate the end of the wicked task. When he found that she had built up the fire and had the kettle boiling and a soup pot bubbling the last lingering threads of doubt and indecision began to slip away. He did not chastise her for invading his privacy. The only thing that annoyed him was that he was hardly presentable and that it was difficult to be manly when clad only in a towel and old coat.

'Are you not frozen?' Innis said.

'I am that.'

'I did not know that sea-bathing was to your taste.'

'It's not,' Michael said. 'But it gets rid of the ticks and sheep fleas.'

'Come in,' Innis said, as if she had already taken possession of the house and he was her guest. 'Take your coat off and stand close to the fire and I will dry you.'

'The dog needs to be fed.'

'Roy will not starve if he has to wait five minutes.'

She reached for the arms of the coat that he had knotted about his chest. After a split second's hesitation he yielded and let her peel the coat from his shoulders.

He was thin and white-skinned, except his hands and face and the vee of his throat which were burned brown by air and sun. He did not concern himself how his body looked for he had no reason to suppose that he was other than handsome and that his vigour, or whatever quality it was that women found attractive, would appeal to Innis too. He remembered how Biddy would fondle him, caressing him as if he were some young godling. How good that had made him feel. He waited for that now, for Innis's touch to light the spark in him, to feed on her admiration.

'You are in need of feeding up, Mr Tarrant.'

'What?'

'Will you be looking at you? You are like a stick, so thin.'

'I've been in the sea, for God's sake. I'm cold, that's all.'

He put his hand to the knot of the towel at his waist and clutched it, keeping his back to her. He peered down at himself, his skin ruddy in the flame of the fire but wrinkled, ribbed with flat muscle with, he had to admit, not a pick of flesh upon him and hardly so much as a wisp of hair except where the towel sagged below his belly button.

Suddenly self-conscious, he pulled the towel a little higher and when she tapped him on the shoulder automatically stooped forward as if for a game of Cuddy-Leap-the-Dike.

The dry towel came down hard and rough upon his shoulder blades. She scoured away at his shoulders and spine with big, vigorous movements as if she were washing a window or whitening a wall. He could feel the abrasiveness of the cloth on the salt on his skin but pursed his lips and said nothing as Innis worked downward and around the flanges that protruded above his hip bones.

'You really are in need of feeding, Michael,' she said again, panting slightly with the effort she was putting into the drying of him. 'I think that what you need is a good wife to look after you.'

He was tempted to turn around. He was not in the least aroused by her ministrations but he still had Biddy on his mind and how Biddy had held him in awe. He clutched at the knot of the towel and stayed where he was, modest even in the face of such intimacy.

Then he said, 'Did you learn to do this for your father?'

'No. No, no.'

'For your brothers then?'

'I have never done it before. Am I good at it?'

'Aye, you are good at it.'

'Turn around.'

'Innis . . .'

'You have nothing to fear from me, Michael. Turn around.'

'What has come over you? If someone were to walk in . . .'

'No one will walk in.'

He pressed his knees together and turned slowly from the waist, brought his feet round after him.

Roy sprawled on the doorstep – the door was still open to admit the fading evening light – as if Innis had somehow influenced the dog too, charged him by silent command to keep watch for intruders.

'Since we are asking questions' – Innis dabbed the damp towel to his hairless chest – 'let me be asking you one: did Biddy ever do this for you?'

He did not know how to answer. He sensed the point behind the question, saw the trap in it. *What you need is a good wife to look after you!* She was seeking to overcome him, to compel his consent by compelling his desire.

His wariness increased. He watched her with more curiosity than need as she knelt before him and with the same rough scouring motion as before dried each of his legs from knee to ankle. There was no significance in it. No mockery, no adoration. She was just making herself useful, without reserve but apparently without design. As if, he thought, she knows that she cannot compete with her sister and that this is her counter-offer, her show of what can be mine.

It was not pathetic, far from it; yet he felt some pity for her and, yielding again, stretched out his hand and brushed her hair with his forefinger. She looked up at him, as if surprised.

'That's enough, Innis,' he said.

'But you are not dried yet.'

'I am dry enough,' he said.

It was coming back, seeping back, not need or want but the unavoidable, inevitable charm, that quality which he had never consciously cultivated but that was his saving grace – except when he abused it.

'I do not mind doing it.'

'I know you don't,' Michael said. 'But you should – mind, I mean.'

'There is nothing wrong in it.'

He took her by the elbow and helped her to her feet. 'Yes, there is.'

'Because of what Father Gunnion would say?'

'Father Gunnion has nothing to do with it,' he told her. 'I wouldn't even let a wife do such a thing for me.'

'What would you do with a wife, Michael?'

Again he could find no satisfactory answer.

'What would you do with Biddy?' Innis said.

She held the sodden towel against her breast. He could see the faint damp stain that spread across the material as if she were bleeding softly within.

The pity that had been in him was suddenly something else, something that he couldn't begin to define. It was not what he felt for Biddy; that, he believed, was safely locked away. It could not be transferred to Innis who was so different from her sister, so candid and consoling that he felt his bewilderment lessen and be replaced by an assurance that had nothing whatsoever to do with Biddy-things.

'Go outside, Innis,' he said.

She was shocked by his abruptness. Hurt flared in her dark brown eyes. He touched her again, protectively. 'I want to dress and I can't bring myself to do it in front of you. One minute is all I ask.'

She could not disguise her relief. Beneath her candour, he realised, lay a great pool of vulnerability. He responded to that quality in her, prompted by a tenderness that he thought he had

sacrificed to little Rose Garrity and again to Biddy Campbell.
'So you are not sending me away?'
'No, Innis,' he said. 'I'm not sending you away.'
'Not ever again?'
'Not ever again,' said Michael.

It was Vassie who carried the news of Innis's engagement to
Fetternish House. She came clambering up from the foreshore
in the middle of the morning. Austin was still at breakfast and
Biddy was alone in the garden cutting roses to decorate the
dining-room.

Biddy was not distressed to learn that Innis and Michael
Tarrant would be united before the priest in the chapel at
Glenarray one Saturday forenoon in a month's time. Innis would
make her promises and at a later date would give serious and
deliberate consideration to becoming a Catholic. Apparently
Father Gunnion's Church required no more of her at present.
No secret would be made of the marriage but it would be
celebrated very quietly, for many friends and neighbours would
regard it as a betrayal of principles, almost as an act of degrada-
tion and would not only boycott the wedding feast but would
avoid all but the most necessary contact with the shepherd and
his bride in future.

Vassie, it seemed, did not care. She had about her, Biddy
thought, a hard, steely quality, like a sheath. It was as if her
mother had not only come to terms with hollow ambition but
had found a strange kind of peace in her isolation, an indepen-
dence of mind as well as spirit.

Biddy led her mother out of the garden on to the grass terrace.
'What did Dada say when Innis told him?'
'Innis did not tell him. I told him,' Vassie said.
'He ranted and raved, I suppose, and threatened to strangle
Michael with his bare hands for corrupting his other daughter.'
Vassie shook her head. 'He accepted it meekly enough.'
'Oh, I see. He was drunk.'
'No, he was as sober as he ever is these days.'
'I cannot believe that he said nothing.'
'He has nothing left to say, Biddy,' Vassie told her. 'He has all
that he wants and he knows that it is more than he deserves. If

Innis decided to marry a Chinaman there is nothing her father could be doing to prevent it.'

'And you, what of you?'

'I am happy to see her married to a man she loves.'

'Even if he is not the man for her?'

'You have no right to say that, Biddy.'

'No,' Biddy agreed. 'I suppose I haven't.'

'You will not be saying it to Innis, not now or in the future.'

'I hope that she will be happy with him. I will tell her that I wish her to be as happy with Michael Tarrant as I am with Austin. Will that be enough?'

'That will be good enough,' said Vassie.

Ten minutes later, after her mother had hurried away, Biddy went indoors and found her husband in the office.

She went to him, put her arms about his neck and kissed him. He looked up, surprised and pleased. 'What's that for, dearest?'

'My sister is to be married to our shepherd in a month's time.'

'How marvellous!' Austin said.

'Isn't it,' Biddy said. 'Isn't it, indeed.'

And, to her astonishment, Biddy found that she meant it.

All her hostility had evaporated. It had never been there at all, perhaps, or had been no more than a manifestation of the disorder that had infected Pennypol down through the years. She no longer hated Michael Tarrant for what he had done to her or for not telling her the whole truth. If he had told her the whole truth at the beginning she would not have found out about herself, would not have discovered all that mattered at the time.

When, later that day, she wandered to the summit of Olaf's Ridge and looked down upon the cottage perched above the Solitudes she felt only gratitude and relief that Michael would not be lost to her as so many others had been lost, that he would be safe with Innis, safe within marriage, safe within reach.

That night in the big four-poster in the bedroom of Fetternish House Biddy made love to her husband with prolonged and desperate fervour and some time in the early hours of the morning wakened to find that poor Austin had died, without a whimper, in his sleep.

It was Willy who first heard it. He sat bolt upright in bed, one arm thrown protectively across Margaret as if the sound itself might harm her.

It was barely daylight. The window of the little bedroom was misted with condensation, the light grey and mysterious. Willy cocked his head and had just begun to wonder if he had had a bad dream when the screaming started again, augmented now by the howling of the dogs from the gunroom.

He flung back the bedclothes and leaped to his feet.

Margaret sat up. 'What is it, Willy?

'Don't know,' he said. 'Might be burglars.'

'Burglars? Oh, God!' She slid out of bed too. 'What should we do?'

'Tell Queenie to bolt her door,' Willy said, 'then go into the kitchen and arm yourself with a knife or a poker – aye, the big poker – and wait there.'

'It cannot be burglars. We have never had burglars on Mull.'

The screaming ceased once more but the dogs continued to fill the house with their mournful howling.

'Wait in the kitchen, dear,' Willy said, then, still in his nightshirt, darted along the corridor and upstairs into the great hall.

Biddy craned over the rail of the balcony, hair flying, nightgown swirling about her. He could see her arms, pale in the gloom, her pale face, mouth open. As soon as she caught sight of him she let out another shriek.

Willy headed for the staircase. 'What is it? What's wrong?'

She did not answer. She vanished.

Willy dashed up the stairs two at a time. He found her at the top, arms spread wide as if in welcome. She did not look like Biddy Campbell at that moment. She looked, he thought, like something wild off the moor, some entity, as she flung her head this way and that and keened. He grabbed her flailing arms and pinned them. She continued to thrash and lash with her head and might have done him damage if he had not caught her by the hair and forced her to be steady.

'Biddy, what's the matter?'

'He's – he's – he's . . .'

'Slowly. Tell me. Is it Mr Austin?'

'In – in – there.'

The instant Willy entered the bedroom and clapped eyes on

his master he realised that the poor chap was beyond human aid.

Austin lay on his back, head square on the pillow, very neat and peaceful, except that his neck was arched and his mouth open and his eyes stared upwards at the plaster ceiling, quite unseeing. There was no sickness, no dribble, nothing to indicate that he had suffered distress. One arm was by his side, the other thrown up and frozen across his chest, the fingers, not yet stiff, fanned over his breast in a gesture so delicate that Willy could almost hear the gasp, the last, astonished gasp that his master had uttered before he passed into oblivion.

Willy tiptoed to the bedside. He placed his fingertips against the side of Mr Austin's neck: cold, cold and pulseless. He leaned across the corpse and looked for signs of life – of which there were none. Then Biddy, big and urgent, came up behind him and he, Willy, pulled away, weeping.

'He is dead? Is he not dead, Willy?'

'Yes.' Willy covered his eyes with one hand. 'Yes, he's gone from us.'

'Is there nothing we can be doing?'

'Nothing. Nothing.' Willy sobbed. 'How long since you found him?'

'Minutes, only minutes. Did you not hear me?'

'Aye, aye, we – we did.'

'I wakened. I put – put my arms around him and he was, he was . . .'

She was calmer now that Willy was here to share her shock and grief and, in fact, appeared to be more in control than he was. She laid a hand upon his shoulder and offered him comfort. Before he quite knew what he was doing Willy took her into his arms and, not daring to look at the corpse of the man he had served so faithfully for almost forty years, pressed his face into the widow's auburn hair and wept.

'We must send for the doctor,' Biddy said.

'Aye.'

'Is Margaret up?'

'Aye, she is.'

Biddy separated herself from him, stepped past him and stood by the bed. She leaned on the upright and peered down at her husband.

'Perhaps we should move him.'

'Don't touch him,' Willy cried out. 'No, don't touch him.'

'At least let me close his eyes,' Biddy said.

'Did you do this?' Willy snapped. 'Did you do this to him?'

'No, I told you – how – how it happened.'

He pushed her to one side then, bending close, placed the tips of his thumbs on Mr Austin's lids and gently closed them. He remained where he was, his tears falling on to the white face. He could hear Biddy just behind him, not keening, not weeping now, just her sonorous breath in the cold, grey room. He leaned and kissed his master on the brow, then, uncoiling, swung round to confront the woman who had become his mistress, who held his fate and future in both her trembling hands.

He swallowed his rancour and said, 'Come away, Mrs Baverstock. I think it would be advisable to leave everything just the way it is until after Dr Kirkhope has seen it. We must have you dressed before he arrives, though.'

Dishevelled and ashen but still peculiarly dry-eyed, Biddy blinked.

'Because there will be an examination?' she said.

'Under the circumstances, I expect that will be required by law.'

'What then, Willy? What else?'

'I'll send telegraph messages to Mr Walter and to Alister Paul.'

'They will come here, won't they?'

'Yes, they will.'

'Will they – will they take Austin away?'

'He'll be buried in Sangster,' Willy stated.

'Not on Mull?'

'In Sangster,' Willy told her, firmly, 'in the family plot. There's nothing you can do about that, Mrs Baverstock. I'm sorry.'

'What can I do, Willy? Tell me, what can I do?'

'You don't have to do anything,' Willy said. 'I'll attend to all the arrangements.'

'I mean – later?'

'That,' Willy Naismith said, 'is something we'll have to talk about, Mrs Baverstock, after the doctor's been.'

'Yes,' she said. 'Yes, after the doctor's been.'

'I'll send Margaret up to help you dress.'

'Thank you, William.' Biddy glanced at the mute and motion-less figure on the bed. 'Would you be good enough to let my mother know what's happened?' She paused. 'Oh, and Michael too, perhaps.'

'Michael?'

'Michael Tarrant.'

'Of course, Mrs Baverstock,' Willy said, biting his lip. 'If that's what you wish for - of course I will.'

Dr Angus Kirkhope was nothing if not thorough. He had dealt with sudden death before, many a time. He had examined young men who had succumbed to insult to the brain brought on by a drastic infusion of alcohol, young women who had tapped out because of some female problem that they had been too ashamed to bring to his or anyone else's attention. He had attended three cases of fatal poisoning, none malicious, a sundry variety of strokes, chokings, drownings and general falling-downs as well as a brace of suicides and a fair bag of unsuspected diseases of the heart in men who were apparently in the pink.

Even before he ordered the removal of Austin Baverstock's remains to the stone room in the back of the old salt store in Tobermory where he performed the post-mortem examinations that the law deemed necessary, Dr Kirkhope had little doubt that the gentleman in question had fallen victim to an occlusion of the coronary artery and that, local gossip notwithstanding, there were absolutely no suspicious circumstances.

An hour's hard work with saw, scissors and scalpel confirmed his initial opinion. What had occasioned the excessive strain that had blown poor old Baverstock's arterial wall, however, was a question that the doctor elected not to answer. In his report to the fiscal he recorded the cause of death as a congenital heart defect and, without further ado, released the body to the undertaker for packing and shipment.

Walter Baverstock, the grieving brother, insisted upon haste. The grieving widow, Bridget Campbell Baverstock, agreed without a murmur of protest. Within seventy-two hours of Austin breathing his last, his body was en route to the mainland, borne away - ironically and rather touchingly - in the hold of the SS *Iona*.

The Broken Heart

Biddy did not travel to Sangster for the funeral.

She remained on Mull, on Fetternish, to acknowledge the condolences of friends, neighbours and employees. She did not – as many supposed she would - invite her mother or sister to stay with her in the big house but rattled about there with only Maggie Naismith and the cook to ensure that she did not, in her heartbreak, fall into a state of collapse.

Tom Ewing called. He found that Biddy was bearing up with remarkable fortitude, very stiff and determined in her resolve to 'carry on' until Naismith, her steward, returned from Sangster to inform her what the Baverstocks intended to do. Meanwhile, Biddy told the minister that she would be grateful if he would conduct a service of thanksgiving for the life of her late husband, a man who had Mull at heart and who, in their few short weeks together, had been unstinting in his uxorious responsibilities and who, by rights, should have been laid to rest on the green hill behind the kirk in Crove where she could be buried by his side, when her time came.

There was too much anger in Biddy to fuel such maudlin sentiment and Tom Ewing did not attempt to point out that she was still a young woman and might very well marry again, or that Austin Baverstock had been an incomer and still almost a stranger in the island community.

Seated in the drawing-room in her dense black day-dress with its jutting cuffs and rigid collar, no ornament upon her save a small Celtic brooch pinned above the shelf of her breast and a black velvet ribbon in her auburn hair, Bridget Campbell Baverstock was no ordinary island wife or, for that matter, no ordinary island widow. Tom did not care to argue with her, not in her present frame of mind.

'The service?' He cleared his throat. 'Do you have any particular date in mind, Mrs Baverstock?'

'Sunday, this coming Sunday.'

'Oh!' Tom exclaimed.

'Can that not be managed?'

'Well, yes,' Tom said. 'It is just that I doubt if Mr Baverstock's relatives will be able to get here without a little more warning.'

'They will not wish to attend.'

'Are you sure?'

'William will be home on Saturday. William will say a few words.'

Tom opened his mouth to protest that it was not usual for house servants to deliver eulogies in praise of deceased masters, but then thought better of it. He understood what Biddy was up to and the reasons for her urgency. A service in Crove would be her gesture of farewell to a man whom she had not known for long or, the minister suspected, known very well. It would also be her revenge upon the Baverstocks for some slight, real or imagined. He did not approve of using the Church in this manner but he simply did not have the heart, or the nerve, to refuse Biddy's request.

'I will not have an opportunity to make an announcement from the pulpit,' Tom said. 'How will you let folk know?'

'I'll send cards,' Biddy said. 'I will also put up a notice in Fergusson's shop window. Evening service?'

'Yes, that would be best.' Tom paused. 'Will your family be there?'

'Certainly, and all my employees.'

'Including Innis's fiancé?'

'He is not her fiancé.'

'Oh, I was under the impression . . .'

'Nothing has been decided,' Biddy said. 'In view of my tragic bereavement Innis may consider it inappropriate to go through with a marriage ceremony in the near future.'

'I understood that it was to be a very quiet Saturday wedding.'

'Michael will be there,' Biddy stated. 'Unless the priest forbids it.'

'I doubt if Father Gunnion will object. After all, your husband was an Episcopalian, was he not?'

'What does that have to do with it?'

'At a sad time like this,' Tom said, cautiously, 'we tend to put our differences to one side, that's all.'

'Good,' Biddy said. 'Good. Now, about the choice of hymns . . .'

She had spent the best part of the afternoon walking the flock with Michael. It was a mixed sort of day with a stiff breeze that brought high clouds skimming across the sea to dapple the distant hills. Across the horizon, though, stretched a ribbon of pure, pale blue, so clear and unblemished that from the crown of Olaf's Ridge you felt that you could sense the promise of fair weather.

Innis was glad to be alone with Michael, walking through the faded bracken and along the sheep paths that connected one expanse of pasture to the next. He took her to see the rams, cropping good grass far out in the west quarter, all dignified and passive and ready to perform. Took her next to the pens where within the next few weeks parcels of lambs would be gathered prior to being ferried out from the jetty at Pennypol in the hold of a steam lighter and conveyed directly to Oban; an experiment in transportation that Thrale and Michael had worked out between them and that Mr Baverstock – rest his soul – had agreed upon only three days before he passed away.

Michael carefully disguised his uncertain mood. He pretended to be entirely dependable and trustworthy and concerned only about what would happen to his flocks if the worst came to the worst and Fetternish was sold. He did not take Innis by the hand; this was no leisurely stroll but a working tour of inspection. But as they returned from the west quarter and came within sight of the tower of Fetternish House, he offered her his arm and let her lean against him for reassurance while he, with great self-control, did not once stare in the direction of the big house, did not once speak the name that was in his mind.

Innis had been three times to call upon her sister, twice with Vassie and once on her own. She had watched Biddy weep and had watched Biddy *not* weep. She had watched Biddy tighten the rein on her emotions until she was so controlled that she seemed remote, drawn so far back into herself that there was no reaching her with tenderness or an exchange of confidences.

Ronan had not deigned to visit his daughter in her time of mourning. He had swallowed the news of his son-in-law's death with a diffident shrug as if to say that he had expected the fellow to fall upon his face sooner or later, that punishment for marrying Biddy had been inevitable, if somewhat drastic.

'She will be back here in the loft with you, Innis, before you can say "Mackerel",' Ronan had predicted with a smirk. 'They will be finding a way to be rid of her, to get her out of Fetternish before the year is much older.'

'How can they do that?' Innis had asked. 'She is his widow. Surely under the law she must receive something?'

'Hah! Do you not think that I have not seen what they can do, those rich folk. They will be having their legal gentlemen sweep it all away from her. There will be nothing left for Biddy at the end of it but the clothes she stands up in and a basketful of bad memories, you will see.'

Vassie hadn't disagreed with him. She had talked to Biddy, however, quietly and soothingly. Mother and daughter had sat under the long windows of the drawing-room for an hour or more, not touching and with not a tear shed and eventually Innis had gone down to the kitchen to talk to Margaret and Mrs McQueen who were understandably anxious about their future. Then she had taken the hounds, Thor and Odin, out for a walk and had thought how subdued the dogs were, as if they sensed that their master had gone for good and that obedience was all they had left by which to remember him.

She had returned to find Biddy and Vassie standing on the gravel before the main door, not talking, but with a secretive, almost furtive air about them as if they had been collaborating on a gigantic plot. When they had looked at her, purse-lipped and grim, Innis had felt a coldness that she had not experienced before, not hostility but a form of calculation which, so tense had she become of late, she assumed was related to her marriage.

'What is it?' Innis had tugged the dogs to her on the leash. 'What have you been saying about me?'

'You? We have been saying nothing about you,' Vassie had told her.

'Why should we be talking about you? It is not *your* husband who has just died,' Biddy had added, sourly.

'Are you saying that I must wait to marry Michael?'

Vassie and Biddy had glanced at each other but Innis had been unable to decide what the look that had passed between them meant.

'We are saying nothing of the sort,' Vassie had told her. 'We are only wondering what will be happening in the matter of the will.'

'Will?'

'To me,' Biddy had said. 'To me, not to you.'

It did not matter to Biddy that Innis would marry in three weeks' time and that her husband was dependent upon Fetternish for his living. Innis had experienced a terrible distrust of her sister, almost as if Biddy had brought this calamity deliberately upon herself simply to prevent her marriage. She had walked back to Pennypol with her mother without saying a word.

Now, a day later, with Michael in the pastures, her fears for the future were eased. He was so calm and confident that Fetternish would prosper that Innis wondered if he had received information that was not known to Biddy, something about Austin Baverstock's will.

When she put the question to him he shook his head. 'It's nothing like that. I think the old boy will have sealed his affairs up pretty well. Even if he did not and the Baverstocks tie the property up in legal tape, Mr Walter is not so daft as to let Fetternish run to ruin. He is making too much profit out of the wool crop to do that.'

'What about the house?'

'Walter Baverstock may wish to close it.'

'Biddy will have no home?'

'She can go back where she came from, can she not?'

'She will never be doing that,' said Innis. 'She has sampled a better life than we can ever give her and my sister is not the sort to give up what she wants without a fight.'

Before Innis could pursue the subject, he put his arm about her waist and kissed her on the side of the mouth.

'It won't matter to us, though,' Michael said. 'If it comes to it, I will go off to look for work elsewhere.'

'And leave me behind?'

'Only until I am settled.'

'Do you mean that you are having second thoughts?'

'Of course not. I just mean that we must be sensible.'

'Sensible? And not marry?'

'Yes,' he told her, curtly. 'Yes. We will marry.'

'You promised . . .'

'Nothing has changed between us,' Michael assured her.

But Innis knew that it had.

TWELVE

A Promise of Fair Weather

Until he returned first to Edinburgh and then to Sangster Willy hadn't realised how much Mull - and Maggie too, of course - meant to him.

The funeral was a grand affair.

All those folk who had spurned Austin's wedding were, it seemed, only too willing to turn out for his burial and were disappointed - actually disappointed - that there was no grief-stricken widow for them to ogle at. Willy was plied with questions from every side. He soon grew weary, then angry, at the impertinence of the Sangster servants who seemed to think that he owed them information and now that Mr Austin was deceased would immediately betray his master's confidences for their amusement.

He visited his children and pampered his grandchildren but, in spite of his affection, felt that he no longer belonged with them. He had become distanced from his past and his offspring, busy with their own lives, would get along better without him. He was impatient for it all to be over so that he could return to the beautiful isle and his beautiful wife.

Neither Mr Walter nor Agnes Paul tried to prevent Willy hastening back to Fetternish as soon as the funeral was over. They assumed that he was still loyal to the Baverstocks and their cause, whatever that cause might be. Mr Walter told him that there were complicated legal matters to be taken care of but that he, and Agnes too, perhaps, would return to Mull very soon to square away the loose ends that Austin's untimely demise had occasioned and to come to some sort of arrangement with the widow.

Willy knew only too well what that meant.

They would try to buy Biddy out or pay her off, twist her out of what was her rightful due. Before he could say 'knife' he would be summoned back to the poky little basement in Charlotte Square or the servants' hall in Sangster, with Margaret feeling like a fish out of water. At all costs he must prevent that happening. Within an hour of stepping through the door of Fetternish House, therefore, soon after he had hugged his wife and devoured the supper that Queenie had prepared, he went upstairs to the great hall to have a serious talk with Bridget Campbell Baverstock.

Widow's weeds suited Biddy. Black clothing made her seem even more desirable and added a dignity that had been, to a degree, absent before.

Willy assumed that she would be over the worse of her shock and, unless he missed his guess, that she would have put grief far enough behind her to give thought to what would become of Fetternish and what she could do to ensure that she gained as much as possible out of her all-too-brief marriage.

He presented himself before the Georgian chair still wearing his travelling jacket, his collar and necktie tight about his throat.

'I'd be grateful if I might have a word with you Mrs Baverstock.'

'Have you come to tell me how the funeral went?'

'If you wish,' Willy said.

'How many were there?' Biddy said.

'The big kirk in Sangster was full to overflowing.'

'Did many travel down from Edinburgh?'

'Hundreds.'

'I see,' Biddy said. 'Well, we will be having our own service tomorrow evening in the kirk at Crove. It will be conducted by the Reverend Ewing.'

'Uh-huh,' Willy said. 'I can see sense in that. I'm sure Mr Austin would appreciate it.'

'Will you say a few words?'

'It's not usual for a servant . . .'

'You knew Austin better than anyone.'

'That's true,' Willy said. 'Yes, I'd be honoured to participate.'

Biddy's eyes were wide open and very clear. Willy doubted if she had shed many tears in the past week. He had negotiated with her father and it had led to disaster but Biddy was her mother's daughter and made of sterner stuff. When it came to material matters, Willy reckoned, she was far more astute than the drunken little fisherman who had spawned her.

She was not yet his, Willy's, employer though, for on paper he was still indentured to the Baverstocks, still nominally 'their man'.

'I'll be straight with you, Mrs Baverstock,' he said. 'I'm worried about my future position on Fetternish.'

'Is it that you are wanting to go back to Edinburgh?'

'Oh, no indeed,' Willy said. 'I would prefer to stay put.'

'Is island life not too dull for you?' Biddy said.

'Not dull at all,' Willy said.

'Well, William, I can give no guarantees. I do not have much security myself and have nothing much to offer you.'

'More than you think, Mrs Baverstock,' Willy said. 'More than you think. That's what I want to talk to you about.'

She signalled him to be seated. He glanced at the vacant armchair, Mr Austin's seat, thought better of it and pulled one of the straight-backed chairs closer to the fireplace. Shifting Odin gently with his toe, he made himself comfortable and began.

'From what I can gather Mr Austin left a very detailed will.'

'Did Walter say as much?'

'Indirectly, yes,' Willy said. 'They are concerned about its contents. So concerned, Mrs Baverstock, that I reckon if you play your cards right you could wind up as a very wealthy woman.'

'And how do you suggest I play my cards?'

Willy paused. He seemed to be listening to something outside, his head slightly to one side. He did not meet Biddy's eye. Eventually, after two or three seconds, the lady of Fetternish smiled and enquired, 'Am I to take it that you would be prepared to work for me instead of the Baverstocks?'

'I would, Mrs Baverstock, if a suitable position could be found for me.'

'What sort of position did you have in mind?'

'Steward. Steward and housekeeper, Margaret and I.'

'Will the Baverstocks release you?'

'I'm not a slave,' Willy said. 'I'm at liberty to work for any master – or mistress – who offers me a suitable position.'

'Very well, Willy,' Biddy said without hesitation. 'I will employ you as my steward and your wife as my housekeeper – if, that is, I have a house. Do you wish me to put something in writing?'

'No, Mrs Baverstock, I'll accept your word as your bond.'

'Very well,' Biddy said. 'Now, tell me, how wealthy am I likely to be?'

'Very wealthy,' Willy said.

'Cannot the will be broken?'

'Not having seen the document and not being that well versed in the law of heritable property I can't say for sure,' Willy said. 'What I can say for sure is that the Baverstocks will employ every legal device that money can buy to make sure that you do not get your hands on all that's due to you.'

'A twenty-six per cent share in the tweed manufactory, for instance?'

'That's it,' Willy said, 'in a nutshell.'

'And a half share in the ownership of the house in Charlotte Square?'

'The Charlotte Square property is still under mortgage,' Willy said. 'But, aye, it is heritable property and I imagine that you, or a shrewd lawyer working on your behalf, might be able to force Mr Walter to put it on the market, if only to establish its current capital worth.'

'Walter would hate that, would he not?'

'He misses his brother more than you can imagine, Mrs Baverstock,' Willy said. 'I doubt if he would want to lose his comfortable home too.'

'Are you suggesting that I should trade on my brother-in-law's grief?'

'I'm suggesting that you must protect yourself,' Willy said. 'May I put politeness aside for a wee minute and speak frankly?'

'I wish you would,' Biddy said.

Willy said, 'They think you're stupid. They think you're a simpleton. They think they'll be able to palm you off with a few thousand pounds.'

'But if the will says . . .'

'They will challenge the will,' Willy said. 'That's how they'll do it. They'll tie up your money and property for years in the hope that sooner or later you'll become impatient and will take what they offer you.'

'It's Fetternish I want.'

'Oh, yes, Mrs Baverstock, I know that.'

'Walter owns half the estate too, remember.'

'That's to our advantage.' Willy drew his chair closer. 'Agnes Paul is the one we have to look out for. She's a dangerous woman who will do anything to get her own way. She has no scruples at all. Mr Walter is sensible, though. And he's hurt and lonely. He'll want things settled quickly – which means, Mrs Baverstock, that he'll want shot of Fetternish as soon as possible.'

'But the wool crop is highly profitable, is it not?'

'That, Mrs Baverstock, is your trump card.'

To give her credit, the tears that Biddy shed during the evening service were perfectly genuine. She was moved by Mr Ewing's reading from Ecclesiastes, for the verses brought home to her just how much joy Austin had taken in the life of the island and what he had found there that she had never known existed. She was even more moved by the reading from the Gospel of St John which spoke of the light of life, the light of the world and of the shepherd as life-giver.

She sat in the honoured pew beneath the pulpit, her family beside her and her servants just behind. She pressed her knuckles into her lap and wept for, that very morning, nature had delivered a sure sign that she had not conceived a child to Austin and that she was to be denied even that consolation.

She also wept when Willy Naismith made his halting speech in a language so simple that it could be nothing other than sincere.

She wept when Innis comforted her, wept when, one by one, the good folk of Crove and Fetternish came and offered condolences once again: Mr Leggat, Mr Kirkhope, Mr Thrale, even the Barretts, boy and man. And Michael Tarrant too; Michael who had been seated at Innis's side along the pew from her, listening to the strange dour language of the Kirk with that same bland, unrevealing expression that so effectively cloaked his thoughts and feelings.

Biddy was not weeping, however, when she spoke with

Michael a second time, separated and briefly parted from Innis, a moment or two before Willy Naismith brought the carriage to fetch her from the gate of the church. She was dry-eyed again, just a little flushed with the emotions that had overwhelmed her within the house of the Lord.

It had been a year, almost exactly a year, since the night of the Harvest Home. Since that night in the Winfield when he had whispered that he loved her, that he wanted her so desperately and urgently that no man would ever want her more. Almost exactly a year since she had felt the sensation in her belly and loins, that indescribable urge or ache that robbed her of all common sense.

As she paused by the gate of the church, her retinue of servants and employees behind her like a little army, her mother and sister visible in the half-darkness ahead, she felt again the thrill of his eyes upon her. And she knew that if he would only say the word she would jettison all her authority, all reason and ladylike civility and would go with him, skulking down into the sheep-smelling cottage at Pennymain, slithering away into the damp bracken, just to have his hands upon her, his mouth, to feel him press and probe and enter her.

It would not matter then that she was the widow of Fetternish, a Baverstock not a Campbell, no longer a country lass but the titular owner of half the northern tip of Mull. Or that he was a Roman Catholic and would soon be her sister's husband.

She said, in a murmur, 'Come and see me, Michael. Come to the house.'

'When?'

'Tomorrow.'

'I am moving sheep tomorrow, Mrs Baverstock.'

'On Tuesday then.'

'I will have work to do on Tuesday too.'

'I see,' Biddy said. 'I see.'

'Unless you order it,' Michael murmured, looking away towards the lights of the village, towards the faint spectral sheen of the September sky and the panoply of stars that lay over the hills and the sea. 'Unless you make me.'

'No,' Biddy said, loudly. 'That will not be necessary.' And then, with a whisk of her jet black skirts, moved past him into the obsequious little crowd of well-wishers that waited to see her off.

Everything was ready, everything packed. She had sponged her dresses, such as they were, and repaired the ragged little thorn tears that marred her working skirts and shifts. She had bleached her drawers and stockings and had ironed them with the heavy old flat-iron that her mother had dug out of the cupboard behind the bed. Had put them, together with the bundle of good new bed linen that Vassie had insisted on buying for her from the store above the haberdasher's in Tobermory, into the old stained leather chest from the loft and had even roped it, ready for the cart that Willy Naismith had promised to send over on Friday, the day before the wedding.

She would be married in white, of course; not a bridal gown, as such, but a plain white dress with borders of lace sewn on to the collar and cuffs and a cupid's bow of seed pearls that Vassie had unearthed from a jar stitched to the bodice to give shape and definition to her breast. There would be no boning, no arrogant bustles or half hoops or any of the other fashionable paraphernalia that turned brides these days into gargantuan grotesques, for Innis Campbell was a country lass, slender as a willow and too slight to carry such a burden.

Besides, there would be few folk, if any, at the wedding service in the public hall that served the parish of Glenarray as a chapel. Michael had no friends in that scattered community, few friends at all, and Mull was far too far from the Ettrick Pen for his family to undertake the journey; if, that is, Michael had seen fit to let his family know of his marriage plans in the first place. He would be served by a groomsman that Father Gunnion had found for him. And Innis would be attended by a bridal maid, a young girl named Bernadette who lived on a farm in Kettlestone and whom she had never met.

She received a taciturn letter from her grandfather, written in a spidery, elongated hand. He wished her well in her marriage but also chided her for not marrying the minister of Crove instead of a Catholic shepherd. She was hurt by the letter's tone rather than its content and not appeased by the two five pound banknotes that were folded into the envelope. Although he did not say so, she knew then that her grandfather would not be at her wedding. The books that he had gifted her over the years were packed away too, however. She would carry them with her to Pennymain, would cherish them and the memory of Foss and what Foss had once meant to her – what he, Evander McIver, had once meant to her – until her dying day.

She was ready for marriage, all prepared and ready ten days before the appointed day, as if her haste might speed on the hour and remove the dull threat that hung over her that Michael might yet change his mind.

She had offered him everything, everything except escape.

She had cooked his suppers, washed his clothes, fed the friendly dog. Had scrubbed the cottage until it gleamed. She had kissed him and rubbed herself against him and felt the wiry strength in his body as she pressed it against her own. She had whispered in his ear that she could not wait for the day when they would be man and wife and that, if he asked it of her, she would rehearse that aspect of marriage too. But he would not, would not allow himself to be caught up and carried away into sinfulness perhaps, go to the confession that would precede a uniting before God in a less than perfect state.

Innis was relieved, relieved but also disappointed. She was not afraid of what he would do to her, of the mysteries that would be revealed in the now-familiar kitchen in the cottage by the Solitudes. She was not afraid that he would hurt her or demand from her anything that she was not prepared to give. She would surrender to him eagerly when the time came. It was just that he did not appear to have to fight against temptation, to exercise self-discipline, to tug himself reluctantly away from her kisses and embraces, as if – somehow – he respected her too much.

On the subject of the duties of a wife Vassie remained silent. Cautious to the last, Innis did not risk raising the subject, for the memory of their last conversation still hung in her mind like a bad odour. In any case, she had her father's lewd babbling to remind her that however cleansed of sexual desire a betrothal and a Catholic wedding might appear to be there lay behind it all the heat and passion and plain lustfulness of a man on top of a woman.

If she had any lingering doubts about her compulsion to marry

A Promise of Fair Weather

Michael Tarrant and the wisdom of her choice of a husband, her father put paid to them once and for all. He, Ronan Campbell, would have nothing to do with her or her damned Pape of a husband. And was it not that she was lucky that he did not throw her out of the house right now and let her damned Pape shepherd take care of her and show her what was what without the benefit of some damned Papish mumbo-jumbo to give it an air of decency, to make her think that there was any more to it than spreading her legs whenever that damned fornicator demanded it? Aye, where would the priest be when she was bucking under the weight of a man, where would the Virgin Mary be when she was writhing and sweating and begging for mercy? And who would hear her prayers when she paid a painful price for her treachery?

She kept away from her father, kept well away from him, indoors and out. He did not have the strength to threaten her, except with his mouth. The weaker alcohol made him the louder became his voice. There was no charm in it now, no sly softness, no wheedling or cajoling. He roared, he raged, he ranted at Innis and at Vassie too – even at the dog, Fingal – from whatever corner he had tumbled into, sprawled there, spraddle-limbed and spavined by the drench of whisky, in a paralysing state of drunkenness which had rendered him, at last, impotent and exposed in all his helplessness.

In ten days' time she would be free of him. She would strive not to carry him with her into marriage as she would carry wistful memories of her grandfather. She would leave Pennypol behind, abandon it, cast it off, shake off the memories of her childhood as she might shake dust from a skirt or dirt from her shoes; all the sorrows, all the disappointments, all the fears and hurts that had been inflicted upon her by a man whose values were cocked by wicked arrogance and the unshakable conviction that his family had failed him, and not the other way about.

She would be cut off from Pennypol by Olaf's Ridge just as completely as Pennymain was cut off from the big house of Fetternish by the tangle of the Solitudes. Her anger at Biddy, her pity for Mam would surely wane in the fair-weather years ahead. But fear of her father would never diminish, for in him, perhaps, she had glimpsed her own weaknesses, her own potential downfall, the farce of selfishness that stood tragedy on its head. From all of this she would be rescued by marriage to Michael. She could not wait for that day to dawn.

It was Willy who found the lawyer. He did it by opening a door that he would have preferred to have kept closed: he wrote to Jack Stockton. Rather to his surprise he received by way of reply a letter not from Stockton in Glasgow but from the legal firm of Ashcroft, Ashcroft & Dunlop in Perth, indicating that they would be delighted to undertake any pieces of business that the Fetternish estate might care to put their way and pointing out, discreetly, that they were specialists in matters of probate, heritage and settlement.

Willy barely had time to show the letter to Biddy and discuss the wisdom of hiring a firm 'blind', as it were, before a carrier's cart arrived from Tobermory bearing, unannounced and unaccompanied, Mr Walter Baverstock in person.

It was quite a shock for Biddy to find herself suddenly confronted by her brother-in-law. At first she did not know how to behave towards him. He looked haggard and had, she thought, lost weight. He was also much affected by the sight of the dogs who, after a little hesitation, padded from their berths by the hearth to sniff at his trousers and tentatively lick his hands.

'Do they miss him, Bridget?' Walter said, thickly.

'Oh, yes, Mr Bav – Walter,' Biddy said, 'I believe they are missing him almost as much as I do.' She allowed her brother-in-law to take her into his arms for a brief, awkward hug. 'Will you be staying for long?'

'Only one night, two at most.'

'I will have Willy make your old room ready.'

'I'd prefer the guest bedroom,' Walter said. 'If it's not inconvenient.'

'It is certainly not that,' Biddy said, pleased by the fact that he deferred to her. 'After all, is this not your house too?'

'Yes,' Walter said. 'Yes, that's what I've come to talk about.'

'I thought it might be,' Biddy said. 'I am surprised that your sister did not see fit to be coming with you.'

'She is – Agnes is – she does not know that I am here.'

Trying not to smile, Biddy nodded to Willy who had been

loitering by the door with Mr Walter's overnight bag in his hand.

'Take it up to the guest room, William. Then would you be good enough to ask Margaret to bring us tea? Is the fire in the drawing-room lighted?'

'It is, Mrs Baverstock.'

'In the drawing-room then.'

'Perhaps Mr Walter would care for something stronger?' Willy suggested as he moved towards the staircase with the luggage.

'No,' Biddy said. 'I think it might be better if Mr Walter kept a clear head just at present.'

'I agree,' said Walter, wearily.

Although sunset was still two hours away the day seemed to be ending prematurely with dusk sifting down over the hills of Ardnamurchan.

Biddy would have had the curtains drawn but Walter, fed and watered, lingered by the tall windows as if to soak himself in the general gloom of the evening or, Biddy thought, to absorb the view from Fetternish for the last time. She did not question Walter's right to be melancholy, did not suspect that it might be an act designed to put her off her guard and weaken her position in the negotiations that were just about to begin.

Walter's return to Mull must be painful and difficult. She had that advantage over him, however, and did not intend to let sentiment stand in the way of hard-headedness for, as Willy had pointed out, the Baverstocks had already behaved abominably by neglecting to allow her sight of the will. The family's lawyers had obviously colluded in this unethical manoeuvre in the belief that Mrs Campbell Baverstock would know nothing of her rights under Scots law and that Walter – Austin's executor nominate – would be able to play fast and loose with her interests.

Biddy prudently waited until tea had been consumed and the tea-things removed. Walter was still loitering by the window, his melancholy tinged with nervousness now. He had no great interest in admiring the view, Biddy decided, but was only using the position to keep his distance. She would have preferred to have Willy Naismith present in the drawing-room but felt sure that Walter would not permit it. She tried to adhere to the advice that Willy had given her, to remain calm and unruffled and keep her anger in check.

'I hadn't realised that it was so – so magnificent,' Walter said. 'The view, I mean. The landscape. I appreciate what Austin saw in it and why he loved Mull as much as he did.'

'Are you for coming back to stay then?' Biddy asked.

'No, I – I fear not.' Walter swivelled from the window and peeped at her almost coyly. 'My business – now that Austin is no longer here to help me – my business in Edinbugh will demand too much of my time.'

'Is Fetternish not your business?'

'Of course. I'm half owner.'

'And who is owner of the other half?' Biddy said.

'Oh!' He seemed surprised. 'You are, my dear.'

'What else do I own?' Biddy said.

'Well, as you'll have seen from the dispositions in the will . . .'

'I have not seen a copy of the will.'

'What!' Walter exclaimed, acting now. 'Did Mr Fanshaw not inform you of its contents?'

'Who is Mr Fanshaw?'

'Our lawyer.'

'The Baverstocks' lawyer?'

'Yes, but he also manages certain of the estate's affairs.'

'So, he is my lawyer too?'

'What?' Walter was puzzled. 'What? Yes, I suppose he is.'

'And should, therefore,' Biddy said, 'be acting in my interests.'

'I'm sure he does. He is, after all, one of the most highly regarded legal gentlemen in Edinburgh. He has handled our affairs for many, many years. And his father before him.'

'I suspect,' Biddy stated, 'that there may be a conflict of interests in the bosom of Mr Fanshaw. It must be hard for the mannie to be impartial since he has worked for the Baverstocks for so long a while. Why have I not been shown my husband's will?'

'Obviously there has been confusion as to . . .'

'Are you not Austin's nominated executor?'

'I am.'

'Was it not up to you to see that Austin's wishes were carried out? To let me know what those wishes were?'

'I thought – I left it to . . .'

'Fanshaw, yes,' Biddy said. 'Come away from the window.'

'What?'

'Come away from the window, Walter. You cannot be hiding all evening.'

'Hiding? I'm not hiding,' Walter protested but none the less drifted into the region of firelight, closer to the sofa. 'Why should I hide from you, Bridget? I have come here specifically to discuss your future, to make sure that . . .'

'That I receive less than I am due.'

'Six weeks of marriage does not entitle you to . . .'

'Ten minutes, ten minutes of marriage entitles me to whatever my husband saw fit to pass on to me.' Biddy had expected more of Walter. She felt temper warm within her and, sitting stiff and upright, inhaled three or four deep breaths before she continued. 'Where is my copy of the will?'

'It will be sent to you, I promise.'

'No,' Biddy said. 'Send it to my legal advisor.'

'What?'

'Mr Fisher Dunlop of Perth.'

'Dunlop is your legal representative?'

'He is. He will be in communication with your Mr Fanshaw.'

'Why – I mean, how did you persuade Fisher Dunlop to act for you?'

'On the recommendation of a friend.'

Walter had forgotten his shyness. He was close to her, leaning slightly forward. His moustache bristled with concern and his eyes were no longer pensive. He seemed, Biddy thought, to have wakened up.

She said, 'I take it that you have had dealings with Mr Dunlop and that you are aware of his reputation?'

'I know of him, certainly.'

'He is, I think, applying for an interdict.'

'A what? A what?'

'I think that is the proper word for it,' Biddy said. 'In any case, Mr Dunlop will be going to court to make sure that we receive a copy of Austin's will and testament without any more delay.'

'Good God!'

Walter plumped himself down on a brocaded armchair, one

of the Sangster exports. He placed his hands on his knees. He shook his head in disbelief, almost in wonderment.

Biddy said, 'Austin left me everything, did he not?'

Walter sniffed, glanced towards the window, then the door, then said, 'It was Agnes's idea. To keep it from you, I mean. She is wounded by Austin's untimely death. Very wounded. I told her that we would not be able to keep the information from you for long.'

'Keep what information from me?' Biddy said. 'How much am I worth?'

'A great deal,' Walter admitted. 'Yes, Bridget, a very great deal.'

'He left me everything?'

'Yes.'

'Austin told me that he would provide for me and that he had made arrangements to that end,' Biddy lied. 'My husband – your brother – was a man of his word. He would be furious at you for the trick you have been trying to put over on me.'

'It wasn't a trick,' Walter murmured. 'Not exactly.'

'What was it then?' said Biddy.

'I have – I have come with a proposition.'

'Put together by your sister, no doubt, assisted by your Mr Fanshaw.'

Walter did not have the gall to deny it.

He moved on hastily, saying, 'Surely it would do no harm to hear what I have to say before you condemn me?'

'I am listening,' Biddy said.

'There is little enough by way of hard cash, Bridget. Austin did not have large reserves tucked away. His principal asset was half ownership of Fetternish. I may as well tell you that if I choose to do so I am entitled to liquidate my holding in Fetternish – house, land and stock. I can force its sale. Unless you can find the capital to buy it from me. Can you do that?'

'Only by selling my half of Charlotte Square,' Biddy said.

'Which, I beg you to remember, is still under mortgage.'

'Even so,' said Biddy, 'the Edinburgh property is worth a considerable sum, is it not? Selling it would give me some sort of money to offer you for your share of Fetternish.'

'That's what you want, isn't it?' Walter said. 'Fetternish?'

'I am, I gather, entitled to more than the value of Fetternish.'

'Don't you understand, my dear, that it will take months, perhaps years, to assess, value and divide what is shared between us. In the meantime there are wages to be paid, on-going debts to be squared up and . . .'

'Money coming in from rents,' Biddy reminded him. 'From wool sales and from my dividends in the Sangster manufactory.'

'Oh!' Walter said.

'Do I not own twenty-eight percentage of the stock?'

'Twenty-six.'

'Very well, twenty-six. And did you not originally purchase Fetternish to provide cheap wool for the tweed-making?'

'Perhaps we did.'

'Walter!'

'Yes, of course we did.'

'And is it not profitable?'

'Fairly, fairly profitable.'

'Walter!' Biddy said again, chidingly. 'I may not know anything about manufacturing but I know enough of farming to be sure that you would not be leasing land and buying more sheep if the estate had been running at a loss.'

'Leasing Pennypol from your mother was Austin's idea; an act of charity, really, done only to please you.'

'Nonsense,' Biddy said. 'Charity had nothing to do with it.'

'What lies has Fisher Dunlop been telling you?'

'I am not needing instruction from a lawyer on how to add up the figures in a profit and loss account,' Biddy said. 'What is your proposition, Walter? That I waive all my rights and entitlements in exchange for sole ownership of Fetternish? Is that what you have in mind?'

'We – we would not see you homeless, Bridget.'

'Hoh!' Biddy snapped. 'Homeless! I am as wealthy as you are, probably, and I will never again be in need of having a roof over my head that is not my own. Homeless, indeed! What is it that you would be offering me, Walter? A cottage by the shore, a loft above the stables? Although you have tried to keep the contents of Austin's will a secret I know what I am worth, not to the penny, not even to the pound, but I can calculate that I have more coming to me than the Baverstocks wish me to have and that by island standards I am rich.'

She got to her feet abruptly, causing Walter to rear back as if he thought that she might strike him. She felt remarkably calm inside, though, all trace of anger gone. She was even beginning to enjoy herself, for she knew that he had seriously underestimated her intelligence, that bred-in-the-bone canniness where money was concerned, her Campbell inheritance.

She said, 'Is it that you thought I would never question the will? Come away with you, Walter, I am not so stupid as to let you just give me what you think I am due. I did not marry your brother to get my hands on his money. I thought that my marriage would be a long one and—'

'Why did you marry him if not for gain?' Walter interrupted.

'He loved me,' Biddy said, offhandedly, then returned immediately to the subject on hand. 'Now that I do not have Austin to guide me I must look out for my own interests. I will be telling you frankly that you have treated me very shabbily. If you had come to me at once with Austin's will in one hand and a proposal in the other I might have been inclined to accept. However, that was not how you and your sister saw fit to deal with me. You have been clumsy, Walter, and disregarding of the law and it will be for my Mr Dunlop and your Mr Fanshaw to settle matters between them, to my satisfaction if not yours.'

'Bridget,' he said, helplessly. 'Biddy, it was not my wish that you be treated in this manner. I would have had you down to Sangster for the reading but Agnes . . .'

'Agnes, Agnes, why do you always blame your sister? You are all the same to me,' Biddy said. 'If it is a proposition you are wanting, Walter, I propose that I trade my share of your house in Edinburgh for your share of Fetternish.'

'No. Oh, no, that would not be fair.'

'To me, or to you?'

'To me.'

'What would be fair then?' Biddy asked.

'If you were also to waive your interest in the Sangster manufactory.'

'Would I not then be killing the golden goose?'

'It isn't your company. My father built it up and I see no reason why you should profit from the Baverstocks' enterprise.'

'Because I am a Baverstock too, whether you like it or not.'

'Unless you marry again.'

'I will not marry again. I will never marry again.'

'Never is an exceeding long time, Bridget.'

She was still standing over him, not deliberately threatening but projecting the dominance of youth and femaleness, an air of assurance that Walter, for all his guile, could not match.

He had to try, though, if only for the sake of form.

He said, 'We will take you to court, you know. We will tie up the settlement of Austin's financial affairs for as long a time as possible.'

'You will not win the case, Walter.'

'Possibly not,' Walter said. 'But there are three of us to bear the brunt of the legal fees which, believe me, will be very steep indeed, so steep that it will drain you of working capital and you'll have to sell Fetternish just to pay the damned lawyers, never mind find my share of purchase money. In the interim, Fetternish will be held in escrow – do you know what that means?'

'No.'

'Right of sale will be granted to a third party at the discretion of the court and you will be allocated just enough and no more from Austin's estate to keep Fetternish ticking over.'

'But,' Biddy said, 'I will be at liberty to sell the wool crop to the highest bidder and, as we both know, the highest bidder will not be from Sangster.'

'That' – Walter paused – 'would be cutting off your nose to spite your face.'

'Because I am also a stock-holder in the Sangster manufactory?'

Again, a pause. 'Yes.'

'The profits from tweed-making would fall.'

'Oh, I doubt that,' Walter said, shrugging.

'Your dividends as well as mine would be much reduced.'

'No, no.'

'At least until such time as the case was settled. And the longer the case runs the less chance there is of a low cost wool crop coming in from Fetternish.'

'If this is Fisher Dunlop talking . . .'

'It is *me* talking, Walter. *Me* – Bridget Campbell Baverstock.'

Biddy stepped back and seated herself on the sofa once more.

She flounced her black silk skirts and fingered the brooch at her breast as if it were a source of inspiration or, perhaps, of courage. 'It is the wool crop that is important to you and you would be doing well to admit it.'

'It is,' Walter conceded, 'a consideration.'

'Consider this then,' Biddy said. 'I will be making you a fair exchange. I will surrender my half of Charlotte Square together with fourteen percentage of the stock in the Sangster manufactory in exchange for Fetternish. Since you have not seen fit to show me the will or any of the documents that would go with it I cannot say how much these exchanges are worth in money terms. But I do know that it will give you what you want.'

'And you will have what you want too,' Walter reminded her.

'That is the truth,' Biddy said.

'All of your stock,' Walter said.

Biddy shook her head. 'I must keep some connection with the Baverstock family if only to protect myself against you. Twelve percentage will be doing very well. For that consideration I will ensure that the whole crop of quality wool that comes off Fetternish is supplied to Sangster at a price below market value.'

'How much below market value?'

'Walter, how can you possibly expect exact figures when you have failed to show me any figures at all? I am offering you a starting point, that is all. If you and I agree on this in the main then we will be leaving it to my Mr Dunlop and your Mr Fanshaw to sort out the details.'

Walter tapped his hands on his knees, beating out a strange little rhythm, while he contemplated the pattern of the carpet.

It was almost full dusk outside now and sea and sky had merged. He did not like Mull, had never liked the place, not from the first. He felt small here, dwarfed by the landscape and the hollowness of the house. There was very little of his brother left on Fetternish, little except the widow and even she seemed somehow transitory. He got up and crossed to the window and pulled one of the ropes that closed the half curtain. He stood for a long moment with the other rope in his fist, staring out into the gloom. He could see the drawing-room, caught and boxed, hanging mysteriously over the lawn like an apparition.

A Promise of Fair Weather

It had been injudicious of him to come here. It had also been wrong of him to listen to his sister's malicious plan to cheat Biddy Campbell out of what was hers by legal entitlement. Austin's wishes were clear and absolute: everything went to his wife; every scrap of furniture, every share, every sheep. Austin, of course, could not possibly have known that he would pass away so soon and that there would be no children, no heirs to inherit the island empire that Biddy and he would build together.

Now it all belonged to the island woman, handsome and shrewd and, in her way, just as ruthless as any Baverstock, even his sister. Bridget Campbell would have made a valuable addition to the family. In a generation her sons would have *been* the family; the Highland branch, at least. The big house on the Atlantic coast would have been part of Baverstock history and they would all have been proud of it. But then poor old Austin had died. Poor Austin's heart had been weak all along and nobody had suspected it. Now all that was left of his brother were memories, memories that Biddy Campbell could never share, along with a neat folio of texts and documents that reposed in a safety box in Mr Fanshaw's Edinburgh chambers.

Walter knew what Fetternish was worth. He also knew what twelve percentage of the stock in Baverstock, Baverstock & Paul's tweed-making factory was worth, down to the last halfpenny.

It was not, as Biddy supposed it to be, a fair trade at all.

Other bits and pieces of money, other shares would come to her to provide a healthy working capital. As executor he would see to it that there was no impediment put in the way of her receiving them. Agnes be damned; it was what Austin had wanted. She, this island woman, was what Austin had wanted and she, if only for a brief and fleeting time, had made his brother happy.

Reconciled, he looked round at her.

'Very well, Bridget. In principle, I agree to your proposal.'

'Fetternish and twelve percentage. And you can be keeping the rest?'

'And we get the wool crop every year.'

'Every pound of it.'

'Done then,' Walter said and gave the curtain rope a tug to close out the early dusk.

* * *

It was well after eleven before Willy brought her the glass of hot milk flavoured with a dash of brandy. She had loosened the binding ties of her mourning dress and reclined in the Georgian armchair in the hall almost as a man would, feet propped up on the crab-claw footstool, hips drawn forward, head resting on a cushion. The dogs had been led away to the gunroom but the smell of them, not unpleasant, still lingered around the huge stone fireplace, mingled with wood smoke and the aroma of the cigar that Walter had smoked after dinner.

Biddy glanced up at Willy with sleepy satisfaction. She had achieved everything – almost everything – that she had set her heart on, or would once the lawyers had thrashed out the details. She felt languorous and satisfied and, if she had been a cat, would have purred loudly.

Willy plucked the glass from the tray and slipped it into her outstretched hand. 'I gather everything went well, Mrs Baverstock?'

'Very well, Willy. Much better than I had anticipated.' She sipped brandy and milk and with the tip of her tongue licked the creamy residue from her upper lip. 'I have you to thank for it.'

'I did nothing,' said Willy modestly. 'Nothing much.'

'No, I would have been floundering without your advice.'

'Did – em – did you tell Mr Walter that I would be staying on here?'

'I did, and he agreed to it. After some argument,' Biddy added, tactfully. 'He will be sorry to lose your services, of course, but he understands that you have a wife to consider now. Where is Margaret, by the way?'

'In her bed. Fast asleep.'

Biddy nodded. 'I have a feeling that we should be making a trip to Perth very soon. It would be no bad thing to consult face to face with this Mr Dunlop.'

'I think it might be wise, ma'am, aye.'

'Will you accompany me?'

'I will.'

'Margaret will not object?'

'No, Margaret will understand the position.'

'We will travel towards the middle of the week. On, say, Wednesday.'

'For how long, Mrs Baverstock?' Willy enquired.

'A week should be sufficient. I take it that there are suitable hotels in Perth where we might be putting up without undue discomfort.'

'I'm sure there are, ma'am,' Willy said, frowning slightly. 'But . . .'

'But?'

'That will mean you will miss the wedding.'

She stirred slightly but the purring little smile did not leave her lips.

'What wedding?' she said.

'Your sister's wedding.'

'Oh, that!' Biddy said. 'I would not be worrying about that, Willy. No, no, I would not be worrying about that at all.'

In retrospect it struck Michael as odd that Roy had not barked, that it was only instinct that wakened him just a moment before she slipped into his bed. A split second later and it would have been too late. If she'd touched him, if he'd felt the weight of her breasts pressing on his chest, her mouth on his mouth, her belly rubbing against his thighs, then he would have been lost for ever and everything that happened afterwards would never have come about.

He was sure of only two things: that it was not Innis who stood beside his cot in the darkness, and that it was not a dream.

As she groped for the blanket that covered him he sat bolt upright and caught her arm. Though the kitchen was as chill as a tomb at that early hour, her skin was warm. She swayed against him and he could hear her breathing, a strange sawing sound, too loud for stealth.

'Michael. Oh, God, Michael.'

It was still pitch dark. There was no light at all save a faint, faint glimmer in the hearth where the ashes of last night's peat fire contained an ember or two. In spite of the shock of his wakening, he was aroused. He could smell her body, heavy and luxurious in the darkness, and bore the whole smooth weight of her against him as she leaned into him. She wore nothing but a slippery undershift. Her hair, unloosened, feathered down across her shoulders. He could feel her face nuzzling, her mouth groping for his.

He pushed her roughly away and got to his feet.

'What time is it?'

'Early, very early. Get into bed. Please.'

'What are you doing here, Biddy?'

Her arms trailed across him. He evaded her grasp only with difficulty, with farcical clumsiness, skipping back and almost tumbling on to the bed again. Roy had wakened at last. He could hear the dog's claws scrabbling on the stone floor and the little uncertain yelps the animal let out, bewildered as he was by the appearance of the woman in the room.

Michael stumbled towards the fireplace. He fished on the ledge, found a match and struck it, saw her standing by the bed, one knee upon the blanket. Saw too the heavy, cotton-lined, tweed cape which had covered her lying on the floor like a snakeskin, her shoes beside it. She seemed huge in the confined space of the kitchen and Roy, even Roy, cowered from her, hackles bristling, not yelping now but growling. Michael found and lit the stump of a candle, stabbed it into a holder and put the holder on the table.

'Biddy,' he said again, 'what are you doing here?'

'I need you, Michael. I need you. Do you not also want me?'

He stepped to one side, away from the bed, keeping the table between him and the woman. He reached down and pressed his hand against the collie's neck, calming him, saying, 'Ssshhh, Ssshhh, there now, there now,' as if the dog were a danger to him, the dog that needed gentling.

Biddy sat upon the side of the bed, one long leg bent beneath her, the undershift hitched up to show him her thighs, her hair, more auburn than fiery in the wan flicker of candlelight, spilling across her shoulder and breast. She had come out of the darkness, walking down in the pre-dawn darkness, down the sandy tracks from the big house, bare-legged, with nothing to keep out the cold but the cape. The sight of her alarmed and excited him and, in spite of his resentment, he remained aroused. He pushed himself against the edge of the table, his fists on the table top, his arms stiff with indignation.

'I'm not your serf, Biddy,' he made himself say. 'I am not here at your beck and call like a slave out of the market. You have no right to sneak into my house in the middle of the night.'

She spoke softly, matching his heat with apparent coolness.

'I have every right,' she said. 'It is not your house; it is my house.'

'Aye, well, perhaps that's so,' Michael said. 'And perhaps it's also true that I am your shepherd. But that does not make me your man.'

'Make love to me.'

'I will not,' he said.

'Do you not want to take me to your bed?'

'Aye,' he said. 'But whether I want to or whether I do not . . .'

'Do you not know that I am a rich woman?'

'Is that the news that Walter Baverstock brought to you?'

'It is.'

'Where is Baverstock now? I'm sure he doesn't know where you are.'

'He has gone back to Edinburgh,' Biddy said. 'He left yesterday morning. On Wednesday I will be going to Perth to consult my lawyer and make arrangements concerning the will. There will be no upsets. Very soon I will be the owner of Fetternish House, and all the land and its rentals.'

'What is that to me?' Michael said.

Biddy said, 'I will be needing a man to share it with.'

'Do you mean that you are already looking for a new husband?'

'It might be that I will take on a new husband – in due course.'

'There will be no shortage of suitors, Biddy.'

'I am thinking, though, that you will not be one of them.'

'Are you asking me a question?' Michael said.

'I am telling you that I could not do what my sister is doing. It would not be right for the lady of Fetternish to marry a Catholic. I could never do that.'

'Then why are you here?'

'Oh, just to see if you can change my mind.'

She settled back, dropping her shoulders against the pillow, one elbow cocked. She looked opulent in the half-light, even in the cold kitchen. In less than a week's time it would be Biddy's sister who would lie there – but not like that, never like that, never with that arrogance, that sensual self-assurance. Whatever power he had had over Biddy Campbell, the fisherman's daughter, had been squandered long since. All that was left of it was a residue of desire, of thrusting male need. He might take her, might teach her a lesson, might even manage to humiliate her for a little while but he would never again possess her as he had possessed her before.

'Is it Innis?' Biddy said. 'Are you afraid of what Innis might say?'

'I'm not afraid of either of you,' Michael said. 'You should not be here, Biddy. It isn't right.'

'I will not be telling Innis, if that is what you are afraid of.'

'I *will* marry her, you know. This – you – won't deter me.'

'Because you love her?'

'Yes.'

'Because you have had me and now you want her?'

'Yes,' he lied.

She unfolded her limbs slowly, almost cautiously, as if they had suddenly become brittle. She raised herself up, breasts thrust out, stomach arched out at him beneath the fine fabric of the undershift that clung to her like silvery-grey dust. He was astonished at her boldness, her precocity, rattled by what he perceived as her sluttishness. She was no longer the gauche country girl that he had taken and seduced, and this was not the time or the place for her to demonstrate her true nature. He felt ashamed, not of what he had done to her but by his failure to recognise her for what she was. It was wrong for a woman – girl or wife or widow – to behave in this manner, to foist herself upon him or upon any man, to offer herself so shamelessly and demand that he serve her.

He felt all desire for her wane.

Biddy said, 'I am not used to being rejected.'

'I can't do what you ask, Biddy.'

'Why?'

'Because it would not be fair to Innis.'

'Do you not know that I am your mistress now?'

'What do you mean?' Michael asked, stupidly.

'I told you; I am mistress of Fetternish.'

'The Baverstocks . . .'

'No, not the Baverstocks. Walter and I have reached an agreement.'

Michael felt his knees grow weak, the chill communicate itself to him, wash suddenly across his flesh, more like water than air. He groped behind him, found a chair, half seated himself upon it and leaned for support upon the table.

Biddy was on her feet again, standing by the bed. She was smiling at him, indulging him now, not taunting. He tried to see Innis there, to merge one image with the other, and found a strange unnatural comfort in the thought of Innis, modest and intelligent and so in love with him that he might do anything with her – or nothing – and she would not complain, would not transform herself into this bizarre cross-breed, this hybrid creature, a woman who had stumbled upon the meaning of power and had, by a disastrous accident, acquired it.

'Are you telling me that I must do as you want me to do,' Michael said, 'or you will put me out of work?' He felt cold, shudderingly cold. Even the words in his mouth were cold, like great gulps of seawater or the water from the pipe first thing on a winter's morning. He swallowed. He said, 'Come Saturday I will marry Innis no matter what you do, Biddy. No matter who you are or what you own. I will marry Innis and be content.'

'You will never be content with her,' Biddy said, scornfully. 'Not you, Michael, not you.'

'Will you put me out of work? Am I being sacked?'

She stooped and dragged the cape from the floor, fanned it out and wrapped it around her. With a passive little motion of the wrists she even unfolded the hood and brought it over her head. She looked at that moment more beautiful than he could believe, her red hair turned auburn in the candlelight, her face framed by fine-cut tweed.

'No,' Biddy said, and laughed. 'I would be a fool to lose you, Michael.'

'What do you mean, for God's sake, lose me?'

She stepped into her shoes and turned towards the door.

'I mean,' she told him, 'marry my sister and be damned.'

'Biddy . . .'

She rounded on him, the laughter gone. There was a strict, almost vicious quality in her voice now, one that he had not heard before, not even when she had been swept by temper or mean moods.

'Not Biddy,' she told him. 'Not Biddy ever again. Even if you are hell-bent on being my brother-in-law from now on I am Mrs Austin Baverstock and you would do well not to forget it. Do you understand?'

He opened his mouth to object, then thought the better of it.

'Yes, Mrs Baverstock,' Michael said, meekly. 'I think I understand.'

Then it was Saturday. Innis stood at the track's end, up among the golden brown bracken, all alone, waiting for Michael to arrive in the borrowed dogcart that would carry them to their wedding, carry them away together into a new life.

She had been awake since before dawn, wide awake, lying for the last time on the straw mattress in the loft of the cottage that had been her home since the day she had been born. Biddy had gone over to Fetternish, Aileen to Foss. Donnie was dead and Neil as lost to her as if the city, like the sea, had swallowed him up. She wondered who was to blame; if it was chance or circumstance, destiny or God that had separated them from one another and had driven them out of Pennypol, or if it was some subtle and indecipherable flaw, not just her father's wickedness, her mother's bitterness, but something unique in each of them that had shaped the past and would shape the future.

The wall that they had laboured to unearth to protect Pennypol from Fetternish had turned out to be no defence at all. In all but name Fetternish and Pennypol had become one and the same.

There were sheep everywhere now, sheep dotted across the moor pastures and up around the calf park as far as her eye could see. If what Michael had told her was true then they were Biddy's sheep on Biddy's land. Her sister had not seen fit to inform them what had taken place or why she, Biddy, had gone off to Perth and what she had had to do to make Fetternish all her own.

Come noon in the chapel at Glenarray Innis knew that she would become part of that same dominion, part of Biddy's empire, dependent upon her sister's whim for her livelihood. She would still have nothing that she could call her own; nothing except Michael whom she loved irrationally and from whom, no matter what Biddy said or did, she could never be parted again.

Undoubtedly there were those who considered her a fool; others, her father among them, who condemned her as a traitor to her heritage; others still who supposed that she had been carried away by sexual desire and were puzzled by the attraction that the shepherd, that skinny incomer, held for her. There were probably even a few, like Grandfather McIver, who were disappointed that she had not moved upward in the world, had not married a man whom they regarded as her peer. Innis had no answer to give to any of them, no excuse for loving Michael Tarrant, none that would stand the test of reason; except that she needed to be this man's wife, to call him her own, and in the binding of the vows to find certainties and purposes that were hers and hers alone.

Anxiously Innis scanned the track that led over to Pennymain.

Before he had left with Biddy for Perth Willy Naismith had arranged for Mr Bell to deliver a dogcart to the shepherd's cottage and yesterday, Friday, Michael had collected Innis's belongings from Pennypol, had carried them up to the track, loaded them behind the pony and had driven them away to his house, to that house which she would share with him for ever more.

Her father had offered no helping hand, of course. He had skulked by the byre with a bottle in his fist, unshaven and ragged, and had jeered incoherently at Michael's efforts and when she had followed Michael up to the track had shouted and shaken his fist. Mam had said nothing, not one word to Michael. She had stood by the cottage door with her arms folded and had watched her daughter and the man who would soon be her son-in-law lug out the clothes chest and baskets of books as if they were thieves whose actions she was powerless to prevent. Mam had said nothing because Dada was watching, and she, Vassie, would not be disloyal; not now, not when she would be left alone with him, chained to him for as long as it took him to die.

It had been a silent, scuffling household that Friday night at supper and there had been no sentimental wistfulness, no regret in Innis when she had gone very early to bed. There had been nothing in the loft except empty chests and, folded neatly on a newspaper, her white dress and underthings, the milk-white stockings that she would put on tomorrow, leaving her worn old work-clothes behind. She had lain alone on the broad straw mattress listening to the waves' soft *pah-dah* on the crescent of sand where the burn ran into the sea; listening to her mother's voice below, a long, undulating murmur of sound, not harsh but insistent, as if she were praying not to God but to Dada, to the wreck of Ronan Campbell or the man that he had been, who, drunk or insensible or merely sulking in dumb pride, gave no answer, no answer at all.

She had been up before dawn and had dressed herself at once in the white dress and had gone down into the dark kitchen and lighted the lamp. She had brewed tea and had forced herself to eat an oatcake to calm the fluttering nerves in her stomach and to ease her trepidation at the thought that Michael might yet change his mind, might not come for her and that she would be left here in her mother's house to wilt and wither away, inch by inch.

It was, thank God, a dry morning with no trace of rain in the high dove-grey clouds that lay calm over the Treshnish and, to the north-west, outlined in the far distance the pale blue-painted mountains of Skye. A little wind off the sea combed the grasses and plastered the dress against her legs and she wished that she had brought out a shawl to keep her shoulders warm. She thought about that while she scanned the fringe of the moor and looked away along the track for a glimpse of the pony and the cart that would bring Michael to her and put an end once and for all to her doubts.

He was late, a half-hour or more late, for the sun was clearing the cloud and the tide had begun to turn and she could see the heave of the weed on the rocks and hear, louder now, the clash of the waves on the sand spit where the currents met.

And still there was no sign of Michael.

Below, her mother leaned on the rusted harrow, that makeshift barrier from thirteen months ago that would never now be replaced. She could see her mother leaning on her arms the way a man does, gazing over the fields and the moor, not looking at her, just watching, waiting and watching for the little pall of dust to rise from behind the crown of bracken, waiting and watching to see her daughter go off, without a sign of blessing.

Innis looked towards Olaf's Ridge where the wind rippled the grazing grasses and tossed among the tall pine trees.

She peered at the spot where the track dipped down through the crumpled rocks, peered so hard that her eyes grew hot and began to water. She shivered in her plain white dress. Not for her the kirk at Crove, the Edinburgh gentry, the trim lawns of Fetternish, a steamship glittering in the bay, the glamour and glory of marrying a wealthy and adoring husband. She did not want that. She did not even mind that she would be married without a friend, not one friend, not even her mother, to see her off and shed a tear of happiness and wish her well on her wedding day.

All she wanted was for Michael to arrive.

She ached with loneliness and fear of loneliness and when she pressed her fingers to her cheeks found that she was crying in spite of herself.

He is not coming, Innis thought. Mam knows that he is not coming. Mam knows that I have been let down. Mam knows that Biddy has taken him from me and that he will wait for her to return, wait for the widow's weeds to fade and for Biddy to blossom again when spring comes, and that then he will marry her or, if he cannot marry her, will become her man. Mam knows that Biddy will have everything she wants, for that is the way the world wags, and that I was wrong to hope for it to be different, for it to come out right in the end.

She glanced down at the wall, at Mam, as if for confirmation, but Vassie had not moved and gave no hint that anything was wrong, nothing that patience and endurance would not cure.

When Innis looked back towards the ridge she saw the little waft of brownish dust that rose from the wheels of the dogcart or from the pony's hooves and, before she could even let out her breath, saw the hat of the man who occupied the board and then his head and shoulders and, without meaning to, began to run towards him, calling out his name.

It was not Michael, though. It was Tom Ewing, Minister Ewing, at the reins of the Fetternish dogcart. He was not alone. On the seat behind him was Quig and with Quig the baby, little Donnie, wrapped up warm and woolly and wide awake, lying in a creel on the young man's knees. Innis drew up short. She waited until the cart came abreast of her and halted. She could say nothing. Her tongue had gone dry as sand and seemed to stick to the roof of her mouth.

'Well, young lady,' Tom Ewing said, cheerfully, 'where might you be going, dressed up so prettily?'

'W-where – where is he?' Innis stammered. 'W-where's Michael?'

'We are going to a wedding in Glenarray,' Tom Ewing said. 'If it is that you are travelling that way too we would be delighted to have your company.'

'Where is Michael?'

'Do not be fretting, Innis. Your man will be waiting for you at the chapel,' Quig told her. 'Mr Ewing has sent him ahead on another cart, for do you not know that even Catholics believe it is bad luck for a bride and her groom to meet on their wedding day before they step up to the altar?'

'Has Michael gone? Has he left Mull?'

'No, no,' Tom Ewing assured her. 'I'm sorry, Innis. I did not mean to alarm you. Here.' Leaning from the board, he offered his hand. 'Climb up and we will be on our way.'

'Have you seen Michael? Today, I mean? This morning?'

'Yes,' Quig answered. 'He is as eager as you are since we had the pleasure of talking to him, of having a wee bit of a word in his ear. Did we not now, Minister Ewing?'

'He will be there, Innis,' Tom Ewing promised.

She stared into his face, so familiar, so friendly, and felt the tears warm her eyes once more. She did not doubt Tom Ewing's assurance that Michael would be waiting in the almost empty chapel where the River Array curved through the plain of the long glen; not even Michael would risk flouting the orders of the minister, let alone the expectations of a priest.

Innis scrambled up on to the board and tucked her white skirts about her knees, keeping her dress as clean as possible. Tom clucked at the pony, one of Bell's sturdiest, and gave a little snap of the reins and the dogcart rolled on along the track with the bracken nodding in its wake.

Innis turned and looked down on Pennypol. Her mother had climbed over the harrow and stood with her hands on her hips, isolated against the dark line of the wall. Her father had come out of the house and, quite separate from Vassie, leaned on the metal with a bottle dangling from his fingers and the wind, like a joke, puffing out his shirt and flicking his greying hair about his head as if that was all it took to make him animate.

Innis did not turn away just yet but took her eyes from the cottage and the folk by the wall and looked, smiling, at the baby nestled in the creel. He was stirring now, curling his tiny fingers into his palms and his blue eyes had focus and, she thought, showed signs of intelligence. Although he was passive, he seemed somehow watchful as if at some time far into the future he might raise the memory of this morning from his consciousness and tell his sons and grandsons that yes, he was there when Innis Campbell wed the Catholic and Pennypol and Pennymain, Foss and Fetternish became linked.

Innis said, 'Did my grandfather send you to see me married, Quig?'

'Aye, he did.'

'Why did you bring the baby?'

'He is to be christened tomorrow in Crove kirk.'

'Is it you who will be performing the ceremony, Mr Ewing?'

'Who else?' Tom Ewing replied.

'Why, Quig, is Aileen not with you?'

'Oh, it will be easier if she is not, if she stays at home on Foss.'

'How did you persuade her to let you take her baby?'

'Because she imagines that it is my child too,' Quig said, with a shrug.

The hot uncertain tears had gone from Innis now. She did not have to look up to know that the wall and her parents and the roofs of Pennypol had slipped out of sight. The track was angled close to the burn now and the dry ground sang under the wheels and away to the west on the headland above the Ards, old Caliach stood watchful and benign in the quiet morning light.

Suddenly it seemed fitting that Quig and Tom Ewing should accompany her to her wedding and Innis felt her heart lift and all concern about her future just up and fly away. With a little

409

laugh, she asked, 'Why, Mr Ewing? Why are you doing this for me?'

'Well, Innis,' the minister answered, 'a promise is a promise, after all,' and, cracking the reins again, steered the dogcart on towards the chapel where Mr Michael Tarrant waited to greet his innocent bride.